D1083373

GATE
OF
RAGE

BOOKS BY C. Y. LEE

Flower Drum Song
Lover's Point
The Sawbwa and His Secretary
Madame Goldenflower
Cripple Mah and the New Order
The Virgin Market
The Land of the Golden Mountain
The Days of the Tong Wars
China Saga
The Second Son of Heaven
Gate of Rage

GATE
OF
RAGE

◆

A Novel of One Family
Trapped by the Events at
Tiananmen Square

◆

C. Y. LEE

William Morrow and Company, Inc.
New York

R0120713712
HUMCA

HOUSTON PUBLIC LIBRARY

Copyright © 1991 by C. Y. Lee

All rights reserved. No part of this book may be reproduced or utilized in any form
or by any means, electronic or mechanical, including photocopying, recording, or by
any information storage or retrieval system, without permission in writing from the
Publisher. Inquiries should be addressed to Permissions Department, William Morrow
and Company, Inc., 1350 Avenue of the Americas, New York, N.Y. 10019.

It is the policy of William Morrow and Company, Inc., and its imprints and affiliates,
recognizing the importance of preserving what has been written, to print the books
we publish on acid-free paper, and we exert out best effort to that end.

Library of Congress Cataloging-in-Publication Data

Lee, C. Y.
    Gate of rage / by C. Y. Lee.
       p.   cm.
    ISBN 0-688-09764-2
    1. China—History—Tiananmen Square Incident, 1989—Fiction.
I. Title.
PS3523.E3158G38   1991
813'.54—dc20   90-26480
                                                                                  CIP

Printed in the United States of America

First Edition

1 2 3 4 5 6 7 8 9 10

BOOK DESIGN BY WILLIAM MCCARTHY

A million voices
crying for freedom
are silenced by guns.

A plastic goddess
erected for democracy
is crushed by tanks.

Tiananmen Square,
the largest in the world,
is washed in blood.

Tiananmen,
the Gate of Heavenly Peace
becomes the Gate of Rage.

1

When Jimmy Hong got into the backseat of the taxi at Beijing Airport, he reached for his wife's hand. "Welcome home, Do Do," he said, holding her hand tightly with both of his. "How was the Moscow trip?"

A reporter for Radio Beijing, Do Do had been invited to Moscow as a member of the Chinese news media to help renew the friendship between the two Communist giants. She moved a little closer to nestle against him.

"The Russians were friendlier than we expected," she said. "We got two free meals and a lot of friendly smiles."

"That was very gracious, considering their severe food shortage," Jimmy said. "When the famous reporter Liu Binyan visited the Soviet Union in 1949, the Russians entertained his delegation royally. But at the end of the trip, they presented him with a bill, charging him for everything except water. And it was at a time when the Soviet Union was China's best friend and long-cherished socialist motherland."

"Thank Deng Xiaoping for his open-door policy," Do Do said. "Who would have guessed that after more than thirty years of isolation, we're being romanced by two superpowers?"

She fished out from her purse a little wooden bear. "For you," she said. "A little souvenir from Leningrad, purchased on March 20, 1980, the day of our arrival . . . the night I missed you the most. Every time you have doubts about your wife, just push the bear down and see what happens. It'll bounce right back, like a *pu dao wen*. It's the symbol of my affection, Jimmy, forever standing!"

Jimmy kissed the bear and squeezed her hand. "I missed you, too," he whispered. "Three weeks are like three years."

When the taxi stopped in front of their apartment building, Jimmy unloaded his wife's battered suitcases and paid the driver. The Gobi wind had melted the snow and cleared the narrow, treeless lane of debris; the full moon and the stars, shining brightly, provided the only light in the darkened street, as the dim street lights had been turned off before midnight to save energy.

They climbed up three flights of stairs with the luggage, panting. But they could not stop talking. Inside their tiny apartment, Jimmy opened a bottle of champagne, poured two glasses, then laid a letter with Hong Kong stamps on the kitchen table in front of her. "Read this," he said.

Do Do, still a bit out of breath, fished out the letter from its impressive envelope. Written on heavy personal stationery was a brief message, the handwriting bold and heavy. It read:

Dear Jimmy and Do Do,

It is all set! I'm finally able to return to China for a visit after more than thirty years, thanks to your connections and efforts.

I have no words to express my happiness at this meeting. I'm so excited that I have to use a marker to hide my trembling hand while I write this note. I'll advise you of the exact date and time of my arrival as soon as I've booked my flight.

All my love,
Your long-missing father, Charles

"Jimmy!" Do Do said excitedly. "How could you hide this from me all the way from the airport?"

"I believe in pleasant surprises," he said, picking up his champagne. They clicked glasses and drank a toast to Jimmy's long-lost father, and another to the American embassy.

Through an enormous effort by the embassy staff, Jimmy and his father had been able to make contact with each other after a long, tireless search.

"Tell me about your father," Do Do said.

"So far as I know," he answered lightheartedly, "he's a nice guy, born in Honolulu, filthy rich . . . probably looks like me, God forbid!"

"Why do you say that?" she laughed. "To me, you're the most handsome man I've ever met."

"I'm glad that beauty is in the eye of the beholder. Do Do, it's fate. If my mother had gone to America with my father, we would never have met. Meeting you was the greatest blessing of my life!"

She looked at him tenderly, sipping her champagne. "Do you know what Elizabeth Morgan said at the airport?" she asked.

"Your foreign-correspondent friend from Los Angeles?"

"Yes, we returned to Beijing on the same flight. While you were busy loading my luggage into the taxi, she whispered to me, 'Do Do, you and your husband only shook hands. What's wrong? Aren't you still married?' "

"What did you tell her?"

"I told her that we Chinese don't kiss and hug publicly. But behind closed doors, it's another story. She raised an eyebrow and said, 'I envy you. When my husband meets my plane, we'll kiss and hug, but the moment we reach home, he'll make a beeline for the TV set to find out how the Lakers are doing.' "

They looked at each other, quiet for a moment. "Do Do," he said, "let's make your foreign friend really envy us." He rose to his feet and picked up his champagne. Without a word, she picked up hers and followed him into their small bedroom.

She unbuttoned the top of her blouse, a gesture that he always found alluring. After a long, lingering kiss, he undressed her. His gentle touch and kisses made her feel like a precious vase being savored by a connoisseur. The whole procedure was like a delicate tea ceremony performed with soothing words and confessions of love. Instead of groaning and moaning, she clutched him tightly, her fingers digging deep into his flesh. Then she begged him to stop. He remained on top of her and waited until she started to move again, inviting him to continue. When it was over, he lay beside her tremulous body feeling gratified . . . happy that the ten years of the brutal Cultural Revolution had not dehumanized them. Both of them had come out of the disaster intact, still capable of loving and caring.

Do Do slept soundly, breathing gently, looking peaceful and beautiful. Jimmy was grateful that their marriage was happy despite the hard life. He thought of China, a country that had never provided an easy life for its people. For almost 150 years the Chinese people had been abused by both foreign powers and their own leaders. The horrors had started in 1840 when the British invaded China and forced the Chinese to smoke opium. In 1900, during the Boxer Rebellion, Germany and seven foreign allies had occupied Beijing; the kaiser had ordered his troops to shoot Chinese on sight. In 1937, the Japanese had almost conquered China, killing millions of civilians and burying thousands alive during the rape of Nanking. Finally, the Soviet Union had exported communism to China, causing a devastating civil war between Mao Zedong and Chiang Kaishek. After Mao's victory, this alien communist system had ravaged China, killing more millions and setting China back almost forty years.

It was not until 1979 that Deng Xiaoping's reforms had begun to revive this sick giant. Instead of being always threatened, China was for the first time being wooed by foreign powers as an equal. It was a miracle.

Lying beside a wonderful wife, with a long-lost father reaching out with love and Deng Xiaoping holding up the sky, Jimmy felt so excited that he could not fall asleep. He got up and finished the champagne, savoring every moment of the happiest day of his life.

2

The China Airline pilot's voice was soft . . . so soft that the passengers could only guess that the jumbo jet was arriving in Beijing and that he was urging everybody to buckle his seat belt. Charles Hong obeyed and heard his buckle click, almost politely. Somehow the atmosphere in the first-class section induced politeness; the stewardess always smiled and talked softly, like the pilot. He had heard that China had entered a new era in 1979, after Deng Xiaoping jailed the notorious Gang of Four, and that freedom, honesty, and politeness had started to raise their beautiful heads.

Charles's seatmate, a Chinese-American businessman from Los Angeles, had given up his seat so that Charles could put up his feet and take a nap. Across the aisle, five men were talking. They were returning from Houston on an oil-refinery–buying trip. Occasionally, they whispered as though the mission had been a national secret. Charles looked back and saw his seatmate lying across two seats, snoring, his large paunch heaving, the buttons on his three-piece suit about to burst.

He looked out the window. At almost sixty years of age, he felt somewhat silly to be so excited, like a young boy about to visit Disneyland for the first time. But he could not help it; he was returning to his motherland for the first time in thirty-two years, and he was about to meet his son, Jimmy Hong, for the first time. Charles had spent almost a year locating Jimmy. It was not until April 1980 that he was able to arrange the trip.

It was early morning, Beijing time. A layer of fog that covered the vast northern plain was lifting. When Beijing came into view, he could see the tree-lined boulevards stretching for miles. The green and yellow tiled roofs of the palaces and temples gleamed in the sun. Beijing always fascinated him, especially the Forbidden City, the stuffy museums, and the colorful mansions. Behind those massive vermilion doors puffy officials and generals plotted murders and coups; political intrigues went on forever.

Now the capital had just emerged from a terrible turmoil caused by Mao Zedong's Cultural Revolution, which had almost wiped out the entire intellectual class in China. Charles Hong remembered that Chairman Mao had said, "The more one studies, the more stupid he becomes." He had heard that for ten years everybody felt unsafe. An engineer was arrested on a bus because he had said that foreigners made better can-openers than the Chinese. Some intellectuals were so intimidated that they walked with their shoulders stooped and their eyes shifting from side to side suspiciously. Charles shuddered, wondering if there were still such tragic figures on the streets of Beijing.

As the plane approached the airport, he could clearly see the intricate alleys called "hutungs," which zigzagged across the sprawling city like little blood vessels. He had heard about Beijing's Ba Da Hutung, or the Eight Great Lanes. In the old days, the red-light district, as famous as Peking duck, had catered to both the rich and the poor. While a Mandarin squandered gold and silver in a first-class singsong house, his sedan chair bearers and servants would spend their brass coins in a lower-class lane. He wondered what the puritanical Communists had done to this pleasure-seekers' shrine.

He was so anxious to meet his son, Jimmy, and Jimmy's wife, Do Do, that he found his hands sweating and his foot tapping the floor nervously. He knew little of North China. During the Second World War, he had gone to Chonqing, the wartime capital. His father had said, "Go help your motherland." In southern China, he had run a scrap-iron business to help resist Japan's invasion.

Now, returning after thirty-two years, he recalled vividly how he had escaped from the wartime capital when Mao's victorious Red Armies swept southward like a tide in the summer of 1948. Pro-Communist and pro-Nationalist students had marched and countermarched; political prisoners had been shot on the street; wild dogs and rats had feasted on rotten corpses. Thousands of people had fled again from their own soldiers, and millions more had been killed. The civil war had crushed the spirit of the whole nation, especially those who had helped win the Second World War. Charles had watched the apathetic survivors wining and dining themselves in a last big fling, getting roaring drunk, ready to perish with Chonqing.

He had wound up his scrap-iron business quickly. He had wanted to take his wife, Mabel, and her mother, Brigid, to his home in Honolulu; but Brigid had insisted that she remain in China to look for her long-lost husband. Mabel was torn between husband and mother.

"Why are you afraid, Charlie?" Mabel had asked. "Communists are not three-headed monsters."

Charles did not want to take a chance. The Communists had already started attacking American paper tigers. As an American citizen, he was an enemy in 1948. Having failed to persuade his family to go with him, he had taken the last plane to Hong Kong without knowing that his wife was pregnant. He had expected to send for her as soon as the political dust settled; but Chairman Mao had lowered the Bamboo Curtain and isolated China for more than thirty years.

As he reminisced, he was suddenly overwhelmed by guilt for having abandoned his son before he was even born. Now, married again, he realized that he had never loved another woman as much as he had loved Mabel, who had given him the two best years of his life despite the horrors of the war. It had almost broken his heart when he learned that Mabel had died of cancer in Hunan in 1979.

The plane finally touched down. He quickly got up and put his coat on.

"First time visiting Beijing?" his seatmate asked. He had returned, yawning and wiping his mouth with a perfumed handkerchief. They had only exchanged polite smiles and a few pleasantries since they had come aboard in Hong Kong. Charles always made a point of not talking to plump men who wore large diamond rings that glittered on their soft, puffy fingers. They were rich and leisurely, always talkative after they had yawned a few times. But in an airplane, he was a captive listener.

"Yes," he said with a pleasant smile.

"My twelfth trip," the man said, "thanks to Richard Nixon, who helped open the China door in 1972. My wife doesn't know how much she has missed. She doesn't care much for the Communists."

He fished out an impressive card. Charles glanced at it. BENJAMIN CHOW, president of several corporations including a Beverly Hills restaurant, the Mandarin Garden. Charles had been there. In front of the restaurant was always a line of Mercedeses that belonged to the staff, parked in order of their owners' rank: manager, maître d', chef, and headwaiter. It had been the flashy owner's advertising. He offered Mr. Chow his own card.

"Don't tell me you're the one and only Charles Hong," Chow said, wide-eyed with surprise, "the hotel tycoon in Hong Kong!"

"I own just a few," Charles said modestly.

"You must come to eat with us in our Mandarin Garden when you're in L.A. Not the food on the menu but what the cooks and waiters eat—the genuine coolie dishes."

Mr. Chow called China a businessman's paradise. Four years ago, he had visited China for the first time and had brought back a few bamboo baskets as souvenirs. The manager of a chain store had seen them and advised him to import them. He had, and now the whole chain was carrying his baskets. Then he started importing pigskin garden gloves, something the Americans scorned at first. Now they could not buy enough, as though the plants would not grow without them.

"I wrote to Deng Xiaoping that year," he said with a big

laugh. "I thanked him for China's pigs, which had made me a multimillionaire."

Mr. Chow had eighty-odd nephews and nieces in China, and the family was growing after each trip. They all wanted to go to America and become millionaires.

"Now they all want a color TV set or a refrigerator," he said with another laugh. "I say why not? Spread the wealth around a little. Just show them that capitalism isn't that bad."

As they were parting, Charles was glad that the pigskin king had slept most of the way from Hong Kong to Beijing. His ears were still ringing from the man's chitchat and explosive laughter.

The customs inspection was simple and swift, the inspectors polite and smiling. Obviously, the previous "American paper tigers" had all become China's best friends. Crowding outside a wide iron fence in the factorylike terminal, hundreds of Chinese faces peeked in anxiously through the iron bars, looking for their visiting relatives and friends.

Charles collected his luggage and waited for the iron fence to open. He would depend on Jimmy, his son, to help him with the heavier bags. In China, there were no porters, he had been told. He scanned the crowd outside the fence, trying to recognize Jimmy's skinny face and drab clothing. He had one of Jimmy's pictures in his office. By prearrangement, Jimmy was to carry a placard with Charles Hong's name written on it. He could see several such placards being waved outside the fence, mostly written in Chinese, but he failed to see his name in any language. As he was straining his eyes, someone tapped him on the shoulder. It was a smiling man in a neat uniform, obviously an official at the airport.

"Mr. Hong?" he asked in Mandarin.

"*Shi di,*" he replied in Chinese, then switched to English. "I'm Charles Hong."

"Please come with me," the man said.

Charles followed him to a side door. Waiting outside was a small group of people. A tall young man stepped forward and bowed.

"I'm James Hong," he said, his voice trembling with excitement. "Welcome to Beijing, Father."

Charles stared at the happy face. Dressed in a dark Mao uniform, his short hair neatly combed and his face clean-shaven, Jimmy looked like one of the Communist heroes depicted on propaganda posters. For a brief moment, Charles felt an urge to embrace his son, but quickly restrained himself, reminding himself that he was now in China, where embracing would probably look as ridiculous as kowtowing in a public place. He extended his hand, which his son grabbed with both of his and shook vigorously for a moment, his eyes full of tears.

Jimmy introduced the rest of the group. Charles shook their hands warmly. When he grabbed the hand of Do Do, Jimmy's wife, he felt a strong urge to embrace her also, but again he controlled his emotions. It was Do Do who broke the rigid custom by flinging her arms around him and giving him a long hug. Fighting his tears, he did not know what to say, but the awkwardness was soon overcome by a wonderful feeling of father, son, and daughter-in-law meeting for the first time.

Do Do was pretty. She wore a fashionable Western red sweater and dark skirt. Charles had visualized a young couple in drab Mao uniforms, undernourished and nervous. The pleasant surprise immediately endeared Deng Xiaoping to him even more.

The others in the group were all government officials. The highest was a Mr. Yeh, one of the four vice mayors of Beijing. The others were general managers and deputy managers of government manufacturing companies that catered to the hotel trade.

Charles was impressed by the suite reserved for him at the Beijing Hotel, the most luxurious in China in 1980. The silk linens, the original decorative art, the imitation antique furniture, the thick carpets, and the comfortable Western sofas were well blended and in good taste. There was a faint detergent smell, indicating that the suite had just been polished and scrubbed.

After Jimmy and two young deputy managers had carried his bags to his suite, they withdrew almost immediately, saying that as an American he probably wanted to take a shower and a nap before Mr. Yeh's welcome banquet. They had heard that Americans showered twice a day. A car would be dispatched to take him to a restaurant at seven. He would have liked Jimmy to stay and chat; he had a lot of questions to ask him, especially about his mother. But somehow China was no longer the China he had known; everything looked a bit strange to him. The family intimacy he had been accustomed to seemed out of place in this rigid society. He decided to take his time. He had a lot to learn about his family and about the country.

Promptly at seven, Jimmy and Do Do came to take him to the banquet in a brand-new Toyota owned by the city. The driver was a young man in a Mao uniform who wore a pair of dark glasses with an American Thrifty Drugstore price tag still tacked on them. Jimmy, riding beside the driver, was quick to explain in English that everybody loved American goods; American price tags and trademarks had become a status symbol.

Do Do seemed relaxed. Sitting in the backseat with Charles, she said that Beijing had rolled out the red carpet to all Chinese-Americans, urging them to return and invest in China's future. She and Jimmy had been excited about Deng Xiaoping's four modernization programs. They had decided to devote their lives to helping build a new China. Do Do was so enthusiastic about China's modernization projects that her voice became tremulous as she gestured and talked.

She was fluent in English. A graduate of the Foreign Language School, she worked as a reporter for Radio Beijing. Charles loved her eager and warm personality, and found her somewhat naive; at twenty-nine, she was still young. Jimmy was also a graduate of the Foreign Language School, now an instructor at Bei Ta, the prestigious Beijing University. Both were admirers of Deng, deeply grateful for Deng's vision of a modern China, a revitalized dragon trying to catch up with the rest of the world.

The wide, tree-lined boulevard was a sea of bicycles. The Toyota weaved through the cyclists precariously, its horn blaring. The driver seemed to enjoy his job enormously, honking like a child showing off a new toy. Several near-collisions almost made Charles's heart leap out of his mouth, but everyone else seemed totally unconcerned.

The Peking Duck restaurant was busy and noisy, full of diners in the large dining hall and in numerous private rooms. Charles saw quite a few Westerners being entertained by their Chinese hosts, struggling with their chopsticks and laughing at their own clumsiness. He heard the familiar noise of the finger-guessing game, with the host challenging his guests in a drinking bout. It brought such a wave of nostalgia to him that the old Chonqing days during the war years came back to him, bringing tears to his eyes.

Mr. Yeh and half a dozen others were in a reserved private room, waiting. Twelve places had been set at a large round table, with matching napkins, cups, glasses, and ivory chopsticks. In the center of the table were four large cold plates, with thin slices of meat, fish, shrimps, and thousand-year-old eggs artistically arranged in flower patterns.

The deputy mayor rose quickly to greet Charles, the fifth-wealthiest man in Hong Kong. Once more everybody shook the millionaire's hand, clasping it between theirs and pumping it vigorously. So far he had not found one limp hand in China; every one of them exuded eagerness, full of enthusiasm and warmth.

Mr. Yeh placed Charles in "*shan zo*," the honored seat, which faced the entrance. Flanking him were two older men in meticulous Mao uniforms, who spoke a dialect that was hard to follow. Mr. Yeh seated himself opposite Charles. Two uniformed waiters passed out hot towels, and everybody wiped his hands. The guest on Charles's right took off his horn-rimmed glasses, wiped his entire face thoroughly, and blew his nose.

Yeh was a good host, gregarious, with a loud laugh. He kept urging his guests to eat, and personally filled Charles's cups and glasses. Each place had two glasses, one for soft drinks and one for beer, a cup for mao-tai, and a covered cup for tea. Charles suspected that Mr. Yeh was pushing Beijing's orange drink, Shanghai beer and wine, Kweichow mao-tai, and Suchow wulung tea, for he had glanced at the business cards of the others who had welcomed him at the airport; they were all representatives of various industries that catered to the hotel trade.

Besides the Suchow wulung, Charles liked the mao-tai, for which he had developed a taste in Chonqing during the war.

Charles enjoyed his host's blatant propaganda, which boasted of China's progress and the people's devotion to socialism. His host cleverly avoided using the term *communism*. Whatever he said was readily seconded by everyone at the table, who nodded and grunted with approval. Many of their remarks were superfluous, like feet added to a snake; but Charles was accustomed to this old habit of Chinese bureaucrats. What annoyed him somewhat was the man on his left, a Mr. Mah, who kept belching and spitting bones onto the table. When a plate of fried little birds was served, he ate all the heads, crunching them with his strong teeth, bones and all.

When a sweet dessert was served, Mr. Yeh proposed a final toast and gave a long-winded speech. He first extended a formal welcome to Charles on behalf of the six million people of Beijing. Then he listed all the possible investment opportunities in China for all patriotic overseas Chinese to consider.

Charles thanked the vice mayor and quipped, "Don't you object to an American capitalist doing business in your heartland?"

Mr. Yeh shot back with a loud laugh, "Don't worry. Our paramount leader, Comrade Deng Xiaoping, has well said: 'We don't care if the cat is black or white. As long as it catches mice, it's a good cat.' "

Feeling exuberant and high on the excellent mao-tai, Charles expressed his interest in investing in a hotel chain for the middle-class Chinese in China. He would commit a hundred million in U.S. dollars and raise another hundred million among his rich friends. The welcome banquet ended with laughter and warm camaraderie. In a triumphant mood, the vice mayor made one more toast to Charles's proposal. Charles returned the toast. When they staggered out of the gaudy restaurant, they took considerable time to say good-bye at the entrance, shaking hands repeatedly and laughing.

On their way back to the Beijing Hotel, Jimmy apologized for Mr. Mah's horrible table manners, explaining that he was the general manager of a Shantung silk factory that supplied sheets and draperies for luxury hotels. He was not a silk expert but a semiretired Communist cadre, commonly known as a *"lao kan pu,"* or "old tree trunk." His silk-factory position was his reward for having been loyal to the party all his life. His deputy, the real expert, would do all the negotiating. Therefore, most of the general managers of China's industries were *"tu bao ze,"* or "native bumpkins," with peasant or military backgrounds. Spitting bones onto the table was their improved table manners, for they had been told that spitting on the floor was impolite.

Charles watched his son's painful apologetic expression and laughed. "Don't worry about it, Son," he said. "When he ate those little bird heads so hungrily, he whipped up my appetite. I won't mind trying one myself next time."

The banquet, the conversation about food and wine, and the drinking bouts had all reminded Charles of the decadent life in the old Kuomingtang days. Was this Communist China? In a way, he was glad. Obviously, the Chinese Communists were changing.

3

Charles Hong decided to visit Mabel's grave in Changsha, Hunan Province in south-central China. Jimmy offered to go with him. Charles was secretly pleased, but protested as a matter of politeness. Since his arrival in Beijing, he had brushed up on his Chinese customs, which he had learned in the old Chonqin days. He remembered that when he was treated for a sore throat in Chonqin, the visiting doctor, to demonstrate his politeness, had declined his fee three times before he accepted it; that was the right amount of protest, dictated by the rules of decorum.

"Can you take the time?" he asked Jimmy.

"I can take a sick leave," Jimmy said. He had come to Charles's hotel room every day to take a bath in a tub with hot running water . . . something rare and precious in China. "Sick leave is the only excuse we can use to get a few days off. All I need is a doctor's slip saying that I have a cold. One of Do Do's distant cousins is a doctor who writes such slips frequently. In lieu of a fee, a pack of American cigarettes or a Japanese ballpoint pen will be gratefully accepted."

Jimmy chatted about irregularities in China as though they were established customs. And he was getting chattier every day. Charles began to feel the warmth and closeness of a father-son relationship, and he was grateful. Completely relaxed, they were now able to talk about any subject without inhibition.

"Besides," Jimmy went on with a short laugh. "It's fun to travel now. Before, you couldn't have dragged me anywhere with five horses. If you took a plane, you could be bumped off just before takeoff because some 'old tree trunk' or high-ranking army officer wanted your seat. If you took the train, the constant singing of 'East Is Red' and the tireless shouting of 'Long Live Chairman Mao' on the radio could drive you insane. All this is gone, thanks to Deng Xiaoping!"

Jimmy worshiped Deng Xiaoping as much as the Maoists worshiped Chairman Mao. Charles was glad. China finally had a new leader who made the intellectuals happy. During China's long isolation, he had been sympathetic toward Mao until the Cultural Revolution.

"Is criticizing Mao still dangerous?" he asked.

"One of our neighbors, a retired railroad engineer, developed a bad habit," Jimmy said. "When he gets up every morning, the first thing he does is to throw his window open and shout, 'Mao Zedong is a turtle's egg!' One day someone reported him to the police. The officer only shrugged and said, 'The turtle's egg is insane, what can you do?' Nobody knew if the officer meant this man or Chairman Mao."

"Yes," Charles said with a smile. "It could mean both are turtle's eggs and both are insane."

They took an airplane to Changsha. To Charles, time was money, even though the short ride in a cramped Russian aircraft was uncomfortable and risky. He had heard that those ancient planes often disintegrated in the air. Newspapers seldom reported such disasters.

But he always felt that life was cheap in China. In the old Chonqin days, the constant Japanese bombing had made him immune to death, which, according to his father, was only a trip to another world. It was probably a very pleasant trip.

The small plane had no more than thirty seats, mostly occupied by two kinds of people, the high-ranking fat army officers and the skinny "tree trunks" who chain-smoked. Charles had a window seat, and Jimmy was assigned to an aisle seat in the back. Jimmy talked to his father's seatmate, an army officer, and requested an exchange of seats. The army officer was reluctant until Jimmy told him that his father was a Chinese-American who was visiting China for the first time. The army officer changed his attitude instantly, smiled, and went back without further protest.

"He must have watched Deng Xiaoping touring America," said Jimmy, settling down beside his father. "He saw how friendly the Americans were."

Two hostesses came by, offering hot towels, candy, and bottled water in plastic cups. The towels seemed the most welcome item. The passengers, almost all males, took off their caps or eyeglasses and scrubbed their faces thoroughly, sighing with satisfaction.

The towels were heavily perfumed. Charles wiped his fingertips. He wondered aloud what to do with the candy. Jimmy dumped his into the magazine pocket in front of him.

Charles smiled and did likewise. In the old Chonqin days, he had often bought candy to toss at beggar boys in the street, thinking it was an act of charity. "I haven't seen one beggar in China," he said. "I must give Chairman Mao credit for that."

"Wait till you go into the interior, Father," Jimmy said. "You must have read that China got rid of all beggars, dogs, birds, and flies. That's not true. The only thing we have really wiped out is venereal disease."

"How did China manage to do that?" Charles asked.

"No place to engage in the act of 'cloud and rain.' Too crowded. Besides, sex is dirty and unmentionable in New China."

Charles looked at his son askance. "Is that why I am still not a grandfather?" he asked.

Jimmy laughed and changed the subject.

The ride was rough, and the noise was so bad that they almost had to shout to converse. Charles was still obsessed with Mabel, the beautiful, cheerful young woman whom he had married more than thirty years ago. He learned as much as he could about Jimmy's childhood in Changsha after the liberation.

Jimmy was happy to report his adventures. Before the Korean War, he had been told to fight insects; during the Korean

War, most of the landlords and beggars had been eliminated, so the government launched a hate campaign against the new enemy—"the American paper tigers." He didn't hate anything; but he enjoyed hitting pictures of "American paper tigers." He told his father about one incident:

Rain was always falling on Changsha. One day it was pouring. Mabel was reluctant to take him to school, but he jumped and cried and demanded to go to school to hit American paper tigers. "Listen, Jimmy," she said, "I want you to know that your father is an American tiger."

After that, he did not want to hit American tigers anymore. Mabel was happy. Carrying him on one arm and holding an umbrella with the other, she hurried along the wet cobblestone street, dodging pushcarts, pedicabs, and water-carrying coolies. When they approached the East Is Red Nursery School, Mabel imitated the water-carrying coolies to amuse him, trotting and grunting. When she put him down, he did the same, trotting, grunting, and laughing.

The school was a two-story brick building that had been confiscated from a liquidated landlord. There were new posters on every wall. Mabel said they were slogans exhorting people to wage an all-out war against imperialists, rats, and insects. One of the largest was a slogan attacking horseflies; it had a swarm of horseflies clustered on it, feasting on a bit of paste. One big boy picked up a rock and flung it at the dark heap. A bull's-eye. He had killed at least a dozen. He dusted his hands and shouted triumphantly, "I did it! I did it! Death to horseflies!"

Jimmy wanted to hit some horseflies. Mabel hushed him and took him to the courtyard where the school custodian was putting up more new posters. That day all the pupils were dressed in blue uniforms. They all wore a red armband on their right arm that said LITTLE SOLDIER. The custodian, an old man with a limp, was putting up two large pictures on a short wall inside the entrance. One picture showed a monster, its fangs dripping blood, one of its hairy hands holding a skinny little man whose eyes bulged and tongue hung out. The poster said, CHIANG KAISHEK AND THE TAIWAN PEOPLE. The other poster was a painted tiger with blood dripping from two bared fangs. On the upper-right corner, a huge clenched fist was raised over the tiger's head like a hammer. The legend said, DOWN WITH THE AMERICAN PAPER TIGER!

"Little soldiers," Miss Feng, the teacher called, "today we're going to hit both the American paper tiger and its running dog, Chiang Kaishek! Those who hit a bull's-eye will win a prize. I want you to pick up two mud balls and hit the targets!"

The custodian always prepared the mud balls in two big buckets. The pupils, laughing and shouting slogans, picked up the mud balls and started pelting the pictures with them. For a few minutes, the balls flew wildly, splashing over the wall. Jimmy picked up one ball and hit Chiang Kaishek. Then he stopped.

"What's the matter?" the teacher grabbed his arm and demanded. "Why don't you throw a second mud ball?"

He did not answer. He just stared at Miss Feng's skinny face, his mouth clamped tightly.

"Answer me!" Miss Feng yelled at him. "Why don't you hit the American tiger? Hit, hit! Hit the American paper tiger!"

After she had shaken him a few times, he still refused. She threatened to punish him, but he only stared, his mouth twisting and tears welling out of his eyes.

Mabel rushed over, removed the mud ball from his hand, and said, "All right, let's go home."

"How dare you!" the teacher shouted, glaring at Mabel. "Who's running this school, you or me?"

"Sorry, Comrade Feng," Mabel said. "I told him his father is an American citizen. That's why he refuses to hit the American tiger."

"You were a stubborn little boy, weren't you?" Charles said, laughing.

Jimmy also told his father about a difficult year when everybody suffered. It was the year his grandfather Hu Yin committed suicide.

"Your grandfather?" Charles asked, surprised. "What grandfather?"

"Grandmother's husband, remember? The military governor of Hunan."

Charles vaguely remembered that Brigid, Mabel's mother, had refused to leave China because she wanted to find her long-lost husband.

It was 1962, Jimmy said, the year of a horrible famine in Hunan, brought about by Chairman Mao's Great Leap Forward campaign. China was still sending ammunition, supplies, and advisers to Hanoi.

Jimmy was Hu Yin's favorite grandson. Every evening he would sit him on his lap, rock him, and tell him stories about his own youth. He had been a beggar, a soldier, and a grave robber who had robbed the empress dowager's tomb and donated the money to the government to fight the Japanese. In that war, the Japanese had shot six holes in his body; Jimmy had admiringly examined every one of them.

"None in my back," Hu Yin had said proudly, turning his back to Jimmy for inspection.

One evening, when Hu Yin was telling stories after dinner, his aide came in and reported that a farmer had been arrested and paraded in the street. The soldiers had taunted him, tortured him, and poured manure over his head. Hu Yin hated such cruel and humiliating treatment of anyone. He asked what the farmer had done. The aide said he had told the truth about the crop failure in his village. The people had been eating grass roots and tree bark, but the provincial party secretary had reported to the central government that Hunan had a glorious bumper crop. He had made up the glowing report to glorify Chairman Mao's collective farming and Great Leap Forward. Nobody dared to criticize Mao.

Angered by such stupidity, Hu Yin ordered his car and went to see the party secretary, who ranked higher than the governor. That night Hu Yin did not come home. The next day the aide returned to say that Hu Yin had been arrested. Two days later, they found him hanging from a beam in the county jail.

Jimmy stopped and swallowed, trying to hold back his tears. "I was very sad," he went on. "Hu Yin was my hero. I thought he was the most powerful man in Hunan. Later I learned how wrong I was. Even Liu Shaoqi, the president, was arrested and paraded with a dunce cap for going against Mao's policies. He also died in jail." He blew his nose and added with a smile, "You can see how happy I am to see the change, Father. From now on, no more dictators, no more tyranny. Now tell me the things about Mother that I do not know."

"What do you mean?" Charles asked.

"The beautiful young lady you married before I was born. Was she a good cook? Did you two quarrel?"

Charles thought for a moment. Mabel couldn't even boil an egg. All the cooking and washing had been done by an amah. They had rarely quarreled, but when they did, Mabel would carry on a cold war for a day or two, refusing to speak to him. Amah had said that every time he was late for dinner, Mabel would pace back and forth in the living room, glancing at her watch. During each cold war, Mabel would swear that she would never wait for him again. But each time the amah asked if she wanted her dinner, she would always say, "Five more minutes. If he does not come home in five more minutes, we'll eat and feed the leftovers to the neighbor's dog." After several more "five more minutes," she would go to her bedroom and pout, refusing to eat. The amah had told him that once in a while she would sneak out of the room to listen for his footsteps.

"Do Do is like that, too," Jimmy said. "She will carry a cold war to bed, sleeping all night facing the wall. Wonder how she can do that."

Charles laughed. "Thank God your mother wasn't like that!"

4

Mabel was buried at the foot of Yu Lu Mountain on a small island in the Xiang River, a short distance from Changsha, the capital of Hunan. Charles and Jimmy took a boat to the isle, taking with them several gifts packed in a large bamboo basket.

The neglected graveyard was overgrown with weeds. Half-hidden in weeds and dried brush, the modest tombstone on Mabel's grave was toppled and broken. Her Chinese name, roughly carved, was still readable, but the dates were gone. Ashamed of its shabby condition, Jimmy started pulling weeds and trying to right the tombstone.

"The Red Guards," he said breathlessly. "They went around breaking tombstones and robbing the dead. Look at some of the graves."

Charles looked around. Indeed, some of the graves looked as if they had been robbed; nothing but heaps of wood and white bones were left. He quietly helped with the weeding, trying to control his grief. Luckily, Mabel's grave had not been tampered with, probably because it looked too shabby.

They cleared a small area in front of the grave and laid down a bouquet of flowers. Both bowed to the grave three times, then stood silently for a few minutes. "Mabel, my dear Mabel," Charles said in English, allowing tears to creep down his cheeks. "Forgive me. Please forgive me."

Jimmy muffled a sob and turned away. He had not visited

his mother's grave for more than a year, leaving it in such an awful state that his heart ached. He wanted to throw himself down and beg for her forgiveness, but in Communist China such an expression of emotion was taboo; he simply could not bring himself to do it. He had brought offerings—a bowl of rice, a whole cooked chicken, a plate of fresh fruit, and six incense sticks. He lighted the incense sticks and laid them in front of the grave along with the offering food. It was a ritual practiced during Ching Ming, the ghost festival when all graves were supposed to be weeded and brush cleared by the loving relatives.

Charles was pleased with this extra tribute. "Jimmy," he said, "I'd like to have your mother's grave rebuilt. Can you find an architect?"

"Architect?" asked Jimmy, somewhat puzzled.

"I want it to be a shrine. Very elaborate. Is it possible?"

Jimmy thought for a moment. "Everything is possible, Father," he said enthusiastically, with a smile. "China is a free country now."

Xiangjiang Guest House, old, huge, and gray, was the only luxury tourist hotel in Changsha. A massive building on Zhongshan Road, it was close to the business center. Since the government's open-door policy, the building had been painted and the service upgraded. On each floor, there was a service desk with a swarm of attendants waiting to do the guests' bidding around the clock, from fetching drinking water to shining shoes. Most of them were aborigine girls from the countryside, healthy and rosy-cheeked. Dressed in white uniforms, they all looked fresh and attractive, smiling brightly, their dark eyes sparkling. They reminded Charles of the popular song he had learned to hum in the old days. The song "Peach Flower River Is the Nest of Beauties" was about the aborigine girls of Hunan. And he could not help humming it when he entered his room.

Jimmy was glad that his father was happy. Even the usual foul Hunan weather had changed. For three days, Changsha had been bathed in bright sun. Every time they returned to the hotel, there was a group of visitors sitting in the lobby waiting to see them. They were mostly strangers who claimed that they were relatives. An American citizen in town was big news. Both Charles and Jimmy had been interviewed. The local evening news had reported the successful Chinese-American who had returned to seek his roots.

This afternoon, as they returned from a visit to Mabel's grave, a family of five was waiting for them in the lobby. Hong Nai Nai, the matriarch of the family, her short hair combed behind her ears and her blue cotton Mao uniform shapeless and drab, stepped forward, sank onto her knees in front of Charles, and started kowtowing to him. It was a shocking act even to the natives, but the sixty-year-old lady was old-fashioned. Besides, she had kowtowed numerous times to the Red Guards and the Communist "tree trunks" in her village during all the anti-this and anti-that canpaigns.

"Uncle Hong," she said in a thick Hunan dialect, "welcome to Hunan. I, your niece, and my brood of four are here to pay you our respects and to wish you ten thousand blessings."

Charles, bewildered and surprised, quickly helped the lady to her feet. The rest of the family, two daughters and two sons, all dressed in drab Mao uniforms, bowed deeply. Hong Nai Nai introduced them and claimed that they were descendants of the Hongs of Hunan and Guondong. By tracing the family tree, she had discovered that she was one generation lower than Charles, therefore Charles was her uncle and her children's granduncle, a true ancestor who deserved the traditional nine kowtows. Charles realized that in China anyone who had the same last name was an uncle or cousin or nephew, regardless of age.

To prevent the family from carrying out such a feudal salutation, Charles bade them to sit down in the numerous rattan chairs in the lobby. Hong Ta, the oldest son, a nervous, skinny man with nicotine-stained fingers, had a favor to ask. He told Charles that their sick father, Hong Kung, still lived in a cowshed in the countryside. He was a writer and had published stories that the provincial party secretary regarded as antirevolutionary. The government had banished him to the country to have his thoughts corrected through hard labor. Now that the Cultural Revolution was over and all the accused had been liberated, the government seemed to have forgotten about Hong Kung.

"He still lives in a cowshed," Hong Ta said in a tremulous voice. "Even though he is free to come and go. But where can he go? It's sixteen miles from the nearest village, and there's only a dirt road with ankle-deep mud. There is no transportation. And we live fifty miles away, with nine members of our family crammed into three rooms. . . ."

"Two sons and two daughters and their children," Hong Nai Nai added. "Nine mouths, all told."

"We have been promised larger quarters by the government," Hong Ta went on, his voice rising in anger, "but promises mean nothing. Our pleas have fallen on deaf ears. And our father is still in jail. . . ."

"Almost like jail," Hong Nai Nai corrected him quickly.

"What can I do to help?" asked Charles, feeling sympathetic but helpless. "I am only a visitor."

"Great-uncle," Hong Ta said quickly, "we have prepared what to say to the party secretary. All you have to do is to accompany us to pay the secretary a visit in his yamen. That's all."

Charles turned to look at Jimmy for help. Jimmy had listened to the family's plight with interest. He had known many families in similar situations, and they had all tried to find a back door to reach the authorities. He wondered what the family had prepared to say to the party secretary. Curious, he nodded to his father.

It was a short distance to the party secretary's office. The waiting room was crowded, mostly with weather-beaten men with wrinkled faces and bloodshot eyes. Hong Ta, now energetic and confident, marched to the receptionist and asked to see the party secretary. The receptionist, a young woman wearing a neat Mao uniform and a pair of fashionable gold-rimmed glasses, ignored him at first, but when she heard the word *American*, she looked up.

"Did you say your 'American uncle?' "

"Yes, my American uncle," repeated Hong Ta, pointing at Charles.

After one glance at the distinguished-looking Charles in his foreign suit, the receptionist nodded and went into an inner room. A moment later, she came out and invited the whole brood of Hongs to go in. In the spacious office, furnished with puffed sofas, a long coffee table, several cuspidors, and pots of houseplants, she asked the Hongs to sit down. She said that one of the deputy secretaries would see them in a few moments.

It was almost half an hour before a man came out. Neatly dressed in a Mao suit, he greeted Charles with little bows and apologized for being too busy and keeping them waiting. Having introduced himself as Deputy Secretary Wang, he offered Charles a cigarette from a cloisonné cigarette box. Charles declined it. The secretary fished one out and lighted it. From his nicotine-stained fingers, he was obviously another chain-smoker.

Hong Ta quickly reached for a few cigarettes and pocketed them. Lighting one, he came to the point. "Deputy Secretary," he said without mincing words, his voice strong and firm, "my granduncle is an American. His wife is an American. My uncle has been telling everybody in America how China has progressed. It's beautiful and clean, its people well fed. There are no flies, no thieves, no beggars. Now many of our American relatives have planned to visit us. If they see us crammed into such a hovel, my father still living in a cowshed, they will think my granduncle is a big liar. And China will lose plenty face. That's why we are here today, requesting better housing for our family, so when our American relatives come, we will not lose face."

"How big a place do you need?" the deputy secretary interrupted.

"At least a five-room flat."

"Five!" the deputy secretary said with a sardonic grin, shaking his head slowly.

"Four then," Hong Ta said quickly. "There are ten in our family. Our father will also join us. We can't let our American relatives visit him in a cowshed."

Comrade Wang changed his expression. "All right. An intellectual should live in a decent place. This negligence will be corrected. This is a special case. I'll see what I can do."

The whole family got up immediately and bowed to Comrade Wang. Hong Ta helped himself to a few more cigarettes.

* * *

To express the family's gratitude, Hong Ta extended an invitation to Charles and Jimmy to see a Hunan opera that night. Hong Mei, his younger sister, was starring in the show. Tickets were hard to get, but since they were for American relatives, he was sure that he could get two of the best seats in the orchestra.

"We have all seen it," he said enthusiastically. "My voice has become hoarse from shouting 'hao hao hao'!"

"We wouldn't want to miss it," said Charles, anxious to see a Hunan opera, which was as famous as the other two Hunan products, hot pepper and passionate women.

The theater was three miles from the hotel. An hour before curtain time, Jimmy started arranging transportation. Several phone calls to get a taxi failed. They decided to take the bus.

At the bus depot, under a dim street light, a crowd of more than fifty people was waiting on a tree-lined boulevard with unfinished tall buildings going up amid old, rickety wooden houses. Obviously, Changsha was one of the cities going through the nation's modernization programs in a big way.

Most of the people in the crowd were dressed in dark Mao uniforms with duckbilled caps, except a dozen or so youths who wore blue jeans and wrinkled shirts with their shirttails hanging out. A few had their shirtsleeves rolled up enough to show their new Japanese digital watches. Complete with dark glasses and long hair, they, too, looked alike.

Jimmy tugged at his father's sleeve and whispered, "Watch out. These young men are looking at you like cats eyeing a goldfish."

"Everyone stares at me as if I were a creature from outer space," Charles said. "I'm used to it."

When the bus arrived, Charles remembered what to do. He put a hand over his hip pocket while climbing onto the crowded bus. Everybody was pushing and shoving. When the bus started and stopped, it jerked and threw the passengers back and forth. Struggling for balance with one hand, Charles still managed to keep his other hand on his wallet.

At another stop, a few passengers tried to rush to the door, pushing and squeezing through the crowd. Charles, almost carried to the door, wondered if he should get off and make way for those who wanted to get out. When the door opened, somebody shoved him from the back. To protect himself from falling on his face, he extended both hands as he stumbled out of the bus. At that split second, someone lifted his wallet, and five young men were running off in different directions. He tried to give chase but did not know which one to follow. He yelled, "Stop them! Stop the thieves!"

Everybody was watching and gaping, but nobody tried to stop the fleeing gang. Soon they disappeared around the corners and into the darkness. The bus was gone, leaving behind a trail of black smoke.

Charles sighed. He should have left his wallet in the hotel room. He wasn't too upset, for he had left all his travelers' checks in the hotel.

He remembered an old story. An accountant had buried three hundred taels of silver. To make sure they were safe, he had put a sign over it that said, "No three hundred taels of silver are buried here." Why he had kept his hand over his wallet, he did not know. Perhaps he was as stupid as that accountant.

Jimmy suggested that they go to the police immediately. At the nearest police station, the indifferent officer on duty produced a sheet of paper and asked Jimmy to fill it out. It was not until Jimmy told him that the victim was an American citizen that the officer suddenly became alert. He called the captain, who came out and invited them into his office. An orderly served tea. All smiles, the captain offered them his own cigarettes from a thin silver case. He was a middle-aged man in a black uniform; his weather-beaten face and large paunch told his life's story, that of a man of humble origins having risen from the ranks. With a thick Hunan accent, he asked routine questions. Charles let Jimmy do all the talking.

By the time they were driven back to their hotel in a police car, it was almost midnight. Charles went to bed, regretting that he had missed the opera. The theft was only an inconvenience. He doubted that the thieves would have much use for his credit cards, for only in Beijing, Shanghai, and Canton were those cards accepted. He quickly put the robbery out of his mind and went to sleep.

He was awakened by a vigorous tapping on the door. He turned the bedside lamp up and glanced at his watch: four-thirty A.M. He wondered what had gone wrong. Sleepily, he put on his robe and padded to the door. Framed in his doorway was Captain Wu, smiling happily. Standing behind him were Jimmy and two other police officers.

"They have caught the thieves," Jimmy said. "They need your signature on some documents."

"Congratulations, Mr. Hong," the captain said graciously. "I think we have gotten everything back, except your credit cards, which were found in an outhouse. I'm sure they will be safe in there, so there's no point in fishing them out. Can we come in?"

"Of course," Charles said.

The hotel had twenty-four-hour service. A maid came in and served everybody fragrant jasmine tea in covered cups. Sipping tea noisily, the captain told Charles that in China nothing would be lost.

"Have you heard the story about a foreign guest who lost a razor? When a hotel maid found it, she immediately took it to the manager, who chased the guest to the train station and returned it."

Charles remembered that he had read about it. It was a disposable razor. "I'm sure everything is safe in China, Captain," Charles said.

"We caught all five thieves. See if anything else is missing besides the credit cards." After another sip of tea and with a cigarette hanging on his lower lip, he fished out a sealed envelope from a pocket and handed it to Charles with both hands. "Please examine the contents and tell me if all the money is returned."

Charles opened the envelope and took out his wallet. He counted the money. Not a Chinese yuan was missing. "It's a miracle, Captain," he said with a smile. "I must say your police work is probably the best in the world. Congratulations!"

Chuckling happily, the captain produced three documents written on police stationery. Charles dutifully signed them, acknowledging the receipt of all his lost property except the credit cards.

The police left about the time Charles was accustomed to having his breakfast. He called room service and ordered his favorite Chinese breakfast—hot bean milk, rice gruel, and boiled salted eggs. Jimmy ordered ham and eggs and coffee.

"Oh, the police told me to ask you a favor," he said.

"Oh? A little gratuity?"

"No. They want you to treat yourself as a Chinese and the theft as a family affair."

"What does that mean?"

"The Chinese have an old saying: Don't expose family ugliness to outsiders."

Charles laughed. "Well, it's a good story. It's hard to forgo the pleasure of telling it."

"Only if you knew how much they went through, Father."

"What did they go through?"

"They mobilized all the security guards, the police, and the army. They cordoned off a radius of five miles around the scene of the crime. They questioned every household and searched some of them. They told everybody how important it was to return the lost wallet to a foreigner, lest Hunan lose plenty of face and foreigners would be reluctant to invest their money here. Sure enough, somebody tipped off the police, and they captured the five thieves before dawn. The captain said they'll get five years."

Charles felt sorry for the gang of five. "Five years of hard labor for lifting a wallet?" he asked incredulously, shaking his head.

During his two weeks in China, Charles had discovered a lot of things that surprised him. Years ago, before the Japanese invasion, he had heard that white men were the real privileged class. In Shanghai, at a public park in the British Concession, there was a sign that said, CHINESE AND DOGS ARE NOT ALLOWED.

Today, many places in China were again not open to yellow

faces . . . such as Beijing's friendship store. Even a Chinese-American like him had to produce identification at the entrance. Today, a foreigner enjoyed the best of everything, but also paid through the nose. The large restaurants had three grades of dinners and service. The gold grade was for the foreign customers, the silver grade for the overseas Chinese, and the bronze class for the natives. An egg dish in a bronze dinner cost one jinmingbi, about thirty American cents; in a silver grade it was sixty cents; in gold grade, $1.50.

During a leisurely breakfast conversation with Jimmy at the Beijing Hotel, Charles learned that when they traveled together, he always paid double—airline tickets, hotel rooms, dinners, and service.

"I also walked on many red carpets with you, Father," Jimmy said, "thanks to your American haircut and American-style clothing. Without them, you would have walked on dirt like the rest of us. That's why Pang Sin has stopped dying his hair black. He has reddish hair, you know."

"Who is Pang Sin?" Charles asked, surprised.

"He's Mother's oldest son by a previous marriage," he said. "I thought you knew."

Charles felt hurt. "Nobody told me. Go on, tell me about him."

"He has red hair and a white man's build, but the rest of him looks Chinese. He said he was the son of an American sailor killed at Pearl Harbor. That's all we know. Grandfather changed his name to Chinese to make him more Chinese."

Charles kept quiet. He did not want to know any more.

"We invited him to see you when you first arrived," Jimmy said. "But he did not show up. He's married to a general's daughter."

"Must be a smart fellow," Charles said.

He decided not to ask any more questions. He only wanted to know the Mabel who had existed after they met. Whatever past she had had was none of his business. He had married a wonderful woman, beautiful, cheerful, loving, and amusing, who had given him two very exciting years.

The limousine was waiting, his bags loaded. He finished

his breakfast quietly and straightened up. "Well, my stomach, the inner man, is satisfied. Time to fly back home and make plans. There's a great job ahead."

On his way back to Hong Kong, he was vaguely annoyed by the thought of Pang Sin, Mabel's other son he had never met. But he was growing increasingly curious about the half-breed with reddish hair and a white man's build. Why hadn't he suspected that Mabel had a secret past? Why had she hidden such a previous marriage from him? Or had it been a casual affair—a sort of one-night stand?

He found the suspicion very painful. He quickly turned his thoughts to China and began to feel excited. All the way back to Hong Kong, he could not keep his mind off her.

5

Sitting in his new house on the Peak, Charles watched through the picture window the breathtaking view of Hong Kong Bay. Twenty years ago, when he had moved there from Hawaii to start his hotel business, Hong Kong had been alluring, like a mysterious mountain shrouded in fog in a Chinese painting. Later, it had become an open book, a receptacle for refugees, adventurers, and fugitives. Many ruthless former Red Guards and unemployables from Communist China had drifted across the border and organized murderous gangs.

Some were even political. He had heard of a gang called the Blue Dragons that plotted to put Jiang Qing, Mao's widow, on the throne and proclaim her the empress dowager of the Blue Dragon Dynasty. According to the police, many convicted robbers, extortionists, and drug traffickers had a blue dragon tattooed on their arms.

Hong Kong was never dull. The British colony was ultramodern and yet backward. The majority of the inhabitants were superstitious, believing in mysticism and fortune-telling. Infidelity and lack of filial piety were destroying traditional Chinese family values. The working class lived from day to day; the rich rollicked in easy profits from wild speculations.

But still it was heaven compared to Mainland China where the Communist leaders constantly toppled each other as if they were playing musical chairs. A president had died in a labor camp; a military commander in chief had planned a coup, and his airplane had been sabotaged and crashed; the Gang of Four, including Jiang Qing who had imprisoned millions, had in turn been thrown into jail. The present paramount leader, Deng Xiaoping, had been in and out of prison several times himself.

Shock waves from China always affected Hong Kong, making people feel on edge. Many had been trying to emigrate. The fatalists were plunging into a decadent life, like the war days in Chonqing. People squandered money. But the elite were still in Hong Kong, building and raking in fortunes. Now that China had opened up, it had become more of a gold mine for smart and daring entrepreneurs. Charles's Hong Kong wife, Aimee, always felt at home here among her relatives and friends. Marathon mah-jongg games and idle gossip sessions in teahouses kept her happy and content. The marriage remained polite and dull, with hardly a harsh word exchanged between them. Questions were seldom asked, jealously was almost nonexistent. Only pride and ego surfaced occasionally to ruffle their domestic tranquillity.

When he thought of Aimee, he invariably remembered Mabel, as if Mabel always poked her head out from nowhere and asked seductively, "Still love me?"

For the past twenty-five years, he had never forgotten their wedding anniversary and her birthdays. He had always celebrated those occasions in an exclusive restaurant alone, ordered two dinners and toasted her with champagne, ignoring the waiter's discomfort. Sometimes a waiter, suspecting that he was being stood up, would say sympathetically, "She'll be here soon, I'm sure."

Quite often he would sit in the living room watching Hong Kong Bay and wishing Mabel were there with him. He never forgot how they had met, and the little episode still amused him. He had been twenty-two, running his father's scrap-iron business in Wuhan. At a party, his American friend Sam Cohen had introduced them. She was eighteen, voluptuous, with a small waist, perfect hips and bust. She had black wavy hair, sparkling dark eyes, sensual lips, and dimples. She was so perfect that he had a sudden feeling of inferiority. He became awkward and began stammering. Sam Cohen recognized the symptoms and appointed himself as "the old man under the moon," a Chinese term for a go-between. But the war interrupted a possible romance.

A year later, they met again at Sam Cohen's party in Chonqing. She had not changed, but he had. The war had toughened him; he was more confident and sophisticated. His heart pounding and hands sweating, he cornered her, and they talked. But a drunken sailor disrupted the party by pestering her and chasing her around. By the time Sam restrained the sailor, Mabel and her mother had fled. Charles had spent several sleepless nights thinking about her and regretting that he had not asked her address.

One day, while working in his office, he had heard on the radio that Japan had surrendered. The happy news made him choke with tears. An eight-year-old war had finally ended. Celebrating the occasion, he poured himself a drink, toasted China's victory, and smashed the empty glass against the wall.

Outside, noises of celebration had started. Hundreds of people had gathered on the street to shout and sing patriotic songs. He hurried to the window to watch. Lion dancers pranced, and firecrackers exploded. He decided to join the celebrants. As soon as he stepped out of the building, he heard a sob. Sitting beside a battered suitcase near the entrance was a pretty young woman. It was Mabel.

She told him that she had quarreled with her mother and walked out. She had remembered where he worked and came to ask for help, but had not summoned up the courage to enter the building. She was so ashamed and so helpless.

He took her home. At his apartment, he gave her his bed and slept on a sofa in the living room. Still a virgin, he had always believed that sex was for marriage. For almost a week, he was torn between that belief and a wild desire to slip into bed with her and make passionate love.

One night, having tossed on the sofa into the wee hours, he finally drifted away in a restless sleep. Suddenly, he was awakened by a soft nude body beside him. He felt her warm breath and a wet tongue licking his ear. "Love me?" she whispered.

After that night, he was happy but tormented and confused . . . happy that he had become a man, a conquering hero who had made a woman moan and groan as though she were drowning in a sea of passion, tormented because he was still torn between his moral code and his wild act. He still believed that sex belonged only to a wedding night. He had thought of marriage many times, but numerous questions kept popping up. Should he marry a virgin or not? The more he thought about it, the more confused he became. Finally, he decided to ask Sam Cohen's advice.

Sam agreed to meet him in a small coffee shop called Little Red Heart in Sha Ping Ba. His heart pounding, Charles drove across town amid debris, burned houses, and collapsed buildings. The Japanese bombing had almost flattened the entire wartime capital.

Sam, bearded and wearing a khaki safari suite, was waiting for him at a corner table in the tiny coffeehouse. He sounded a little patronizing, but Charles did not mind. Sam was a lady's man and a good teacher on the subject.

"So you've met a girl," Sam said. "It's about time, Charlie. I've been wondering if you were a eunuch or what. Describe her. I won't be able to write the right prescription unless I know something about the subject."

"Well, she is young and pretty," Charles said hesitantly, not too sure how to describe her without revealing her identity. "And she is kind of . . . experienced."

"So you have slept with her?" Sam asked with a raised eyebrow.

"Y-yes, many times. But I can't fool around with a woman unless I marry her. That's my problem."

"Are you in love?"

"Yes, but she is kind of experienced."

"What's wrong with that?"

"I always thought a man should marry a virgin. Shouldn't he?"

Sam took a sip of coffee, gave his cigar several puffs, and said, "Marriage is like a business partnership, Charlie. If I want a business partner, I'd rather have someone who is experienced. If you are in love, never let that bother you. Never!"

Charles's eyes sparkled; it was exactly what he had hoped to hear. He asked anxiously, "Would you marry an experienced girl yourself, Sam?"

"Of course I would. Like dancing, it's a lot more enjoyable to dance with someone who knows how and doesn't have two stiff left legs."

"That's what I thought," Charles said with a happy smile.

"That's it, then!" said Sam, putting out a hand for him to shake. "Let's set a date to tie the knot. I'll give her away if she needs a father. Does she have a father?"

Charles did not know.

Sam went on, "I'll bet your parents have been badgering you to give them a plump little boy so they can rock him on their knees. I know all Chinese parents do."

"They sure do, Sam. Well, if you think virginity isn't that important, then it isn't. I can sleep on that. Thanks a lot, Sam."

"Good! If you need any more advice, let me know. Since she is experienced, I don't suppose you need any pointers in the sex department—or do you?"

"If I do, I'll call," said Charles, blushing a little. He was tempted to tell Sam who the girl was, but changed his mind. When they walked out of the café, Sam put a fatherly arm around him and hugged him affectionately.

"Charlie," he said, "one last piece of advice. Love is like a plant. It dies easily from neglect. Keep it fertilized."

"Fertilized? With what?" he asked, looking puzzled.

"Say 'I love you' once in a while. It's the cheapest fertilizer there is, and a woman loves it."

The new house he and Aimee had bought was above May Street, an area where no Asians had been allowed to live or own property. After the Second World War, the law had changed, and many Chinese moved to this "forbidden" area, living side by side with retired British generals and admirals.

The house had been expanded by the last owner, Admiral Harrington of the British Navy, retired. It consisted of seven bedrooms with views, a library, and an office. A servants' quarters had been added in the back beside the huge, ultramodern kitchen. It was rumored that the admiral was a gourmet and glutton, with his gallbladder and liver ruined by too much good food and wine. He had sold the house to Charles, moved to Scotland, and become a vegetarian, nursed by many nieces and grandnieces who smothered him with love. Charles still kept the admiral's portrait in the living room as a warning against overeating.

He loved the place for its fantastic view. Aimee loved the address, which represented money and prestige. Whenever she told people where she lived, she seldom failed to add, "It's above May Street."

As Charles watched the bay through the huge picture window in the living room, the sun was setting. In the distance on the Kowloon side, he could see Shanghai Mary's all-girl crew washing a luxury liner in exchange for the ship's leftovers. Shanghai Mary was Aimee's best friend. She operated a fancy restaurant in Kowloon called the Golden Phoenix, which featured gourmet food made of leftovers. The American sailors, hating their own chow, happily dined on Golden Phoenix's gourmet dinners without knowing that they were actually devouring leftovers from their own ships' galleys.

It was rumored that the restaurant had many secret rooms in which orgies were staged. Its street was handsome, lined with trees and American dollars; nearby were little lanes full of money changers, whores, and pickpockets. Foreigners found the area exotic, colorful and exciting, happily allowing bar girls to drain their wallets in American-style bars. Aimee spent most of her evenings at the gaudy restaurant playing mah-jongg with idle rich ladies. All scandals were aired amid giggles and frowns; politics was discussed with exaggerated disgust.

Shanghai Mary, her enormous body encased in a colorful Hawaiian muumuu and her round face heavily made up, was a middle-aged matron with a loud laugh. Charles had learned that there was not a serious bone in her fat body, and she was horribly ignorant. People had overheard her ask a foreigner if the popular Gorbachev whom everybody talked about was a famous Indian guru. She knew of only one American president, Richard Nixon. She encouraged free speech, including profanity, and had many racy stories to tell.

Charles avoided Shanghai Mary's restaurant. But he was glad that his restless wife had a place to go and that Shanghai Mary kept her busy and entertained.

This Sunday evening, Aimee came back unusually early,

bringing with her Dr. Wei-ming Fu. Charles had seen Dr. Fu's ad in almost all the Hong Kong papers. The leading *feng shui* expert in the colony, Dr. Fu hired himself out to analyze new buildings' topography to see if their "wind and water" were in harmony. Even the Bank of America had followed his advice and made certain changes in its bank building to balance its yin and yang.

Charles did not believe in Dr. Fu's gibberish, no matter how famous. But he received him politely and ordered tea. Dr. Fu had no time for tea. He immediately started examining the floors, doors, and windows, and knocking on the walls.

He was a fiftyish man with dark skin, sunken cheeks, and a short chin that sported a thin goatee. When he finished inspecting the living room, he asked to see the rest of the house. Aimee sent for her personal maid, Woo Mah, to show him the other rooms.

While waiting, Aimee asked, "Charles, do you know our house number?"

"Of course," he said, surprised. "One Twenty-four."

"We must apply for a new number," she said.

Charles was taken aback. "Why?"

"Because four is pronounced '*se*' in Chinese. It means death. One Twenty-four means one or two people in our house will die."

"Who said so?"

"Dr. Fu."

"Look, Aimee, we all die."

"What's so bad about changing the house number? With all your connections, one phone call from your secretary will do it. Do you know what else Dr. Fu said about the unlucky number four?"

"I don't know," he said wearily. "Frankly, I'm not too interested."

"I'll tell you anyway. Today, everybody is praising Deng Xiaoping's government. He has turned a new page for China. But in four years it will collapse, because four means death."

"Hogwash!" said Charles, trying to soften his harsh words with a smile. "Aimee, Deng Xiaoping's government will last as long as he lives, and he will live forever. You know why?

Because when I visited him a few months ago, I saw a miracle. His cigarette smoke curled up and formed three words, 'I never die.' "

Dr. Fu said that the house was sitting on the forward part of a dragon, slightly askew, so evil spirits could enter easily. To correct this, the front door should be moved one foot to the east to balance the weight and make the dragon more comfortable. The master bedroom window should either be covered or moved toward the east three feet to avoid facing the jagged skyline of Hong Kong. Jagged objects were evil, a disruptive force to good *feng shui*.

Charles absolutely refused to have the door moved. After consultation with Dr. Fu, Aimee finally accepted a compromise. Since evil spirits could not make turns, a nine-dragon screen would be placed inside the front door to make the entrance crooked.

After Dr. Fu's visit, Charles became more alienated from his wife. Every time he saw the gaudy nine-dragon screen, he remembered Mabel; every time his teenage son, Raymond, practiced his drums, he thought of sending him to China for better education.

China had become his new love.

6

Do Do had been brought up in Hunan by a middle-class family, a rare breed, for China, as she remembered, primarily had only two classes—the rich and the poor. Her father, an herbalist of modest success, always dreamed of becoming rich. He experimented with herbs, trying to invent a pill that would cure the common cold, which was the plague of the chilly and wet province. All the children had perpetual runny noses and nasty coughs. Do Do remembered that her playmates had all developed the habit of wiping their noses on their sleeves. She did not adopt the habit because her father had threatened to cane her buttocks if she did.

But her father's invention never helped her colds. Instead of wiping her nose with her sleeve, she sniffled. When she grew up, her mother always stuffed her pockets with little handkerchiefs. For that she was grateful; by the time she went to middle school, she was neat and tidy, without any bad habits.

At home, relatives and friends referred to her as "Thousand Gold," a polite term for all daughters. But her father gave her a bad name, Do Yu, or "Surplus," to fool the evil spirits. In Hunan, people believed that evil spirits always seduced pretty and lucky girls. To show the evil spirits that this girl was no good, a bad name was necessary. It was not until after the Communists had liquidated all ghosts and evil spirits along with landlords that her parents changed her name to Do Do, meaning "Plentiful," a lucky name.

Do Do remembered her childhood without much pleasure. There was little entertainment. Her mother used to take her to see public executions on the military drilling ground in the center of the city, behind the governor's yamen. They were quite festive, like social occasions. The condemned men were first paraded along the main thoroughfare. Standing on horse-drawn carts, they looked proud and daring, singing and chanting slogans as though they had suffered great injustice. Once she saw a man stripped to his waist, his muscles rippling, demand a whole chicken as his last meal. On his back he bore a placard with his crime written in classical Chinese language, which Do Do was too young to read. A soldier bought him a whole chicken dinner from a food peddler. He ate it ravenously, spitting out bones noisily. Between swallowing and chewing, he scolded the government in a heavily accented dialect. It was the only time he had enjoyed freedom of speech.

At the execution ground, he was helped down from the cart by two soldiers who made him kneel and told him to bow his head. The man refused; he kept talking and shouting and beating his bare chest, swearing that he would come back and haunt those who had condemned him. Suddenly, Do Do's mother put her hands over Do Do's eyes. There was a shot. The executioner had put a bullet through his skull. When Do Do was permitted to see, the man had toppled on his face, blood still spurting from the hole in his head.

Do Do asked her mother why people loved to watch public executions. Her mother whispered, "They are fascinated by the freedom of speech the condemned enjoy. Sometimes they speak everybody's mind."

Even though she had attended many executions, she had not become immune to killings. She hated blood. During the anti-insects, anti-birds and other harmful vermin campaigns, she had refused to kill even a fly.

But Chairman Mao had done a great deal of good for China and her family. Her father became an admirer of the Chairman. He studied diligently everything Mao had written. Her mother was offered a job in a hospital, making money like a man. She became a nurse and taught Do Do everything she had learned. Everybody had a job. Many contagious diseases disappeared. Communists were no longer called "bandits"; they were treated as China's saviors and addressed as "Comrade." "Mister" and "Miss" were eliminated from the Chinese vocabulary; there were no more wives or husbands; all married people were called "lovers." It took years before Do Do's parents could call each other "Lover." This change was the only thing her father disliked about communism.

Both her parents had died of hardship and stroke. She had missed them so much that she often wept secretly when she was alone. Now that China had entered an exciting new era, she no longer had time to think of her parents and be sentimental.

It was a bright day. She returned home for lunch. Jimmy had cooked two of her favorite dishes—mushui pork and scallion fried eggs. He had left them in the new Japanese refrigerator Jimmy's father had bought for them. After Charles Hong's visit, their two-room apartment had become a conversation piece and a gathering place for friends who enjoyed their twenty-five-inch color television, another of Charles's gifts. Occasionally, some friends would bring their dirty clothes and wash them in their brand-new washing machine. Charles had talked about giving them an automobile, but both of them declined, saying that only maniacs would drive in Beijing traffic.

Do Do heated the dishes in the microwave oven and enjoyed them with a bowl of rice that had been kept warm in a Japanese rice-cooker. The cooker was the only modern gadget that they had bought with their own money, and it had cost them two months of their combined salaries.

There were two notes beside the dial telephone left by Jimmy: "Call Mark Hansen at Beijing Hotel, Rm 551. He has brought you something." "Call Yun Mei. She's like an ant on a hot stove. She's waiting for your rescue. A mystery to me."

She and Jimmy often communicated in English, a habit they had adopted as students at the Foreign Language School. She ate as she made the calls. The kitchen was so small that everything was within easy reach—phone, writing pads, assorted pens in a bamboo holder, and the rice-cooker. She could even reach for food in the refrigerator without getting up from her chair. The oblong dining table also served as their office desk, and it was long enough for an overnight guest to use as a bed.

She felt lucky that Jimmy was a tidy man and did not mind sharing all the household chores. The tiny apartment was cramped but was never dirty or dusty. Everything had its proper place except the few pots of houseplants, which they moved around trying to achieve the best aesthetic effect.

Neither of the two callers were in. She left messages for them to call back. She would be home for the two-hour siesta, then she would ride her bicycle back to her Radio Beijing office in the Broadcasting Building, a short distance from her home.

She enjoyed her work as a reporter and translator. Her recent assignment was to read all the American news magazines, especially *Newsweek* and *Time*, and translate all the news articles and comments that had something to do with China. She tried to be accurate, knowing that the translation would be channeled to the top leaders in Zhong Nan Hai, the nerve center of the party hierarchy. She had been told that the translation rarely arrived at its destiny without some alterations, for top leaders did not like bad news. Before Mao died, good news was all he wanted to hear, she had been told, for the Chairman had high blood pressure and gallbladder problems.

She was a fast worker, and her working hours were flexible. Sometimes she would spend hours in the field, talking to foreign reporters. If she had not been conscientious, she could have taken a four-hour siesta and nobody would have known.

After lunch, she washed the dishes, watered the houseplants, and called Jimmy at Bei Ta. Jimmy was the only assistant professor who had his own phone on his office desk, again a gift from his father. Before they had their own phones, they had had to share community phones, blocks away. Usually, a neighbor was assigned to answer a community phone. Every day, he was found delivering messages like a marathon runner, rain or shine.

"Jimmy," she asked, "who is Mark Hansen?"

"Who knows?" Jimmy said. "He only said he's a friend of my father."

"What did he bring?"

"He didn't say. Just something for you. Probably your sewing machine. He sounds like a pleasant fellow. He can say 'nin hao,' 'zai chian,' and a few other Chinese words. Another one of those Americans who love to practice Chinese on you. Did you call him?"

"Twice. Why didn't you call?"

"But he asked for you. All right, I'll call. Go take a nap. You sound tired."

"That's all right, I'll call again," she said, hanging up.

Jimmy was always helpful. She had never heard him say no to others who needed his help. He and Pang Sin were so different, coming from the same mother. When she remembered that she had almost married Pang Sin, she shuddered. A narrow escape.

It was at the height of the Cultural Revolution. She, Jimmy, and Pang Sin were all Chairman Mao's Red Guards. The schools were shut down. Jiang Qing of the Gang of Four was their commander in chief. They had been ordered to destroy the "four olds," meaning China's four-thousand-year-old culture. They were encouraged to struggle against the intellectuals, invade their homes and ransack their belongings. If they found Mao Zedong's works covered with dust, they would make the owner kneel down and recite a few passages; if he failed, they would accuse him of being a hypocrite who had bought Mao's books not to read but to display.

On that particular afternoon, they found such a "hypocrite," a professor of philosophy at Beijing University. Pang Sin, the group leader, forced the professor's son to thump his father's head on the cement floor. The son, also a Red Guard, obeyed to show his lack of emotional ties, a prerequisite of a good Red Guard. He banged his father's head on the cement until it became a bloody mess. The professor's wife cried and begged him to stop. When she fainted, Pang Sin, his face flushed with excitement, applauded and encouraged the son to keep showing his Red Guard spirit.

Jimmy had tried to stop the son from killing his father, but Pang Sin pushed him away angrily. Do Do was shocked. Had she been engaged to a heartless, bloodthirsty maniac? When she saw Jimmy walk away from the accusation meeting in disgust, she followed and caught up with him. That was when her feelings for Pang Sin died.

Mark Hansen was waiting for her in the lobby of the Beijing Hotel. He was a tall, blond young man, deeply tanned, wearing a rumpled checked shirt and gray gabardine trousers. He greeted her warmly.

She liked him immediately, telling herself that here was a sincere American, an honest reporter with a firm handshake. "Have you eaten?" he asked in Chinese.

"Is this a real question or just a greeting?" she asked, laughing.

"Both," he said. "I was told that besides '*nin hao ma*,' 'have you eaten' is the most popular greeting in North China. It happens that I'm hungry at the same time. Are you?"

"No, but I'll have a cup of tea."

"Follow me."

Mark picked up a box and walked toward the enormous dining hall in the hotel. "By the way," he said, "this is for you. Your father-in-law said you are an anchorwoman at Radio Beijing. You may want to watch yourself. So he sent you a video-cassette recorder."

"Thank you very much," she said, taking the box. "I'm not an anchorwoman, only a reporter. But I'm delighted to have the gift. Both Jimmy and I are movie addicts. Now we can watch all the X-rated films."

Mark looked at her with raised eyebrows. "Oh?"

She laughed. "Most of the American movies are forbidden in China, and ancient. To the government, they are all X-rated. We had not heard of Paul Newman until recently."

They took the nearest empty table. The dining hall was almost full, with most of the tables occupied by foreigners and their Chinese guides or translators. White-uniformed waiters and waitresses stood in groups waiting for signals. Mark raised a hand. A waiter sauntered over with a stack of menus, which he tossed into the middle of the table, unsmiling. He was a skinny young man with thick black hair and a gloomy, narrow face. Do Do had not seen a happy waiter in any of the luxury hotels in Beijing.

"Are you sure you don't want anything to eat?" Mark asked as he scanned the impressive two-page menu.

"I'm sure," she said, wishing she could give the waiter a kick in the shins for looking sour. She always felt uncomfortable in the company of a foreigner if people were rude or the place was dirty. Luckily, Mark Hansen did not seem to notice the waiter's insolence. He ordered a pork chow mein, coffee, and tea.

"On the phone, you described yourself as tall and blond," she said. "There were three in the lobby. I almost went to the wrong guy."

"Sorry," he said. "I should also have told you that I have a long nose."

She laughed. She thought that he could be very handsome if his nose were a bit smaller. "Dustin Hoffman is not bad-looking," she said. "He has a nose even bigger than yours. How did you know my father-in-law?"

"Everybody in Hong Kong knows Charles Hong, the hotel tycoon. All the foreign correspondents want the best living quarters in Hong Kong that don't cost an arm and a leg. Only Charles Hong has them. And he's friendly and approachable. The moment you mention somebody he knows, he'll take you to dinner."

"How do you like China?" she asked.

"Wonderful! Marvelous!" he said. He poured out what Do Do had heard from other foreigners, who had breathlessly described the impressive tree-dotted boulevards, the massive modern buildings under construction, the spotlessly clean homes of the ordinary citizens, the country's elimination of crime and inflation.

"Hey," Hansen added, "I even heard about a tourist who couldn't get rid of an empty ballpoint pen. Every time he tossed it into a hotel wastebasket, the maid fished it out and a hotel clerk chased him to the airport to return it. It happened twice. Is that true?"

Do Do was a little disappointed that Mark Hansen was so naive as to believe such a story.

"Where else have you visited besides Beijing?" she asked.

"Only Beijing. My third time. I have a busy schedule this

week—the Summer Palace, the Forbidden City, a school, a factory, a worker's home. The guides all speak English with a British accent. Charming!"

Do Do was familiar with the authorized itinerary for foreigners. She began to feel a little uncomfortable, wishing he would leave China soon, while he still had such a good impression.

"How long will you stay this time?" she asked.

"Who knows? I'm here to open an office for AP News Bureau in Beijing. It will be the first foreign news bureau in China, I'm told."

Do Do knew it was not true, but she decided to keep quiet. Let him enjoy the illusion for a while longer. When the spell was broken, she would invite him home to have jiaozi. Then he would see how she and Jimmy really lived. They could have a Qindao beer and a good laugh together. But China was still a fabulous market, with a billion potential customers for American businessmen. She hoped it would compensate for his disappointment in the real China, which sooner or later he would see without rose-colored glasses.

Having met Mark Hansen, she rode her bicycle to the *People's Daily*. The Beijing streets were less jammed before three in the afternoon, as it was still siesta time. She peddled energetically, dodging pedestrians and other vehicles like a circus cyclist. By spending two to three hours on a bicycle every day, she had built up stamina and kept her girlish figure, but her thighs seemed to bulge with muscles. Jimmy hated chopstick-like legs, for which she was grateful.

The *People's Daily* was housed in an enormous courtyard with Chinese palatial buildings on each side. The place was full of bicycles, parked amid many potted plants. Do Do went to the eastern building where reporters and copy editors worked in partitioned areas. The office was strangely quiet; phones rang only occasionally, and voices were kept low. Many workers were reading instead of writing; cigarette smoke was heavy.

Do Do found Yun Mei at her small desk writing furiously, her pretty face pale and her long, wavy hair falling over her shoulders. She was one of the daring women who had got rid of her shapeless Mao uniform and had her hair done at a beauty parlor. She wore a pink silk blouse and a short skirt that barely covered her knees.

"Sorry I'm late," said Do Do, taking the chair beside her friend's cluttered desk. "Now tell me what's wrong."

Yun Mei seemed relieved to see her. They had been classmates in the Foreign Language School, and best friends for years.

"You won't believe it," Yun Mei said with a grimace. "I quarreled with the managing editor. I never quarrel, you know that."

"I know," Do Do said. "But why tackle a big man like the managing editor? He holds your rice bowl."

"He almost broke it," said Yun Mei, her eyes reddening with tears. "I'm in a terrible jam, Do Do. Next week I'll be demoted. I'll be a proofreader, reading things that'll bore me to death. I want to write. I want to travel and interview people. I need your help. I want you to talk to the turtle's egg and see if you can change his mind."

"I don't know him that well."

"He made a pass at you in Moscow, didn't he?"

"Yes, but I can't use that to blackmail him. What's wrong? Why did he demote you? Did you reject his advances?"

Yun Mei, almost in one breath, told her what had gone wrong. She had returned from Shandong Province and written a report on a new company called Jewels of Mountain Tai. It manufactured artifacts of Shandong jade, mostly jewelry and carvings of vases and Chinese mythical animals. The company had almost gone bankrupt and badly needed foreign investment and joint-venture partners. She had been assigned to interview the management and to write a promotional article. She submitted the article, but when it came out, she was shocked. The managing editor had personally rewritten it without consulting her. She stormed into his office this morning and demanded a retraction.

"Why?" Do Do asked, surprised. "Chang Ming isn't a bad writer."

"I don't mind his rewrite, good or bad. But he made a liar out of me!"

"Oh?"

"Read this," said Yun Mei, producing the article from her drawer. "He gave the company a glowing report, saying that the exquisite jade carvings were such hot items that seventy-five thousand pieces were sold instantly to a dealer from Canada. The jade jewelry was shipped all over the world. The company could hardly meet the enormous demand. The company was swamped with sales contracts that were piled three feet high. It would take the company years to fill the orders.

"The conclusion is even more ridiculous," Yun Mei fumed. "It boasts that their carving experts have learned their skills from their ancestors, an art form that has been kept a secret in their families for thousands of years. And they will continue to serve the customers to show their love for socialism." She tossed the article onto her desk with a grimace. "I'm going to throw up!"

"What did you write?" Do Do asked.

"I praised the natural beauty of Shandong jade, its quality, its color, and its usefulness. I said it had a tremendous potential as a source of foreign exchange only if the material could be turned into interesting art objects. But the company needed new investment and a new team to improve the workmanship and the marketing. I told the truth!"

"Yun Mei," Do Do said, "you also attempted to smash many rice bowls."

"But the damned company is about to go bankrupt!" Yun Mei said heatedly, her face flushed and her eyes burning with impatience. "We don't want to merely survive, we want to succeed. We want to join the flourishing family of the industrial democracies! How can we compete simply by telling lies?"

Do Do watched her friend, somewhat amused. She thought that Yun Mei was more eloquent and even more attractive when she was incensed. "Yun Mei," she said, "let me talk to him. I know how to handle his type. By the way, did he proposition you?"

"Him!" Yun Mei almost shouted. "I'd rather sleep with a donkey!"

All the heads in the room turned. A few giggled. "Let's go talk in a teahouse," Do Do whispered.

7

The wind churned up the fallen leaves on the street. Jimmy could feel sand hitting his face, and a few grains had already got into his eyes. He leaned against the force of the wind and peddled his bicycle energetically, blinking his eyes, trying to get comfortable. By the time he arrived at Bei Ta, tears had washed out the sand from his eyes. The wind had made the short journey from his home to the university very strenuous, but the effort had toughened him, and he often philosophized, "Nothing is all bad."

He arrived at his class on time. The classroom was packed, as usual, for his was one of the most popular at Bei Ta. Called "English Proficiency," the class required each student to give a three- to five-minute talk on a given subject. Last week's subject had been "Fortune." It was a vague subject; he had selected it to test the students' attitude toward fortune and how they interpreted the term. Most of his students were about ten years younger than he. All of them were the product of the Great Cultural Revolution, exposed to a period of insensitivity and brutality as they grew up. When the Red Guards staged so-called struggle meetings against capitalist roaders and counterrevolutionaries, some of them had watched their own parents insulted and beaten. They had been praised as Chairman Mao's "brave little soldiers" for not showing emotion. It was believed that many of them had been dehumanized and that their own individuality and independent thoughts had all been smothered.

Jimmy was surprised by the results of last week's test. Twenty percent of the students were interested in material fortune; 70 percent believed in spiritual fortune; the rest did not care one way or another. This small group had said that the world was a sea of bitterness; there was no hope and no future, since fortune was beyond anyone's reach.

Happy about the positive results, Jimmy had graded their little speeches generously. One student in the "spiritual fortune" group had impressed him particularly. The young man believed that "fortune" meant "satisfaction." Like the maid in his family who enjoyed cooking—she was happiest when she was in the kitchen chopping and stir-frying dishes. By doing a good job, she also made others happy. In his own case, the student said, he would be the happiest if he could find a cure for cancer, regardless of whether he made any money. It was a bit high-sounding, but his voice was forceful and sincere, and Jimmy had given him an "A."

"Good afternoon," he greeted his students pleasantly as he walked into the classroom. The students returned the greeting in unison. "Today, I want you to choose your own subject for your proficiency speech. Any subject. No restrictions."

A few students looked disappointed, but most of the young faces brightened. He opened his file and called out the name of the first speaker.

A young man with bushy hair stood up and cleared his throat. His subject was "Don't Judge a Person by His Looks."

"In my village in Honan," he began, "we have two girls called 'Stupid Sister.' The first one got the name because she was too pretty. Her parents gave her this ugly name to fool the evil spirits. The second one was called 'Stupid' because she was slow in movement; she had big feet and thick lips. The pretty one was charming and clever; she loved money and a good life, and she attracted a Shanghai gentleman who promised her the moon. One thing led to another. She became a Shanghai prostitute and died of AIDS. Everybody in my village shed tears for her misfortune. The elders quoted a saying, 'Cheeks rosy, life thin.'

"Nobody chased the second 'Stupid Sister.' She had all the days and nights to herself, raising chickens. She sold the chickens on the free market and made more money. She expanded her chicken farm, hired a college graduate who knew scientific chicken farming. In three years, she bought the first private car in Honan. She lived in a two-story brick building furnished with American sofas, Japanese refrigerators, color TV and VCR. She has everything but a boyfriend. She is my sister. Anybody interested?"

He bowed and sat down, provoking a lot of laughter. Jimmy did not know if he was joking or serious, but his talk was clear and interesting. He gave him a "B+."

The next speaker was a serious-looking young man wearing thick-rimmed glasses. He spoke in a deep voice. "My subject is an old saying, 'Hanging out a goat's head but selling dog meat.' Deng Xiaoping's New Socialism, they say, is to make theory of 'Work more, get more.' So we work more. People eat better, production increases. Color has returned to women's faces and clothing, shapely legs are no longer hidden in baggy trousers. Comrade Deng said to critics recently, 'Don't fart too soon. This New Socialism is pragmatic, but we will still have public ownership. We will make some people rich first, so they can help the rest get rich later. Through this process, we will eventually enter Lenin's Utopia, the ultimate goal of communism.'

"Remember, this is Comrade Deng speaking. He is not going to abandon public ownership. But how can you become rich without private ownership? This New Socialism looks like a horse with a donkey's tail to me! Therefore, the whole open-door movement is only 'hanging out a goat head but selling dog meat.' "

He finished the speech with a nod and plunked down on his seat without bowing. The class applauded him wildly. A few looked shocked, staring at Jimmy for his reaction.

Jimmy was surprised. He admired the young man's courage. Such open criticism of the paramount leader was unprecedented in his class. Perhaps freedom of speech was now tolerated; perhaps it came from Deng's open-door policy. Many of his students were the children of old cadres in power. Again it was a good sign; he wanted to give the student an "A," but changed it to a "B+," just in case Comrade Deng did not like it and blew his whiskers.

Jimmy had been told that the happiest man in the world is the one who is anxious to go to work in the morning and anxious to return home after work. If that was the case, he could be considered a happy man. Nearing home, he peddled more energetically. His home, although cramped and not very comfortable, seemed to have a certain magnetism. The closer he got to the dilapidated brick building, the stronger the pull.

He raced up the three flights of stairs and felt proud of the fact that he was not even out of breath. He smelled cooking; it was his favorite dish, eggplant cooked in soy sauce, garlic, and hot pepper. Breathing deeply, he walked into the kitchen and greeted the two ladies cheerfully.

Yun Mei was a frequent guest. She did not even bother to stand up. She waved at him with her left hand, as she was busy cracking watermelon seeds with the other. The kitchen table was full of melon-seed shells, cups, and glasses.

"Jimmy," said Do Do, adding water to the wok and covering it with a lid. "Congratulate Yun Mei. You know the old saying 'Old Man Sai loses his horse. Who knows it's a blessing in disguise?' "

"Come here," said Yun Mei, pointing at her left cheek. "Kiss here."

Jimmy pecked her cheek and was overwhelmed by her perfume. Yun Mei had been totally Westernized except for her taste in food. Her English accent was British, her manners American, her perfume French, but her favorite food was still Cantonese, especially the bizarre dishes such as snapping turtle stewed with chicken feet, snake soup with shark's fins, and rice gruel with a few slices of black thousand-year-old eggs.

"Congratulations," Jimmy said. "What's the good news?"

"She quarreled with her boss and was demoted," said Do Do laying the table for dinner. "Because of that, she got a better job."

"I'm submitting my resignation the first thing in the morning, thanks to your loving and helpful wife."

"Oh?" Jimmy looked at Do Do inquisitively.

"I introduced her to a foreigner, Mark Hansen," Do Do said. "He hired her right away, like love at first sight."

"Who's Mark Hansen?" he asked.

"Have you become an absentminded professor already?" Do Do asked with a laugh.

Jimmy snapped his fingers. "Of course! The American who left you a message. That's fast work. You ought to run a computer dating service."

"Jimmy," Yun Mei said with a scowl, "do you always think of romance? He's opening an office in Beijing, and he's looking for an assistant."

Do Do said, "So Yun Mei says the hell with her old job! She falls right into this God-sent opportunity, making three times as much money. She was depressed, you know. So I called Mark Hansen. He invited us to have a drink. If she hadn't been unhappy, nothing would have happened. So there you are, a blessing in disguise."

"Do you like the man?" he asked, pouring three glasses of wine.

"Don't rush her," said Do Do, laughing.

The cheerful conversation was interrupted by yelling in the next apartment. The neighbor's window was thrown open, and a man's cracked voice could be heard shouting toward the street below, "Mao Zedong, you are nothing! Mao Zedong, you're just a bag of wind!"

"Oh my God! It's Mr. Yang again," said Do Do, quickly closing the window. "Mao Zedong is dead. Doesn't he know?"

"He's insane," Jimmy said sympathetically.

"I'm glad he is," Do Do said. "Otherwise the security guards would have hauled him to jail a long time ago."

Yun Mei hurried to the window to look. "He's putting out a banner."

The banner was a piece of four-by-four white cloth on which a slogan had been written: ALL YOU SLAVES, ARISE! ARISE!

"He sure has guts, insane or not," Yun Mei said admiringly. "Maybe I can write an article about him for an independent publication."

A woman's voice was heard pleading with the man to stop

shouting insults about Mao Zedong. But the man kept scolding Chairman Mao like an irate man berating a misbehaving street urchin.

"See what you've done, Mao Zedong! You've given everybody a rice bowl, but you've taken away our rice tub. What's the use of a rice bowl if there's no rice?"

The neighbor woman tried to drag him away from the window. "Listen, neighbors!" she shouted. "My husband is insane! Don't believe a word he says!"

"How long has this been going on?" asked Yun Mei, bringing out a pad from her handbag to take notes.

"Since Deng Xiaoping announced his open-door policy," Do Do said.

"I don't think he's insane," Jimmy said. "Deng criticized Mao, too. This man thinks he's safe."

The argument next door was getting more heated. There were sounds of a scuffle.

"We've got to stop that before someone gets hurt," said Jimmy, starting for the door.

"I'll go with you," said Yun Mei, following.

After Jimmy and Yun Mei had left, Do Do finished cooking. She had made one soup and four dishes . . . a treat. Without guests, they had only two dishes, a vegetable and a meat. She had been told that it was what Mao Zedong always had when he was alive, two dishes when dining alone and four dishes when entertaining guests. It was no secret that Mao had been a frugal man. He had only a few changes of Mao uniforms; two were saved for formal occasions, a light one for summer and a dark wool one for winter. But Mao had more women companions than changes of clothing. Even when he was dying of Parkinson's disease, he would walk with a young secretary on his arm.

Do Do had always admired Mao despite his mistakes, but her faith had been shaken during the Cultural Revolution. It was only after he had died that people dared to speak their minds. She wondered if her neighbor, Mr. Yang, was clever, speaking his mind under the guise of being insane. Who was he? She was curious. Since the Cultural Revolution, nobody associated with his neighbors; people distrusted each other—

it had become a habit. Even if the husband and wife next door were trying to kill each other, nobody would give a damn.

The door was thrown open. Jimmy and Yun Mei helped Mr. Yang into the room, followed by his haggard wife, her clothes torn and hair disheveled. Mr. Yang was about sixty. He had a gaunt face and sunken eyes, his T-shirt bloodied and his baggy trousers also torn. He grimaced as if he were in great pain.

"He's trying to kill himself," Yun Mei said. "His wife can't manage."

"We'd better call an ambulance," said Jimmy, picking up the phone.

"Sit down, Mr. Yang," said Do Do, helping the man sit at the kitchen table.

Subdued, the man sat and bowed his head. His wife thanked everybody profusely. "He has cancer of the stomach," she said. "Every time he has an attack of pain, he goes berserk. I don't know what I'd have done without your help, Mr. Hong. You're all so kind!"

Jimmy was arguing with somebody on the phone. He slammed down the phone and exploded, "Goddamn!"

"What's the matter?" Do Do asked.

"The hospital refuses to send an ambulance unless it's an emergency. They claim that if the patient can still walk, it's not an emergency."

"Call a taxi," Do Do suggested. She turned to Mrs. Yang and asked her to sit down. "It's dinnertime. You may as well eat with us."

Mrs. Yang declined the invitation but agreed to have a cup of tea. Yun Mei started asking questions. Mr. Yang was quiet, still grimacing in pain. Mrs. Yang did all the talking.

Mr. Yang was a retired engineer from Tianjin. On July 20, 1976, a disastrous earthquake had wrecked Tangshan in Hopei Province, destroying property and killing people with a force equal to four hundred atomic bombs. Do Do remembered the official casualties, 240,000 killed, a quarter of a million injured. Mr. Yang joined the rescue team. For a week, he dug out the dead and the dying from the ruins; he ate and slept among corpses; both the rescuers and the rescued were crying for help.

But help came at a tortuously slow pace. One day, Hua Guo-feng, the successor of Chairman Mao, proudly declared that China had declined aid offered by the United Nations, France, England, and the United States. He said to reporters, "For-eigners want to come to China to give us help. But China is self-sufficient. We don't need any help from outsiders."

When this message was broadcast, Mr. Yang dropped everything and left the disaster area. He returned home a changed man, quiet, gloomy, antisocial. He acted so abnormal that he was fired from his job. He and his wife moved to Beijing, where they lived on his retirement check. After he had been told that he had cancer the previous year, he began shouting insults out the window to nobody in particular. It got so bad that he became violent and often attempted to kill himself by throwing himself out of the window.

While Yun Mei was interviewing Mrs. Yang, Jimmy was still talking on the telephone, pleading with the taxi company to send a taxi. His face flushed, his hands trembling, but his voice still patient, he said, "Look, Comrade, we don't have American money. . . . Because we've spent it."

Yun Mei took the phone and barked into it, "Look, Com-rade, I'm from America. My uncle is dying! I'll pay you foreign exchange rate . . . fifteen renmingbi . . . about five American dollars. I'll even throw in a pair of dark glasses as a tip. . . . Yes, American-made. The trademark and price tag are still on them, intact!"

"Fifteen renmingbi?" Mrs. Yang said. "That's half our month's income! We can't afford it!"

"Don't worry," Jimmy said. "We'll all chip in."

"Fuck them all!" Yun Mei said after she had hung up.

8

Charles Hong was disappointed by Richard Tan's disinterest in China. He was determined to change his best friend's anti-Communist stand. When Deng Xiaoping's book was published and forty million copies were distributed, Charles ordered two thousand copies and sent them out in lieu of New Year's cards. Richard Tan certainly needed a copy. China was on the world map again, with foreigners pouring into the country to talk business and visit the Great Wall.

Charles had collected many of Deng's pictures, had them framed and hung them in his office. There were pictures of Deng swimming, playing bridge, shaking hands with other world leaders, laughing and joking. The one that dominated all the others was Deng's photo on the cover of *Time*, enlarged several times and hung directly behind his desk. He made a note reminding himself to send a copy of Deng's photo to Richard.

This die-hard anti-Communist was beginning to irritate him. He would consider his effort to change Tan's opinion of China his first call of duty. The self-made shipping tycoon was so rich that he could fill everybody's rice bowl in China for years without having to pawn any of his eight hundred–odd ships.

Since his first trip four years ago, what happened in China had become Charles's main interest. He had subscribed to *People's Daily, Inside China, Ta Kung Pao, Evening News, Hong Kong*

Times, and many magazines and small gossip tabloids published in China and Hong Kong. From those publications, he read about China's booming economy and the newly created ten-thousand-yuan families, which included illiterate fishwives who sold fish on the street and had accuminated ten thousand yuans in the bank. There were stories about farmer-peddlers who built brick houses and decorated them with pianos and sewing machines, upstart young entrepreneurs who rode around on Japanese Yamahas in American cowboy boots, showing off their fashionable dark glasses of different styles with trademarks and price tags intact. Some had girlfriends riding on the back in matching tight jeans and colorful boots, their long, wavy hair flowing in the wind. Pedestrians dodged them and gawked at them with envious eyes. Some papers predicted that soon the ten-thousand-yuan families would be scorned like black-and-white television sets. Color TV, VCRs, refrigerator-freezers, and washing machines would be the new status symbols. Some farmers who raised chickens, ducks, and hogs had already acquired all of them. A few millionaires had even built Western-style houses and furnished them with Western furniture and pianos that nobody played.

Charles read all the editorial comments including those published in Communist papers. While the gap between the rich and poor widened, the intellectuals organized groups demanding freedom and democracy. Charles and Jimmy often discussed China's problems on the phone. Both considered Mikhail Gorbachev a new leader who would lead the entire Communist world to peace and prosperity. Charles was excited about his son's deep involvement in Deng Xiaoping's four modernization programs. Jimmy had volunteered as a guide for visiting professors and scholars from America. Do Do had been busy interviewing foreigners, and engaged herself in all kinds of cultural-exchange activities. She even introduced the American "doggy bag" to Chinese restaurants. When leaving a banquet, she never failed to carry away a few bags of leftovers for the skinny students at Bei Ta. The practice raised many eyebrows, but Do Do criticized her critics by saying, "Why slap your own face red and swollen to look healthy?" Charles applauded such a rebuke and enjoyed telling it at dinner parties.

But Sir Richard Tan's political prejudice still annoyed him. Tan was a stubborn man of the old school who had started as a clerk in a shipping company. Now he was one of the two largest shipping tycoons in the Orient. He had two dozen children from a wife and two concubines; he had been knighted, awarded numerous honors and a seat on the boards of some of Hong Kong's most prestigious corporations. His business card was large and impressive, full of awesome titles in both the private sector and government.

Bigamy was a crime in Hong Kong, but Richard Tan lived harmoniously with his three wives in a huge mansion in Kowloon. The government looked on his domestic arrangement benevolently, with one eye closed, treating his bigamy as a man's bad habit. Charles never stopped marveling at Richard's three happy women under one roof. He was also amazed by Richard's brood of children, aged from toddlers to grown-ups, all well behaved and properly educated.

He and Tan often met their close friends at the Turf Club and other prestigious places where businessmen congregated. They also conducted social and business meetings in exclusive restaurants without their wives. In Hong Kong, nobody had to lie to his wife about where he had dined or why he had returned home late at night. Many rich Hong Kong ladies enjoyed all-night mah-jongg games; they also demanded that no questions be asked. If a woman caught her husband cheating, she simply ignored it or found a way to get even, such as buying an extra mink coat that she didn't need, or allowing bugs to ruin it in a neglected closet. A few jealous wives even spread rumors about beauty salons where male beauticians offered extra services. The ladies said that if a man could spend a night with a singsong girl, there was no reason why a wife could not enjoy the skills of a gigolo.

This morning, Charles received a phone call in his office from Richard Tan. He was surprised, for they seldom called each other at their offices for fear their employees would eavesdrop. During their last conversation, Charles had been miffed by Tan's growing militant stand against the Communists. Tan had likened Communist China to a hungry cat that eyed Hong Kong as a tasty goldfish in a tank. Many anti-Communist organizations in Hong Kong had invited him to come aboard with his checkbook, either as a sponsor or an honorary chairman. He supported them all, especially the one headed by his good friend David Loo, an influential legislative councilman. Loo praised and publicized his goldfish analogy, and Tan was pleased.

"Do you know what Deng Xiaoping said this morning?" Tan asked. "I heard it on my radio."

"What did he say?" Charles asked, knowing it was something negative . . . possibly another rumor.

"Deng made it clear that Beijing would take immediate action if Hong Kong ever became a base for anti-Communist activities."

"So stop supporting them!" Charles said.

"But this saber-rattling can't be ignored, Charles."

"What have you in mind?"

"You and I should not put all our eggs in one basket. Suppose Deng turns off the water supply? This colony will immediately become his barbecued duck. This is no laughing matter. We've been friends for over twenty years. It's my duty to inform you that I'm leaving for Manila tomorrow to open a new office there. I'd like to invite you to go with me. You should spend a few days there to explore some investment opportunities. All business, no politics, I promise, so we won't quarrel and spoil the trip."

Charles accepted the invitation. Aimee had been pressing him to invest in Canada and America. But he had committed himself to invest in China. The Philippines, however, was a Third World country; he did not mind exploring some investment opportunities there, too.

They arrived in Manila the next evening. The red-carpet treatment accorded two of the richest men from Hong Kong made them feel like visiting statesmen. They had the Presidential Suite at the Ritz. After two days of meetings and banquets, Richard Tan heaved a heavy sigh and told Charles that since he was going to open an office of his shipping company in Manila, he had arranged a little private ceremony that would bring it good luck.

"What private ceremony?" Charles asked.

"I've ordered two virgins," Tan said with a little chuckle. "The lucky red color will bless any new business venture. This is an old tradition, you know that."

Charles knew that Richard was one of the few old-fashioned businessmen in Hong Kong who still followed mildewed old traditions. Because of the likes of Richard Tan who kept the old traditions going, there still existed in the colony an underground virgin market. Virgins, believed to be the fountain of youth, not only brought good luck to new business ventures but also provided "elixirs" to men with sexual dysfunctions. Most old men knew that a few Chinese dates inserted into a virgin overnight and taken with breakfast the next morning would not only revitalize a man but prolong his life. Charles had heard friends swear that such a tonic was even better than bears' paws, male seals' sex organs, or rhino horn, the three most potent aphrodisiacs. When he thought about it, he could not help shaking his head and laughing.

"Don't tell me you have stage fright, Charles," Tan said with a little chuckle. "A veteran like you!"

"Well," said Charles, still laughing, "I haven't threaded a needle for so long that my eyesight might fail me." Then he became serious and added, "Richard, I'm surprised at you."

"Lucky red or not," Tan said, "this is only a gesture . . . a good excuse to have a good time. Be my guest, Charles. I've engaged two of the most beautiful virgins in Manila. The go-between may have some beet juice hidden in them, but what the hell."

Shortly before midnight, a skinny girl of about fifteen, heavily made up and gaudily dressed in a Chinese embroidered gown, arrived at Charles's suite with the proper credentials— birth certificate, horoscope, and proof of virginity, all notarized. She did not smile or flirt like a paid singsong girl. Businesslike and unsmiling, she disrobed, laid her clothes carefully in a pile on a chair, and climbed onto the bed. She lay there quietly and stared at the ceiling, waiting for the ceremony of being deflowered. She looked tiny on the enormous bed, a pitiful child, her breasts the size of oranges and her skinny legs stretched like a chicken's wishbone. Charles felt so revolted that he tossed some money on the bed and ordered her to get dressed and leave.

When he came out of the bathroom, she was gone. He called the desk. There was a night flight back to Hong Kong. He could still make it. He left a thank-you note for Tan at the desk and took a taxi to the airport.

After the Manila trip, he was more determined than ever to put all his eggs in one basket—China.

A week later, he called Tan and apologized for his sudden change of mind in Manila. After he had hung up, Aimee came in with a copy of the *Hong Kong Standard*, one of the major English language papers in the colony. She had got up unusually early, looking fresh and bubbly in her tailored suit, a handbag on her arm.

"Charles," she said excitedly in English, showing him an article in the paper. "Please read this. Isn't it God-sent?"

It was a story about an old British nobleman who was offering to sell his title. For $100,000, the purchaser could obtain a registered peerage complete with a copy of the Domesday Book, a gold signet ring with the family crest, a family tree, and membership in the Manorial Society of England.

"Why is this God-sent?" he asked with a frown.

"You've always wanted a title, haven't you?" she asked.

"No, I've never wanted a title, and never will!"

"No matter. Here's one for sale."

"Aimee, I don't buy titles."

"What's the difference?" she said. "Tell me what in the world is not bought. Everything is bought."

"Aimee," he said, trying to sound patient, "would you wear a borrowed mink coat and claim it's your own?"

"That's a silly comparison. I'm talking about buying, not borrowing. Charles, even Richard Tan has a title. He did not even finish high school."

"Well, he earned it."

"You're much more qualified to have a title. Each time I watch Richard Tan eat at a banquet, I'm embarrassed. He has such horrible table manners! He sucks in his breath, smacks his lips, and belches. Ugh! Look at his wife, an ignorant woman who waddles on her high heels like a peasant. Everybody kisses her coarse hand and calls her Lady Tan. Gad! Charles, everybody thinks you deserve a title. I've called the governor's wife. She said that unfortunately Queen Elizabeth has stopped granting titles in Hong Kong. But right away an ad pops up in the paper offering a title for a measly hundred thousand dollars. It's God's will, Charles. . . ."

"Aimee," he interrupted, his voice still patient, "first, I would not bad-mouth Richard and his wife. They're our friends. Please forget about the title."

"Charles," she said, smiling again, "your birthday is approaching. Can't you allow me to give you a gift of my choice?"

"Of course. But not this registered peerage complete with a copy of the Domesday Book. I'm an American. Americans do not have titles."

"To tell the truth, I've already bought it for you."

Charles stared at her, shocked. "You've what?"

"I've bought it at a ten percent discount. I've met the seller, a distinguished English gentleman with a monocle and waxed mustache. He's terribly nice. He kissed my hand and all that. Charles, from now on you're a 'Sir,' and that's that!"

9

Do Do invited Mark Hansen to a home-cooked dinner. Yun Mei volunteered to make jiaozi, the meat dumplings that Marco Polo turned into ravioli in Venice. Yun Mei had fast hands. Since *pao jiaozi* (making meat dumplings) and *da ma jian* (playing mah-jongg) were two of the most popular pastimes in China, Yun Mei was always in demand. She hated mah-jongg games, but she could turn out jiaozi like a machine, her fingers flying. Like mah-jongg players, she chatted and told stories while wrapping jiaozi. This evening, she was telling stories that made Jimmy smile, frown, look worried and embarrassed.

Do Do, chopping vegetables and slicing meat on the dining table, made comments, adding tidbits of her own. The tiny apartment was full of cooking smell, chitchat, and laughter.

Two pots of food were simmering on the stove. Hansen sniffed and wondered if anything was burning. His question provoked such hilarity that Yun Mei ducked under the table to laugh. Jimmy explained to Hansen that it was the smell of a spicy Hunan dish. Hansen threw his head back to laugh, almost tipping his chair over. This provoked another round of guffaws.

Yun Mei told Hansen the story of Mr. Yang, the engineer who shouted, "Mao Zedong is a turtle's egg!" through the window. "What happened to him?" Hansen asked.

Do Do's eyes reddened. She kept chopping for a few moments. "He jumped out of a hospital window," she said quietly.

"Three stories high," Jimmy added.

"Let's not talk about tragedies," interrupted Yun Mei, finishing her last jiaozi.

"I forgot," Jimmy said. "Mr. Hansen has brought a bottle. Shall we open it?"

While Jimmy served the wine, Yun Mei resumed her storytelling. "Talking about hospitals," she said, "you won't find one in China that is managed by a doctor. All Chinese hospital heads are retired military men or "old tree trunks." When you see a street sweeper or a garbage collector, he might be a neurosurgeon."

"That's not a joke," Do Do said.

Jimmy changed the subject, He did not want Hansen to get the impression that China's medical system had been turned topsy-turvy by amateurs.

"Mr. Hansen," he said, "I'm intrigued by American fashions. Do your movie stars still attend Beverly Hills parties in Rolls-Royces but in blue jeans with holes in them?"

"I don't know," Hansen said. "I'm not interested in movie stars and their lives. But I'm intrigued by Chinese fashions. I've seen some eye-popping clothes worn by your women."

"What clothes did you see that almost popped your eyes out?" Yun Mei asked.

"I saw a woman wearing a T-shirt without a bra, and a skirt that was shaped like a fishtail."

"I bet she's in jail now," Jimmy said.

"I would like to know," Hansen said, "is China so liberated?"

"That's our fishtail skirt," Do Do said, "designed by a film actress. She designed miniskirts, pagoda skirts . . . hundreds of skirts. My favorite is a four-piece skirt with slits showing a lot of flesh, but it hides the whole leg. It's terribly seductive."

"Mark," Yun Mei said, "you ought to distribute this sexy skirt in your country. All those women with fat legs, thin legs, or bowlegs will gobble them up, and you'll be a millionaire."

Jimmy was glad that they had stopped talking about tragedies. "Have you heard about the new fashion in cutting a watermelon?" he asked.

"No," Hansen said. He was interested in anything new in China. Pen in hand, he was ready to take notes.

Jimmy said that the old art of melon-cutting, like the tea ceremony, was being revived. It included cutting off each end of a melon, pushing a mold through it, and taking out the middle. Each mold had a different design, the most popular being a lotus flower. When a lotus flower–shaped middle was sliced, it made a plate of beautiful flower-shaped watermelon slices. If it was for the emperor, the seeds had to be picked out; if it was for a prime minister, the melon had to be sliced more than six times; for the common people, the melon had to be eaten in four pieces, seeds and all.

While they were talking and laughing, someone knocked on the door. Do Do opened it and found a smiling man who introduced himself as a gas-stove inspector. He said that the gas company had received reports of a gas leak in the neighborhood. He would like to take a look.

He was a quiet man, businesslike. His hands were smooth and slender. After the inspection, he bowed and left.

"He's a security man," Yun Mei said. "I know him. He turned his back to me, did you notice? God, we're in trouble! We're fraternizing with a foreigner."

"Security man?" Hansen asked lightheartedly. "I'm not a rightist or leftist. I'm in the middle knocking out a report as objective as possible. What does he want to know?"

"Just don't let them get hold of your notebook," Yun Mei said. "All those words sound like secret codes. 'Push a mold through a watermelon.' My God! It can be interpreted a million ways!"

Mark Hansen returned to Beijing Hotel in his Toyota, somewhat worried. The home-cooked meal had been excellent; he had liked every dish except the one that smelled burned. But the unexpected visit from the gas inspector bothered him. He had been told that foreign visitors, expecially foreign correspondents, were watched by the Security Bureau and half a dozen other foreigner-watching organizations within the government. A Chinese diplomat had assured him that as long as Deng Xiaoping was at the helm, there was nothing to worry about. He shrugged as he entered his two-room suite at the Beijing Hotel, which had become his office and living quarters.

The desk called to tell him that he had a package. Hurrying down to fetch it, he saw some Chinese men in the lobby glancing to right and left. Were they security people watching him? he wondered. Suddenly, he felt uneasy.

Back in his room, he found that his package had been tampered with. He bolted his door. Feeling silly, he unbolted it, almost laughing at his own paranoia.

The package contained a tape cassette. Because of Do Do's dinner invitation, he had had to decline an invitation to attend a lecture at Beijing Normal University. His friend Professor Shen had enclosed a little note in the package. "I taped the lecture for you. Thought you might want to hear it. In case your friend's dinner turned out to be lousy, you won't kick yourself in the shin for missing the lecture."

Hansen smiled as he slid the tape into his recorder. Professor Shen had been his guide during his first visit to China. Shen had learned as much about America from him as he had learned about China from the helpful, gregarious professor, who had even adopted the American name Frank Shane.

The lecture was brief, delivered by some students who were leaving for America to take up advanced studies in social science. The keynote speaker, president of the Normal University, had just returned from a U.S. visit. His lecture was blunt and daring. He told the students that nuclear weapons were no longer the criterion for judging a country's strength. Soviet Russia, a superpower, was a good example. Now the country was yelling, "uncle," begging for help. Why? Because several decades of communism had given the Russians not Lenin's Utopia but Stalin's hell. He urged the students to study hard and join the Communist party, just in case China refused to change.

"The future is in your hands," he shouted so loudly that he almost cracked his voice. "Communism has created a new feudal class that is worse than those warlords before the liberation. Even the reform advocates have no idea what has become of the country. You all have heard the line 'Let's cross the river by groping around the pebbles.' That means even our paramount leader, Deng Xiaoping, has to grope around to solve China's problems. Hell, isn't that the blind leading the blind? As I say, the future is in the young people's hands. Remember that!"

Mark Hansen shut off the recorder and poured himself a glass of wine. He felt good. If a university president could give a public speech as daring as this one, the country must be on the right track.

To discuss the hotel project, Charles had visited Beijing twice in two months. Each time, he and various government officials had dined and discussed the sites, the plans, and the building designs. The joint venture seemed to sail in smooth wind, although at a snail's pace. A cautious man, he did not mind the slow progress.

During his third trip, he decided to spend a few more days in Beijing with Jimmy and Do Do. He brought Raymond with him so that Raymond could get acquainted with his half brother's family. Charles always enjoyed eating the little dishes cooked by Do Do with cheap materials. Having learned that the expensive items such as fish and meat needed ration coupons, he told Jimmy and Do Do to forget them. They could have the best of everything in a restaurant, but it was the home-cooked dinners he wanted, regardless of ingredients.

The family dinners were always a success, with a lot of side dishes of preserved vegetables. The main courses were usually five-spiced chicken livers or red-cooked beef gristle. This time it was a fish head cooked with bean cake, hot and spicy. To Charles's surprise, Raymond, who often picked at his food in Hong Kong, ate the coolie dishes with relish. It seemed that the stranger the food, the better he liked it.

Barely sixteen, Raymond was extremely curious about China and its different life-style. Totally relaxed, he kept asking silly questions. Jimmy and Do Do answered them patiently amid loud chuckles.

"If you have more than two babies," Raymond asked during the dessert of fried bananas, "does the government really impose a fine and send you the bill?"

"That's right," Jimmy said. "It's like speeding. You get a ticket."

"You have no babies. Do you get a reward?"

They all laughed.

"No reward," Jimmy said. "Probably a letter of congratulation from some party chief."

"As a grandfather," Charles said, "I'd rather hear some little feet padding around my rocking chair."

"Raymond, hear that?" Jimmy said with a laugh. "You'll have to share this responsibility when you grow up."

"Grow up! I am grown up!"

"Don't we know!" Do Do said, winking. "The way you ogled the young ladies when we visited the Great Wall yesterday!"

Again they all laughed.

Charles was happy that Raymond had changed from a gloomy boy to a happy teenager, naive but hungry for knowledge. After dinner, when he was ready to go back to his hotel to attend a meeting, Raymond asked him, "Dad, can I spend the night here with Jimmy?"

"Where can you sleep?" Charles asked. "The kitchen table?"

Raymond looked from Jimmy to Do Do. "Why not?" Do Do said. "The kitchen table has always been our guest bed."

"As a matter of fact," Jimmy said, "we have two guest beds, the kitchen table and a folding cot. Army surplus, we bought it for five jinmingbi . . . About two dollars. Raymond, take your pick. I recommend the cot, so you won't fall off the table and bump your head."

Charles shook his head. Raymond had a $120 room at the Beijing Hotel, but he preferred a used army cot in a tiny apartment.

"How is the hotel project progressing, Dad?" Jimmy asked.

"So far, so good," Charles said. "I hired the best architect in Hong Kong. He did a terrific job. But the design seems to disappoint the Chinese officials. They give me the impression that they want a chain of Hiltons or Marriotts. But what I have in mind is a Chinese Holiday Inn in each major city, catering to the natives and those foreign visitors traveling on a tight budget. Well, we'll see."

After dessert, he asked Jimmy, "Do you know Miss Mao Ling? She's supposed to be a famous interior decorator. She'll present her interior designs tonight."

"Glad you mentioned it," Jimmy said, "the one and only Miss Mao, a former Miss Macao. Thrice divorced, a shark who bites off more than she can chew."

"She looks anything but a shark," Charles said. "A lovely purring cat is more like it. She has attended all the meetings, always smiling and agreeing with everybody."

"Dad, you need protection," Jimmy said with a laugh.

"I'll offer my services," Do Do chimed in quickly.

"A delegation of three men will be there," Charles said. "I'll be well protected. I like a shark in cat's skin. It'll be a challenge. She must have torn quite a few hearts to pieces."

"No broken hearts," Jimmy replied. "All her ex-husbands said it was worth it."

"In other words," Do Do said, "she's a whore who is worth all the trouble and money."

The appointment was for 8:00 P.M. As soon as Charles returned to his hotel suite, he called room service and ordered a carton of Lucky Strikes, three coffees, one Irish coffee, and a soft drink for himself. The three Chinese negotiators and Miss Mao were always punctual and thirsty for coffee and American cigarettes. It had become a ritual, smoking, sipping coffee, and talking about the hotel project. They had gone over the blueprints many times. Each time, they had made some suggestions for minor changes, and he had promised that he would consult his architect. Now it was Miss Mao's turn to present her designs for the interior. He expected another long evening of discussion, rounds of coffee and cigarettes and polite chuckles.

Exactly at eight, the phone rang. Miss Mao was calling from the lobby. "Come right up, please," Charles invited. A nonsmoker, he opened all the windows behind the heavy drapes.

The air was smoggy outside, but it would be better than stale cigarette smoke choking up the room.

He answered the gentle knock and opened it. Framed in the door was the smiling Miss Mao, a mink stole on her shoulders, a Gucci handbag in one hand, and a large album under her arm. "Hello," she said pleasantly.

While greeting her and shaking her hand, he looked past her and discovered that there was no one else. "Where are the others?" he asked.

"I'm alone," she said. "They didn't come because they know nothing about interior decoration. May I come in?"

"Of course." He stepped aside. She walked in mincingly, leaving behind a trail of intoxicating perfume. She put her album on the coffee table, her mink and handbag on a chair, and sat down on the long sofa, crossing her shapely legs.

"I see that you have brought your designs," he said, anxious to see what she had done.

But she was not in a hurry to discuss her work. "Yes," she said, reaching for her handbag on the chair. She fished out a golden cigarette case and matching lighter. Charles quickly took the lighter and lit her long, slender cigarette. After a puff, she went on, "Did you have a nice trip, Charles? May I call you Charles?"

"Of course," he said. "Shall I call you Ling?"

"It's about time we got rid of the formality," she said with a little laugh. "After all, we've met many times, and I feel I've known you for a long time. In fact, each time I've gone to Hong Kong, I've stayed in one of your hotels."

"Do you go to Hong Kong often?" he asked.

"Constantly," she said. "My home is in Macao. Each time I go home, I take a side trip to Hong Kong to do some shopping." Tonight she was talkative, speaking English in a sing-song voice. Her makeup was light, with the right amount of eye shadow and lipstick. Her jet-black hair, swept up into a bun, made her look taller and complemented her melon-seed–shaped face. Her dazzling diamond earrings matched her diamond choker. She was wearing a plunging cardigan that was beautifully embellished with gold floral and geometric designs. Her thin silk pants revealed an excellent contour of hips and legs. During the past three meetings, she had worn a Mao tunic like the others, except that hers had been well cut . . . Even fashionable. Still, Charles watched her and marveled at this stunning change.

The coffee and cigarettes arrived. Just as Charles was about to sign the check, she stopped him.

"Why pay for so many cups of coffee if nobody's going to drink them?" she said. "Three dollars a cup. You should deduct nine dollars from the bill."

"That's not really necessary," Charles said.

"Let me ask him." She turned to the waiter and asked him if it was all right to return the coffee and deduct the charge. The waiter smiled and nodded. "See?" she said triumphantly. She picked up the pen and changed the total on the bill with a flourish.

"Do you want anything else?" asked Charles, feeling a bit uncomfortable about the change.

"May I have a whiskey?" she asked.

Charles ordered a whiskey. She asked the waiter how much that would be. The waiter said twelve dollars.

"Ridiculous!" she said. "A whole bottle of Johnny Walker costs only twenty-two dollars in the gift shop. Can you get us a bottle from the gift shop?"

The waiter shook his head. "It's against the house rules, ma'am. But the room service can offer you a bottle for thirty-eight dollars."

"That's highway robbery!" she retorted with a snort.

"It's still cheaper by the bottle." The waiter smiled, looking at Charles for help.

Charles put a fifty-dollar bill on the tray and said quickly, "Bring us a bottle. And keep the change."

They discussed her designs, which occupied only two pages of her portfolio. The rest were her previous drawings. The designs for both the lobby and the rooms were gaudy, full of luxurious furnishings and antique decorations. Charles studied them, his face expressionless. Miss Mao stared at him anxiously, waiting for his comments.

"Ling," he said with an apologetic smile, "I'm afraid this is not what I have in mind. I'm trying to build a chain of hotels for the convenience of the natives and travelers of modest means. Your designs are for the rich."

Looking disappointed, she lit another cigarette. "Look, Charles," she said, blowing out smoke heavily to show her irritation, "China is a poor country. How can you squeeze anything out of the natives? Last year a builder from America was interested in investing in public housing. We laughed our heads off. No family in China pays more than ten yuans a month for rent, rich or poor. We asked him if he was in the charity business. That sent him packing. You are investing for profit, are you not, Charles?"

"Of course," he said. "Isn't every businessman?"

"You are ready to sink millions into this hotel deal. The location we selected for your pilot hotel is on Chang An Boulevard. Do you think the government will build a modest hotel there? It's almost like putting a little pawnshop on Wall Street."

"But that's what we've agreed all along," Charles said.

"You don't know how the negotiators negotiate in China, Charles," she said after a few more puffs on her cigarette. "They agree on a lot of things at the beginning, just to get the project started. They know we are all in this business to make money, especially foreign exchange. How else can you do that unless you aim your guns at the rich foreigners? Eventually, you will come around to see the government's point of view. I hope I've already turned you around, Charles."

She refilled both their glasses and daintily dropped an ice cube into each. Charles was disappointed. The three negotiators from the government had impressed him as knowledgeable and sincere; he could not believe that they would hide their intentions and fool him. He had repeatedly emphasized his point before they started the negotiations two years ago. He wondered if this glamorous lady was telling the truth. Probably not, he decided.

He closed her album and picked up his drink. "Let me sleep on this for a few days, Ling. I'm sure we'll find a common ground on which we can build the hotels to satisfy everybody."

"Well, cheers!" she said, proposing a toast.

She began to look a bit tipsy, her face pink and her hands fluttery. And she giggled more easily. She pulled her earrings off, tossed them onto the coffee table, and stretched her legs. "Do you mind?" she asked. "They pinched. I have no holes, see?" She leaned close to show him her earlobes.

"So I see," he said, overwhelmed by her strong but pleasant perfume. She stayed close and wriggled her body to make herself comfortable. With her face so close to his, he could almost feel her breath. He peeked down her sweater. Her breasts, half-hidden in a lacy brassiere, looked firm and full, her skin white and smooth.

"You know," she went on, "in the Orient, you have to be careful. I know of a girl whose ears were torn. You know why? A thief grabbed her earrings and ran. It happened on a busy street in broad daylight. Imagine that!"

"I hope she didn't wear diamond earrings, like yours," he said, enjoying her perfume and the warmth of her body.

"I put all my diamonds in a bank vault," she said. "Only a fool wears the real thing these days. I don't care where. Here or in America. Tell me about your family."

He told her about his family without mentioning Aimee. She told him about hers without mentioning her three divorces. She was the only daughter of a Macao jeweler, retired. She had come to Beijing three years ago to help China's modernization programs. The government treated her royally, and she loved it. She was confident that China would catch up with the West and eventually become the biggest tiger in the gang of four tigers, with Singapore, Taiwan, and Hong Kong tagging along behind.

Suddenly, she changed the subject. "Oh, you have such strong legs," she said, touching his thigh. "Do you ride bicycles a lot?"

"No, I climb a lot of stairs," he said. "I avoid elevators if I can."

"No wonder you are so strong." She began to massage his leg, first with one hand, then both hands. "I've learned Swedish massage. Do you want me to give you one, from head to toe?"

"Why not?" he said, trying to lie down on the sofa.

"Don't you want to be more comfortable?" She glanced at the bed in the back of the suite.

Taking the hint, he moved to the enormous double bed.

She took off his coat and made him lie on the bed on his stomach. Then she slipped off her shoes and started massaging his toes. Her manipulation was so good that he could not help humming.

"You are good," he commented.

"I know," she said. "I spent five thousand dollars on the lessons, all scientifically designed to benefit the human body and induce pleasure."

She squeezed and kneaded his muscles, working her way upward. When she reached his torso, her hands became more dexterous, traveling up and down, lingering on the sensitive areas. Charles, realizing that this was no longer Swedish massage, was somewhat surprised. But it was so pleasurable that he lay without resisting. He wondered where she had learned these skills. They were worth every penny of the tuition she had paid.

"Feel good?" she asked.

"Not bad," he said. It was really marvelous, but he refrained from saying so, unsure of what she really wanted.

"You know," she went on, "my girlfriend and I took the same course under the same tutor. You know what my girl-friend said? She said we could become rich by doing this."

"Open a massage parlor?" he asked.

"No!" She laughed. "Who wants to slave in a massage parlor making peanuts? Heard the story of the two Shanghai sisters who murdered a man with sex? They received two million dollars in insurance money. A perfect crime." She laughed again. "Don't be alarmed. If I wanted to murder you, I wouldn't tell you. Besides, I can't claim your life insurance."

"Why are you doing this to me?" he asked amid some groaning. "It's hard work."

"I enjoy it," she said. "I'm always attracted to mature men. You are strong, solid, and successful, full of wisdom. That's terribly attractive!"

She pulled up his shirt and kissed his back. "Take your clothes off," she said, and started to unbutton her own cardigan.

Riding him astride, she responded to his entry with a low moan. She had a beautiful body, her skin smooth as jade. Her eyes half-closed, her head thrown back, she rubbed her own breasts as she increased the rhythm. He synchronized his movements with her thrusts. After a frenzy of action, she suddenly uttered a cry as if in agony, then flopped on him, her body wet and trembling.

"I'm finished," she whispered. "Now it's your turn."

"That's not necessary," he said, giving her soft rump a gentle pat.

"Don't you want to finish?" she asked.

"I try to economize," he said with a little laugh.

She rolled off his body and nestled against him. "You are fantastic! Did you enjoy it?"

"I never had it better."

"Really? I don't believe you."

"If I die now," he said, "I'd say to Yen Wong, the king of ghosts, 'Send me back, I want to die this way again and again.' "

With a laugh, he rose and got dressed. They returned to the sofa, and he refilled their glasses. She said, "If we do it in Bei Dai Ho, you won't be so nervous."

"Was I nervous?" he asked.

"Because you couldn't finish. Your mind was on your business. Probably thinking of your wife, too. Let's take a trip to Bei Dai Ho. I know a cozy hotel there. We can stay there a week in isolation. There is no noise but the singing of birds. It will soothe your soul, drive away all your worries about business or wife. . . ."

"Why do you keep saying my wife?" he asked.

"You are not happily married," she said. "Why deny it?"

Charles was surprised that she knew so much. He kept quiet. She urged again, "Let's go to Bei Dai Ho. I'll make all the necessary arrangements. I know the manager of that cozy little hotel." She gave him another kiss and begged, "Shall we? Please say yes! Please!"

The temptation was so strong that he found himself mumbling a hesitant yes.

The next morning he woke up with a bad headache, the worst hangover he had ever experienced. Sobered, he realized what he had done and began to worry. After taking two aspirins, he jotted a short note to Miss Mao on the hotel stationery, telling her that he had to leave Beijing unexpectedly ahead of schedule.

On his way to see Jimmy and Do Do, he posted the letter, praying that she would take the hint. He definitely did not want to be her number-four ex-husband and say, "It's worth all the trouble and money."

11

"This is for both of us," said Do Do, giving Jimmy an opened letter from Hong Kong.

"Who is it from?" Jimmy asked. They had had dinner and were finishing a bottle of wine that Mark Hansen had brought them.

"Read it," said Do Do, clearing the dishes away. "You have a funny brother. We ought to help him."

"Pang Sin?"

"Pang Sin! Does he ever need our help?"

"Oh, you mean Raymond," said Jimmy, his face brightening. He fished the letter out from its stamp-covered envelope. "Look at the stamps! What a waste! He needs help, all right."

"Don't forget, your father's rich."

"Spoiled brat!" Jimmy said with a chuckle.

He read the letter, written with a marker in a heavy hand on his mother's expensive stationery:

Dear Jimmy and Do Do,

Father says you two are busy help build China. Can you find me a job? I can type 30 words a minute. I ride bike pretty good. And I love Beijing. I'd like to work with you to help build China. Sounds terrific! Can

I help? Looking forward to seeing both of you again
soon.

Love,
Raymond

"Where can we find him a job?" Do Do asked. "He can type
thirty words a minute."

"Do you need a delivery boy at Radio Beijing?" Jimmy
asked. "He rides a bike pretty good, too."

"Considering his grammar," Do Do said, "we'll send him
right back to school. How old is he?"

"Sixteen?" Jimmy wondered. "He still hasn't finished high
school. Something's wrong. Do Do, we'll take on the responsibility for Raymond's education."

"You mean baby-sit him."

There was a knock on the door. Jimmy answered it and
welcomed the visitor with a hug. A former schoolmate at the
Foreign Language Institute, Jane Lo was now an actress who
always looked worried. With her constant frown, she played
tragic roles successfully in films. Approaching thirty, she was
beautiful and fashionable. Today, she wore a tight shiny
cheongsam and carried a white shoulder bag. Do Do thought
her perpetual frown was the result of her divorce, but Jimmy
suspected that Jane was frigid. There were rumors that Jane
was promiscuous and George Lo fickle.

"You just missed a good dinner," said Do Do, hugging her
friend. "Jimmy cooked it. It was so good we don't even have
any leftovers."

Jane said with a laugh, "I'm glad. If I put on another ounce,
I won't be able to get into this cheongsam." She made a turn
like a model, expecting comment.

Jimmy thought Jane had the best figure in Beijing, but he
refrained from praising it. "Have you seen George?" he asked,
knowing that she still carried a torch for her ex-husband. Somewhat old-fashioned, he had hoped that they would reconcile
and prove all the rumors and speculations wrong.

Jane made a face and snorted. "I'll never look at that man's face again. I fell in love with his back. That's enough of a mistake."

"You fell in love with his back?" asked Do Do, raising her eyebrows inquisitively. "What do you mean?"

"He played Yu Fei on the stage," Jane said. "Before that historical war hero went to fight the northern barbarians, he always stripped to the waist and knelt in front of his mother, begging her forgiveness. Remember?"

"That's a famous historical scene," Do Do said. "On his back there's the famous tattoo 'Die for my country.' How can anyone forget such a scene?"

"I was the best calligrapher in the company," Jane said. "Before every performance, I had to paint that tattoo on his back. By the time I had written it fifty times, I was head over heels in love with that damned back. Who'd suspect that above a handsome back is the dirtiest mind I've ever known!"

"I didn't know that," said Jimmy, surprised.

"Now you do. You can forget about me going back to him. By the way, where is he? Have you two seen him?"

Jimmy still believed that she was in love with the man, but he decided not to get involved. "No," he lied.

They talked about her new film, which was to be released soon. It was about a Communist cadre, the chairman of a local committee in a small southern town. He was upright and energetic, and a loyal adherent to revolutionary causes. But he condemned an innocent man to prison with manufactured evidence so that he could steal the man's wife. The film was a bold indictment of the Communist "tree trunk," a hypocrite and wife-stealer. Jane played the condemned man's tragic wife, who finally committed suicide. She hated the part.

"I'm quitting," she announced. "I'm going to America to study drama. No more stereotypes and stylized acting. Every time I must cry, I have to smear pepper in my eyes. Another one of those tear-jerkers, I'll lose my eyesight! If you see George Lo, please let me know and tell me how to find him."

"I thought you never wanted to see him again," Jimmy said.

"I meant socially," Jane said. "I have some business to settle with him."

"What business, Jane?" Do Do asked. "If it's shady, we don't want to get involved."

"Have you heard of something called alimony?"

"Of course."

"It's a Western product. Since Deng Xiaoping opened China to the West and started importing everything from the West, why not alimony? I'm going to America. I need the money."

"You need a lawyer for that," Jimmy said.

"I've got one. All I need is to find the bastard. Will you help me?"

"We'll try," Do Do said.

"I've got to run," she said after a quick sip of coffee.

Just as she was getting up to go, there was another knock on the door. Jimmy answered. Pang Sin sauntered in. He had dyed his hair from red to blond, and his fashionable gabardine suit was meticulously pressed. Despite his slightly slanting eyes, he looked more Western than Oriental. Jane stared at this tall, handsome man and changed her mind about leaving.

Jimmy was surprised by his half brother's visit. He hadn't seen him for several years. Acting like an American, Pang Sin hugged him and patted his back affectionately.

"How are you, Younger Brother?" he asked.

Jimmy had always hated Pang Sin's opportunistic personality. In the past, when the leftists were in power, he had dyed his hair black and become a foreigner-hater; when the country befriended the West, he had changed his color again, trying to look like a foreigner. Now Jimmy was rather amused by Pang Sin's "dogtail grass on a mud wall" policy. He had swung with the wind again.

"You look good, Pang Sin," he said.

"Aha!" said Pang Sin, walking toward Do Do with open arms. "My favorite girl!"

He hugged Do Do and planted a long, noisy kiss on her cheek. "How are you, darling?"

"You're getting more American, Pang Sin," Do Do said with an awkward smile, wriggling out of his arms. "Have you learned all this from watching American films?"

"You haven't introduced us," Jane said. She had returned to her seat.

Do Do introduced them quickly. Pang Sin shook Jane's hand warmly. "I've seen you many times." As he snapped his fingers trying to remember, Jane named a film she had been in.

"Of course! *The Bitter Sea.* You are . . . you are . . ."

"You see?" Jane said. "Nobody remembers a sad woman." She flapped her long eyelashes and added. "If you see a woman crying on the screen, it's me."

Pang Sin looked at her appreciatively and gave her his business card. "Call me if you need help."

He returned to his half brother. "Jimmy," he said. "I heard that your old man became a 'Sir.' That's quite an honor. Was he knighted by the queen?"

"If he was, we were not invited to the ceremony," Jimmy said. "How did you find out?"

"It's all over the Hong Kong gossip tabloids. I'd like to pay him a visit and offer my congratulations. Where does he live in Hong Kong?"

Jimmy hesitated. Charles had already told him not to be surprised if someday people started calling him "Sir." It was a birthday gift from Aimee. He had accepted it to avoid a quarrel. Now he had found it to be quite useful; he had walked on a lot more red carpets. But he wanted Jimmy not to publicize it in China.

"It's a family honor, Jimmy," Pang Sin said. "All of us ought to share it."

"Where were you when Jimmy's father visited Beijing?" Do Do asked. "You were invited to meet him."

"I was out of town," Pang Sin said. "I'm a businessman."

"Are you still married to that general's daughter?"

"Do Do, you're still the same, with a sharp tongue. But you're much prettier, I must say!"

Do Do made a face. Jimmy poured a cup of coffee for him.

There was a heavy knock on the door. It was Pang Sin's young chauffeur in dark glasses. He said that the street urchins were all over Pang Sin's car, touching it and kicking it. They had better leave before the beggars dirtied it.

"Shit!" said Pang Sin, putting down his coffee quickly. He got Charles's Hong Kong address and started to leave. At the door, he turned and pointed a finger at Jane Lo. "Don't forget to call me, darling," he said in English.

"He gives me goose pimples," Do Do said after Pang Sin had left.

"I like him," Jane said, tossing Pang Sin's impressive calling card into her bag with a calculating smile.

"Good luck," Do Do said. Knowing that Jane Lo was Pang Sin's equal in dirty tricks, she was not worried.

12

The banquet room at the Beijing Hotel was ready to entertain three hundred intellectuals, the cream of the arts in China. Charles Hong was the host. He had arrived with his son Raymond, who had just enrolled at Beijing Middle School. Jimmy had told him that if a Chinese citizen paid the bill, he could save 50 percent; but Charles wanted to pay the full amount, U.S. $6,000. His whole purpose was to entertain the friends of both Jimmy and Do Do, and to help China make some foreign money.

His hotel project had been progressing slowly in spite of red tape; his enthusiasm for Deng Xiaoping's reforms and open-door policy had turned him into a supersalesman for China. He had talked all his rich friends in Hong Kong into investing in various businesses in China. Even his staunch anti-Communist friend Sir Richard Tan had reluctantly sunk a million U.S. dollars into his hotel venture.

Among the invited guests were writers, composers, poets, musicians, actors, and directors who had had been forced to sweep streets and clean latrines, carry night soil and work side by side with farmers and laborers. This dinner was to honor the arts, the previously disdained professions that were now noble undertakings under Deng's reform.

The large banquet room was luxuriously decorated with silk embroideries, couplet scrolls, and paintings by famous artists.

Thirty round tables, covered with the best linen, were glittering with fresh flowers, cut glass, silver dinnerware, and exquisite porcelain. The food was the hotel's best, prepared with all the available delicacies from the high mountains and deep seas, including bird nests, sharks' fins, bears' paws, sea slugs, and an imperial fish dish with electric blinking eyes.

The guests arrived early, chatting and laughing. Charles toasted their health, the arts, and China's future. As he glanced at the three hundred beaming faces looking at him anxiously, he decided to discard his prepared speech, which discussed how the horrible Second World War had devastated China and how the Communist Army had helped defeat her enemies. In a spontaneous brief talk, he emphasized the positive, instead.

"I have a vision," he said. "In ten years, China will no longer look like a sick old man. The people will all live in tiled houses. *Everybody* will have ten thousand Yuans in the bank. The present policy of 'six yeses' and 'six nos' will become reality. Yes for free education, free medical care, for huge shopping centers, theaters, and entertainment complexes. Above all, free speech! There will be no more carrying water on shoulders, no more wood-burning for cooking, no more squatting in outhouses, no more sponge baths in kitchen sinks, no more running back and forth between homes and public telephones, and no more black-and-white televisions. How do you like that?"

There was enthusiastic applause. One man raised his hand and shouted, "And no more 'old tree trunks' riding over our heads!"

There was more applause and some laughter.

The next speaker was Liu Bo, introduced by Jimmy as one of the most outstanding writers in China. His daring investigative reporting had won millions of admirers. Even though he had been jailed numerous times and cleaned thousands of latrines, nothing could daunt his anger against corruption and injustice.

Charles expected Liu Bo, a fierce speaker, to pound the table while scolding the government. But to his pleasant surprise, Liu was subdued, middle-aged and mild-mannered. He spoke in a calm voice, a faint smile on his deeply wrinkled face. He wore a baggy Western suit, his red tie soiled and a bit awry, his hair long and windblown. He looked like a tired accountant who hadn't straightened out his own finances.

The applause was thunderous. He had to keep leveling his hands to quiet the audience. First, he admitted he was a Communist party member, having started on the revolutionary path through self-abnegation. He had denied bourgeois ideology and individualism, which in simple terms were self-interest and selfishness. He had been told that individualism was the original sin, but like Adam and Eve he and a woman, now his wife, couldn't help stealing the forbidden apple, resulting in numerous "thought reforms." Today, the burden of this "original sin" was being lifted. People were told to eat the forbidden apple. Self-interest gave people incentive to better themselves; selfishness encouraged corruption. So it was up to the individuals, especially writers, to separate the two, encourage the former, and expose the latter.

"Historically," he said, "dictators and tyrants hate intellectuals because they can tell a good apple from a bad apple. The moment you find intellectuals mistreated, you know something is going wrong. There will be martial laws and secret executions. Class struggle will produce class distinctions. The lords will live in palatial mansions, and the people will sleep in cockroach-infested squalor. The lords want robots, not intellectuals who spread diseases called freedom and democracy."

His talk was brief, an attack on the party without mentioning the party as such. Charles fidgeted as he listened, but the audience drank in every word like hungry children licking ice-cream cones.

Mark Hansen, sitting beside Yun Mei, was dazzled by the gathering of the poor and famous. Yun Mei was busy pointing out who was who. He was also amazed by the contrast between the elegant surroundings and the shabbiness of the guests, who looked like a bunch of homeless people invited to a state dinner at the White House. A few hours before, he and Yun Mei had had lunch at the famous May Fourth Restaurant. Most of the customers there had been dressed in patched clothes of blue cotton cloth. They sat on stools around crude, unpainted wooden tables. A few waitresses in soiled white smocks and caps served rice gruel and cabbage-filled dumplings, their fingernails long and black. When a table became empty, they loaded the dirty dishes on a tray and swept the scraps of food onto the floor. There were flies buzzing around, and the cement floor was slippery with grease. Under the tables, a few dogs cleaned up the bones and gristle. Mark compared the two places and was flabbergasted by the difference. How could this be a classless communist society?

He took out his notebook to jot down a few notes, but Yun Mei tugged at his sleeve. He stopped and looked at her quizzically, suspecting that she wanted him to be more cautious.

"Look at that young woman at the next table," she whispered. "She's an actress, Jane Lo. She knows all the racy stories in Beijing. Interested in scandals? I'll introduce you."

Mark almost blurted out a yes, but he checked himself. He was not sure if Yun Mei was testing him, trying to find out if he was a womanizer. That was the last impression he wanted to give to anyone in a foreign country. "No, I'm not interested," he said firmly.

Raymond Hong, sitting between two teenage girls, was enjoying everything. He had never had so much attention from girls in Hong Kong. May Fong, bespectacled, had short hair combed behind her ears. She was chubby and awkward, with a round face. Her blouse and skirt were "native," which meant shapeless. Yin Yin Mei was slim and pretty, with long, wavy hair falling down her shapely back. Her hairdo and fashionable Western clothes attracted a great deal of attention. Raymond had overheard a man saying to another, "There's a film star from Hong Kong."

Both girls were from Raymond's middle school. Jimmy had invited them to be Raymond's dinner companions. The two girls took care of him like two protective hens, filling his glasses and cups, and piling food on his plate. They also wanted to practice English with him, so their conversation never stopped. Yin Yin chatted about rock and roll and film stars; May, a little less talkative, discussed heavier subjects.

Raymond, to his own surprise, found himself knowledgeable and eloquent on many subjects. He had an answer for almost everything; if he wasn't sure, he shrugged. His face was getting red from drinking too much of the wrong things. In front of every guest, there were two tall glasses, one small cup, and one teacup. Yin Yin kept filling the tall glasses with beer and orange soda, the small glass with mao-tai, and the teacup with wulung. Raymond, floating from the strong mao-tai, drank and ate whatever was offered to him.

"Have you seen much of Beijing?" Yin Yin asked.

Raymond shrugged. "Not much."

"I'll show you around," she offered. "There are a lot of beautiful places in Beijing."

"If you're interested in out-of-the-way places, I'll take you," May said.

"Do you like this place?" Yin Yin asked.

Raymond shrugged.

"This place is for government and party leaders to dine and entertain. It must have taken your brother a lot of *gwansi* to get it for this banquet."

Raymond knew that *gwansi* meant "connections." "I bet," he said. He turned to May and asked, "What out-of-the-way places?"

"Oh, hidden places . . . places the tourists don't see."

"You have to get special permits to see them," Yin Yin interrupted. "And they're dirty and smelly."

"But colorful," May said.

Raymond was more interested in the hidden places. Both girls offered to be his guide and named many interesting places in their separate itineraries. Raymond was too fuzzy to recognize any of the names; he was getting increasingly high.

The dinner was a tremendous success. When it was over, it took Charles almost an hour to shake everybody's hand, and exchange pleasantries and calling cards. Some guests staggered out of the restaurant laughing and chatting. For some intellectuals, it was their first banquet in ten years and the first time they had talked so freely. A few of them laughed heartily for no good reason, for they had not laughed like that for more than ten years.

Back in his hotel suite, Raymond opened the door for his father. "Dad," he said, "I had a good time."

"Son," Charles said, "I'm glad you're enjoying Beijing."

"Thanks a million, Dad." He threw his arms around his father and hugged him. The show of affection surprised Charles. Raymond had never hugged him voluntarily before. When Charles closed the door behind him, he was choking with emotion. It was the first time Raymond had ever thanked him for anything.

Pang Sin became totally infatuated with the vivacious, winsome Jane Lo after they had had a cup of tea at the Lido Coffee Shop near Tiananmen Square on Chang An Boulevard. He had had a hard time inviting her out. She seemed to know his weakness: the harder to catch, the better the trophy.

He and his wife lived in a three-walled compound of modern high-rise apartments, guarded by army sentries. The building was reserved for high government officials, military officers, and their families. The luxury apartment had been assigned to his wife, the only daughter of General Han, a member of the Central Military Commission. Pang Sin always felt like a guest. The general was cordial but aloof, acting as though his daughter had married him by mistake. Even Pang Sin's wife treated Pang Sin like a decoration and tool. The more his wife demanded his conjugal services, the more he found home-cooked meals tasteless. He often dreamed of stealing a bite elsewhere when nobody was looking.

Jane Lo was quite a bite; he had been racking his brain to find a love nest or appropriate rendezvous without creating a scandal. His wife's family was ultraconservative. One mishap and he could be banished forever from privileged society.

He was very uncomfortable when Jane Lo requested that he take her to visit the stores that were reserved exclusively for

102 ♦ C. Y. LEE

the party and government elite. She wanted to buy some "privileged food," which she could not get in the regular markets.

He could have used an official car, being a family member of the general, but he thought better of it. In his own Toyota, he drove to pick up Jane at the southwest corner of Tiananmen Square. The traffic was heavy, but he could outmaneuver even the brash young cabdrivers. They blasted him angrily with their horns, a special language that had been developed among the drivers in Beijing. Pang Sin knew them all and responded with his own horn. An excellent driver, he braked and swirled to avoid collision.

Jane was at the appointed corner, waving at him as he approached. She got in beside him and thanked him in a breathless, sexy voice. He put on his oversized dark glasses to hide his identity. His heart pounding, he inhaled deeply her pleasant perfume and began to count the out-of-the-way hotels where he could rent a room for a few hours. He glanced at her marvelous legs, generously exposed under her tight, short skirt. She was easily the most desirable vixen who had stepped inside his car.

"What do you want to buy?" he asked.

"Oh, many many things. Cosmetics, canned food, Yuban coffee, etcetera etcetera."

"You need foreign exchange to buy American products," Pang Sin said.

"Can you buy them for me? I'll give you the money. I'll appreciate it."

Being able to go into such a store was his trump card. He decided to use it cleverly and strike a hard bargain. He had already selected the hotel. But she wasn't a prostitute; he must be careful and more subtle. He suggested dinner and dancing at the International Hotel, a luxury hotel that catered mostly to foreigners. There, they would be less likely to run into Chinese, especially high government officials. Jane accepted the invitation after a lot of "ohs" and "ahs," saying that it all depended on whether she could break another engagement.

"Take me to the food store first," she suggested.

He took her to a shop called Number 53, a few blocks east

of Zhong Nan Hai. It was an ultramodern building with large plate-glass windows. A small plaque nailed to a post beside the driveway identified the place as Peking Food Supply.

There was no waiting line outside, no housewives clutching dog-eared jinmingbi and ration coupons, looking worried and harassed. Instead, there were chauffeured limousines, jeeps, vans, three-wheeled vehicles, and food trucks clustered on the sidewalks near the entrance. Several chauffeurs squatted in the shade, fanning themselves with palm-leaf fans and picking their teeth, waiting for their masters or mistresses to finish shopping.

The huge store was stacked with food items. Jane Lo made a beeline for the meat section, where chickens, pork, fish, and all kinds of seafood were displayed. Jane stared at the meats like a hungry child in a candy store. In ordinary markets, she had to fight for a skinny chicken or half a catty of pork, mostly fat. This was heaven. She secretly stuffed some money into Pang Sin's hand and whispered, "Some of everything, please."

Pang Sin started giving orders, but the sales clerk demanded to see his membership card. "I forgot to bring it," he said with an official air.

The clerk still demanded his membership card.

"I'll bring it tomorrow."

"Buy your food tomorrow then," the clerk said.

"Do you know whom I'm buying the food for?" Pang Sin asked, irritably. "General Han Wen-bing!"

"No membership card, no purchase," the clerk repeated, and turned away from him.

"What's your name? What's the number of your unit?"

Pang Sin's authoritative voice alerted a few other clerks. A fat man in a bloodstained white apron came over to inquire what the problem was. Pang Sin told him. The man sided with the clerk and still demanded his membership card.

"Where is the phone?" Pang Sin asked angrily. "Let me call General Han Wen-bing!"

The bluff worked. The fat man said, "All right, just this time."

After they had bought a bit of everything for a total of five hundred jinmingbi, he took Jane to Number 83, a store on South Chaoyangmen Avenue a few blocks further east. A tall brick building, its windows were shuttered with red-painted boards.

"What is this place?" she asked.

"Wait and see," he said with a smile.

At the door, a doorman demanded a special purchase card. Pang Sin used the same bluff and easily gained entrance. Inside, all kinds of books and magazines, both Chinese and foreign, were displayed. With a tinge of pride in his voice, Pang Sin told Jane that the store was reserved exclusively for the highest government officials and party leaders.

The place was quiet . . . so different from the jammed ordinary bookstores in Beijing. A few customers standing in front of shelves were leafing through books and magazines. Two elderly men in Mao uniforms were sitting in rattan chairs, reading and making their selections. Most of the publications for sale were marked For Internal Information Only.

Jane knew they were forbidden books, not sold in ordinary bookstores. She wanted to buy some American novels, especially those by Jackie Collins. But Pang Sin took her to a special section in a corner. On the shelves were all kinds of love stories, including the famous *Jin Ping Mei*, a banned novel about a sexy lady and her love affairs. There were other pornographic books and magazines, complete with photos or drawings, mostly published in Japan and Hong Kong.

He picked one and showed it to her. "I'll buy you one of the best," he said. She glanced at the title: *Eighteen of the Most Pleasurable Positions.* "Japanese etchings," he said. "You can't buy it anywhere, even in Japan."

The salesgirl wrapped it, stealing glances at Jane.

"Hungry?" he asked after he had paid.

She ignored the question, saying that she must go home to put the meat in her refrigerator. What luck, he thought, taking it as a hint. They did not even have to go to a hotel.

She lived alone in a remodeled courtyard in the eastern city. The hutungs were neat and clean, but barely wide enough for his car to pass. In Beijing, a courtyard was usually shared by four families, each occupying a wing; in the center was the community yard, or garden. But Jane's courtyard seemed more crowded. Children were crying and women were yelling. Through the entrance, he could see laundry and bedsheets hanging everywhere like a forest.

"Do you want to come in for a cup of tea or to wash your hands?" she asked. "My roommates are entertaining a lot of their friends tonight. You might meet a mutual friend or two."

The information was like a bucket of cold water poured over his head. The last thing he wanted was to meet a lot of people, some of whom he might know. In Beijing, gossip was a favorite pastime, and it always reached the wrong ears.

"Thanks but no," he said quickly with a false laugh. "I have good kidneys."

The lie worked nicely, and she went in with the food.

They had dinner in a Russian restaurant near Ha Te Men. The interior was old and gaudy with gilded carvings. Besides the portraits of Mao Zedong and Lenin, there were some ancient Russian tapestries hanging on the walls.

The borscht and black bread were filling and good. But Jane was thinking of her mother's cooking. With all the meat in her refrigerator, she had already lost her appetite for foreign food. She picked at a meat dish with a name she could not pronounce, wondering if Do Do had called. She was anxious to settle her divorce, get some money, and go to America. She was sick of China.

Pang Sin was like a cat anxious to steal the goldfish. As soon as he finished his dinner, he paid the bill and rose.

"Now let's go dancing," he said, dabbing his mouth with his napkin. "The band I have in mind is from Hong Kong. The music will melt your heart."

"I can't stay long," she said.

The dance hall was in Jian Guo Hotel in the eastern city, a huge basement decorated with glittering lights and Western abstract paintings. The five-man band was playing softly in a corner. Most of the customers were middle-aged businessmen from overseas and a few Caucasians. The women, all Chinese, were dressed in Western clothes, some in tight blue jeans and cowboy boots. Most of them were quite pretty.

Pang Sin glanced around from behind his dark glasses. No familiar faces. He relaxed and ordered gin and tonic, Jane's favorite drink.

Six men were talking loudly in English at the next table. One seemed to be a China expert, lecturing the others about business opportunities in China. He assured his listeners that both Zhao Ziyang, the premier, and Hu Yaobang, the general secretary of the party, advocated reform, openness, and learning from the West. Both openly acknowledged Mao's errors.

"Ben," one man interrupted him. "Don't forget that Mao's contributions to China outweigh his mistakes. For one thing, he drove many of us out of China in 1949, and see what happened. Some of us became millionaires!"

Pang Sin had heard that before, and it always provoked some laughter.

He danced a slow fox-trot with Jane. When the music ended, they returned to their table. Jane suddenly felt a hand creeping up her thigh under the table. She pushed it away and called the waitress.

"What do you want?" Pang Sin asked, surprised.

"I want tea."

"Tea? Why fill yourself with tea? How about another gin and tonic?"

"Pang Sin, I don't like this place."

"Why? Famous band, rich customers from all over the world. Everything is high class."

"Look at those women," she said with a snort. "They're all prostitutes. And the cement floor. God, you call it high class?"

"Two more drinks," he said, hoping the gin and tonic would help his cause.

"One more dance, and we'll go," she said. She stood up and looked at him as if she were saying, "Let's get it over with."

Clutching her tightly, he danced to the soft beat of the music. She followed well. He felt her breath and her warm, soft body. Her perfumed hair brushed his face, and her breasts moved with his chest. Enjoying the tickling sensation, he clutched her more tightly. Soon he started licking her ear and whispering endearing words.

She didn't resist. When they returned to their table, she

excused herself to go to the ladies' room. He was happy; he was sure that the fish was about to bite.

Jane passed the ladies' room without entering. She turned around the bar and hurried out of the building. On the street, she took a deep breath of the night air and sighed with relief. She was familiar with the area. She walked briskly three blocks to a bus stop.

It took her almost two hours to get home by bus after several transfers. The hutung was quiet but well lit by the full moon. Crickets were singing everywhere, and a rooster crowed in the distance. Roosters used to herald the dawn, but now they crowed anytime aimlessly, and she wondered why . . . probably confused by all the political upheavals and endless campaigns against this and that. She glanced at her watch. It was almost midnight.

"Hello, Jane," a voice said behind her.

She turned sharply. Pang Sin, grinning, took her arm and started guiding her toward his Toyota parked nearby. "You can't slip through my fingers so easily." His breath was heavy with liquor.

"Let me go," she said, trying to free her arm.

"Not yet, bitch," he said in English. "We haven't had dessert yet." He opened the car door. "Get in."

She hesitated, wondering if she should obey or scream. He was drunk. She had had some experience with drunks. Avoiding violence was the first rule. She climbed in.

"You have nice breasts, you know that?" he said, trying to kiss her.

As she tried to get out of the car, he pushed a button. There was a click, and all the doors locked. "How about a hug?"

"Not tonight," she said.

He started the car. "Where are we going?" she asked.

"Let's take a ride to the West Mountain," he said. "Move over a little. The way you sit, I can put an elephant between us."

The car roared out of the hutung at high speed. Her heart was pounding. He made several sharp turns and drove recklessly down the boulevard that led to the western suburb.

"Slow down, please!" she said, a bit frightened now.

"Custom-made car," he said drunkenly. "It only goes fast. Do you want me to drive upward? I can do that, too. Love is all-powerful!"

She remained stiff and quiet for a moment, praying that nothing would happen. At an intersection, he ran a red light and made another sharp turn, tires screeching.

"Where are you taking me?" she asked, really alarmed now.

"West Mountain," he said. "I know a cozy little hotel there."

"I'm not going to any hotel with you! Let me out!"

"In a little while, you'll see the countryside. They all do it in the bushes. The girls all know where. They can find a spot where no insects will sting their bare bottoms. If you know where to find such a spot, we won't go to a hotel."

"Slow down!" she screamed.

The car swerved, narrowly missing an electric pole.

"Stop the car!" she cried, trying to put her foot on the brake.

"Okay, okay," he said. He stopped the car and again tried to kiss her. She struggled, twisting her head to avoid his mouth. He gave up and brought out a bottle of whiskey from under the seat. She wondered if he was going to hit her with the bottle.

"Will you marry me?" he asked.

"Yes, I'll marry you. Please let me go!"

"Promise?"

"Promise."

"Good. I want to disinfect you after your roommate used you last night."

She stared at him as he opened the bottle and poured the whiskey over her groin.

During the Cultural Revolution, "Dare to scold your father and beat up your mother" had been the revolutionary vanguard's first requirement. Both Jimmy and Do Do had witnessed the total destruction of filial piety and other Confucian virtues. They had watched a new crop of youths coming of age who enjoyed urinating on food piles, throwing rocks at passing trains, and locking up their parents in cowsheds. Suddenly, in 1985, six years after the end of the Cultural Revolution, the government rehabilitated the long-dead Confucius, who had been condemned as a corrupting force in a socialist society. The new campaign was to promote honesty, propriety, and respect for elders, especially parents and teachers. Flyers were distributed to schools urging students to bow to their teachers in class and greet them with 'Nin hao.' Some incorrigible youths had obeyed the instructions with comical exaggerations. Jimmy had seen students bowing to their teachers so low that they looked like inferiors bowing to their superiors in a Peking opera; a few greeted their teachers like peasants and coolies, by asking, "Have you eaten?"

But on the whole the students had become more polite and respectful. Jimmy even found gifts on his desk, mostly from female students who enjoyed his casual method of teaching. One day he brought home four pairs of mittens, all handmade with his name embroidered on them.

At home, even Raymond started bowing to him. Raymond seemed to enjoy his life in Beijing. He had turned down his father's offer to rent a place for him; he liked Jimmy's cramped apartment and slept well on an army cot in the living room. Both Jimmy and Do Do enjoyed his company and tolerated the chaos created by a teenager's idiosyncrasies and bad habits.

Raymond was inquisitive. At the dinner table, his appetite for food was as big as his curiosity. Jimmy was glad. He fed his half brother everything he could think of, from coolie food to stories about Mao Zedong's women.

"Raymond," he asked one evening, "who told you to bow to me every time you see me?"

"Our teacher," Raymond said. "He also told us to greet the elders every day. In the case of an older brother, it's 'Older Brother, good morning,' 'Older Brother, how are you?', 'Older Brother, good-bye.' If I finish my dinner sooner than you do, I should lay down my chopsticks politely and say, 'Older Brother eat slowly.' "

"That's overdoing it a bit," Jimmy said. "I'm glad you haven't started using all those greetings. Let's save our breath to discuss more interesting things."

They turned to weightier subjects.

"What's Three, Four, Five?" Raymond asked, devouring Do Do's jiaozi, his favorite.

"That's the newest slogan since Confucius was rehabilitated," said Do Do, carrying more food to the table. "It means five emphases, four beauties, and three loves."

She explained that before Confucius' rehabilitation, the five emphases were eating, drinking, entertainment, nice clothes, and plenty of money. The four beauties meant a beautiful lover, beautiful working place, beautiful home, and beautiful decorations. Three loves were love of fame, fortune, and family. Now the five emphases were culture, politeness, hygiene, discipline, and morality. The four beauties were beautiful heart, beautiful language, beautiful behavior, and beautiful surroundings. The three loves had become love the motherland, love the Communist party, love socialism.

Before Confucius' rehabilitation, China's noble class consisted of peddlers, street cleaners, stevedores, farmers, cooks, steelworkers, barbers, and grammar-school teachers. Now the high-class people included engineers, doctors, technicians, reporters, judges, writers, lawyers, and scientists.

"For the first time, we intellectuals are climbing the social ladder."

At school, Raymond had learned a lot of limericks, all about the social changes and new trends started by Deng Xiaoping's reform policies.

"Are you two Communists? he asked.

"Are you kidding?" Do Do said. "We have the worst background—educated bourgeoisie. Everybody wants to be a member. Without being a member, you can't get the best jobs. It's a vicious circle. That's why we're so poor. A houseguest has to sleep on a secondhand cot."

"We'll get you a bed, Raymond," Jimmy said with a laugh. "We're climbing the social ladder."

"Don't you believe it," Do Do said. "The party leaders still claim that they are people's servants and that we people are the masters. Recently, a factory worker came to Radio Beijing and demanded to appear on our program. We asked him what he wanted to say. He spoke his mind. 'Fellow countrymen,' he said, 'we masters live in shacks, but our servants live in mansions in Zhong Nan Hai. We masters ride bikes to work, but our servants ride in chauffeured limousines to Bei Dai Ho.

What kind of social system is this?' We kicked him out before we got ourselves in trouble."

"What's Bei Dai Ho?" Raymond asked.

"The best summer resort in China, where our servants go for vacations and to hold meetings," Do Do said.

"Do you still want to become Communist party members?" asked Raymond, getting more interested in the subject.

"Not anymore," Do Do said. "Times are changing. Some of my friends are hiding their membership. Jimmy, have you heard this joke? Two lovers are discussing whether they should have sex. The man says, 'I must be frank with you, I have a social disease.' The woman says, 'Thank you for your frankness. I also have a secret. I'm a Communist party member.' "

Jimmy didn't laugh. He was on tenterhooks when Do Do talked negatively about the Communist party. Afraid that Raymond might get the wrong impression, he changed the subject.

When dinner was over, there was a knock on the door. Raymond leapt up and opened it. Pang Sin, looking harassed, stepped in.

"Just in time for coffee," Jimmy said.

"Meet Raymond, Pang Sin," said Do Do, clearing the table. "He's Jimmy's half brother. That makes you a half-half brother, or is it double-half brother?"

"You always joke," Pang Sin said with a grimace. He shook Raymond's hand and sat down at the table.

"You look terrible," said Jimmy, pouring a cup of coffee for him. "What's wrong?"

"I shouldn't have come the other day," Pang Sin said with a sigh. He looked at Raymond and hesitated.

"You can air any dirty linen here, Pang Sin," Do Do said. "Raymond is family."

"Remember that bitch I met here a few weeks ago?" Pang Sin asked.

"Jane Lo," Do Do said. "It was love at first sight. Why do you call her 'bitch'?"

"I got a letter from her lawyer this morning. She's suing me for rape."

Raymond sat up and listened, his interest perking up.

"Did you rape her?" Jimmy asked.

"Of course not! I just poured some whisky over her legs. That's all. I was a bit drunk. Listen, Jimmy, I can't afford this kind of publicity. If this lawsuit gets into the papers, I'll be in terrible trouble."

"Hey," Do Do said, "if they kick you out of the party, you're a master again!"

Pang Sin looked at her with a scowl; he didn't know what she was talking about.

"Pang Sin," Jimmy said, "what do you want us to do?"

"Talk to the bitch. Reason with her. Tell her not to go through with her goddamn lawsuit. Tell her nobody is going to win . . . we'll only get our names ruined. Who knows it wasn't she who seduced me? Maybe I can sue her for blackmail."

"Did she seduce you?" Jimmy asked.

"Of course she did! Didn't she wink at me? You all saw it!"

"She did stay a little longer," Jimmy said. "She was about to leave."

"You see?" Pang Sin said triumphantly. "The moment the bitch saw me, she was thinking of a trap."

"Don't call Jane a bitch, Pang Sin," Do Do said. "She's a family friend."

"But I'm family. Think about me, Do Do!"

"How did she seduce you?" asked Raymond, getting more interested. "Did she take her clothes off?"

"She spread her legs, if you really want to know."

"Oh, yeah?" Raymond asked. "What did you do?"

"All right, all right," interrupted Jimmy, throwing up his hands. "We'll talk to her when we see her."

"Listen, Jimmy," Pang Sin said, "this is urgent! You've got to call her right now, before the news of the damned lawsuit leaks out!"

"What if she refuses to drop the lawsuit?" Jimmy asked.

"Ask her if she'll settle out of court in private. Since she's a family friend and I'm family, we'll settle right here."

"Can I watch?" Raymond asked excitedly.

14

Mark Hansen often asked himself why his assistant, Yun Mei, was so interesting. His only answer was that it was because she was so rebellious. One day he asked her, "Yun Mei, why are you so rebellious?"

Yun Mei refused to tell him. Hansen regarded her as a tragic figure; all her laughter and gaiety were only a cover. For interviews, she always took him to those who had suffered the cruelest fates, whose lives had been ruined and whose futures shattered by others.

The latest man Hansen had interviewed was a medical doctor named Yao who lived in a hut and raised chickens. He was making a good living peddling live chickens and eggs on the street. His downfall as a doctor had started during Mao's Great Leap Forward in 1958. Hunan, the rich rice bowl, suffered a terrible famine that year. The party leaders, in order to glorify the results of Mao's Great Leap Forward, falsified the record of the province's harvest. Before they were inspected, farmers were told to fill their barns with hay and cover the hay with a layer of grain. Soon Hunan became known as a model province where "every barn was full." Such a glorious report deprived the province of famine aid a year later. More than a million people died of starvation. Yao was one of the doctors sent to Hunan to treat widespread disease caused by malnutrition. He was so incensed that he exposed the party leaders' fraud. As a result, he not only lost his job but was banished to a border province to work as a laborer. When he was finally rehabilitated twenty years later, he had lost his medical skills and decided to abandon his profession altogether.

After Hansen had written several stories about such tragedies, he wanted a change of pace. Yun Mei said that the government had started promoting "glorious reports" again to glorify "the million-Yuan families" among the farmers. Several propaganda organizations had even printed limericks describing farmers' new life-styles: rice machine-polished, eggs fried sunny-side up; chickens, ducks, and pork in every bowl. Watches, bicycles, sewing machines, and radios were no longer fashionable; now desired items were color TVs, refrigerators, washing machines, and VCRs. The government also advertised a ceremony to be held in Hopei Province celebrating the occasion of a farmer buying his first private automobile. Hansen checked the date: He had missed the ceremony by two days. He stamped his foot and blamed himself for being unable to read Chinese.

To compensate for his loss, Yun Mei took him to the nearest million-yuan family for an interview. The nervous millionaire, uncomfortable in a Western suit, complained that he missed being poor. Now he was a fresh-flower farmer in Tung-xien, just outside Beijing. His family of five lived in a two-story brick building surrounded by fruit trees. They missed their hogs and chickens roaming in and out of their two-room shack. Now that those animals were gone, only a lazy dog and two alley cats remained as their companions. Every day, curious visitors, mostly strangers, came from afar to admire their modern house and their luxurious life-style. They must answer hundreds of letters every month, praising the party, which had made them rich. Because of all that, the farmer had developed a chronic headache. His wife was laid up with a cold, an ailment the family had never had before. He concluded the interview with a heavy sigh. "It's hard to raise flowers, but to live a millionaire's life is even harder."

The wife, bundled up, was lying on a sofa. She interrupted her own coughing and said to Yun Mei, "What bothers him the most he did not tell you. Everybody puts out a hand and asks for a loan. Don't translate that, or the foreigner might think China is full of beggars."

Yun Mei translated it anyway.

Hansen asked Farmer Ding what he was going to do with all his money. Ding shrugged. "Build a house for each of my three children, two sons and a daughter. The daughter costs more, for she needs a dowry. For my wife and myself, we'll travel . . . get away from this cage in which we are only strange animals on display."

"What about your farm?"

"Lease it."

"Become a landlord?"

Farmer Ding grinned. "Why not? Nowadays everybody wants to become a landlord."

Yun Mei knew a theatrical makeup artist called Fat Wong who opened a beauty salon in Wang Fu Jin and wanted some publicity. Hansen happily obliged him. He found Wong talkative and eager to please, going out of his way to show his services and equipment. He even gave Hansen and Yun Mei free haircuts. Hansen enjoyed the complete treatment, which included a shampoo, facial massage, and the beating of the shoulders. For a woman customer, the services included makeup, plucking the eyebrows, piercing of ears with loops included, and a wrinkle treatment. Yun Mei also accepted two bottles of wrinkle-reducing ointment made of ginseng and pearls. The two ingredients had been proven effective in rejuvenating skin for thousands of years.

Traditional Chinese women used to strap their breasts in; now ladies wanted them out. Fat Wong offered services in making breasts big and firm through exercise and massage. He said that his best customers in this department were newlyweds and those who were engaged to be married. Hansen asked him about the costs. Wong told him in English that if a woman wanted everything on the menu, it would cost five hundred jinmingbi . . . about a year's salary for an average working man or woman. Hansen was surprised; the place was packed to capacity with women of all ages going through the rigors of every kind of treatment. Razors were clicking and electric gadgets humming.

"How can an average worker afford this?" he asked.

"They can't," Fat Wong said. "But beauty has been dead in China for forty years. Now everybody wants it, thanks to Deng Xiaoping. Ladies organize clubs where they pay a monthly fee into a fund which they spend by turn in my shop. They buy one machine to develop breasts and they use it by turn. Do you know how much a Western suit costs? More than a year's salary. So half a dozen men chip in to buy an expensive suit. They, too, wear it by turn. Chinese are starved for fashion and beauty. If you want to invest, this is the right business to get into."

Hansen visited a dress store full of magazines displaying the newest fashions. A big crowd was outside gawking at things they had never seen in public before—seductive brassieres and panties. In the men's department, three-piece suits, silk shirts, cowboy boots, jeans, and gold chains were all displayed with huge price tags fastened to them. Again there were more gawkers than paying customers.

Yun Mei tugged at Hansen's sleeve when a couple walked out of the door. The young man had his brand-new silk shirt unbuttoned, showing his new gold chain that rested on his hairless chest. The woman also had her new silk blouse unbuttoned, showing a new pink brassiere that barely covered her full breasts. Complete with fashionable dark glasses, they stepped onto the busy street, arm in arm, drawing many eyes, some curious and some disdainful. To Hansen, it was quite a sight.

Yun Mei told Hansen that China also had many homeless people, even though rent was subsidized by the government. She took him to the Sino-Japanese Hospital, a brand-new facility in the Eastern City where the massive building awed the ordinary people. Most of them thought such a place was only for the privileged few. As a result, the hospital was never full. Those in the know often took advantage of the vacancies and spent a few comfortable nights there free of charge. All **they** needed was some symptoms of a disease. Flu was the easiest to fake; with a bit of hot pepper smeared in the eyes, a man could look awfully sick. While visiting a ward in the hospital, Hansen heard a lot of coughing.

"Those who cough the loudest are the freeloaders," Yun Mei told him.

She took him to a middle school nearby one early morning. In the school compound, the students and teachers were like ants, busily moving beds out of the classrooms. Others were sweeping, dusting, and putting desks and chairs back. Garbage was being collected and carted in barrels to the public dump in a three-wheeled truck. Just before eight o'clock, everything was in order. Bells rang and classes started. Hansen learned that every weekend the school turned into a hostel for tourists passing through Beijing. The school earned extra income, and the students and teachers made some pocket money.

Hansen visited many of the out-of-the-way places with Yun Mei and explored several levels of Chinese society. He felt lucky that he had a guide like Yun Mei. His articles were fresh and different. But Yun Mei herself still remained a mystery to him. He wanted to know her better. He wanted to interview her for an article, but she always declined.

He was tired of frequenting Beihai Park, the Summer Palace, and the Western Hill, eating Peking duck, Mongolian hot pot, imperial food, and other expensive foods. Both he and Yun Mei agreed that they would eat with the coolies for a change. She took him to a small restaurant south of Xidan Intersection. The place was crowded, almost choking with cigarette smoke and the pungent smell of spicy food. They ordered beef noodles and a few other nameless dishes. Hansen found it adventurous to eat anything without asking what it was.

"Well . . . in Rome do as the Romans do," he said, plunging into a bowl of stew. He ate with crude bamboo chopsticks, sucking in air noisily, like the other diners. He chewed and smacked his lips, half suspecting it was some kind of wild-animal meat. But Yun Mei assured him that it was only pork heart and lung with some gristle . . . her favorite. His favorites were the slippery eels cooked in Chinese leeks, and hairy crab steamed in garlic. There were two side dishes of peanuts and chilies that came gratis with all the main orders.

Yun Mei ate quietly, as if deep in thought. Suddenly, she blurted, "I wonder if Deng Xiaoping is imitating Mao Zedong. Both are tricky."

Hansen glanced around to see if anyone was listening. Luckily, the customers, mostly workers with coarse hands and leathery faces, were too hungry to pay any attention to idle conversation. Besides, he doubted that they understood English.

"Why do you say that?" he asked.

"Mao was tricky," she said, sucking in air to cool her tongue. The food was hot and spicy.

"That's not news," he said with a smile.

"Before the Korean War," she went on, "he declared that the more a man studies, the stupider he becomes. After half a million men were killed in Korea, he heard a lot of criticism about the stupidity of the war. But he came out smiling, saying that he welcomed criticism. He called the intellectuals' criticism 'gentle breeze and fine rain.' He started a campaign called 'Let a hundred flowers bloom.' Since he openly welcomed freedom of speech, everybody started talking. A storm of complaints and protests poured out like water out of a broken dam. Then Chairman Mao threw his huge net and caught all those who had dared to criticize his erroneous policies. So you see? The 'Let a hundred flowers bloom' movement was only a trap."

"Why do you mention it now?" Hansen asked.

"Remember," she said, her voice lowered but angry, "the movement was immediately followed by his antirightist movement. Hundreds of thousands of intellectuals were singled out for public humiliation. Many were imprisoned, and some were even executed." She stopped, her eyes red and moist. She took a deep breath and remained silent for a moment, trying to control her emotions.

Hansen had heard about the post–Korean War period. He even remembered Mao's slogan "Let all the demons and devils, ghosts and monsters, air their views freely. Let all the poisonous weeds sprout and grow profusely so that we, the people, can take steps to wipe them out!" He remembered it because the slogan wasn't stuffy, but interesting and folksy in Mao's usual style.

"Yun Mei," he said, "you haven't answered my question. Why did you mention it now? It came out of the blue. You surprised me."

She pulled herself together. "I've wanted to tell you this, but it's only safe to do it in a coolie place. I'm cynical. You still look at China through rose-colored glasses."

"Oh?" Mark looked at her inquisitively.

"You've been praising China's freedom of speech too much, Mark. How can you be sure this is not another 'Let a hundred flowers bloom' trick?"

Hansen scratched his chin. He had just filed another report about China's new freedom of speech, describing how anyone could post his opinion in big letters on the "Wall of Free Speech." He shook his head, amused.

"Yun Mei," he said, "You're going to turn me into a suspicious old lady. What am I going to write about now?"

"Why don't you write something on the light side?" Yun Mei suggested. "Some of the Communist papers are full of stories that sound pretty funny. No foreign correspondent has ever reported on them."

"Can you give me a few examples?"

Yun Mei fished some clippings out of her handbag and translated:

"Item: China has discovered a formula for hair-growing. It is called One-oh-one. The article claims that if a man has lost one hundred hairs, the drug will help him grow one hundred and one hairs back.

"Item: In Liaoning Province, the Communist medical authorities claim that eighty-three cancer patients in that province have completely recovered after taking a new drug called Shrink. A malignant tumor as big as a fist in a sixty-eight-year-old male patient vanished after only one injection of Shrink.

"Item: A twenty-four-year-old female army doctor on Hainan Island is described as a miracle woman with magic eyes that can kill cats and dogs. They can also determine the sex of unborn babies."

Hansen laughed. "Are these reports serious?" he asked. "Or just a bunch of jokes?"

"If they were jokes," she said, "they're not funny and nobody would read them. Because they're dead serious, they attract wide attention. Medical researchers have spent time and money to investigate these miracles."

"You mean people really believe this crap?"

Yun Mei nodded gravely.

Do Do finished her assignment and took an afternoon off to polish her report at home. She was surprised to find the apartment unusually tidy. Obviously, Jimmy had tidied it up, picking up Raymond's clothes from the floor and folding them, something Raymond rarely did. The boy was spoiled rotten by his mother. She smiled as she thought of Raymond. Neither she nor Jimmy had regretted inviting him to live with them, despite the inconvenience. Jimmy had said he was grateful that Raymond did not smoke pot. Nor was he the product of the Cultural Revolution. The boy's only fault was leaving his clothes around.

She made a pot of coffee, sat at the dining table, and relaxed, counting her blessings. She had read an article about housework in an American magazine. In the old days, men used to gather wood, process grain, make tools, and butcher animals. Today, men came home, turned on the TV, threw their feet on the coffee table, and asked, "What's for dinner?" The article further stated that when a Western man does not idle, he tinkers. He rarely lifts a finger to help his wife with her endless household chores—cooking, cleaning, laundry, mending clothes, etc. When the wife hears an outburst of profanity, she knows that he has clumsily hammered his thumb while tinkering, and it is she who rushes to him with the medicine kit.

While reading the article, she told herself how lucky she was not to have married such a man. She also felt lucky that she had enjoyed a variety of assignments in her job. Her newest subject was free enterprise in China, a thing that was nonexistent before Deng Xiaoping's reform. She had discovered that most of China's new enterprises were family-owned. They employed almost forty million people grinding out food, clothing, vehicles, electrical appliances, and all kinds of consumer goods. She had found that Beijing and Shanghai had the largest number of entrepreneurs, and more than 20 percent of them were from Wenzhow City in Zhejiang Province.

As clothiers, Wenzhow businessmen netted more than U.S. $50 million a year. They had branched out to all the other provinces in China, like a giant octopus. In Kunming alone, there were ten streets named Wenzhow. The sudden prosperity had brought men and women to the major cities to open restaurants, dance halls, gambling houses, and even brothels in thoroughfares and back alleys, catering to the new rich. Those supporting new ventures in town made enormous profits. Even a small restaurant owner made twenty times more a year than an average worker.

She also discovered that not all the new rich were happy. They were getting increasingly nervous for fear they would lose their wealth in another political upheaval. A great many of the entrepreneurs were sending money to foreign banks in Canada, Mexico . . . even the Bahamas. If they could not buy foreign exchange legally, they bought it on the black market. By greasing the proper influential palms, they were able to send their relatives overseas to build their foreign nests.

The free entrepreneurs were changing China so fast that Do Do felt dizzy while she was reporting it.

There was a knock on the door. She opened it, hoping it was not a long-winded visitor.

Yun Mei, smiling, stepped in. "You look so cheerful," Do Do said. "What's new this time? Money? A promotion? Mao Zedong turning in his casket?"

"Nothing of the kind," said Yun Mei, taking a chair at the dining table. "I just enjoy my new job, thanks to you."

"I see romance in the air," Do Do said with a laugh.

"No comment," said Yun Mei, helping herself to some watermelon seeds in a plate.

"What do you do?"

"I gather material for his articles. And I translate, of course. The Communist publications are so dull that I sometimes fall asleep in the middle of a sentence. But lately I've discovered some tidbits that lightened things quite a bit. Mark Hansen is a meticulous reporter. He never reports anything without a thorough investigation.

"Last week I showed him an article about a woman in Tung-xien outside Beijing. It reported that she had given birth to quadruplets, one of which had two heads. The health authorities planned to dispatch a medical team to study this phenomenon. Mark wanted to report it, and dragged me to visit this farm family. We spent almost all day looking for the family. When we finally found them in a shack in a dirt compound, the toothless mother-in-law declared that the published story was a mistake. It was her hog, not her daughter-in-law, who had the quadruplets. The two-headed one? It died, and the family ate it. We wasted all day, but we had a good laugh."

"I'm glad you like the job," Do Do said. "Even wasting time sounds like fun."

"I never thought I'd have so many fringe benefits working for a foreigner. I don't mean medical insurance, paid vacations, or anything like that. I'm approached every day by people looking for foreign connections. Suddenly, I've become one of the most popular women in Beijing!"

She got up, patted her stomach, and laughingly declared that this was the disaster area. Two inches of expansion in two months. She had been showered with dinner invitations, free rides in limousines, free tickets to closed film screenings, and lots of gifts. Her apartment was full of trinkets; some of the boxes had still not been opened, but were stacked ceiling-high in her bedroom.

"Today, foreign connections are as important as *gwansi*, or back-door connections," she said. "You have no idea how many people want to go abroad and are looking for foreign sponsors."

"You and Mark Hansen can make a fortune," Do Do said with a laugh. "You two can go into business together and open an office called 'Foreign Connection Agency.' "

"You know what?" Yun Mei said. "This white man is a strange hombre. He isn't a bit interested in money. He could easily bring duty-free TV sets to China to sell. A man approached him for a deal, and he threw him out."

She suddenly stopped laughing and became serious. "Listen, Do Do, there's something you ought to know, and pass the information on to Jimmy and your father-in-law. That big bash your father-in-law threw for the intellectuals at the Beijing Hotel may have displeased some old fogies in Zhong Nan Hai. I have a cousin working there. She tipped me off."

"How could anyone criticize an overseas Chinese for entertaining some intellectuals?" Do Do said. "Thanks for the tip, but I don't think there's any need to worry."

"Do Do," Yun Mei said, "if the dining hall was bugged, a lot of remarks made during the dinner could have stung a few ears in Zhong Nan Hai. Especially Liu Bo's little speech."

"Nothing spoken on that day was more critical than those big posters on the freedom wall," Do Do said. "I read some posters a few days ago . . . one almost called for another revolution. Jimmy said that those writers are still teaching, laughing, and giving the Zhong Nan Hai residents a piece of their minds. Jimmy firmly believes that we've already had a revolution. Deng Xiaoping isn't stupid enough to smother the voices of the intellectuals again. He himself was a victim during the Cultural Revolution. Look at his son, pushed off a balcony by Red Guards and crippled for life. Don't you think he has learned a lesson?"

"I hope he has," Yun Mei said. She was unconvinced, but she did not want to argue, knowing that Jimmy's father had been investing heavily in Deng's four modernization programs.

"Come and have dinner with us again," Do Do said. "And bring Mark Hansen. Jimmy's half brother has moved in with us, but this table is still big enough to seat five."

"Mark Hansen will come to eat your jiaozi anytime, rain or shine, typhoon or earthquake," Yun Mei said.

She left Do Do's apartment laughing, but deep down she was worried.

15

Both Do Do and Jimmy were home early. Do Do was busy cooking a five-course dinner to celebrate Raymond's graduation from middle school. In Beijing, cooking was the only entertainment for those who could not afford to eat out. Raymond's average grade was a "B-," a marked improvement over his high school grades in Hong Kong. The boy enjoyed the spartan life in Beijing and the casual chitchat with Jimmy and Do Do. The tiny apartment was often full of laughter and rock and roll music. The cooking smell of hot, spicy food always lingered.

As Raymond found Do Do outspoken and interesting, he felt completely at home in her company, except when she teased him about his love life. When he was embarrassed, Jimmy would chide her for being too frank.

"She's a woman with only one long tube stretching from top to bottom," Jimmy whispered.

"What does that mean?" Raymond asked.

"A woman has nothing to hide. An old Chinese saying."

"Wish my mother was like that," Raymond said. "She's kind of complicated."

When he thought of his parents' frozen faces, he shuddered.

The phone rang. Jimmy answered it.

"Raymond," Do Do said, "who are you serious about, Yin Yin or May?"

"Both," Raymond said. "Tell me about your own love affairs. You dropped Pang Sin for Jimmy, didn't you?"

"That's no secret."

"How did it happen?"

"It was during the height of the Cultural Revolution . . . during a 'struggling against rightists' meeting. Pang Sin tortured an old professor by making his son bang the old man's head on a cement floor. When his head became a bloody mess, I made up my mind to switch horses. Jimmy looked as if he was about to throw up. When he rushed away, I followed him. I caught up with him and took his hand. We've been holding hands ever since."

"So you two walked into the sunset," Raymond said.

"We walked into the sunrise," Do Do said. "We were full of hope for the future. We had nine years of excitement. We went through ups and downs. We believed that every twist and turn, no matter how troublesome or dangerous, strengthened our relationship."

"I wish Mom and Dad had this kind of relationship."

"I wouldn't wish the Cultural Revolution on them, though, no matter how it might have strengthened Jimmy and me."

While they were chatting, Jimmy was still on the phone. When he finally hung up, he looked disturbed. "My father is unhappy about his joint venture," he said. "He has been pouring money into the hotel project, but nothing is happening."

"Jimmy," Do Do said, "you know Chinese red tape. When any project requires ten men's signatures, it always gets bogged down. If one of the ten refuses to put his chop on the document, the whole thing is beached until he changes his mind."

"What damned fool would refuse to approve a project that will only benefit China? It's all good for the country . . . a tremendous contribution to Deng Xiaoping's Four Modernization Programs!"

"That reminds me," said Do Do, snapping her fingers. "I wonder if there's some truth in Yun Mei's inside information."

"What inside information?"

"She said somebody in Zhong Nan Hai told her something that we ought to know. Your father's literary party displeased quite a few old men in Zhong Nan Hai. They felt threatened."

"That party was perfectly harmless," Jimmy said, surprised. "Why would they feel threatened?"

"Who knows what they think?" Do Do said pensively. "Maybe it's true that whatever the intellectuals say or do, it looks like a threat."

"No, no," Jimmy said, pacing the floor, worried. "The government can't be that stupid. Someone is offering China a hundred hotels on a silver platter. Would they throw them away because this someone has entertained some intellectuals?"

Do Do shrugged. "They may think the hotel project is a giant Trojan horse, have you thought of that? Let's eat. Let's celebrate Raymond's graduation and his coming of age."

Raymond grimaced.

Mark Hansen's office in the Beijing Hotel became a popular stopover for his friends and colleagues. It was cozy and convenient. When the hotel was full, his office couch served as a comfortable bed.

One morning the hotel manager knocked on his door just after a friend had sneaked out with his luggage. The manager, a stout man with a large, dark face, was accustomed to all types of foreigners and gave no one special treatment. He wore elevated shoes so he could stand tall and equal when he argued with a white man. He confronted Hansen with his thumbs hooked in the vest of his three-piece suit, his legs apart, and a heavy scowl on his face. He demanded to know who had just moved out.

Hansen told him the truth . . . a friend who could not find a hotel room in Beijing.

"Mr. Hansen," the manager said, "I'm afraid I'll have to evict you for letting an unpaid guest sleep in the hotel. This is highly irregular, and this rule must be enforced."

Yun Mei was in the next room. Knowing how difficult it was to find office space in Beijing and that there was a two-year waiting period, she rushed out and tried to charm Manager Hu. In China, a pretty girl was the best troubleshooter if she could giggle, flap her eyelashes, and flatter. Yun Mei did all three and softened Mr. Hu's belligerent attitude considerably.

When Hu began to smile, she suggested a compromise: Hansen would pay a double room rent for the guest, plus his promise not to cheat the hotel again.

After Hu had left, Hansen almost lost his temper. "Why did you say I wouldn't cheat the hotel again? It wasn't cheating!"

"I wish it had been," Yun Mei said heatedly. "I'd like to cheat the pants off all of them!"

Hansen cocked an eyebrow inquisitively. He was surprised by such a blunt answer, and the way she had changed from charming to bitchy amused him.

"I don't understand," he said.

"That's what I mean . . . cheating them," she said, still breathing fire. "The 'old tree trunks' can use the hotel free. They even evict guests to accommodate their own friends and relatives. Hell, we can't take this lying down! We'll cheat!"

"How?" Hansen asked. He was getting curious, wondering if there was an interesting story in this for an article.

"We have an old saying, 'Money can make a ghost mill grain.' With a little money, you can do anything. By tipping the service boy on this floor a few dollars, you can start a hotel business yourself. You can offer overnight accommodations to all your stranded friends. There won't be any more problems, I guarantee!"

"You mean the service boy is a hotel informant?"

"A spy! But cheap! They all are. They're the eyes and ears of the management. Otherwise how would the manager know you had an overnight guest?"

Hansen laughed. He found Yun Mei an invaluable assistant. He had learned from her how to predict events, how to interpret official reports, and how to find newspapers tidbits that might have hidden meanings.

"Every time you find the bylines of Fang Lizhi and Liu Binyan in the *People's Daily*," she said, "you know the liberals have gained an upper hand. This sort of thing is like a Chinese political barometer. You can almost tell when the reformers are winning. The moment an anti-rightist's articles appear on the front page, you know the hard-liners are gaining power. The seesaw war in Zhong Nan Hai never stops."

She also told him how to recognize stories written by hard-liners who "sold dog meat by hanging out a sheep's head." She showed him an article that eloquently defended freedom, saying that freedom was sacred, but argued that it could become a two-edged butcher's hatchet if wielded by the wrong people, such as counterrevolutionaries. "If a driver of a car has total freedom," the article said, "he can go out and smash properties, run over pedestrians, and wreak havoc on society. Therefore, the freedom promoted by the Communist party is the exact right amount of freedom that everyone should fight for."

Yun Mei showed him another article that defended the appointment of a retired army man to head a university. The article admitted that the old army man was not well educated, but he had acquired invaluable experience, gained through a lifetime of manual labor and numerous life-and-death battles with enemies. Therefore, he was an excellent role model for thousands of young people in high educational institutions, a man to be emulated. The article concluded by saying, "We challenge you to find a man who is better qualified to be a university president."

There was also an article attacking capitalism. It said that communism was born in 1917 during Russia's October Revolution. Capitalism was invented in 1584 during Europe's Industrial Revolution. It was four hundred years old. What had it accomplished? Nothing but exploitation of the Third World. Communism is only sixty-seven years old, but look at its glorious accomplishments in such a short time!

The same article also pointed out that in America, crime was rampant because of racial, religious, and sexual discrimination. In an accompanying table, statistics showed the rapid increase of murder, rape, and robbery in all major American cities. The article ended with the conclusion, "If this is capitalism, who needs it?"

"Mark," Yun Mei said, "such articles might fool a lot of people. But what intelligent person will buy this kind of communist logic? You can also tell when the editors are unhappy; they will sneak a little story onto the back of the page as a token protest. Here's an example. This little story says, 'A young Shanghai woman was pregnant for five years. Her worried family hired a fairy godmother to diagnose the problem. Since the world was full of war and violence, the pregnant young woman had prayed for a son who would be the most polite in the world. That was the young woman's problem, the fairy godmother said. She suggested a cesarean section. When the surgeon opened her up and looked inside, he found a set of twins with long beards, refusing to be the first one to be born. They kept bowing to each other and saying, 'After you. No, after you.' "

"You know," Yun Mei said seriously when she finished the story, "this is supposed to be a true story, like all the other stories about miracles, only the part about the twins was fabricated by editors as their commentary."

"How do you know?" he asked.

"I have informants all over the Beijing press," she said with a grin.

Raymond had a busy social life. He dated many girls and was anxious to sleep with them, but he could not find the courage or the place to do it. Some girls were not too interesting. Finally, he discarded them all except May and Yin Yin. He treated them equally well, taking them out alternately on weekends. They toured out-of-the-way places on bicycles, ate ethnic food in dirty restaurants, attended student meetings, and argued on issues. Both girls had passed the entrance examination for Beijing University and had enrolled in the languages department.

The pretty one, Yin Yin, was aggressive. He found her charming and sexy, a good companion. The plain one, May, was scholarly and knowledgeable. She and Raymond exchanged English and Chinese lessons and carried on serious discussions. May was a conservative, the daughter of one of the hard-liners in the government. But by associating with Raymond, she began to change. She often looked at Raymond dreamy-eyed behind her thick glasses, and agreed with him instead of defending her own ideas.

One evening, Raymond took Yin Yin home for dinner. Do Do had promised to cook them a few spicy dishes. As soon as he opened the door, he yelled, "The hungry wolves have arrived!"

There was no answer. He found a brief note on the kitchen table.

"Dear Raymond, Jimmy and I have to attend an urgent meeting. Sorry no hot, spicy dishes tonight. Take your guest to one of those 'little eat' places in the Farmers' Market. Here's a ten yuan. Be my guests. Love, Do Do."

"Shoot!" Raymond said. He put the ten-yuan note in his pocket and crumpled the note. "Let's go!"

"I'm not really hungry, are you?" Yin Yin asked.

"Not really. We can eat later. Want to play gin rummy?"

"Let's talk," she said, throwing herself on the sofa in the small living room. "Do you sleep behind that sheet?"

"Yes. I forgot to take it down. Sorry." He quickly took the sheet down, revealing his army cot. He picked up some of his clothes from the floor, threw them on the cot, and covered it with the sheet. Then he sat beside her with a sigh.

"Okay, let's talk. What do you want to know?"

"When you take me out, is May jealous?"

"No, she's a bookworm, not the jealous type. Besides, she knows nothing. She doesn't even know we've kissed."

"Did you kiss her?"

"I'm not attracted to her physically. Not like this, anyway."

He grabbed her and kissed her. She kissed him back, her tongue darting in and out of his mouth. While kissing, she reached down and started to unzip his pants.

"No," he said, pushing her hand away. "My brother might pop in any moment. I don't want to get kicked out of this place."

"All right," she said, throwing her legs on the coffee table. "Let's talk. What do you want to know?"

Raymond was always curious about women's sex lives. The more he read about them, the more he became interested. "How do you amuse yourself?" he asked.

"Well," she said. "I watch TV, I listen to music. . . ."

"I mean when you're hot," he interrupted.

"When I'm hot? I do what everybody else does. I fan myself."

"No, no. I mean when you're sexy."

"You mean masturbation?" She laughed.

"Yes, how do you do it?"

"I do nothing."

"I don't believe you. According to scientific research, ninety-nine percent of women masturbate."

"I don't want to talk about it. Why do you want to know?"

"It's kind of exciting to think about it. Do you really use a hairbrush?"

Yin Yin jabbed his forehead with a finger and laughed. "Hairbrush? What for? Spanking myself for being naughty?"

"How about the water faucet in the bathtub?"

Yin Yin laughed even louder. "You mean making love to a water faucet in a bathtub? How silly can you get?"

"I read about it," he said.

Yin Yin couldn't stop laughing.

"Listen," he went on, "I read about women using the pulsating warm water from a water faucet. The article says thirty-five percent of women use it to amuse themselves."

"Where can you get that in China?" she said after her laughter subsided. "We only have pulsating warm water in Zhong Nan Hai and the luxury hotels. What else did you read?"

"Don't tell me you never masturbated," he said, glancing at her white shapely legs on the coffee table, swallowing. He was getting increasingly excited as he talked about sex and watched her legs.

"I didn't say I never masturbated," she said. She glanced at his pants and found the bulge growing bigger. "Do you really want to know?" she asked.

"Yes. How do you do it?" he asked anxiously.

"I lie on top of a pillow, cross my legs tight, and do a little rumba, that's all. Come here."

She got up, went to the door, stood beside it, and lifted her skirt. He was so aroused that he almost threw caution to the wind.

"Let's go to the bedroom," he said.

"What if your brother pops in? Come here."

"What are we going to do?" he asked, going to the door.

"Do you have a condom?" she asked.

"No."

She fished one out of her skirt pocket. "Put it on."

He fumbled with it nervously and dropped it.

"Let me," she said. She picked it up and put it on for him.
"Why do it here beside a door?" he asked.

"Because we can hear people coming. If we hear the door click, I can just drop my skirt and you can pop your little bird back, like the cuckoo in a cuckoo clock."

It was his first sex experience in Beijing. He liked it a lot.

18

Raymond had packed his belongings in three suitcases and a tote bag, ready to move to the dormitory at Beijing University, where he had enrolled in the languages department. He was going to miss the tiny two-room apartment, for which Jimmy paid ten yuans a month plus a small utility bill. The most expensive items in the apartment were the color television set and the private telephone, which had cost U.S. $500 to install. Do Do said that they could have got it for fifty dollars if they had waited, but they would have had to wait two years.

Raymond hated the phone. Every time his mother called, he had to answer a lot of silly questions. Did he bathe every day? Did he take his vitamins? Did he eat a lot of vegetables? Did he wash his fruit? He answered all these questions with a simple "Yes," fidgeting and waiting to hang up. When Do Do watched his restless legs, she always mumbled with a worried look, "Raymond, go to the bathroom."

He was glad that his mother had not visited him, for he had lied about the living conditions—soft bed, bathroom, maid service, and so on. He slept on an army cot behind a bedsheet, which he took down every morning. He took cold showers in a communal bathroom three flights down. In the winter, he sponge-bathed in the kitchen. He had not lied about maid service; Do Do had hired a Henan peasant girl to scrub and wash three times a week.

He was looking forward to living in a university dormitory with seven other students who treated him warmly and were anxious to practice English with him. Some were familiar with American politics and rock stars. A few could even recite the Pledge of Allegiance, sing "The Star-Spangled Banner" and "Home on the Range."

He picked up the phone and called a taxi. Do Do had told him that whenever hiring a taxi, he had better mention American dollars, or he would wait forever. She had also told him always to discuss the fee first.

Within twenty minutes, a cabbie stomped upstairs and knocked on his door. He was a skinny young man wearing a colorful Hawaiian shirt, with a cigarette hanging from his lips.

"How much does it cost for you to take me to Beijing University?" Raymond asked. He had forgotten to discuss the fee on the phone.

"Let the meter tell you," the cabbie said with a shrug.

"Forget the meter. How much?"

"Five dollars, American money."

He paid him. "Here's an extra dollar for helping me with my bags."

The cabbie selected the two smallest suitcases and carried them downstairs, inhaling deeply on his American cigarette.

Raymond picked up the two heavy bags, a bit confused by China's new trend; everybody was talking about progress, but people seemed to be getting damned lazy and money crazy. With a shrug, he followed the driver.

In the evening, the apartment was choking with cooking smells. The television was on. Michael Jackson in a tight black leather outfit was singing and dancing. Jimmy ate quietly, his eyes glued to the TV screen. Do Do winced. She never cared to look at the energetic Jackson with his girlie face and makeup.

"Too bad he's not a woman. He's so pretty," Do Do said.

"Don't you miss Raymond?" he asked. "I came back this afternoon and saw the bedsheet gone and the army cot folded. I began to miss him. This place is not the same anymore."

Do Do also found the place different. The bantering and

laughter were gone; there was no more disco music from Raymond's hi-fi. No more sighs and smacking of lips in appreciation of her garlic and hot-pepper cooking. Raymond never openly praised anybody or anything he liked, but never failed to show his appreciation with simple gestures. When he found his clothes washed and clean, he always grabbed Do Do by her shoulders and planted a noisy kiss on her forehead.

On weekends, after dinner, they used to pull the bedsheet aside, remove the cot and the table, and dance. Sometimes one of Raymond's girlfriends would be there to make a foursome. Raymond would invent new disco steps, turning and gyrating comically. He was quite funny, athletic, and graceful. All the girls wanted to marry him, the best catch in town. They all tried to become Do Do's best friend, hoping that she would help. But Do Do never played favorites; Jimmy also seemed reluctant to play "the old man under the moon," the matchmaker.

"What does his dormitory look like?" Do Do asked.

"Eight boys sleeping in four double-decked bunks," Jimmy said. "A long table in the middle for eating and studying. Everybody cleans his own mouse droppings and picks up his own clothes. Dirty sock smell strong. Beds never made. That's about it."

"Wonder why he was so anxious to move. He slept well and ate well here. We always welcomed his girlfriends. And he likes my bean-cake dish."

"Every boy of nineteen has weird ideas," Jimmy said. "He has his reasons for moving. I'm sure male hormones have something to do with it."

"Don't be ridiculous," Do Do scoffed. "How can he do anything with seven other boys watching?"

"You can do a lot behind a bush at Beijing University. To tell you the truth, I'm worried. He might get one of the girls in trouble."

"Relax," said Do Do, laughing. "When I washed his blue jeans, I found a few condoms in his hip pocket."

They heard Raymond's cowboy boots stomping upstairs. He came in beaming, slightly out of breath. "I forgot my toothbrush," he announced.

"You forgot something else, too," Do Do said. "Did you eat?"

"Yes," he said. Seeing unfinished food on the table, he picked up a piece of bean cake with his fingers and stuffed it in his mouth, groaning with pleasure.

"Raymond," Jimmy said, "you look like a cat that has just swallowed a poor little bird. You're still under my supervision. I want you to watch your step at the university."

Do Do had fished out a packet of condoms from a kitchen drawer. She handed it to Raymond. "This is what you also forgot. I almost laundered them. By the way, a few of them looked like they'd been used and washed. Don't you know that used ones are not safe?"

Raymond grabbed the packet and stammered something unintelligible. "Thanks, got to go!" He hurried away, again forgetting his toothbrush.

Jimmy, leaving for home in the late afternoon, saw a poster outside the university. The writer was unhappy with Deng's wishy-washy attitude toward China's freedom movement. He said that in late 1984 Deng had outlawed the Freedom Wall and announced his Four Cardinal Principles of Socialism. While criticizing Mao, he had also declared that China, contaminated by bourgeois poisoning, could only be saved by dictatorship of the proletariat, Marxist Leninism, and Mao Zedong's thought. Now, after three more years, Deng still had not shown any real interest in political reform. He suggested that Deng release Jing Sheng from jail and reread Jing's book *The Fifth Modernization —Democracy*.

The poster bothered Jimmy. He hurried home and told Do Do about it. Do Do had seen the same poster elsewhere, and she expressed her admiration for the writer's courage. But Jimmy thought the man was trying to stir things up. He believed that the so-called fifth modernization would only hinder the progress of Deng's economic reforms.

"I'm surprised at you, Jimmy," Do Do said. "Jing Sheng is still treated as a hero at your university. You're the only intellectual who hates him."

"I never said I hate him," Jimmy protested. "I only said China is not ripe for him. He rushes things."

"You never approved of the Freedom Wall," Do Do said. "It is the only symbol of freedom of speech."

"Do Do, I did not disapprove of the wall. I only said that Deng Xiaoping has his plans all worked out. Nobody should be so impatient as to criticize him. We should give him a chance."

"I tell you, all crows are black!" Do Do said coldly.

It was their first political quarrel. Before it became heated, he picked up his books and left the apartment. Riding back to the university, he felt sad. What had happened to Do Do? Politically, they had seldom disagreed. Why was she so touchy about his criticism of the Freedom Wall?

They had been happy for more than eight years. He remembered when he was leaving Changsha eight years ago. She had followed him to the train and ridden to Beijing with him. He had kissed her for the first time. They had had little to say; they just sat close together, quietly enjoying the soothing feeling of being in love. Even the monotonous clickety-clack of the train had sounded like music, heralding a happy new future for both of them.

They had read the first "big character" poster on Beijing's Freedom Wall that criticized Mao Zedong's mistakes. On December 15, 1978, they had for the first time in years dined in a restaurant to celebrate an important date—the day America recognized China. The next year, Deng Xiaoping had gone to America for a nine-day visit. Every day, Jimmy and Do Do had glued their eyes to the TV screen watching Deng's every move, listening to his speeches, his laughter and folksy chitchat. They had admired his farsightedness, his charisma, and his easygoing manners. Now something seemed to be going wrong. What had made Deng Xiaoping change? Why was he casting a shadow over freedom and new hope? What had happened?

19

Charles Hong had been wondering what Pang Sin looked like, being half Caucasian. Whenever he thought of Pang Sin, he felt a faint stab of jealousy for that nameless sailor who had sown a wild seed in Mabel before he had. He also wondered who that sailor was. Was he still living?

This train of thought always brought back vivid memories of Mabel, of the exciting days of their life in Chonqing, of the horrors of war, the tears and laughter amid air raids, wild parties, and painful separations.

For the past four years, since 1982, he had been going to China every year . . . sometimes twice a year, to discuss joint ventures and to see Jimmy and Do Do. His hotel-chain proposal, after lengthy negotiations, had been beached like a ship. He didn't know why.

He did not blame anyone. He had learned that the Communist red tape was such that dozens of seals and signatures were required on numerous contracts for an enormous project like his. Everything involved in building a hotel needed the approval of many department heads, who were always reluctant to sign for fear of failure. Nobody was willing to risk his job by sticking his neck out for a new venture. Charles had been told by many Hong Kong businessmen that joint ventures were the most bothersome type of business in China. The first year was usually consumed by meetings and banquets because the government officials involved in joint ventures received no personal gain; wining and dining the foreign partners were their only fringe benefits. If a joint venture failed, all those who had risked their names on contracts could lose their jobs. Jimmy had said that the trend was, "Let's talk-talk, eat-eat. The hell with signing!"

Charles had long since stopped being impatient. He loved going to China anyway. He was always royally treated. He enjoyed the nostalgia. Besides, Mabel was buried there. On each trip, he would visit her grave in Hunan, lay a bouquet of flowers, and reminisce for hours, searching his memory for moments of their hazardous but happy life together during those war years.

In March of 1986, when Premier Zhao Ziyang submitted the nation's ambitious Five-Year Plan calling for decentralization of industrial decision making and encouragement of free markets, it was big news, a major step toward capitalism.

In the same month, Deng Xiaoping hinted that he would like to retire from his party posts and let the younger generation take over. Again it was exciting news, for politically China was moving toward Western democracy.

In August, China's bond market opened in Shenyang, a northeastern city in Manchuria. It was the first concrete evidence of capitalism being revived in China.

In September, China's first stock market opened in Shanghai. Thousands of people flocked to Shanghai to trade stocks on the exchange. A clear sign that China was on its way toward complete economic liberalization.

Charles was happy for his motherland and for his extended family in Beijing. Aimee also seemed to be happier. In a surge of energy, she had the house refurnished. She had blended Oriental furniture with the best Western sofas, mirrors, and expensive home-entertainment systems. The thick Chinese rugs, the cloisonné tables, and exquisitely carved jade and cinnabar art objects displayed in curio cabinets gave the new home added elegance. She also kept her figure and her youthful look; she was one of the most fashionable and photogenic ladies in Hong Kong whose pictures often appeared in the society pages.

She was also generous to charities. Her most famous act of

mercy had been to provide the poor fishermen of Aberdeen with free health care. A few years ago, she had hired Dr. Robert Barfenker, a Los Angeles expatriate, to tend the sick; she had even donated a houseboat for the doctor to use as his floating clinic. But the charity work had not lasted long. In less than a year, the doctor had abandoned the boat and disappeared. According to Shanghai Mary, he had married a rich widow and declared that he would never again depress the tongue of a stinking fisherman. It had become a joke that Hong Kong gossips never tired of repeating at the dinner table.

But most of Charles's friends envied him. He had married a woman who was beautiful and almost half his age. He always had an eye for youth and beauty. He once declared jokingly that the greatest contribution of China's reform was to get rid of the baggy Mao uniform, which ruined one of the world's five marvels—the divine shape of a young Chinese woman's body.

It was a bright winter day in Hong Kong in early 1987. The air was crisp, with only a gentle breeze to sweep the smog away. Charles relaxed in his living room, enjoying a pipe and the sight of the busy bay through the picture window. He visualized Jimmy riding his bicycle home from Beijing University after a day's teaching, his shoulder bag bulging with his students' English compositions. The thought of his son always soothed him. By talking to Jimmy every weekend on the phone, he had learned a great deal about his life and work in Beijing. Jimmy had even read some of his students' papers to him on the phone. His students loved to read the classics and were fond of quoting Shakespeare, Hemingway, and John Steinbeck. Sometimes colloquialisms would pop up in the classroom, picked up by his students from American tourists in parks, zoos, and restaurants. Recently, Jimmy reported that he had heard one of his girl students say, "Oh, fuck up!" He asked her if she understood what it meant. She said, "Of course. It means be quiet."

Charles was also delighted to learn that Raymond had adopted some good habits, such as picking up his own clothes. Jimmy had reported that Do Do should take all the credit. When Raymond had lived with them, Do Do used to pick up Raymond's clothes from the floor, fold them, and lay them neatly on a chair. Every time Do Do tidied Raymond's corner, he became neater for a few days. It seemed that the more Do Do cleaned his corner, the more he tended to take care of himself. They never criticized him; they found that the little brother was sensitive and responsive to hints. While living with them, he even helped wash chopsticks and rice bowls. Now that Raymond had moved to a dormitory, Charles wondered how he liked his new life. Aimee wrote to him constantly, demanding to know everything . . . his bed, his towels, his underwear, his toothbrush; were they clean and in good shape? Did he take his vitamins?

The maid brought in the mail. There was a postcard from Raymond addressed to his mother: "Mom, everything is fine. Don't worry your pretty head off about me. A big hug for Dad. I love you both. Raymond."

Charles was satisfied. Raymond was finally severed from his mother's umbilical cord. The boy would develop an independent spirit, which Charles valued above anything in his children.

He picked up a copy of *Hong Kong* magazine and leafed through it. One article, "One of the Pillars Is Cracking," attracted his attention. It said that in China three men were holding up the sky: Deng Xiaoping, the chairman of the Military Commission; Hu Yaobang, the party chief; Zhao Ziyang, the premier. But one of the pillars that supported the sky was cracking. Now people were beginning to feel unsafe under the sky. The pillar about to crack was Hu Yaobang. Is another Cultural Revolution in the making? the author asked.

The article went on to analyze the crisis, believing that a new power struggle was getting more heated in the Communist hierarchy, with several hard-liners locking horns with Hu, who depended on Deng Xiaoping for survival. But Deng was about to abandon his protégé and throw him to the wolves.

Meanwhile, the article reported, the students at the University of Science and Technology in Anhui Province were planning a demonstration demanding better campus living conditions, freedom of the press, and democracy. The student unrest was also spreading to other universities.

Jimmy reported that the unrest had been started by Fang Lizhi, the vice president of the university. He had told intellectuals to throw off party domination by straightening out their "bent backs." Such bold talk had stunned the students and made him an instant hero of the democracy movement. His follow-up speeches shocked the party leaders even more, and electrified the entire intellectual society. In the fall he went to Shanghai and told a Tongji University gathering, "Speaking quite dispassionately, I have to judge this period of socialist revolution a failure in every aspect of economic and political life." He reminded the students that democracy is first and foremost a question of rights of individuals and that individuals are the ones who must struggle for them.

His vast audience immediately responded to his call for such a struggle. At one university after another, the students flocked to hear him; freedom of speech spread like wildfire, with ordinary citizens laughing and cheering in public places, criticizing party leaders and high government officials by name.

Charles had heard Fang's name before, but had never thought that an astrophysicist would become such a powerful student-mover. Jimmy was sad; the disruption upset orderly progress and many plans, including his own vacation in Hong Kong.

When Deng Xiaoping fired Fang from his job along with two other well-known dissidents, Liu Binyan and Wang Ruowang, he also expelled them from the party. Charles followed the events closely. The government act backfired; student unrest revived all over the country.

Early one morning, Sir Richard Tan called Charles. "Have you read the Joint Declaration on the return of Hong Kong to China in 1997?" he asked, his voice excited.

"That's old hat," Charles said. "It was signed in 1984, more than two years ago."

"Listen, when I read the 'one country, two systems' rule two years ago, I wasn't too worried. Now, with the power struggle getting worse in Beijing, we know the country is not ruled by a system, but by men. Deng Xiaoping promised that China would not meddle in Hong Kong's politics. Can he live fifty more years to guarantee that? With his chain-smoking habit, I doubt that he can live to one hundred thirty."

"Why are you so worried all of a sudden?" Charles asked.

"I stopped paying attention to China. I only worry about Hong Kong. Now I realize that China and Hong Kong are like teeth and tongue, inseparable. A lot of people are predicting turmoil in China. Aren't you concerned?"

"I'm glad you've started paying attention to China instead of just counting your ships."

He remembered the day the Joint Declaration was announced. It had hit Hong Kong like an atomic bomb. Even though people had talked about the British government's intention to relinquish the colony, not many people had believed it would materialize. When the Joint Declaration was signed in Beijing, everybody was alarmed and started talking about moving to Canada or Brazil; everyone wrote to relatives inquiring about immigration laws and housing prices.

"Richard," Charles said, "I suggest that you and I organize a delegation and pay Deng Xiaoping a visit. We ought to hear directly from Deng what he has to say about Hong Kong's future."

For the first time, Richard Tan agreed with him wholeheartedly.

A delegation of twenty of the richest men in Hong Kong left for Beijing on a foggy morning in a chartered DC 10. Some brought their wives and their wives' personal maids. One of the wives even brought her own hairdresser.

The Chinese government wanted to put the delegation in the luxurious government guest house Fishing Terrace, where all visiting heads of state stayed. But by a hand vote, the delegation declined such noble treatment, despite their wives' protests. The men knew that a government guest house would be full of hidden bugs and spies who doubled as servants. The wives wanted to boast about their stay at the most prestigious address in China. To compensate them for their disappointment, the husbands gave them two days of sightseeing and shopping with unlimited funds.

A trip to the Great Wall was the first thing on many ladies' agendas. But Aimee's first priority was a visit to Raymond's dormitory at Beijing University. She had little interest in climbing walls or touring palaces and museums; lately she had seen enough of China on television. Besides some tall buildings, most of the big cities were full of bicycles and dirty side streets with rundown buildings.

The morning after their arrival, five official limousines were dispatched to Beijing Hotel to bring the delegation to the People's Great Hall, where a meeting with Deng Xiaoping was scheduled.

Deng was waiting for them in a cushioned chair when they arrived. Smiling broadly and chain-smoking, he rose to meet the visitors and shook their hands warmly, one by one. Deng looked healthy and spirited. He had a strong grip, shaking hands firmly with his guests. He had an amazing memory, immediately addressing each man with his correct name and title. As he talked, he kept smoking and flicking cigarette ashes into a brass cuspidor beside his chair. He politely inquired about everyone's business and encouraged their investment in China.

Two translators, a man and a woman, sat behind him, but since everybody spoke Mandarin, the translators became secretaries, taking notes and occasionally repeating certain words that Deng had missed. His Szechuan dialect was perfectly understandable. He listened intently and laughed easily, not at all like Mao Zedong or Chiang Kaishek, who were so stiff and rigid that nobody had ever dared to laugh during a meeting.

After a lengthy discussion of the 1984 Joint Declaration and about Hong Kong's future, Charles asked Deng the most important question . . . a question that concerned every Hong Kong resident, especially the rich. He said, "Chairman Deng, the Joint Declaration has spelled out everything quite clearly. Since you made it happen, all Chinese in the world owe you a deep gratitude. But in order to carry out your 'one country, two systems' policy through the life of the contract, what guarantee can you give us?"

"Guarantee?" Deng laughed. "The sun provides light, the rain supplies water. Do you ask for a guarantee? Don't worry.

China will keep Hong Kong intact for fifty years under the 'one country, two systems' rule. In fifty years, if Hong Kong keeps prospering and benefiting China, no fool would try to change it. What better guarantee is there?"

He rose and started shaking everybody's hand, signaling the end of the meeting. In parting, he added with a smile of confidence, "Don't worry, Hong Kong will be Chinese."

The delegation was pleased. Hong Kong had been a foreign colony for more than a hundred years. It was every Chinese's wish that one day it would be Chinese. On the way back to the hotel, they savored these words, feeling proud. But soon a delayed reaction jarred some members of the group. Sir Wei-on Shu, the film tycoon, remembered that in 1949, when the Communists first occupied Shanghai, Chairman Mao had said to the Shanghai capitalists, "Don't worry, Shanghai will remain a capitalist city." But in less than six years, all the capitalists had been liquidated and their properties seized.

As soon as Sir Wei-on Shu mentioned the fate of Shanghai, all the others claimed that they were thinking exactly the same thing. The example of Shanghai was most disturbing. Two days later, Richard Tan called a meeting in the hotel to encourage emigration to Europe and America. He also urged that privately held companies go public so that they could get their original investments out and let the public money run their various enterprises.

Charles Hong had never said a harsh word to his best friend, but Tan's suggestion angered him. He stood up and accused Tan of betraying Deng. "Deng has created a miracle," he said heatedly in Cantonese. "In seven years, his reforms have pulled China out of poverty and isolation. How can you pull the rug out from under his feet now? What's happened to your conscience?"

"My conscience has nothing to do with it, Charles," Tan replied with a smile, keeping his voice low and friendly. "But one must move out of his house before it catches fire."

"How can you be so sure the house will catch fire?" asked Charles, still incensed by Tan's plan. "If we did as you suggest, there would be a drain of both talent and capital, and Hong Kong would be finished. I say that such a drastic move would be disastrous to the economy of both Hong Kong and China."

"Who worries about China?" Tan asked bluntly. "The Communists have persecuted capitalists since the Russian Revolution. China has savaged her own economy with Marx's snake oil. How can you be sure that Deng will not force the same oil on us in ten years?"

There was some grumbling; obviously the majority agreed with Tan's assessment. Charles got up and stalked out.

Back in his own suite, he was surprised to find Aimee and Raymond arguing. Aimee was red-faced, pacing the floor and shouting. Raymond, slumped on a sofa, looked dejected, his battered suitcases sitting at his feet.

"Charles," Aimee said, "I've taken Raymond out of that damned Chinese university."

"Why?" asked Charles, surprised.

"That dormitory is infested with rats and cockroaches. . . ."

"That's not true!" Raymond said. "They're not rats. Only a few harmless mice. We even feed them."

"Did you hear that?" asked Aimee, her voice rising. "They are raising rats in their dormitory. These people are uncivilized. They live in that filthy place like savages. My God! I saw cockroaches crawling all over their table, and a rat almost bit me!"

"That's not true!" Raymond protested. "A little mouse ran over your foot, and you almost jumped on a chair. You threw a book at it and almost killed it. You were hysterical!"

"Charles, I'm tired of China and I want to go home. I suggest that you take Raymond with you if the ingrate refuses to go with me."

With a snort and a toss of her head, she stormed out of the hotel suite.

20

Charles regretted that he had spoken to Richard Tan so harshly in front of their peers in Beijing. Several times he picked up the phone to apologize but changed his mind. Aimee had sided with Richard. She was disgusted with Beijing and the Communists. She said that besides a few tree-lined boulevards and some showy buildings, she had not seen any real progress. In the airplane flying home, Raymond had blatantly defied her by blowing a kiss to the city and saying, "I shall return."

That remark had made her so angry that she had raged, "Who is he, anyway? General MacArthur?"

Charles sympathized with Raymond, but the boy had gone back to his old morose and rebellious ways. This irritated him. He had seldom spoken harshly about the boy, now he started speaking out. But Aimee put all the blame on Raymond's Chinese education.

He had just finished his breakfast in his study, served by his number-one boy, Ah Hing. Aimee marched in. He was surprised, for she seldom got out of bed before noon, and she always knocked. She had adopted many nice Western manners that pleased him, but this morning she looked like a shrew, her hair unkempt and her nose flaring. Laying a morning paper on his desk, she demanded, "Did you read this?"

He glanced at the headline: GOVERNOR PLEASED WITH HONG'S PLEDGE.

"What's wrong with that?" he asked.

"Why did you make such a pledge to the Hong Kong governor?" she asked, her voice low but angry.

"Because I don't want to pull up all my stakes and flee," he said. "The governor asked me to set an example, and I did."

"You can stay, but I don't see the point of publicizing your pledge. All your kind words about those country bumpkins in the Forbidden City sound silly. All my friends believe that you've become a card-carrying Communist. It's stupid!"

He stared at her, dumbfounded. He had never heard her call him stupid before, and the word stung him. "Aimee," he said, trying to remain calm, "what do you want? Do you want a divorce?"

"You can't get rid of me that easily," she said. "If you keep pledging your devotion to Deng Xiaoping and his henchmen, I'll take my half of everything and move to New York."

"Suit yourself," he said. Feeling his blood boil, he rustled his paper and tried to read. He had made a pledge to himself never to lose his temper. But Aimee's harassment began to chip away at his patience. He heard her voice, but tried to let the words go in one ear and come out the other. Still, it was not easy to ignore her when his nerves were getting raw.

In his room nearby, Raymond started playing his CD player so loudly that a heavy drumbeat pounded on Charles's eardrums mercilessly. All his life he had hated rock and roll, thinking it was no better than noises made by a demolition crew.

He tossed his paper away and marched to his son's room. "Raymond," he shouted above the music, "don't you have anything better to do?"

"Like what?" asked Raymond, hardly moving a muscle in his unmade bed.

"Do something useful! Read a book!"

Raymond shrugged.

"Shut this damned noise off!" he ordered. When Raymond ignored him, he went to the CD player and switched off the music. Standing over him he gave his son a tongue-lashing, accusing him of being dirty and lazy. "It's about time you learned some manners and respect!" he shouted.

Raymond yawned. "How can I be respectful?" he said. "The son of a rag lord with a purchased title!"

The remark hurt Charles like a knife twisting in an old wound. Furious, he slapped Raymond hard on the face. Stunned, Raymond stared at him, his lips trembling. Without a word, he got up, pulled out his suitcase, and started packing.

Charles took a nap after lunch. It was a ritual, especially on Sunday. Raymond had not called. Aimee acted like an ant on a hot stove, running from one room to another, constantly glancing at her watch, consulting with Charles, calling everybody she knew.

"Aimee," Charles said, "it's no use calling your friends. The boy has his own friends. And don't expect him to come home today. He has taken his suitcase with him."

"If he does not come home for dinner," she said, "I'm going to call the police."

She did not have to call the police; an hour later the police called, saying that Raymond Hong had been arrested for shoplifting an expensive suit and a gold watch at Yen An Department Store. Aimee was hysterical.

"Why would he do a thing like that?" she wailed. "A suit and a gold watch! That's exactly what I offered to buy for him on his birthday! I even got his size and the color he preferred. Where is he? Yen An or the police station?"

Charles always rubbed his face with a hand when he felt distressed, a habit he had developed during the Second World War. He did it subconsciously, as if misery and depression could be wiped off like dirt.

"Aimee," he said, trying his best to remain calm, "the boy is spoiled rotten. Please leave him alone. If he's in jail, I'll ask my attorney to get him out. Go take a nap, or go play mahjongg at the Golden Phoenix."

"Oh, why? Why? Why would Raymond do a thing like this to torture me?"

"He's not trying to torture you. He's protesting my purchased title. I can even see tomorrow's headlines: SIR CHARLES HONG'S SON JAILED FOR SHOPLIFTING."

Aimee threw up her hands with a heartrending moan of despair. Collapsing on a sofa, she started to cry. Charles put an arm around her and said soothingly, "Aimee, this is not the end of the world. We have a lot of relatives in America. Take him to California for a visit. Uncle Chang will cheer you up and straighten Raymond out. He raised twelve children, and knows how to deal with brats."

"It's all the goddamn Communists' fault!" she said. Feeling better, she wiped her tears and blew her nose.

Two days later, Aimee received a postcard. A simple message was scribbled unevenly with a pencil, "Mom, I've gone back to Beijing. Raymond."

Charles did not show it, but Raymond's postcard hurt him. What had he done wrong? he wondered. Perhaps he had neglected his family and paid too much attention to his business. On the other hand, he had abandoned Jimmy before he was ever born, yet Jimmy was so different . . . warm, friendly, and concerned. Why? Was it because one was the product of capitalism and the other the product of communism? he wondered.

21

Arriving home early, Jimmy planned to grade his students' essays before Do Do returned. He would like to spend the rest of the evening sipping tea and talking. He and Do Do had not relaxed together for quite a while.

He made some tea and took out the papers from his briefcase, glad that his students' handwriting was neat and easy to read. Some were flowery and slanting, others rigid like prints. A few were even scented.

The first piece was a short composition by a pretty girl. His red pencil in hand, he started reading:

Title: Where Is New China?

One early morning in 1950 Mao Zedong heard his daughter sing, "No Communist party, no China." Mao corrected her by saying, "No. China existed long before the Communist party. You should sing, 'No Communist Party, no New China.' "

In those days, Mao was clear-minded, truly interested in changing old China into a new and strong independent country. But what happened in the process? Did power corrupt him? Where is the New China now?

Jimmy thought the composition ordinary, but the writer was idealistic. He gave her a "B."

The next article was entitled "Waiting." It had a promising opening:

> Two people are quarreling. One said to the other, "I will outlive you!" The other shouted, "I will outlive you. Just wait and see!"
> Both waited. After one has outlived the other, he is still waiting. Every day he waits to get up, to eat, to dress, to pay his debts; he waits for sunrise, sunset; he waits to go to bed, to get sick, to die. . . .
> After the Communists have outlived the Nationalists in China, life has become so meaningless that one only spends his time waiting.

Jimmy did not like the pessimistic tone, but it somehow reminded him of his father's defunct hotel project. Charles had a vision of a chain of hotels in all the major Chinese cities catering to everybody, not just the foreign businessmen. He emphasized the service instead of luxury. Every morning there would be a copy of a morning paper outside every door; rooms would be cleaned and fresh bedding changed without disturbing the guests; there would be free haircuts and shampoos on request; in every room there would be color TV, maps, transportation timetables, and important phone numbers; there would be a twenty-four-hour restaurant with polite waiters. Charles had everything well planned and had laid out millions of dollars to start the project, but why was it stalled? What had happened to those people who had wined and dined him and had enthusiastically supported the project? Why had it also become a waiting game?

The essay echoed Jimmy's own mind. Feeling a bit sad, he gave the student an "A−."

The third article sounded like a joke, written by a male student who often yawned in his class. Entitled "The Marriage of China and Taiwan," it was bold, brief, and to the point:

> The doctor asked a patient why one of her breasts was larger than the other. The patient said that her husband liked to hold one of them in sleep. The doctor said

that he also held his wife's breast while sleeping, but her breasts were still of equal size. The patient replied, "But my husband and I sleep in different beds."

Today everybody talks about the marriage of China and Taiwan. One side proposes "one country, two systems." The other side says that if they marry, they must sleep in one bed, or nothing will be normal, like the woman's breasts, one big, one small.

Jimmy vaguely remembered that he had heard the joke before, but it was clever of the student to put a meaning to it. Not too bad. He gave him a "B+."

He took a sip of coffee and was about to read the next piece when there was a sharp rap on the door. "Damn," he mumbled, rising to answer it. He hated the interruption.

When he opened the door, his eyes widened in surprise. Standing in front of him, smiling uncertainly, was Raymond, his shirt wrinkled, his tight blue jeans dirty, a duffel bag on his back and a battered suitcase in his hand. After they stared at each other for a brief moment, Raymond dropped the suitcase, and they threw their arms around each other.

"You son of a gun!" Jimmy said. "What happened to you?"

"I'm homeless," Raymond said.

"Come in!" said Jimmy, picking up his suitcase. "Who kicked you out? Dad or Mom?"

"I kicked myself out," said Raymond, following his brother into the kitchen.

"Don't say anything!" Jimmy said. "I want Do Do to hear it, too. Hungry? Thirsty? What d'you want to eat? Do Do will pick it up on her way back."

He grabbed the phone and dialed a number rapidly. "Do Do," he said excitedly. "Hurry home! Bring some food. I've taken in a homeless boy. He's starving!"

22

China's freedom movement was a hot topic in Hong Kong. Shanghai Mary decided to unveil her secret to Charles Hong.

She had heard that his father had aided Dr. Sun Yatsen's 1912 revolution with time and money; during the Second World War he had again supported China's war effort against the Japanese by sending Charles to China to import scrap iron, which China needed for manufacturing ammunition. She now needed Charles's help in her underground work. New electronic equipment had been installed in the basement of the Golden Phoenix, where half a dozen workers communicated with various student organizations in China daily, exchanging information and sending aid through secret channels. The camouflage was almost perfect.

Everybody enjoyed drinking and eating at the Golden Phoenix; gossips poked fun at British royalty as well as Deng Xiaoping and his Communist "yes" men. It was the only place where one could curse any powerful world leader without lowering his voice, for those who patronized the restaurant were all considered to be drunks. As the corrupt life blatantly unfolded around Shanghai Mary, the Golden Phoenix seemed the last place to foment any idea of a high calling.

But Shanghai Mary was worried. The democracy movement's cost was mounting; it could hardly be covered by the income from the restaurant alone. To her, the most distressing problem in Hong Kong was the rich people's indifference. "Who cares?" they would say. "We've already bought homes in Canada." The general mood in the colony was to abandon ship when the time came.

She called Charles and asked for an appointment. He agreed to meet her at his office. She had met him a few times through Aimee and had given him the impression that she was an unreliable, happy-go-lucky woman who rollicked in a rotten life. She decided to correct this impression. In serious business, she was punctual and tidy. Her clothes were plain; she wore no wig or makeup.

When she was ushered into Charles's enormous office, he did not recognize her at first. When he did, he hid his surprise, pretending that she was an old family friend. He wondered why she had wanted to see him.

After a warm greeting, Shanghai Mary got down to business immediately. The momentum of the freedom and democracy movement in China must be kept up, she said. Repression was increasing; the party was again tightening controls, trying to strangle the chickens by the neck. Would Charles Hong help?

"Can I call you Mary?" Charles asked.

"Of course. I'll call you Charles. After all, Aimee is my best friend."

"Mary, don't think I'm not patriotic," he said quietly. "My father always wanted me to do whatever I could for China. For the past several years, I've been doing nothing but trying to help the motherland. Now you want me to donate money to destroy it."

Shanghai Mary was stunned. "Why do you say that?"

"I believe that the freedom movement should try to change the government, not overthrow it."

"Charles, we cannot change the soup without changing the ingredients."

"I know, your idea is to throw out the whole pot, but . . ."

"Charles, Communists are always a violent bunch. China will never have peace if we don't throw out the rascals."

"That's not what my son and I think. Sorry, Mary. If you need money for some charity, I'll be happy to . . ."

"No, no. I'm not in the charity business." She rose quickly

and smiled. "I'm not offended by your refusal, but I'm surprised that you're not surprised."

"Should I be?" he asked, also rising.

"I'm a different Mary . . . uglier without makeup, begging money for a revolution. Aren't you surprised?"

"Not really."

Shanghai Mary shook her head. "I don't think even your wife knows what I'm doing."

"I'm sure she doesn't."

"Shall we keep it this way? She is emotional. You are discreet. I trust that you will not blow my cover."

"Why should I? We're both trying to build a better China, but in different ways. You may prove that your way is better."

She extended a hand. "Thank you."

He shook her hand, surprised at how strong her grip was, even though the hand looked puffy and soft.

"I've never visited you, correct?" she said.

"Correct," Charles said with a smile.

"Why don't you come to dinner at the Golden Phoenix sometime?" she invited.

"Not until you've stopped selling leftovers, Mary," he said with a chuckle.

"You know that, too?"

"Every Sunday morning I watch your girls scrub foreign ships, and foreign sailors load your sampans with crates and garbage cans."

Shanghai Mary laughed. "I hope you can't smell it across the bay."

"Mary, it's no secret. One of my foreign friends swore that he had eaten your delicious ginger beef. It was made from his half-eaten New York steak from his own cruise ship. He said he loved your Shanghai Mary sauce, but refused to learn what it is made of."

Laughing loudly, Mary said good-bye. After she left, Charles was depressed. China seemed to get deeper into trouble every day.

In the evening, an unexpected visitor cheered up Charles Hong. He arrived in a red Jaguar. Ah Hing, the number one, brought in a calling card that had many impressive titles, including president of Fu Xing Corporation, with offices in Beijing, Shenzhen, and Hong Kong. For a brief moment, Charles wondered who he was. After he had read the name Pang Sin a couple of times, he suddenly realized that it was Mabel's firstborn.

Charles had never met him, but when the visitor was ushered in, Charles was highly impressed. The tall, good-looking man in an expensive tailored suit, with charming manners, was indeed a welcome sight.

After a handshake, he could not help throwing his arms around Pang Sin. After all, he was a son of Mabel, the only woman he had ever loved.

He immediately sent for Aimee. When he proudly introduced Pang Sin to her, he blurted out, "See? A product of Communist China!"

After their greetings, Aimee looked Pang Sin up and down. She was impressed, too.

"He is the son-in-law of a general," Charles said, "a member of China's Military Commission."

Aimee feigned surprise; she already knew. "Are you on the commission, too?" she asked.

Pang Sin laughed. "Nobody on the commission is less than eighty years old. Do I look like an old man?" He took the opportunity to describe his father-in-law's agility and longevity and his importance in the military and party hierarchy. It somehow changed Aimee's impression of the Chinese Communists. They were not all country bumpkins, after all, she thought. The general sounded like a nice gentleman, educated in Soviet Russia.

"He's probably very good-looking," she commented when Pang Sin finished talking. "I can tell much about him just by looking at you." She laughed.

Her happy voice told Charles that she had shaken off her nasty mood. She had even become a little giggly. For that, he was grateful. Perhaps Pang Sin would bring harmony and peace to the house. He suggested that he move in with them.

"We have seven bedrooms and half a dozen servants, and

there are only two of us. You can come and go as you please, and eat well."

"That's right," Aimee agreed eagerly. "All we have to do is tell Ah Hing to lay one more pair of chopsticks on the table. After all, you are family. Charles has spoken often about your mother. I feel I know her quite well. Will you move in?"

Pang Sin was delighted. He had already fallen in love with the house.

"Give some parties," Charles suggested. "Invite some of your friends here to spend a weekend."

"And bring the general, by all means," Aimee chimed in. "And all your in-laws. They are our relatives, too."

"We'll treat you as our stepson," said Charles, putting an arm around Pang Sin's shoulders. "That settles it, Pang Sin. China and Hong Kong will be one big family soon. It's about time we got to know each other better."

23

Pang Sin drove to Charles's office in a rented Toyota half an hour ahead of his appointment. He wanted to give Charles the impression of being punctual and reliable. Hong Kong was still building. The streets were getting noisier and more crowded in the midmorning. It seemed that the city was growing bigger, taller, and gaudier every day. The pedestrians, carrying parcels and baskets, scurried like busy ants; they dodged automobiles like matadors fighting relentless bulls. He loved Hong Kong. In certain areas, there was a touch of London, which he had seen in films—Victorian buildings, double-decker buses spitting black smoke, churches with belfries. In the distance, new buildings rose majestically, tall and massive, with colorful laundry flapping on the balconies.

The morning air was cold and fresh. The breeze from the bay had cleared the smog. The smell of spicy food from food stalls faded as he turned into Queen's Road. Suddenly, ultramodern skyscrapers appeared, their facades shining in the morning sun like giant mirrors. Fashionable people, clutching purses or briefcases, hurried in and out of office buildings; late-model cars crawled in heavy traffic. Waiting at traffic lights, he listened to disco music, his eyes following ladies crossing the street. He had never seen so many attractive women before; now he felt like a cat living amid bowls full of delicious goldfish.

After he had parked the car in Charles's modern building,

he rode in one of the four elevators to the penthouse floor, breathing deeply the perfume a few ladies had left behind. The luxurious office suite, decorated with various tall houseplants, had a breathtaking panoramic view of the bay. A smiling secretary, recognizing his name immediately, ushered him into Charles's spacious office. Sitting behind his huge mahogany desk, Charles was talking on the phone. Pang Sin took a seat in a group of sofas and relaxed. The secretary asked him if he wanted coffee or tea. He declined. He fished out a cigarette, lit it with a bejeweled lighter, and waited.

When Charles finished his phone conversation, he came out from behind his desk with an extended hand. After warm greetings, he joined Pang Sin on the sofa. He sized him up again.

"I still can't believe that I have a new addition to the family," he said happily. "Now tell me about your plans in Hong Kong."

Pang Sin told him that he was in an excellent position to help China earn some foreign exchange, for he had important connections in the commercial sector in Beijing and Shanghai. He knew many heads of China's large trading companies. They were all anxious to sell their products to America. "To open the American markets for them is my job," he said enthusiastically. "This is the area I need help."

Charles smiled. "Well, Pang Sin, you've come to the right place. I assume that you'll act as an agent, instead of buying and selling."

"That's right. I don't intend to invest cash in this business except the overhead. I shall be happy to split the commission with you. . . ."

"No, no," Charles interrupted him quickly. "My help is free. What products do you have in mind?"

"Anything," Pang Sin boasted, "but I want to be selective. Silk products are the most profitable. Antiques, cloisonné, cinnabar, lacquer, jade and ivory carvings, and other high-priced items are what China is also anxious to export."

"I'm glad you mentioned this," Charles said. "I heard that the Marriott Hotel chain has already sent an interior decorator to Shanghai to select Chinese artifacts to decorate their lobbies. It's about time that we introduce Chinese arts to America instead of peddling chopsticks, back scratchers, and folding fans.

As a matter of fact, I have two American importers who have leased office space in one of my hotels. I still have their business cards."

He took two cards out of a desk drawer and gave them to Pang Sin. "So your company is called Fu Xing."

"Yes, sir," Pang Sin said.

"Fu Xing is a lucky name. It means rebirth. I like that. It's exactly what China needs . . . rebirth. We are all excited about China's future. When are you going to move in? Aimee says your room is ready."

Pang Sin had already fallen in love with the Hong mansion. "Are you sure it is all right?" he asked modestly.

"You are family," Charles said. "Since Raymond went to live in Beijing, the house feels empty. Where are you staying now?"

"With a friend," he lied. He was staying in a modest Kowloon hotel called the Hamilton Plaza. Its rickety elevators were always crowded with heavily made-up, giggling young women. Some of them looked as if they were still in their teens. At night he often heard sounds of door-scratching. The night before, someone had scratched on his door, but he had been too sleepy to get up and find out who it was.

"Why don't you move in tonight?" Charles suggested.

Pang Sin decided to stay at the Hamilton Plaza one more night. He wanted to find out who those door-scratching cats were.

"Not tonight," he said apologetically. "Tomorrow for sure."

24

Pang Sin enjoyed the Hong mansion. He had no idea if the seven servants—four males and three maids—knew who he was. They were polite, and seemed to have a puzzled look on their faces when he talked to them. He could speak some Cantonese, but when the servants talked among themselves, they spoke a different dialect. He could hardly understand them. The way they talked in low voices and stole glances at him made him a little uneasy. He wondered if they were discussing why their employer had a son who had a big nose and blond hair. When nobody was looking, a maid had even ogled him.

The meals were good. But he enjoyed the native dishes more, especially what the servants ate themselves—a lot of salted fish and preserved vegetables.

Aimee had instructed the chef to cook some Western food for him. He appreciated her concern, but the New York steaks and Southern fried chicken all tasted a bit peculiar. He did not mind; after he had poured enough Worcestershire sauce over them, he couldn't tell the difference. During the Cultural Revolution days, he had developed a cast-iron stomach.

His days in Hong Kong were often topsy-turvy. The Fu Xing business had expanded to Sheng Zhen, the economical zone, with a Hong Kong office in Kowloon. But it was only a shell without a business. As the president of the company, he crossed the border two or three times a week. His wife had moved to an apartment in an ultramodern building in Shen Zhen, demanding that he visit her at least three times a week. He began to dread this conjugal duty. His father-in-law, General Han, had been an illiterate farmer before he joined the Red Army. His participation in the Long March had qualified him as a "tree trunk" of the highest rank. In the army, he had taught himself to read and write. Today, he was regarded as a soldier-scholar; his calligraphy was in big demand. He still disdained Pang Sin's bourgeois background.

Living in Hong Kong, Pang Sin was amused by the capitalists' caste system. Even the servants had rank. In the Hong Kong mansion, Ah Hing, the number one, was the commander in chief. He always walked ahead of Ah San, the number two. When serving dinner, Ah Hing carried the meat dishes and Ah San brought in the vegetables and rice. In the kitchen, the chef was the master. While he was cooking, he made a lot of noise to show his authority by banging his wok with his Chinese spatula. He never washed vegetables or dishes; such work belonged to his assistant. Sweeping and general cleaning were jobs for the maids. Along with the deaf gardener, the maids ranked lowest among the household staff.

Aimee seldom saw Pang Sin. This morning she made a point of having breakfast with him. Wearing an alluring silk robe, she descended the staircase mincingly. Half an hour late, she apologized that she had overslept.

Pang Sin knew all the good manners. He greeted her with a kiss on her cheek, then pulled out a chair for her. Woo Mah served them ham and eggs. Aimee preferred Woo Mah to wait on them because her personal maid did not understand English. With Pang Sin, Aimee always spoke English, as she did not want the servants to gossip about what they said.

After some small talk about the weather, Pang Sin tried to find out how Aimee and Charles could help with his business. All he needed was connections in Hong Kong.

Aimee had no interest in Pang Sin's China business. She had even objected to Charles's hotel project in China.

"I have two best friends," she said. "One is Shanghai Mary. The other is Dr. Fu, known as the Golden Rooster. Do you know him?"

"The famous fortune-teller?" he asked.

"Yes. But he is not a fortune-teller. He is a prophet. Last year he sent Charles a New Year greeting card. He enclosed a poem, something like this:

" 'The Master of Tao empties his heart,
Strengthens his mind,
Exercises his ambition,
And makes full his belly.'

"Excellent philosophy," she said. "I memorized it. I recited it to Shanghai Mary. It will save her soul. She's so ambitious that she even sells American leftovers to make money. You have met her, haven't you?"

"Not yet."

"You will, at my New Year's party. A few years ago, Charles got a speeding ticket. Dr. Fu immediately sent him this bit of wisdom on a postcard:

" 'Hasten slowly:
You will arrive sooner.'

"I love that, and I posted it on Charles's bathroom door so he can stare at it every morning and think about it." She laughed.

"But Charles is no pushover," she went on. "Dr. Fu always quotes the old saying to him, 'Big tree catches wind. Why be such a big tree?' Charles always retorts, 'No big wind has toppled this big tree yet.' Dr. Fu said that Tao is like gentle water, it can drill holes in a rock. I believe it. It tells people to have patience. I'd like you to meet him. His predictions are so accurate that people call him half human, half spirit. He can see past and future. Nothing escapes his thousand eyes."

Pang Sin was somewhat disappointed. Ghosts and spirits did not interest him. "What did he predict that came true?" he asked.

Aimee said after a sip of coffee, "Remember Governor Sir Edward Yaude of Hong Kong? He died of a heart attack during a state visit to Beijing last year. Dr. Fu repeatedly warned that the governor's Chinese name, Yau De, would jinx his trip. The character contains a date . . . September 6, 1986. The character 'De' consists of the words 'heart under earth.' The name Yau De foretold the exact date of the governor's death. Isn't that odd? Dr. Fu said that if the governor's name had been translated differently, he would still be sitting in his office puffing on his pipe today. Too bad. Do you have a problem?"

He had many problems, but most were unmentionable.

"What do you wish to know?" she pressed on. "Your immediate future?"

"Everybody wants to know his future, immediate or not," he said with a chuckle.

"The immediate future can be told in a turtle's shell. Tell me your birth date."

After she had jotted down Pang Sin's birth date, she told Woo Mah to bring a phone to the table. She dialed Dr. Fu's number. She greeted him warmly on the phone and requested that he give her stepson's future an analysis through his golden turtle's shell.

The turtle's shell divination did not take long. The answer was, "Spring water in the desert is a short distance away." Aimee congratulated Pang Sin and encouraged him to pursue whatever he had in mind, for he would surely get it. Dr. Fu was never wrong.

Pang Sin thanked her. What he had in mind was making ten million dollars without having to smuggle opium for Bean Cake Two.

It was Sunday morning. Pang Sin had just finished an unpleasant phone call to his wife. She did not believe his excuse of marathon business meetings with foreign investors. She accused him of using it as an excuse for not going home. The quarrel upset him.

As he lay on his double bed, staring at the ceiling and worrying, he heard a gentle knock on the door. "Pang Sin, are you in there?"

He opened the door to Aimee's smiling face. She was dressed, ready to go out. She wanted him to drive her to the New Territories. "It's a beautiful day," she said. "I'll wait outside."

The sun was warm. The gardener was pruning the shrubs when Pang Sin came out of the house, dressed for a spring outing. Aimee was standing beside the Rolls-Royce at the entrance, waiting, a large handbag hanging on her arm and a mink stole around her shoulders.

"Would you care to drive?" she asked.

He opened the car door for her. She thanked him and climbed in, leaving behind a trail of delicate perfume.

"I'm going to do some shopping in the New Territories," she said as he got behind the wheel. "The merchants in the countryside are more polite and more honest."

Her chitchat about the weather and the countryside was pleasant and friendly. At a busy intersection, she stopped talking.

He glanced at her. She looked very proper, her head held high and her hands folded, very much like an aristocratic lady being chauffeured to church. During the trip from Hong Kong to Kowloon, she changed many times. On busy streets, she remained distant and unsmiling; in quiet areas, she became chatty. The moment the car reached the suburbs, she relaxed again. She told him to stop the car at any scenic spot he chose. "We have all day," she said. "We can enjoy the ocean and have lunch at a peasant restaurant. Are you hungry?"

"Any time you wish to eat, Mom," he said.

"Call me Aimee." She frowned. "Don't call me Mom, please. Well, there is really not much to do in Hong Kong. You either take a leisurely ride in the New Territories or play marathon mah-jongg with friends. Men are different, of course. They take frequent trips to Singapore or Manila, not necessarily for business. I have eyes and ears in all those places, you know. They are men's paradises. What do you do exactly in Hong Kong?"

"Not very much. I'm trying to make business deals for China."

"Hong Kong is a business town. In business, it's a free-for-all. People grab and run, like thieves. I don't blame them. Nineteen ninety-seven is hanging over everybody's head. People worry about their future."

"What are your thoughts about 1997?" he asked.

"I told my husband that if he didn't do anything before the

Communist takeover, I'll take my share and fly. I even have a friend looking for properties for me in Bel Air and Century City in California. But California earthquakes give me second thoughts." She sighed. "I might look around in New York or Florida. I don't know. There! We can stop at that open restaurant and have some tea and dim sum in the sun."

Pang Sin slowed down and stopped at a teahouse that had an old cloth sign hanging outside the two-story building. There were several tables on the terrace. Most of the customers looked liked peasants; they sat at crude tables, eating, drinking, and smoking. Dogs, chickens, and ducks wandered around nearby.

They took a table near the entrance. A smiling waiter served hot towels and tea. Aimee ordered in Cantonese. The pungent smell of the countryside, a mixture of animal manure, wildflowers, and hay, carried by a gentle breeze, was not unpleasant. It reminded Pang Sin of his post–Cultural Revolution days when the Red Guards were banished to the countryside to work with the farmers. Chairman Mao had called it May Fifth School.

Aimee poured tea for him. "Do you have some fun in Hong Kong?" she asked.

"Quite a bit," he said, taking a sip of the hot jasmine tea. She was very attractive, probably not too much older than he.

"Are you a Communist?" she asked.

"No," he lied.

"I don't trust them," she said. "I'm glad you're not a member."

"Why?" he asked. "Don't you think the Communist government has done a great deal of good for China during the past ten years?"

"What have they done? They planted some trees. They don't trust the people, and they don't trust each other. My father was a Communist sympathizer when Mao kicked Chiang Kaishek to Taiwan. Mao didn't trust my father. My old man died in jail. Our property was confiscated. Mao and his handpicked heir, Marshal Lin Piao, didn't trust each other. Lin planned a coup, and Mao had him murdered. Deng Xiaoping and his handpicked heir, party chief Hu Yaobang, did not trust each other. Deng had him fired. Now it's rumored that Deng and his second handpicked heir, Premier Zhao Ziyang, are quarreling. Who knows what will happen? You see? Nobody trusts anybody in China. Why should I trust them? Tell me, what fun have you had in Hong Kong?"

"Well, nightclubs, good food, good scenery."

"You've only scraped the surface. Hong Kong is really a sinful town with a lot of people putting on an act."

The waiter brought the food, little dishes of tidbits—steamed buns with meat and black bean paste fillings, braised chicken feet and duck feet, red-cooked pork gristle, shrimp pouches, and sweet rice cakes. Aimee filled his teacup.

"The dim sum are safe to eat, all thoroughly steamed," she said. "They are not as clean as food at home, but a lot tastier. I like an adventurous life, don't you?"

"Yes," he said, biting into a hot bun.

"Tell me about your father. Is he a white man?"

"Yes," he said. "He abandoned us when I was little, so I didn't know him at all."

"Who was your mother? Charles talks about her, but never told us a thing about who she was."

"She was the daughter of the military governor of Hunan."

"Oh?" she said, quite impressed. "She must have been very pretty." She looked at him longingly. "I can tell."

Pang Sin could almost feel her caressing eyes; he began to feel uncomfortable.

She went on, "We are not related by blood, you see. We can be close friends. Do you agree?"

He did not know what to say. Was she giving him some kind of hint? He smiled and ate another bun to avoid giving his opinion.

"Pang Sin," she asked, "if you had a choice between wealth and happiness, what would you choose?"

He slowly wiped his mouth with the towel. "I don't know," he said. "I've never thought about it."

"Of course you'd choose happiness," she said.

He helped himself to more food, avoiding her eyes.

"Do you know any good summer resort in China?" she asked.

"Bei Dai Ho, the best," he said after a sip of tea.

"Is the place busy and crowded?"

"All government and party leaders go there for vacation and to hold meetings."

"If I go to America, I want to go to a place that's farthest away from Hong Kong. . . ."

Suddenly, she threw down her chopsticks and rushed into the teahouse, hiding her face with her handbag. Pang Sin gave the street a sweeping glance. He saw another Rolls-Royce driving by, churning up dust, with chickens and ducks scattering and cackling in alarm. Somewhat puzzled, he waited.

Presently, Aimee reappeared, glancing around. She returned to her bench and wiped her fingertips with her towel hurriedly.

"I saw Sir Richard Tan's wife. She loves to gossip."

She threw a few bills on the table, took a sip of tea, and rose. "Take me back, please."

Riding back to Hong Kong, she sat beside him looking dignified. She didn't speak until they reached her house. "Please drive me into the garage."

Inside the garage, just as Pang Sin was turning off the engine, he felt a warm hand touching his face. She turned his face around gently and gave him a long, lingering kiss on his mouth.

Pang Sin arrived at Bean Cake Two's headquarters in Kowloon about midnight. Bean Cake always discussed business after midnight, as if the darkness of the night could hide his shady deals.

Pang Sin had been Bean Cake's confidant during the Cultural Revolution, when both were Red Guard leaders. Together they had robbed and beaten many rightists, counterrevolutionaries, capitalist roaders, and other hooligans. Bean Cake had become a leader by showing his courage in struggling against his own parents. Pang Sin loathed him because of his superior air.

In Hong Kong, Bean Cake had built up his power base and commanded two hundred thugs. Some of his gang members were brutal former Red Guards from China. They seemed to roll in money in several areas—money laundering, smuggling antiques from China, extortion, and murder. Since Bean Cake was always looking for new partners for new rackets, he had invited Pang Sin to discuss possible joint ventures.

In his spacious office behind a dilapidated warehouse, Bean Cake bolted the door after he had admitted his old friend. He was a muscular man in his early thirties, his narrow face scarred and tanned. He offered Pang Sin a cigarette. Pang Sin never turned down Bean Cake's cigarettes, because they always gave him a marvelous high.

"Now, Older Brother," said Bean Cake, putting his large feet on the desk as he puffed, "I hear that you have moved in with Sir Charles Hong. You've climbed high."

"He's my stepfather," Pang Sin said with a modest smile.

Bean Cake's eyes, looking like two little slits, opened wide. "A general for a father-in-law and a hotel tycoon for a step-father! What luck!"

"What business proposal d'you have in mind?" Pang Sin asked. He knew that Bean Cake had been smuggling Chinese treasures to Hong Kong from Canton . . . treasures that the Red Guards had confiscated during the Cultural Revolution— antique paintings, jewelry, cloisonné, lacquer, jade carvings of statues and mythical animals . . . things that were forbidden by the Chinese government to export. Pang Sin had long since wanted to dabble in smuggling. After all, the confiscated goods belonged to all the Red Guards.

"The opium raised by the ethnic Katchins over the Burma border is the best," Bean Cake said. "If we can transport it to Yunnan Province, I have a channel that can make it appear in Hong Kong like a gopher from one hole to another. But the border crossing is a problem. Any ideas?"

Pang Sin thought for a moment. He shook his head. He had no idea, and he did not want to get involved in opium smuggling.

"I have an idea," said Bean Cake, after inhaling deeply some cigarette smoke. "But it needs a little help. In fact, I have two proposals that will cash in on your connections handsomely. I've made some investigations. The Yunnan-Burma border is guarded by your father-in-law's troops. Nowadays most troops are self-supporting. If we have the general's cooperation, we'll see a bottomless gold mine. Better than oil. Oil can be ex-hausted, but opium? The supply is permanent as long as the Katchins don't become extinct."

"What is the other proposal?" Pang Sin asked.

"How much is your father worth?"

"My stepfather."

"So much the better," said Bean Cake, blowing his cigarette smoke across the table noisily. "There will be even less of an emotional tie. You were a good Red Guard, I remember. . . ."

"What's the proposal?" Pang Sin asked impatiently.

"You haven't answered my question. How much money does Sir Charles Hong have? One billion? Two billion?"

"How do I know? I never asked, and I don't work for him."

"I know. Almost two billion, counting his holdings in Hawaii. He has a son called Raymond . . . a wild kid but a gem on his father's palm. Hold the boy for a few days, and we can pluck a few apples off this huge money tree."

"Kidnapping?" asked Pang Sin, shocked.

Bean Cake nodded. "Christmastime he'll return to eat his mother's turkey. All you have to do is to tip me off when he'll return to Beijing. We'll pick him up before he reaches the airport. As easy as flipping your hand. I think a ransom of five million is fair and reasonable. Your cut is twenty percent. A cool million for just a phone call." He stared at Pang Sin and chuckled.

26

Raymond was happy to be back. The university readmitted him, but he had to wait for a space in the dormitory. So he opened his old army cot and hung up the bedsheet again in Jimmy's apartment. Jimmy was surprised that he preferred life in China to Hong Kong's freedom and luxury. While Raymond was devouring his favorite dish, Hunan bean cake, Jimmy looked at him and shook his head, amused.

A major in languages, Raymond was no longer interested in studying. A "B−" was his highest grade, but he had made tremendous progress in Mandarin, speaking it like a native.

"Pang Sin loves your house in Hong Kong," Jimmy said. "The way you love your cockroach-infested dormitory. He's staying in your room until he has his own room furnished to his own taste."

"It will be full of nudes," Do Do said with a grimace. "By the way, Raymond, I hear that your grades are not very good. But I must say your Mandarin is perfect. When you and your girl-friends are together, you are like birds that never stop chirping. I think it's the only way to improve language . . . talk a lot."

"I'll credit his progress to hormones," Jimmy said with a little laugh. "Raymond hardly talks to anyone except girls."

"By the way," Do Do asked, "who is your favorite, Yin Yin or May?"

Raymond shrugged. "Flip a coin," he said with a grin. "No,

I know what's my favorite—your bean cake, soft and tender
. . . the best!"

"Raymond," Jimmy said, "if I were you, I'd stop making it
behind a bush. Insect bites and ant stings on the bare bottom
make the whole experience like . . . like . . ."

"Like scratching an itch outside a leather shoe," Do Do said
helpfully.

Jimmy snapped his fingers. "I'll tell you what, Raymond.
Every Thursday night Do Do and I go to a political meeting.
This place is empty for a couple of hours. Since we cannot do
anything about your urge, we don't want you to get caught
behind a bush. Your mother would die of shame and whisk
you out of your school faster than last time. You know that,
don't you?"

Raymond hated to discuss his sex life. But he was glad that
he would have a couple of hours every Thursday night.

"What political meeting?" he asked. "I attended a few last
week."

"Raymond," Jimmy said, "I'm responsible for your education and your welfare in Beijing. You're not even a Chinese
citizen. Don't get involved."

"Okay," Raymond said with a shrug.

"Jimmy, I forgot to tell you," Do Do said, "the Alliance has
scheduled an urgent meeting for tomorrow night."

"Tomorrow night?" Raymond's face brightened. He could
hardly wait.

The urgent meeting was held at Bei Ta to protest the removal
of Hu Yaobang from his party chief post. Hu had been soft in
dealing with the students, and the hard-liners had uncere-
moniously sacked him.

Do Do and Jimmy attended the meeting called by Freedom
in Action, an organization that had close ties with Hong Kong's
Alliance of Democracy. The meeting was held in a large au-
ditorium at Beijing University, chaired by Professor Feng and
attended by representatives from all educational fields, the media, and the arts.

After Professor Feng's brief opening speech, he introduced
the first speaker, Wei Wen-ho, a graduate student who had

recently returned from America. A UC Berkeley graduate, he was an intense-looking young man with scanty hair, thick glasses, and a clear, high-pitched voice. He talked about democracy and prosperity.

He said that when he first arrived in San Francisco, he had found himself in a dazzling world of consumer luxury. He had been to the fashionable department stores, amazed at their glitter and beauty. Shoppers ascended or descended on escalators as if they were touring the Ninth Heaven. When he walked into the section that displayed radios, video recorders, television sets, and VCRs, he almost shouted, "What wealth! What wonders!" When he toured the candy, toiletry, and cosmetics sections, he could not help breathing deeply the marvelous fragrance and marveling at the incredible array of merchandise.

Then he talked about the long food lines, the shortage of housing, the dirt on the streets, the lack of freedom in China. He compared the two societies and came to the conclusion that communism had failed miserably.

After thunderous applause, Professor Feng introduced the next speaker, a young woman from Hong Kong. She looked stunning in a white sweater and red skirt, her dark hair falling to her shoulders in the latest Hong Kong fashion.

She spoke in a clear, singsong voice. She said that the Freedom Action and Alliance of Democracy were twin sisters. Both were engaged in collecting evidence of government corruption and exposing it to the press and other media on the mainland and Hong Kong. She had learned that the elite class operated the largest mainland company in Hong Kong, headed by the sons of party leaders. They sold Chinese products to foreign traders below cost and pocketed enormous commissions; they peddled government influence and forged government documents. By affiliating with the Benevolent Association for the Blind, the company had gained the status of a charitable organization, and all its income was tax free.

She said that she had made friends with a member of the elite clique. She had already obtained some interesting information that she hoped the public would soon read in a few Hong Kong publications.

During the question-and-answer session, there was some heated debate about the word *revolution*. Violent or not, it could mean overthrowing the Communist government. By a voice vote, the meeting decided to adopt the word *glasnost*.

Suddenly, Do Do stood up and said that she worked for the news media. She believed that China had not changed politically during the last few years. Nobody in high place had really embraced democracy except Hu Yaobang, even though the word had been used loosely by many party leaders.

"I say all crows are black," she shouted. "The so-called right and left are always clashing for personal power. We must throw the rascals out!"

Jimmy sweated as he listened to his wife talking so vehemently against the party. He was shocked.

As he tried to stop Do Do by tugging at her blouse, a man responded by shouting, "What's wrong with revolution? How can you clean the house without revolution?"

Professor Feng quickly closed the meeting. "Tonight we are here not to overthrow the government," he said. "We are here to help the government reform. That's all!"

On their way home, Do Do and Jimmy kept quiet, both knowing that whoever spoke first would start an argument.

27

Mark Hansen extended a home-cooked dinner invitation to Jimmy and Do Do, but discovered that his microwave oven was out of order. When he tried to make a reservation at the restaurant, Yun Mei stopped him, telling him that dining in his private quarters was more desirable.

"What about food?" he asked.

"Leave that to me," she said.

They moved the two desks to the center of the office, covered them with a hand-embroidered tablecloth bought at the gift shop in the hotel, then set the table for four.

Yun Mei knew what Jimmy and Do Do liked: the "little eats" at Dong Dan Market on Wang Fu Jin, the famous food street in Beijing. Hansen wanted to buy his guests a gift; she also knew what to buy. Hansen had collected many gifts from his Chinese friends—folding fans, hand-carved chopsticks with his name on them, and other little trinkets. His favorite was a glazed statue of Deng Xiaoping that could not be toppled. Every time it was pushed down, it would bounce right back; it was a popular toy called *pu dao wen*, a gift from Do Do and Jimmy.

"I want to give them something different . . . something useful."

"I know exactly what they need," Yun Mei said.

Hansen loved surprises. Without asking questions, he got into his car and let Yun Mei be the "backseat driver." At Dong

179

Dan Market, Yun Mei took him directly to a mutton stall that sold all kinds of mutton—boiled, steamed, and barbecued. The market was buzzing with activity. "Little eats" restaurants lined the street, with customers sitting at crude wooden tables eating noisily with relish; the food peddlers sang out their wares in cracked voices, and cooks hit their woks with their spatulas loudly as they stir-fried their specialties. The whole area was covered by an aroma of spicy food.

They bought barbecued mutton on sticks, fried prawns, steamed buns with shrimp inside, and a few stir-fried dishes, which filled all Yun Mei's stack bowls.

Then they drove to Liu Li Chang, Beijing's cultural center outside Zhen Yang Men Gate. It was a long cobblestone street lined with bookstores and antique shops. Some of the buildings were gaudy with palatial designs; there were also small stores with humble fronts and cheap signboards. Yun Mei told him that Liu Li Chang meant Glazed Tile Factory, established by the Ching Dynasty emperors, who needed enormous amounts of glazed tiles for their palaces. After the palaces were built, the workers lost their jobs, and they started selling books in the area. As a result, they built a booming cultural center. Besides books, most shops sold antique paintings and calligraphy by famous scholars.

Chinese stationery, writing brushes, and intricately carved inkstands were packed in brocade cases. Ink sticks all bore lucky sayings in gold letters, making a writing set a remarkable collector's item. The stores also sold chops, or seals. In China a chop was a person's signature, used everywhere, on checks, documents, and personal letters. Some were elaborately carved in different styles.

"That's it," Yun Mei said in one of the stores. "Their chops are worn and cheap. Buy each of them a chop."

They selected two chops made of Ta Li stone, smooth and shiny. The shop owner prepared the gift certificate, so Do Do and Jimmy could come in to select the characters' style to be carved on them.

Hansen also bought two writing sets, one for Yun Mei and one for himself.

When they returned to the Beijing Hotel, Jimmy and Do Do

were already in the lobby waiting. Jimmy was always punctual, sometimes arriving half an hour ahead of the appointed time.

"It's embarrassing, arriving so early at a dinner party," Do Do said as they rode the elevator up to Hansen's floor.

"Why embarrassing?" Jimmy said with a laugh. "That means I'm anxious to taste Mr. Hansen's cooking."

"I planned to impress you with how good a cook I am," Hansen said. "But you caught me bringing food from Dong Dan Market. Now I'm embarrassed!"

The dinner was served with style, complete with candlelight, soft music, cut glasses, and silver chopsticks; fresh flowers supplied by the hotel's flower shop decorated the glittering table. Hansen, familiar with many Chinese customs, made his guests sit in chairs that faced the entrance. After he poured everybody a cup of mao-tai, he proposed a toast to China's *glasnost* and *perestroika*, two words that were becoming popular in Beijing. Then he presented his gifts.

Do Do had never had a decent seal. The gift certificate almost brought tears to her eyes. She got up and planted a kiss on Hansen's cheek. He touched Yun Mei's hand.

"Without Yun Mei, I could have bought you a panda bear," he said with a laugh.

The food was still warm. Yun Mei, acting as the hostess, passed the bowls around. Each dish was the guests' favorite; as Jimmy helped himself, he couldn't help humming and smacking his lips. They dined leisurely, toasting each other, joking and laughing and relaxed. The conversation invariably turned to politics. Somehow Yun Mei could not help discussing Mao Zedong and all his failures.

But Jimmy gave Mao a lot of credit for building up China as a world power, to which Hansen agreed. Yun Mei kept giggling; Do Do was making faces. "Mark," Yun Mei said, "do you still look at China through Technicolor glasses? If so, our media did a good job brainwashing you."

Jimmy began to worry. Politics usually ruined a party, creating heated arguments and alienating friends. But Yun Mei seemed to enjoy attacking Mao in a cheerful mood.

"Mao has a double personality," she said. "From one corner of his mouth, he pleaded for revolutionary equality; from the other corner of his mouth, he declared that his words were law. So the law his words became. By quoting him, you could get away with murder. During the Cultural Revolution, I participated in many arguments. The one who could quote Mao always won. If you argued that red was black, you could win by just saying, 'Chairman Mao said so.' Mao made himself the emperor of China."

"Come on, Yun Mei, be a little merciful," Hansen said with a laugh. "When Mao died, he didn't have anything. I understood that most of his holdings were books. He didn't even have a bank account."

"Mao didn't need any money," Yun Mei said. "Money can't buy everything. What you need is power. Want a car with a chauffeur? A private jet? Summer vacation? A luxury villa in Bei Dai Ho? Servants and maids? The best cook to prepare anything your heart desires? Snap your fingers and there they are, everything at your disposal. What did Mao need a bank account for?"

"Mark," Do Do chimed in, "that's why those old men in the government and in the party are scared to death to lose their positions. They'll hold on to their titles until they drop dead."

Jimmy quickly changed the subject. "We've brought you something, too, Mark" he said, digging out two cartons of Lucky Strike cigarettes from the tote bag beside his feet.

Hansen stared at the cigarettes, surprised. "Thanks," he said apologetically. "But I don't smoke."

"It's very useful," Do Do said. "Cigarettes will open doors and speed up things and make your daily life a little easier. When you want a taxi, you tip the doorman a pack of cigarettes and he'll get you one in twenty minutes; if it's American cigarettes, he'll bring you a Mercedes in ten minutes."

"Do you encourage people to smoke?" Hansen asked.

"Why not?" Do Do said. "Those who accept bribes deserve an early death. Let them smoke to their heart's content."

"Don't believe her," Jimmy said. "Deng Xiaoping is a chain-smoker, and he is way over eighty. He still can swim a mile or two every morning."

"Well, in that case," Hansen said, accepting the cigarettes

with a smile, "I'll see to it that I put the gifts to the right use. By the way, what happened to that charming actress, Jane Lo?"

"She sued somebody for rape," Jimmy said. "They settled out of court. Jane used the money to go to America. Pang Sin was too drunk to rape anybody. A successful blackmail."

"Now she's embraced bourgeois liberalization wholeheartedly," Yun Mei said.

"Are you right or left, Mark?" Do Do asked.

"In American political terms, I'm a liberal," Hansen said. "Perhaps a little left of center. In this country, I'm totally confused by your left and right."

"In your country, the right is conservative," Jimmy said. "Here, it's the opposite. The Gang of Four were leftists; Deng Xiaoping is a rightist. Leftists resist change, oppose individualism, freedom, and democracy. Rightists are practical. As Deng says, as long as a cat catches mice, it's a good cat, regardless of color. That's why China is in good hands, as long as Deng is the helmsman."

Do Do made a face. "Leave the cooking to the chef. Jimmy says that even in his dreams. Deng sacked Hu Yaobang, a true believer in liberalism. Deng changed color."

"There are certain fish in the deep sea that change color," Jimmy said. "Why? For protection. For survival. Any temporary change of color always alarms a lot of people unnecessarily."

Do Do made another face. Hansen caught it and glanced between them inquisitively. Do Do laughed. "We have no lovers' quarrels, only political quarrels. We claw each other's eyes out. Anyway, a lot of us like to pour out our inner thoughts to a foreigner. Only with a foreigner can we talk freely; it's a rare treat."

"Mark," Yun Mei said, "you're going to be a very popular fellow in Beijing if you're a good listener."

There was a knock on the door. Hansen opened it. Two Chinese men in Western clothes greeted him in English, their eyes searching the room, studying the visitors.

"What can I do for you, gentlemen?" Hansen asked.

"May we come in?" one of them asked.

"Sure," Hansen said. "We're finishing dinner. If you want to use the phone, you're welcome."

"No, no," the first one said. "We'll just ask your guests a few questions. Sorry for the interruption."

"Ask whatever you want, officers," Do Do said. "How are Qiao Shi and all his little spies?"

Hansen knew that Qiao Shi was the Chinese security chief. His agents were everywhere, and would barge in without identifying themselves. Mark was glad none of his guests seemed to be alarmed. As he invited the two "little spies" to sit down, he opened a carton of cigarettes and offered each of them a pack. The two men declined, but their eyes sparkled. When Hansen insisted, they accepted the gifts eagerly. After a few routine questions, they shook everybody's hand and left.

"Well, that was a breeze," Do Do said, "thanks to Lucky Strike."

"Mark," Yun Mei said, "I've got a title for your next article: 'American Cigarettes—the Best Troubleshooters in China.' "

28

Mark Hansen always believed that romance and work should not mix. But every time he started writing, he saw Yun Mei dancing on the blank sheet of paper in his typewriter, cheerful and mischievous. When she was late for work, he began to imagine all sorts of things. Had her alarm clock failed to wake her up? Or had she been involved in a traffic accident? She liked to speed on her bike in the crowded Beijing streets.

This morning she was almost an hour late. He had called her apartment three times, and there was no answer. He didn't really need her this morning, but why was he so worried?

It was a cloudy winter morning, windy and gloomy, but when she finally breezed in, she seemed to bring sunshine into the small office.

Instead of explaining why she was late, she said cheerfully, "You know why many people in Beijing walk around blinking their eyes, twisting their mouths, and muttering to themselves?"

"Must be the Gobi wind," he said with a laugh, tremendously relieved that she was safe. "It can blow a ton of sand into their eyes."

"No, they are trying to look crazy. You know why?"

Hansen shrugged. "Beats me."

"To avoid responsibility," she said, fishing papers out of

her tote bag at her desk. "If someone makes an awful mistake, he has a ready excuse. He's crazy."

"That's ridiculous, Yun Mei. You know that."

"Yesterday Deng said that he might say crazy things and that he won't be responsible. I see red lights blinking all over Beijing. Danger signs all over. So I dropped in on a fortune-teller this morning. He studied my horoscope and saw me escaping disaster in the Year of the Rat."

"Is that why you were late?" Hansen asked. He looked at her and felt amused. Her hair was somewhat windblown, her face flushed to a healthy color, her eyes sparkling despite the Beijing sand. He controlled a strong desire to go over to her, take her in his arms, and kiss her deeply. He still wasn't sure who she was. Sometimes she looked like one of James Bond's one-night stands—clever, knowledgeable, secretive, with a mission but terribly attractive. She liked to talk about working girls, waitresses who jumped from one job to another, like herself. She said she hadn't met a Chinese girl who didn't want to meet a white knight, Chinese or foreign, who would swoop down from heaven, sweep her off her feet, and carry her off on a winged white stallion.

"Isn't that every girl's dream?" Hansen asked with a laugh.

"Not mine," she said. "I admire a good writer more than a dashing white knight . . . some kind of bookish fellow like Václav Havel, that Czechoslovakian playwright, you know. I watched him on TV last night. He has no winged white stallion. He is not handsome. He is even a little stooped. Are you a good writer or a hack?"

"What is your definition of a good writer?"

"Someone like Václav Havel. I've read most of his plays. He held writing seminars in little theaters; he advocated a gentle revolution without violence, a revolution that is a little playful, a little humorous, even a little romantic. He calls it Prague Spring. I predict that he will succeed."

They often discussed politics and world affairs. He was amazed at how much she knew. Though a bureau chief of a large Western news organization, he had not yet read much about Václav Havel. "What kind of gentle revolution are you talking about?" he asked.

Now she looked serious. She asked, "What's the real strength of communism, Mark?"

"The working class, of course," he said.

"Phooey!" she responded. "China's working class has never been happy. Look at Poland and that union guy called . . . what's his name?" She snapped her fingers.

"Lech Walesa?"

"Yes, Lech Walesa. He invented Solidarity. He smiles a lot, but is he happy?"

Hansen didn't know what she was driving at, but he was familiar with Marxist theory: After a proletarian socialist revolution, class exploitation would be replaced by a system of "from each according to his ability, and to each according to his needs."

"That's a lie," she retorted. "Mao Zedong had forty years to test that theory. What happened? China is still backward. This process of proletarian socialist revolution is for the chickens. I say Karl Marx is a fake!"

As she spoke, she looked incensed, her voice strong, her eyes almost fiery. As she snorted and blew her hair, she seemed to become more attractive. He wondered what would happen if he kissed her. Would she walk out and never come back? It was a dreadful thought, and he decided not to try.

Hu Yaobang died of a heart attack. Do Do and many of her colleagues at Radio Beijing cried unashamedly. Some rushed home, unable to continue the day's work.

Back home she turned on the television. There was talk of Premier Zhao Ziyang being considered to fill Hu's job as general secretary of the party, with Vice Premier Li Peng becoming premier. It was bad news. Li Peng was a hard-liner, scornful of the intellectuals. Do Do poured herself a glass of mao-tai, not to celebrate but to drown her sorrow.

Hu, the champion of reform, had been called China's Mikhail Gorbachev. He had promoted individualism, freedom of speech, and democracy; he had openly opposed collective behavior and the "big pot of rice" policy, which made everybody eat out of one big pot regardless of talent or diligence. He had been Deng Xiaoping's protégé, and Deng had installed him as party chief in 1981. He had been the intellectuals' patron and protector. In protecting them, he had been toppled and disgraced; he had shared brutal blows along with those who demanded freedom and exposed corruption.

The phone started to ring in Do Do's apartment. The first caller was Mark Hansen. He said that numerous foreign correspondents had come to Beijing to find out what was going to happen in China. He asked Do Do to grant him an exclusive interview. She told him to come in two hours. She wanted to present all the facts to a foreign reporter without going through channels, without censorship to muddy the water. Her department head's warning was still ringing in her ears, "We reporters are either artists or housemaids. We either paint a glorious picture or sweep the dirt under the rug. To do otherwise is counterrevolutionary."

Jimmy returned looking haggard. The university had reacted to Hu's death with an uproar that must have been heard in Zhong Nan Hai. Thousands of students were holding a meeting to discuss Hu's memorial. Jimmy found Do Do in a chair, staring blankly, her eyes wet with tears. He made some strong coffee, knowing that she had been drinking. As they sat in the cluttered living room sipping coffee, waves of sadness overwhelmed both of them.

Do Do got up, sat at the kitchen table, and jotted down the dates of some important events. "Jimmy," she said, "I'm going to give an exclusive interview to Mark Hansen this afternoon. He wants my view of China's recent events and upheavals as a private citizen, not as a government reporter. I'm going to tell him all the facts without the government guidelines. I know we have differences of opinion and we quarrel about them. But this time I'm not going to lie. When Mark Hansen's article comes out, I hope you'll understand."

"What are you going to tell him?"

"Deng Xiaoping betrayed Hu Yaobang."

Jimmy stared at her, speechless. He was shocked.

"How can you tell a foreign reporter such baseless speculation? His article will be reprinted everywhere. Do you have proof?"

"I don't need proof. The facts are screaming in our faces."

"Your only proof is the stupid old saying 'All crows are black.' "

Jimmy's face had reddened with anger. His strong reaction made her wonder if she should be a little more subtle. But she felt that she must say what she believed. And this was a rare opportunity to air it worldwide.

It was their bitterest quarrel. Soon after Jimmy had stormed out, Mark Hansen arrived with Yun Mei. They had brought a tape recorder.

Yun Mei did not look as neat and tidy as before. Her hair was unkempt, her lipstick smeared, and her eye makeup stained by tears. Hansen, also looking gloomy and haggard, asked Do Do's permission to use the recorder during his questioning. She didn't care. All she wanted was to pour out all her thoughts, all the facts she knew, and all her pent-up feelings about the Communist government.

She started with the days when the sun began to shine on China, after the death of Mao Zedong and the rise of Deng Xiaoping. Nineteen eighty-five had been the best year. China's economy was booming, friendship with the West was warm. Deng Xiaoping smiled, joked, and relaxed with guests from friendly nations. China was in the hands of three major players, who were all close to Vice President Bush.

In 1985, America became China's best friend; America promised to push China into the modern world of technology. And China was on her way to join the world community of democracy. Do Do remembered how excited the whole nation had felt. Every morning all the public parks were full of students studying English, practicing conversation and reading American publications aloud. Foreign visitors found the scenes on public ground refreshing and fascinating. Young people studied, elderly people practiced t'ai chi. At night, disco music blared on radios and tape recorders, which young people carried everywhere. They shook their shoulders and snapped their fingers to beat time. In public places, they crowded around foreigners, asking questions and making friends. It was an unprecedented flow of friendship and goodwill between China and the West, all started by one man, Deng Xiaoping.

In March of 1986, Premier Zhao Ziyang submitted the nation's ambitious seventh Five-Year Economic Plan. In that year, Deng Xiaoping declared that old fogies in the party and the government should resign, and he himself would take the lead. That was when the octogenarians began to grunt and groan, reluctant to give up the positions for which they had fought all their lives. A few old men swore privately that they would cling to their power no matter what, and refuse to yield the rewards of their struggles: palatial homes, foreign cars, servants, and almost unlimited use of government facilities.

Deng Xiaoping changed color; he joined the hard-liners and refused to step down. Soon the government warned against "bourgeois liberalism."

At the end of 1986, the first bombshell was heard in Shanghai—Jiang Zemin, mayor of Shanghai, banned student demonstrations; police and students clashed. The country was in trouble again. The government and the academic community declared war against each other. The mayor of Beijing announced that he had uncovered a counterrevolutionary plot to overthrow the Communist regime. The end of happy days.

But Hu Yaobang still supported the students. In early 1987, he was fired.

Do Do told Mark Hansen the details of all the recent events and turmoil. She believed that China's fundamental problem was China's old rulers, the new feudal lords. Living inside the Forbidden City, behind the facade of magnificent palaces and the serenity of lush gardens and lakes, those rulers had for forty years fooled the people. Under the outward calm and harmony, there were always power struggles, political intrigues, coups d'état and plots for murder, which proved that the history of China was one of the most violent in the world. The Forbidden City was an unlucky place to live and work, and yet its power-hungry residents remained until they were carried out in pine boxes. It was an address as glorious as the White House or Buckingham Palace, but the most bloody.

As a reporter, Do Do was familiar with all the squabbles behind those massive walls. Deng, like Zhou Enlai, always tested the wind with a wet finger. That was why he had survived many ups and downs and wound up always standing, like a *pu dao wen*. She could see how he and the hard-liners had ganged up on Hu, who had not only suffered humiliation, but had also had his life's dream crushed. China's Gorbachev, the only hope, had died not of a heart attack but of heartache. Do Do wanted Mark Hansen to tell the world China's true tragedy. And to say it on the record.

Hansen was willing. He and Yun Mei spent almost two hours with her, but were a little disappointed that she did not have anything new to say. She was just angry. After they had left, she brooded. Suddenly, she remembered a meeting that she was supposed to attend with Jimmy.

Jimmy went to the meeting alone at Beijing University, attended mostly by professors and student leaders. It was a small gathering; the atmosphere was tense. When he arrived, Professor Wen, a mild-mannered man, was speaking vehemently, demanding that the planned parade to celebrate the May Fourth Movement be moved ahead two weeks to mourn Hu Yaobang's death. Jimmy was surprised that the gentle, forever smiling professor could be so fiery.

Sitting in a back row, he scanned the filled classroom to see if Do Do was in attendance. The rift between them bothered him, but for the sake of family harmony, he had avoided argument. He missed her cheerfulness and smiles; her joking and teasing had been replaced by long silences, loud rustling of newspapers, and banging of dishes and bowls. Each time he attempted to touch her in bed, she would turn her back to him.

He had tried to please her by preparing good dinners for her, but she never came home in time to eat them. Some of his students reported that his wife was everywhere, giving speeches and interviews to foreigners. He was sorry that she had become a political fanatic, unable to remain calm and analytical.

Now at the meeting, he glanced around again to see if she was in the audience. On the platform, Professor Wen was speaking, gesticulating wildly, his face red with excitement.

"The Old Guard is entrenched," he shouted. "Their only qualifications are loyalty to the party and a tenacity to preserve their own power. If the movement is to succeed, China has to abandon communism and uproot the Old Guard. We have all the elements of success on our side. May Fourth is one; Gorbachev's pending visit is another; but Comrade Hu's death is the best, and we must take advantage of it. As the old saying goes, 'Always strike the first blow to gain the advantage.' "

A hand shot up in the audience. When she rose to speak, Jimmy immediately recognized Do Do. Her voice had become hoarse from talking, her hair disheveled. The change in her was shocking. In Jimmy's eyes, she was no longer a loving wife, but a woman who ignored her own appearance and all her wifely duties. She had abandoned reason, tolerance, and logic, charging like a Don Quixote fighting windmills.

"I agree with you a hundred percent, Professor Wen," she shouted. "Hu Yaobang was the only man who promoted the intellectuals to responsible positions, but the hard-liners murdered him. Now the Old Guard are trying to isolate us, sabotage our work, and make our lives miserable again. We must immediately let the world know all the facts. We must expose their stupidity and corruption. Their sons and daughters are all profiteers. They laid their hands on state-subsidized materials and sold them to foreigners. By making enormous profits, they created disastrous inflation, yet the Old Guard blamed it on the reforms. But we cannot fight corruption without freedom of the press."

As the audience responded with enthusiastic applause, Jimmy rose quickly and left the meeting. He knew that the protest would be big and controversial; the extremists would use Hu's death as a pretense to overthrow the system. China would be split beyond repair. With a saddened heart, he hurried home, wondering if his marriage was also damaged beyond repair.

29

Raymond found the people in Beijing getting more quarrel-some. While visiting markets and zoos, going to theaters and discos with his girlfriends, he saw people shouting and fighting at the slightest provocation. He strolled into a shouting match between two men on Chang An Boulevard. They were waving their hands wildly and yelling at the top of their voices, spray-ing saliva. Raymond watched, fascinated. It interested him be-cause he could hardly understand a word. It seemed to him that while quarreling, people used a brand-new language.

Yin Yin, his date, dragged him away from the crowd. She said in English, "Just two sexually frustrated guys fighting over a woman."

"They must be using a lot of dirty words that I don't know," he said, turning his head to look.

"Raymond," Yin Yin said, "if they had more outlets, they wouldn't quarrel. Every time we spend a few hours in your brother's place, you're sweeter, too."

She asked him if he wanted to join the big parade tomorrow. Yes, he had promised to march with May, who had never missed a meeting or a demonstration. And she always carried a banner or a poster when she marched. She had even made one for him to commemorate Hu's death.

"Too bad," Yin Yin said with a wink. "Your brother and sister-in-law will be busy all day tomorrow."

Whenever Yin Yin gave him such a hint about sex, he always felt blood rushing to his groin.

As they walked past Tiananmen Square, they saw hundreds of students laying funeral wreaths in Hu's memory. New posters had been put up on the square's "triangle corner," where people gathered to read, jostling and craning their heads for a better view. Forgetting about sex, Raymond shouldered into the crowd, dragging Yin Yin with him. He was always curious; he never missed any excitement, and the freedom movement was terribly exciting. The new poster, larger than all the others, urged all the students to organize for a coordinated demonstration. It also announced a plan to procure a large wreath to lay at Tiananmen, calling for donations to buy a wreath and black armbands. Under the poster was a large, empty washbasin for the collection.

Raymond dug out two 10-yuan bills from his trouser pocket and tossed them into the basin. To his surprise, people around him all started throwing bills and coins into it. Yin Yin opened her purse and donated all her cash. A package of condoms fell out of her purse. She quickly retrieved it. Raymond almost laughed aloud.

Back at Beijing University, the students had organized a group called the New Thinking Society. They openly solicited donations at the university's main gate. A huge donation box had been set up, adorned with Hu's funeral portrait. Raymond, easily moved, took out all his cash—four more 10-yuan notes and some change—and deposited them in the box.

Inside the university, more than six thousand students had gathered; some were from the People's University twelve miles away. Shouting slogans and waving banners, they started marching out of the campus, many holding hands and others linking arms, singing the Chinese anthem. May spotted Raymond and dragged him to her group. Yin Yin, who did not want to lose him, quickly linked arms and joined the marching crowd. They walked toward Tiananmen Square singing and chanting patriotic slogans. Soon thousands more students from other schools joined the procession, some on bicycles. The police did not stop the parade; some even waved and smiled.

Raymond was so excited that he totally forgot Jimmy's warning, "Don't get involved." He began singing lustily, his deep voice rising above the others.

May was one of a dozen students assigned to hold aloft a twenty-foot-long white sheet of cloth. It bore two big black characters: CHINA'S SOUL. They surged toward the monument to the People's Heroes. Hundreds of wreaths were being laid around it, with people bowing and weeping. Some distance away, Raymond saw Do Do giving a speech on a stool, her high-pitched voice projected like that of a trained actress.

"Freedom of the press tells you what is wrong with the country," she was shouting, "like a doctor telling you what is ailing you. But the government says freedom of the press is a counterrevolutionary gimmick to subvert the Communist party. Comrade Hu Yaobang did not agree. He argued and pleaded with the other leaders to defend this right. He died for our cause. He was crushed by a tyrannical force that wants to set China back another twenty years. He was murdered by the enemies of democracy!"

She was fiery, her hair loose, her voice hoarse and hands gesturing wildly, attracting a great deal of attention and applause. Raymond applauded her enthusiastically, shouting, "Bravo, bravo!" A camera bulb flashed nearby. Yin Yin tugged at his sleeve.

"Quiet down," she whispered. "Someone is taking your picture."

There was a loud cheer elsewhere. Everybody turned his attention to four young men who were scaling the monument. They nimbly climbed to the top and draped the monument with the CHINA'S SOUL banner. A student raised a middle-aged man's arm and shouted, "The characters on this banner were written by our famous calligrapher, Professor Yang. Only he can write in a style that shows such sorrow and strength!"

Responding to the thunderous applause, Professor Yang bowed. Many more cameras clicked, light bulbs flashing.

Besides speeches and shouting of slogans, there were singing and dancing. The students almost turned the affair into a carnival. Some young people became stand-up comedians lecturing the ordinary citizens and joking about the hard-line leaders. A few even became cocky. Jimmy watched and listened with a heavy heart. He found Raymond, and again warned him not to get involved.

"You may sing and dance and play your guitar," he told his brother. "But let the others shout slogans and make jokes. Remember, you are not even a Chinese citizen." For this advice, Jimmy was roundly booed by some of the students.

As the mood was getting more festive, students began to pitch colorful tents. Raymond started teaching his fellow students the latest disco steps. Jimmy went around and asked his students to dance and sing, to have a good time. "Stop criticizing the leaders," he advised earnestly. "Have some respect for the elders. Don't destroy their dignity."

But most of the students ignored him. They kept putting up posters, drawing caricatures, and telling insulting jokes. Jimmy read a few and began to feel sympathetic with those being attacked. One particular poster bothered him the most: "Those who ought to live have died; those who ought to die are still enjoying their ginseng soup in Zhong Nan Hai, still belching from overeating, still breaking wind that can be smelled miles away."

Do Do had been so busy that she only went home to sleep for five or six hours. Her main activity was organizing "democratic salons." The participants squatted in circles on the lawns of universities and public parks to hear speeches. She had recruited many famous speakers, the most prominent being Fang Lizhi and his physicist wife Li Shuxian; U.S. ambassador Winston Lord and his wife, novelist Betty Bao. Such democratic salons became so popular that one of the student leaders, Wang Dan, organized more than twenty, beating Do Do's total by six.

Jimmy became more worried. He remembered the old saying, "A cornered dog will jump a wall." Every morning, when he left his apartment, he left a note on the kitchen table telling Do Do what to find in the refrigerator for her lunch and dinner. Instead of arguing with her, he often ended his note with an old saying or a subtle hint that he objected to the cruel way she was treating the leadership.

He wondered about Deng Xiaoping's health. How could the chain-smoking old man take so much abuse? He was so worried that he even started monitoring his whereabouts day and night.

On the day before Hu Yaobang's official funeral, Do Do returned home early. She looked upset. For days, she and Jimmy had communicated only on paper. Jimmy was happy to see her and was ready to end the cold war with some conversation.

He opened a bottle of champagne that his father had sent him. "Do Do," he said, as he poured champagne into two glasses. "When I watched the freedom movement, I wondered how the top party members felt, especially Deng. Some banners called him many dirty names. One said, 'Little Bottle, how muddle-headed you are'! Throughout Chinese history, no leader has been attacked like that except during a revolution. I hear that the leadership is highly insulted by the students, whom they call a bunch of brats whose mouths still smell of their mothers' milk."

"Jimmy," Do Do said, "this is a revolution. The leadership knows it. They have talked about a bloody crackdown. They have reiterated Mao Zedong's famous saying, 'Power grows out of the barrel of a gun.' If it were not for Zhao Ziyang, the army would have arrived and started shooting by now."

Jimmy knew that Zhao was in sympathy with the students; he had advocated persuasion instead of confrontation. He was one of the few who had escaped the students' attacks.

"I just heard some bad news," Do Do went on, gulping down her champagne. "Zhao and the hard-liners just had an argument. Zhao offered to talk to the students, but the hard-liners refused to let him. Then he said, 'I have the support of the people.' Deng Xiaoping lost his temper. He retorted, 'I have the army. You have nothing!' Jimmy, the Communists always resort to violence. It's about time you realized that and supported the revolution!"

She finished her champagne in one gulp and left.

Jimmy was speechless. Zhao was also Deng's hand-picked

heir. How could they quarrel like that? He remembered that Liu Shaoqi had been Mao's chosen heir, and Mao had imprisoned him. Liu had died in jail.

Sitting at the kitchen table and agonizing over China's future, he wept.

30

Pang Sin dreaded visiting his father-in-law, the general, who was over eighty and a veteran of the Long March. General Han lived in a palatial courtyard home near Zhong Nan Hai, with a sloping tile roof and vermilion gate guarded by sentries and two enormous stone lion dogs. A tall brick wall shielded the entire compound, making it invisible to passersby.

For an unexplained reason, Pang Sin and his wife were summoned to the general's residence. Pang Sin had visited his father-in-law only twice before; each time he had felt like a crime suspect brought to the yamen of a magistrate to be questioned. But he expected to enjoy a sumptuous meal to be served by a horde of maids at a dining table as large as an average citizen's bedroom. The house was Chinese, but furnished with modern luxury—color TV, refrigerator, freezer, and a piano that nobody played. The three bathrooms had the latest French flush toilets, bidets, and bathtubs for bubble baths, with constant running hot water, an unheard-of luxury, even though the general still enjoyed a sponge bath, a habit formed in the old army days.

Pang Sin kept thinking of the dinner to neutralize his distaste for the visit. His wife, Ginger, which sounded like "Golden Sister" in Chinese, was not too keen about visiting her parents, either. At the gate, a sentry recognized the red flag of their Toyota and saluted. They got out of the car and went in the vermilion door, walked across the landscaped court-yard of fish pond and miniature mountains with waterfalls. In the main building, the general was enjoying a bowl of ginseng soup on a deep down sofa. His wife, watching Peking Opera on their color console, called out their names in an excited voice.

Both Pang Sin and Ginger bowed to the general. Her mother turned off the TV set and joined them at a group of sofas in the middle of the living room. A maid, without being told, poured tea for everybody from an enormous warmer.

General Han looked at his only daughter critically and frowned. Traditionally, she was called "a pearl on the palm of the hand" or "a thousand gold." The sight of her always invited his scrutiny to see if she was in good health. "You look thin, Ginger," he said. "Don't you eat well?" "Ginger" was the only English the general knew. Pang Sin had been surprised that he accepted his daughter's English name; he was known as extremely anti-West.

During the conversation, the general's wife hardly spoke. While the general talked, he rarely looked at Pang Sin, even when he was speaking to him. Pang Sin felt nervous, secretly wiping his hands in his trouser pockets, anxiously hoping that the general would get down to business.

Finally, after he had finished his ginseng soup, he said, "This is a family meeting. Whatever is discussed today is strictly private. You all understand."

"Yes, Father," Ginger said. She glanced at Pang Sin, who nodded repeatedly with a grin.

"First, the country is going through a disaster," the general went on, his face expressionless, his voice strong and clear despite his age. "All because of the three pigheaded men, Deng, Hu, and Zhao. Now that Hu is gone, there is one less pebble in the shoe. Those ignorant students, whose mouths still smell of their mothers' milk, are blind. All they want is to love the West more, give the West more, and embrace their so-called democracy more. Luckily, the hard-liners in the government are building up strength to counteract this falling-all-the-way-to-the-West trend. This is good. An excellent opportunity to weaken the hard-liners, too."

He glanced at Pang Sin, who looked a bit puzzled. Han

smiled patronizingly. "I know this is over your head, Pang Sin. Let me make this clear before I go on. The hard-liners are Marxists and Mao Zedong's running dogs. Communism will never cure China's problems. Nor will capitalism. Only a good strong ruler like Bismarck or Emperor Chien Lung can rule a country like China. The Chinese people are like a dish of sand; without a true feudal system of a strong monarchy, they will remain as loose sand. My point is, to get rid of both the left and the right, we must encourage them to fight! Let them fight until they vanquish each other, so that a true leader may rise and take over the devastated land. Mao's wife Jiang Qing, almost succeeded, but she was such a suspicious and jealous bitch that she alienated so many followers and wound up in jail."

"General," said Pang Sin, having worked up enough courage to ask a question that had started gnawing at him, "are you anti-Communist?"

"I am anti-Communist and anti-West," the general said. "Both Stalin and Mao Zedong were ruthless bandit kings. They only used communism to gain power, without knowing that communism almost ruined both China and Russia. I am also anti-West because America is tricky. The United States has never fought a foreign war on its own land; whenever there was a world conflict, the Americans only participated at the very last moment. Like the two world wars, they came in near the end and reaped all the war booty. They seized enemy property and resources and forced all the enemy scientists to work for them. America is a clever imperialist country that nobody should trust. Have you heard of 'the fisherman's double gain'?"

Pang Sin was familiar with the tale, but before he could answer, the general went on, "When a clam was sunning itself, a crane came to peck at its flesh. The clam clamped onto its beak and refused to let the bird go. They starved to death. When a fisherman found a dead clam and a dead crane on the beach, he took them home and cooked himself a good oyster-crane dinner." He paused for emphasis. "This is what we ought to do . . . be the fisherman. Do you understand?"

Pang Sin wondered why the general had refused to look at him while he was talking to him. Now he knew; he looked like a Westerner. "Yes, I do," he said. "What do you want us to do?"

General Han looked at him for the first time, pleased that his son-in-law was not as slow-thinking as he had thought.

He said that the students would riot in a few days. He had arranged for some unemployed workers to destroy some property and set a few fires. The strategy was to arouse public anger against the students, giving the hard-liners an excuse to crack down. Like the oyster and the crane on the beach, both would wind up dead. Then the true ruler would rise to power and save China.

"As to what you can do," General Han added with a faint smile, "I understand that you have moved to Hong Kong and started your own business."

"Yes," said Pang Sin, recovering from his shock.

"How well do you know Hong Kong? Do you have connections there?"

"Father," Ginger said with a proud little smile, "Pang Sin's father is a British lord in Hong Kong."

"Oh?" the general opened his eyes wide in pleasant surprise.

Pang Sin made an attempt to correct his wife, but he decided not to. It was the first time he could put his chest out in the general's house. The general's eyes began to meet his with a twinkle.

"I also have some connections in the underworld," he said modestly.

"That will come in very handy," the general said. "If the student movement spreads to Hong Kong, can you start some disturbances there? I don't want any burning or looting, but some rock-throwing and window-breaking will serve the purpose. Use those who look like students, and pay them enough so that they will not talk."

"Who is going to pay them?" Pang Sin asked.

"Your wife," the general said without hesitation.

Pang Sin looked at his wife, who looked somewhat puzzled at first, but her father's stare made her smile and nod. In the past, a stare had always been his message: "Obey my order and everything will be all right."

The dinner was as sumptuous as ever. The general not only

looked at Pang Sin when he addressed him but also treated him as an equal, laughing and heaping food on his plate. At the end of the dinner, Pang Sin was so tipsy that he had to be taken home in the general's chauffeured limousine, since Ginger had not learned how to drive.

31

Back in Hong Kong, Pang Sin remembered his father-in-law's parting words: "You're doing this to save China, Pang Sin. China and Hong Kong are like Siamese twins with one nerve system. One sneezes and the other will, too. Do a good job in Hong Kong!"

Worried about the job, he avoided Aimee as much as possible. He did not want to become too deeply involved with her. On the surface, he was still her stepson. The thought of a double relationship began to make him uncomfortable. Politically, he had a job to do; he must remain alert, watching and listening, studying Hong Kong's every reaction to China's disturbances and upheavals. Since the Beijing students' democracy movement had started, the Hong Kong students were ready to join. Pang Sin followed the news closely. In China, the more the leadership tried to limit demonstrations, the more defiant the students became; the more the government attacked "bourgeois liberalization," the more the students embraced it. Fang Lizhi became a hero, worshiped by the liberals in Hong Kong. When Deng Xiaoping had attacked Fang, Hu Yaobang had sided with Fang, and had also become a hero. China sneezed and Hong Kong was sneezing, too. The political turmoil in both places was one. As more Hong Kong people joined the student movement, the colony became jittery. Some people were packing, ready to take shelter overseas, as if a hurricane were about to hit.

Every day, Pang Sin spent a few hours in teahouses listening to political arguments. Enjoying freedom of speech, both sides shouted. Corruption was the first chicken bone in most Hong Kong people's throats. Many banged on tables and argued pro and con, getting red in the face. Some of them even came to blows.

One humid evening, Pang Sin went to Hong Kong University to attend a public meeting organized by some Hong Kong students. He saw many familiar faces in the audience, all well-known figures in the media and the arts; even the Communist Xing Hua's new bureau chief was there. The hall was packed. Pang Sin took a seat in the last row.

Professor Feng delivered the first speech. A skinny middle-aged man in a baggy Western suit, with a mild cough, he punched the air emphatically as he spoke.

"J. F. Kennedy said, 'Ask not what your country can do for you, ask what you can do for your country.' "

"God! Rhetoric, rhetoric!" a man mumbled.

"Sh-sh!" a woman hushed him. She was young and pretty. Professor Feng's rhetoric went on:

"In our country rose a man called Hu Yaobang. Since his passing, his ghost has been waving at us, beckoning us to follow. But many of us are reluctant to move. Tonight we are gathered here to organize a movement that will be remembered as the greatest freedom movement in history!"

Thunderous applause brought many people to their feet. The young woman clapped wildly with tears in her eyes.

Professor Feng proposed a plan to enlist all the students in Hong Kong as freedom fighters. "The students will be our vanguard!" he shouted. "We will support our fellow freedom fighters in Beijing, we will raise the fundamental question in everyone—how much can we do for our country? During the Cultural Revolution, Jiang Qing only asked the students how much they could destroy, for she admired Stalin and Hitler. Her Red Guards became China's Hitler Youth. They set China back more than a decade! In this freedom movement, we must undo the damage. We must ask those 'old tree trunks' to get off the people's backs!"

Some heated discussion followed after Professor Feng's speech. Some suggested posters to expose corruption, naming names of rotten sons and daughters of some party leaders, generals and high government officials; others advocated demonstrations; still others wanted to stage hunger strikes. A few wondered where the funds would come from. Everything cost money.

"Yes," one man shouted, "even hunger strikers need medical care and, God forbid, funeral expenses." A few people laughed. It was the only laughter heard during the long meeting.

Professor Feng raised both his hands and declared that money was no problem. Many compatriots in Hong Kong had already pledged financial aid. All he needed was brainpower.

"Speaking of brainpower," he shouted, "may we take this opportunity to ask for volunteers? We need you to organize a 'think tank' for a world-shaking event that will change history!"

At the end of the meeting, Pang Sin volunteered. Feeling like a double agent, he went to see Bean Cake Two.

Bean Cake Two was practicing kung fu in his warehouse headquarters when Pang Sin arrived. "Come to my office," he said in Cantonese, wiping his long, narrow face with a towel. "Glad you're back, I've had more thoughts on the two projects I told you about."

"I want to see you about something else," said Pang Sin, following him.

Bean Cake sank into his rattan chair behind the crude desk and fished out a pack of cigarettes. He offered Pang Sin one, but Pang Sin declined.

"So you have a third project to propose," said Bean Cake, drawing deeply on his cigarette.

"How many hoodlums do you command?" Pang Sin asked.

"Now, Older Brother," Bean Cake said with a scowl, "don't ever call my men hoodlums. That's a term used only by my enemies. Some police officers call them Blue-Red brothers."

Pang Sin had heard of the Blue-Red Gang, a crime organization originated in Shanghai in the 1910s. In the old days, they had controlled the labor unions and many corrupt politicians in China. Even warlords had joined.

"How many members do you have?" he asked.

"About three hundred."

Pang Sin calculated the pay. Three hundred would cost thirty thousand Hong Kong dollars. He would deduct 10 percent for himself. He told Bean Cake the plan. The Hong Kong students would start a protest demonstration to support the Beijing students. He wanted Bean Cake to stage a destructive demonstration in both Hong Kong and Kowloon to discredit the students. The pay was good. H.K. $80 for each Blue-Red brother for an evening's easy work.

Bargaining was a Hong Kong custom. Bean Cake haggled and increased the pay to H.K. $95, taking a 10 percent cut for himself. Pang Sin signed the deal, and they reminisced about the Cultural Revolution days when they had smashed schools, sacked homes, and carried away treasures. They had enjoyed the rampage with the blessings of both Chairman Mao and Jiang Qing. But this time it was different; Pang Sin wanted to know what steps Bean Cake would take to avoid going to jail.

"Ease your mind, Older Brother," Bean Cake said with a smile. "Would I operate without police help?"

Two days later, the Hong Kong students demonstrated to support the Beijing students. They paraded on the main thoroughfares, waved banners, and shouted slogans. More than three hundred Blue-Red Gang members, disguised as students, did a good job of breaking windows and looting stores during the students' demonstration in Victoria and Kowloon. Nobody was fooled. The newspapers dismissed the riot as the handiwork of some street hoodlums who habitually looted during all disasters—fires, typhoons, and political upheavals. This time they shouted the wrong slogans and waved banners with misspelled words. In spite of their horn-rimmed glasses and other props, none of them looked like students. One paper asked facetiously, "We have never seen so many students with so many scars and tattoos before. Is there a university of crime in our crown colony now?"

A few rioters were arrested, but nobody confessed, because of the gang's code of silence.

Pang Sin told Bean Cake that he was unhappy with the riot job. Bean Cake argued that open rioting was not his line of expertise. His specialty was underground work—smuggling, kidnapping, and extortion. He wanted Pang Sin's answer to his two previous proposals.

"We can make a lot of money together," he said. "It's stupid to mobilize three hundred brothers to do a job for half a bowl of rice while you and I can make ten million dollars sitting on our butts."

Pang Sin knew that Bean Cake was talking about kidnapping Raymond Hong. Ten million dollars was a lot of money.

32

Raymond always dragged May to the Peking Opera, which she hated, but she went along just to please him. She also acted as his interpreter, explaining things that Raymond had not known before. Everything in the opera fascinated him—the glittering costumes, the acrobatic fighting, the females playing male roles and vice versa. He had learned that when an actor blew his whiskers, he was angry; when he lifted his leg and waved a whip, he was mounting a horse; when a stagehand threw a red flag over his face, he was killed.

May preferred to take a walk and chat, or have a bowl of hot beef noodles in some coolie restaurant. It was a sunny Sunday afternoon. To avoid going to the theater, May suggested that they take a walk in the park. They had participated in the students' demonstrations in Tiananmen Square for several days. The demonstrations seemed to have run their course. The students were tired, and their annual final examinations were looming over their heads. As the crowd thinned out in the square, something new was happening in parks and other public places. Some extremists were organizing "political salons," inviting the public to listen to lectures and participate in political discussions.

Raymond had found that going out with May was different from dating Yin Yin. May was knowledgeable, familiar with American history and literature. She had read *The Grapes of*

Wrath five times. Yin Yin liked movies and discos. She avoided talking about politics, and always turned serious discussions to casual chats on film stars and scandals. She laughed and giggled a lot. Raymond enjoyed both girls, depending on whether he wanted to enrich his mind or please his body.

This morning, as he and May walked leisurely in the Beijing Zoo, May talked about death. She sounded solemn, like a priest delivering a sermon. She seemed to have a death wish, talking about self-sacrifice for the cause. She believed that meaningful death should serve a useful purpose. Raymond hated the subject, but he was not bored, wondering if May was serious. She sounded so weird that he listened.

"If I'm killed fighting for a cause," she said, "I'd like my death to inspire others to fight for the same cause."

"I'm not easily inspired," Raymond said with a grimace. "What cause is worth dying for?"

"There are almost two billion people in this world who are still struggling under feudal systems without freedom," she said. "Fighting for their freedom is the greatest cause I can think of. But it won't be easy. As the old Chinese saying goes, 'A good thing must suffer.' "

"So you are willing to suffer?"

"And sacrifice, if necessary. If I must be sacrificed, so be it!"

"May, what's the matter with you? You talk as if you had already been placed over a pile of wood, and some savages were about to roast you for supper."

"Raymond," she said seriously, walking almost like a zombie, her voice distant, her eyes far, far away, "I have a premonition. Someone will soon lift the Iron Curtain high enough for two billion people to take a peek at how the rest of the world is faring. When that happens, those who have been enslaved will struggle to be free, and there will be a bloodbath."

"Who will lift the Iron Curtain?"

"Mikhail Gorbachev."

"Two billion people! The Soviet Union has only half a billion."

"The Chinese will be included. But the Chinese rulers, through history, never believe there is another world. Even as late as the nineteenth century, a Chinese emperor still refused to believe that the world was round. He declared, 'We have our own astronomy. It's a lie for the foreign devils to say that the world is like a rice ball and that people are walking on it like ants.' 'China is the whole world' is still China's rulers' mentality. Now, since the liberation, they have declared China's own human rights; they refuse to recognize progress; they are still sitting in the bottom of a well looking up at the sky and believing that the sky is just a little square."

She talked about China's first emperor, Shih Huang Ti, who burned books and buried scholars alive for inner security; he built the Great Wall to ward off foreign invasions. "That was the typical behavior of a feudal lord. He did not care what was going on, as long as he was safe in his own little world. Therefore, knowledge was what he dreaded most. As Fang Lizhi said, "Only with knowledge will we be able to overcome the violence of ignorance at its roots. Without knowledge, nonviolence can deteriorate into begging, and history is unmoved by begging."

All this talk was a little over Raymond's head. "How old are you, May?" he asked.

"Twenty-two," she said, surprised by such an irrelevant question. "Why do you ask?"

"Nothing," he said. He was impressed. "You've changed so much that I can't believe my ears."

"Before I met you, I was a little frog in the bottom of a well," she said. "I saw the world only as a little square of sky."

"Have you been to Hong Kong?" he asked.

"Never. I haven't been anywhere except Shanghai. What's Hong Kong like?"

"Like Shanghai, I guess. Do Do, Jimmy, and I are going to spend the summer vacation with my parents in Hong Kong in June. Why don't you come with us?"

"Is this an invitation?"

"It certainly is!"

"Don't you ask your parents first?"

"What for? We have seven bedrooms. When we have extra guests, they always say, 'Stay for dinner. It's only one extra pair of chopsticks on the table.' "

The zoo was full of people. Most of them wore Western-style jeans and shirts. Some women were even dressed in miniskirts. The drab Mao uniform and duck-tongue caps were gradually disappearing. The children, brightly clothed in yellow, red, and blue, no longer had runny noses. Some were rosy-cheeked, outgoing, waving and giggling. When foreign visitors requested pictures, they happily clamored to pose, making funny faces and saying, "Cheese!" Cameras clicked. Friendly greetings were exchanged. "How cute!" "What darlings!" were heard everywhere. Most of the young people conversed in English; their cassette recorders filled the air with Western music and good cheer. The zoo was as festive as the Tiananmen Square during the student demonstrations a few days earlier.

Raymond was happy. At home, he did not have to lift a finger to do anything; here, it was refreshing to do everything for himself . . . even wash his own clothes and his own rice bowls. Here, he had a choice of two girlfriends; he rode bicycles with them, picnicked on Kentucky Fried Chicken, and kissed them on park benches. At home, expensive gifts were piled in his room, seldom touched; here, a cheap folding fan, a small soapstone panda, a teacup with his name on it were his treasured gifts from his friends. When May or Yin Yin invited him home for a home-cooked meal, he always felt hungry as soon as the cooking smells began to fill their parents' tiny apartments. In Beijing, he never experienced the boredom or indifference he used to feel at home in Hong Kong.

Hand in hand, he and May strolled past the various animals. A monkey scratched its stomach. Another kept saluting and begging for peanuts. A little panda bear rolled over to please its mother. A polar bear stood on its hind legs, pawing the air. In the distance, peacocks screamed and lions roared.

"Why are you so quiet?" May asked.

"I'm thinking how happy I am in China," he said, squeezing her hand. "I think I'll never live in Hong Kong again. Just go there for visits."

"Never say never," May said. "Once I told myself that I would never cry. And I've cried three times since then. Look, there's a 'democratic salon' meeting. Let's go!"

She dragged him to a large crowd a short distance away. They shouldered into the crowd and found two dozen people sitting in a circle on the grass, surrounded by an audience five deep. One scholarly-looking man in a loose Western suit was standing in the middle, talking, provoking laughter and giggles in the audience.

". . . how to measure poverty in China?" he was saying. "Use toothpaste. The majority of more than a billion people in China don't use toothpaste, not counting babies and old folks without teeth. Why? Because they cannot afford it. The government says the only thing that we're overproducing is people. Thanks to Mao Zedong, who encouraged gun-fodder production during the Korean War.

"Today, the government forced thirty million men to have vasectomies. Some doctors and hospitals are making easy money selling certificates without surgery. Meanwhile, the government boasted new medical success in restoring virility in men; it also boasts the production of test-tube babies. Result? More babies! But there's a law saying that nobody should have more than one baby, or pay a heavy penalty.

"You all know that the professors in China are poorly paid. Some of us have to spend part of our time shining shoes and peddling stationery for extra money. Where can we find money to pay such a penalty? Recently, New China News Agency admitted that many teachers have become Buddhist monks just to get enough to eat. At the same time, the rich can buy *chi pao*, the Mandarin-style gown in Beijing, price tag twenty-five hundred American dollars. I am making an equivalent of fifty American dollars a month. If I don't spend a cent, it will take me four years to buy a *chi pao* for my wife. No wonder my wife is divorcing me!"

The audience laughed and applauded. The professor wiped his brow with a soiled handkerchief and continued. "The *chi pao* was created by Li Wen-ping's tailor shop. Li was a fashion model, now a designer and multimillionaire. She has designed clothes not only for the wives of high government and party officials, but for the wives of leaders in Japan and Singapore. She is for free enterprise. Good! We are for it! But . . ."

He paused for emphasis. After a sweeping glance, he went

on, "If you want free enterprise, you have to have *gwansi,* the right connections. Those who can provide gwansi are swamped with gifts. One higher-up in the party said that on his birthday he received a bottle of wine which he auctioned off for one thousand American dollars. Another cadre received so many foreign cigarettes as gifts that he had to sell some of them on the open market. One of my friends recently bought a carton of American cigarettes on the open market. He opened the package and found two thousand American dollars in it. Now this friend spends all his money buying cigarettes on the open market, hoping to hit another jackpot."

When the laughter subsided, Do Do jumped out of nowhere and clapped. "We thank Professor Ding for his eye-opening revelations. But all this kind of talk will be censored if we try to publish it. That's why we must air it at political salons such as this. I can see quite a few foreign friends in the audience. Those who want to volunteer as translators, please raise your hands."

Raymond's hand shot up quickly. Do Do saw him, and they exchanged smiles.

"Any more volunteers?" she asked.

Quite a few more hands went up. A tall, bearded foreigner raised his hand. "Hey, lady," he said, "I don't need a translator. I followed that gentleman's tales word by word. Funny stuff, but there's nothing new. You say you don't have freedom of speech. The fact that you're here telling funny stories about your leaders is proof enough that you do have plenty of freedom."

"Wait a minute, mister," Do Do said. "Have you read anything like this in print? Bribery and kickbacks in high places have all been censored."

"Don't tell me about bribery and kickbacks," the foreigner said. "We have plenty of that in America. You must have read about our defense-industry scandals. A toilet seat for the army cost five thousand dollars. Heard about that? The recent Savings and Loan scandal . . . it'll cost billions of dollars of taxpayers' money to bail out the crooks. Listen, don't tell me I don't know China. I lived in Shanghai for five years when I was a kid. I saw beggars dying on the streets. I saw warlords acting like bandits. Hey, lady, even my son is an old China hand. He's made dozens of business trips to China since Deng Xiaoping opened the door."

"Did he make any money?"

"Of course he made money. So did China. What's wrong with two thousand bucks hidden in a carton of cigarettes? The only thing wrong is that the damned fool didn't open his gift package, and sold it to somebody else."

He was getting red-faced as he harangued Do Do. When his embarrassed wife grabbed his arm and dragged him away, he turned and shouted his last advice, "Lady, don't rock the boat!"

33

There was another lull in Tiananmen Square. Mark Hansen would have loved to stroll in the square watching children fly kites and old men practice t'ai chi; the atmosphere there was always soothing, especially in May when trees were lush and flowers blooming. But the square had changed. Some students still camped there, the Gobi wind blew debris around. The colorful kites of all shapes and forms were missing; whiffs of urine drifted in the air. Hansen could smell it blocks away.

It was a bright Sunday morning. He waited for Yun Mei in the hotel lobby. They had agreed to spend a day relaxing, revisiting some of Beijing's attractions that Hansen had loved. Recently, he and Yun Mei had visited a few of his favorite places in Tiananmen Square—the History Museum, the Monument to the People's Heroes, the Mao Zedong Mausoleum, the cluster of ancient palaces in the Forbidden City that housed the emperors of the Ming and Ching dynasties. They had walked through some of the eight hundred gaudy buildings that had been built by a million craftsmen and laborers. But its history was depressing, full of murders, intrigues, bloody battles, and deliberate fires set by court eunuchs, who got rich off the repair bills.

Yun Mei arrived breathlessly. She was always in a hurry, as though she were perpetually late for important meetings. She blamed her tardiness on the horrifying traffic. Hansen always advised her to pedal her bicycle carefully. He would rather see her late than find her in a hospital.

"Today you are the boss," he said as he rose to meet her in the crowded lobby. "I will follow you to the edge of heaven: old Chinese saying."

"I never heard such a saying," she said with a little laugh. She was dressed in a short black skirt, white silk blouse, and comfortable white walking shoes, her hair tied with a blue ribbon. She looked fresh and pink, a picture of health. "I have prepared a list. Take your pick."

Hansen scanned the list. There were many places he had not visited before, such as the Altar of Land and Grain in Sun Yatsen Park, the Workers' Cultural Palace, the Military Museum, the Beijing National Library, the Chinese Art Gallery. . . .

He returned the list to her. "Sorry, today I'm not in the mood for culture. May we have a pot of tea on Beihai Lake? Can you take me to Zhong Nan Hai?"

Yun Mei widened her eyes in mock horror. "Can you borrow a bullet-proof helicopter from Washington? That's the only way you can land in Zhong Nan Hai, and only for five minutes. Then we'd find ourselves in the Security Bureau's interrogation rooms, our hands cuffed and our feet chained."

"Just joking," he said, laughing. He almost felt relaxed. "Let's go wherever we can have the best jasmine tea."

Beihai Park, northwest of the Forbidden City, was the former playground of the emperors. China's Dragon Lady, Mao's widow, Jiang Qing, loved the place so much that she had entertained there constantly. It was a huge park with a lake for fishing and boating, built by the Mongol emperor Kublai Khan six hundred years ago. Hansen and Yun Mei, after a brief visit to the Nine Dragon Wall, took a ferryboat to the jade island where they ordered dim sum and tea at the Fang Shan Restaurant. Nearby was the famous White Pagoda, thirty-six meters high, shining in the bright sun like a giant Chinese ginger jar. The food served in the restaurant was prepared from recipes favored by the late empress dowager. There were 120 courses to choose from, plus numerous royal pastries.

With the beautiful panoramic view of the lake, dining or

taking tea on the Jade Island was one of the greatest pleasures in Beijing. Hansen stretched in his rattan chair with a sigh. For the first time, he felt completely content and happy.

"Is that a happy sigh?" asked Yun Mei, pouring a cup of jasmine tea for him.

"Yun Mei," he said, "we've known each other for quite a while now."

"Are you counting the days?" she asked.

"And hours and minutes."

"That's not a good sign."

"I hate to see them pass by so fast," he said. "If I had a time machine, I'd like to make time go so slowly that a minute would become a day and a day become a year."

"My God, you'd be bored to death."

"With you, it would never be boring."

She looked at him tenderly. He took her hand and held it. He had always wanted to ask her about her past. Today, he had an uncontrollable desire to know everything about her. "Who are you, Yun Mei?" he asked, unsmiling, his voice serious. "Where are you from? Who are your parents? It's about time I knew you better."

She lowered her eyes, struggling with indecision. Suddenly, without a word, she opened her purse, fished out an old photo, and showed it to Hansen. It was a picture of a handsome man, wearing a silk gown, and a young lady sitting on a Chinese ancestral chair beside him. In her lap was a little girl bundled in a blanket.

"My parents," she said. "The picture was taken when I was three months old." As she spoke, her eyes reddened and moistened with tears. She stopped and wiped her eyes with a finger. "Sorry. Every time I talk about my family, I embarrass myself."

"I'm sorry I asked," he said, returning the picture to her. "Let's change the subject."

"No, I want to tell you more if you're interested."

He squeezed her hand. "Of course I'm interested. My shoulder is ready if you need it."

"Every girl in China has a sob story," she said. "We're always looking for shoulders to cry on. But most of our stories are true . . . father liquidated, mother died, daughter escaped to Hong Kong and became a maid or a prostitute. Her only crime was being too rich, too educated, or talking too much. Those who remained behind envy those who have escaped. My grandfather was rich and a scholar who worked for the Kuomindong. That was a double crime. He was shot. My father had bleeding ulcers. He was denied medical treatment and died a painful death in jail. My mother killed herself by jumping off a five-story building. You probably think I'm a Taiwan agent spreading anti-Communist propaganda. But it's a true story. Ask Deng Xiaoping. His own son was pushed off a building and crippled."

After she blew her nose, she smiled. "Well, now I feel better. Now you know why I'm so rebellious."

"Why didn't you escape to Hong Kong?" he asked.

"I can't swim," she said. "Many girls have drowned. I have a better idea. I want to cross the ocean on a ship. You know what? I applied for a passport, and I got it. All I need is a visa, which is the hardest to come by, because in getting a foreign visa, Chinese *gwansi* is almost useless."

Nearby, a middle-aged man was reading a paper and stretching his leg on a railing like a ballet dancer. Another man and his young daughter were roller-skating hand in hand. The lake was dotted with rowboats; palatial buildings, hills, and distant trees were silhouetted against the morning sky like Chinese paper cuts. There was disco music in the air, coming from cassette recorders carried by young couples dressed in Western clothes. Hansen looked around. He could hardly tell there was trouble in Beijing. On this little island, he only found peace and calm, even a bit of gaiety.

The middle-aged man finished his leg-stretching exercise. He folded his newspaper carefully. Passing by Hansen's table, he smiled and offered him the paper. Hansen accepted it. He invited him to sit down and have a cup of tea. The man, speaking excellent English, thanked him and took a chair beside him. He seemed eager to talk to a foreigner. Hansen introduced himself and Yun Mei; the man offered each of them a calling card. He was a professor at Ching Hwa University and a Ph.D. from Harvard. With a laugh, he said, "Such a card would only bring me trouble in the old days. Now I've dug them out of a buried jar and started using them again."

Hansen also offered him his business card. When Professor Ling read it, his face brightened. "I write, too," he said. "I write fiction. But I don't tell anyone about that except foreign friends. In Beijing, I just jokingly tell people that I'm a professional liar. Do you know how I became a writer of fiction? By writing confessions. I had to lie all the time." He threw his head back and laughed.

Hansen found Professor Ling a delightful man, easy to talk to, open, and knowledgeable, the kind of man he had always wanted to discuss China's problems with. Hansen asked him who would win the power struggle in Zhong Nan Hai, the right side or the wrong side.

"In China, there is no such thing as the right side or the wrong side," Professor Ling said. "We have an old adage that says, 'He who is victorious becomes a king; he who is defeated becomes a bandit.' Chang Kaishek called Mao Zedong a bandit all his life, so did millions of others. But Mao finally became a king, therefore he was right. One day when the Communists are vanquished, they will become bandits again, and then they will be wrong again. That's the facts of life in China." He glanced around and sighed. "Good. I don't see any public security guards around."

"How can you tell who is a public security guard?" Hansen asked.

"You can smell them a mile away," the professor said. "They have the same height and the same age. They are all dressed in Mao uniforms of the same color and cut. They all wear a duck-tongue cap. And they have all acquired a habit of looking around without turning their heads, like this." He demonstrated by rolling his eyes right and left comically. "I know some of them personally. In fact, two of them are my former students. During the Cultural Revolution, some Red Guards searched my house and carried off all my valuable books and records. Through the tips of those former students, I bought most of my books back for a dollar a pound. But my phonograph records are lost forever. 'Tennessee Waltz' and 'Doggie in the

Window' are my favorites. I still can hum them." He hummed a few bars and laughed.

"What do you think of China's future?" Hansen asked.

Professor Ling suddenly became serious. "People have lost faith. This is a terrible loss. They live day by day. They don't put any effort or energy into doing anything. The young people smoke and loaf. They will watch American movies all day if they can wangle a ticket to those 'internal' film shows. In twenty years, there will be no cure for China except a war with a superpower. Then China will be destroyed and start all over again."

Hansen was somewhat taken aback by such a bold statement. Before he could say anything, the professor went on, "When I was a child, I saw a Western missionary pass brass coins to starving farmers and tell them to believe in God. Many of them embraced Christianity because they could get ten cents apiece. Today, the majority of the Communists have become party members because they get better jobs and can have special privileges and benefits. So they are like those ten-cent Christians. They put out a hand and say, 'I believe in God. Ten cents, please.' I wonder how many party leaders are real Marxists. I suspect that the whole Zhong Nan Hai is a fake. You look at one of its buildings. The whole edifice is only a facade with painted windows. The fake building was built to hide the nerve center of China from spyglasses, but it is quite symbolic. Some soothsayers said it is bad for *feng shui*. It will bring disaster to the entire area. I believe it."

He stretched his arms and sighed. "I can only talk to a foreigner like this. What a relief. What luxury. Thank you, thank you!"

After the professor had left, Yun Mei picked up the paper he had left behind. "Oh, my God!" she said, reading the front-page editorial. "This is terrible! Terrible!"

"What does it say?" Hansen asked anxiously.

"The government accuses the student demonstrators of being a bunch of troublemakers scheming to overthrow the government. This is like throwing gasoline over a dying fire." Looking agonized, she blurted out angrily, "How stupid!"

* * *

Two weeks later, on May 4, Hansen was awakened by the
phone from a deep sleep. Yun Mei's voice was excited, reporting that the *People's Daily* editorial had churned up a big
storm. Those strong words accusing the student demonstrators
of being a bunch of troublemakers had angered the entire intellectual community; the student leaders demanded a retraction of the editorial. They also wanted a direct dialogue with
Li Peng. Now the government threatened a crackdown, and
the students were planning a massive march. Some had even
pledged to start a hunger strike. "Do you want to interview
some student leaders?" she asked.

Hansen was wide awake now. "No," he said. "I want to
talk to some ordinary people. I want their opinions of the student movement. Can we meet at some teahouse near Tiananmen Square?"

She told him that she was now at a teahouse at Farmers'
Market run by a Cantonese couple. She and a few friends were
having tea and dim sum. "Come over. You'll eat all kinds of
tidbits and hear all kinds of talk." She gave him directions.

Hansen arrived after fighting traffic for almost forty minutes
in his car. He easily found the teahouse. Noisy, gaudy, and a
bit shabby, it was famous for braised goose feet. Yun Mei was
waiting for him at a corner table. "My friends have left. They
all have jobs," she said.

"What did they tell you? Are they worried?" Hansen asked.

"They all support Deng. They believe Deng has distanced
himself from the hard-liners. He has repeatedly declared that
the intellectuals are not such undesirables, but part of the
working class. There's a musician I know slightly. Want to talk
to him?"

"Yes," he said eagerly.

She caught the musician's eye and gestured for him to come
over. Yee, a long-haired young man, picked up his guitar and
hurried over. It was not often that a pretty young lady wanted
his company. He was also delighted to see an American, for
he was obsessed about practicing English with foreigners. Hansen turned on his tape recorder and asked him if he minded.

"I don't mind, if you give me a copy," he said.

He was quite fluent in English. He liked to use slang words. He even punctuated his sentences constantly with "you know," an annoying habit that Hansen loathed but tolerated.

"Deng Xiaoping?" he said. "he's full of shit, you know. He's only interested in promoting economic reform, you know. The hell with democracy, you know. The king in *The King and I* said, 'It's a puzzlement.' You know."

A new bowl of goose feet arrived. Yun Mei picked up one and placed it on Yee's plate. Yee gobbled it down hungrily. Hansen was worried that he might choke on the little bones. But Yee, after having swallowed the meat, spat out all the bones onto his plate and helped himself to another foot.

Hansen didn't care for such exotic food, but the tea-sippers were all talkative and anxious to express their opinions. The atmosphere was almost like that of London's Hyde Park; the soapbox orators had a lot to say, and most of them spoke some English. Over three pots of Black Dragon tea, Yun Mei invited several more people to their table to share their braised goose feet. To Hansen's surprise, they all wanted to talk about Gorbachev and his state visit on May 15. Yee had even written a song in English to celebrate the occasion. Without being asked, he picked up his guitar and played a flowery overture, then sang in his nice baritone voice:

> "Hee ah yah, Hee ah ho
> Some twenty years ago,
> A big bear was snarling
> A fiery dragon was spitting fire;
> A guy called Nikita
> Banged a UN table
> With his smelly shoe;
> A fellow named Mao Zedong
> Squared off to strike a blow.
> The world was trembling,
> 'Cause both were wild,
> With nuclear weapons piled high.
> Nikita shouted,
> 'We'll bury you!'
> Mao Zedong shouted,

224 ◆ C. Y. LEE

*'If a billion people spit,
We'll drown you!' "*

He played a little bridge and went on singing:

*"Hee ah yah, hee ah ho.
Not too long ago
The big bear stopped snarling,
The fiery dragon stopped spitting fire.
A guy called Gorbie
Smiled his big smile;
A fellow called Little Bottle
Talked a minute a mile.
When both refuted Marx and Stalin,
The Chinese Berlin Wall was fallin'.
When Gorbie and Little Bottle meet
In the People's Great Hall,
We'll hear nothing but Indian love call.
When thirty years of rivalry end
With firecrackers and a big cheer,
We'll all stand up and toast
With good vodka and Qingdao beer!"*

He ended the song with another bridge, his fingers flying, his soft voice humming, "Hee ah yah, hee ah ho."

Two swarthy men in Mao uniforms stood up from their table and approached him. "You," one said. "Come with us!"

Yee looked up and smiled. "Ah, long time no see," he said in English.

"You, too," the other man said to Yun Mei.

"Wait a minute," said Hansen, shooting up to his feet. "What have they done? They are my guests!"

The agents ignored him and repeated their order. When Hansen protested again, Yun Mei turned to him and quietly shook her head. She stood up and agreed to go with them. So did Yee.

When Hansen got up to follow, one of his other guests tugged at his sleeve and told him to sit down, whispering,

"Never argue with security guards. If you do, they will turn a little questioning into a trial. Such nice goose feet! I'll have another."

Burning with anger, Hansen forced a smile. While eating, he wondered where to find a *gwansi* that would get Yun Mei out. Perhaps his friend at the American embassy could help.

It was barely light in the morning. Hansen was already on the phone, talking to Edward Johnson, the cultural attaché at the American embassy. He was sleepy-eyed, pinching his nose to keep himself awake. He had not slept much, having tossed all night, worrying about Yun Mei.

"I called the Public Security," Johnson told him. "They said all you need is to prove that Yun Mei is working for you as an assistant and that you are responsible for her actions, then they will release her. Do you have any kind of document that'll prove her employment?"

"That's no problem," Hansen said with a sigh of relief. "Thanks, Ed. You're an excellent *gwansi*."

"Don't say that," Johnson said. "If the wrong side wins in this power struggle, American connections will be poison again. Good luck."

Hansen had no contract with Yun Mei. So far, all the agreements between employer and employee had been oral. Just as he had started to type a contract, Yun Mei came in looking chipper and tidy, her Western dress laundry-fresh.

"Good morning," she said, planting a kiss on his cheek.

"Is this a hallucination?" he asked, staring at her in surprise.

"Pinch yourself," she said with a laugh.

"Who got you out?"

"My *gwansi*," she said. "I happen to have connections with some inside people at all levels, right, left, or in the middle."

She turned on the radio. Voice of America was profiling Hu Yaobang in Mandarin. Hansen poured two cups of coffee, sat down beside Yun Mei on the sofa, and listened. He had been surprised by Hu's popularity, a man admired almost as much as Zhou Enlai. Some foreign correspondents believed that if these two men had had a free rein in governing China, the country would have become a respected world power, perhaps more influential than Japan, Taiwan, and Hong Kong combined. They could have given communism a good name.

"Hu was a little man," the commentator said, "even shorter than Deng Xiaoping. Some people compared him to a duck. He walked like a duck and quacked like a duck, but he was not a duck. He was a giant; he just acted like a duck to fool his enemies, who finally cooked him like a Peking duck."

The commentator discussed Hu's background; he was a southerner whom Deng Xiaoping had chosen as his heir apparent. He had fallen out of Deng's favor by cackling like a chicken and flying like a bird, violating many of the party codes. His major crime was his sympathy for the democratic movement. His other offenses included his fetish for fashionable Western suits, his good command of English, and his ability to handle a knife and fork correctly at the dinner table. Once he had even committed a cardinal sin by suggesting that China ought to get rid of chopsticks for better hygiene. That suggestion had infuriated a lot of old men. Hu's fall from power had rocked many fence sitters. Suddenly, there was a tremendous revival of Karl Marx and Mao Zedong's thoughts. Decentralization of authority was attacked; centralized control by the party was announced. Democracy became a taboo again. Zhong Nan Hai was now tolling the funeral bell for China's freedom. Some believed that Hong Kong would be colored red after 1997. That was the greatest fear of the intellectual community. That was why the uproar in the intellectual community could be heard all over the world; that was why the students had poured out of their classrooms again. Tiananmen Square had once more become the symbol of their struggle.

Hansen switched on the television set. Sure enough, the propaganda war had already started. The commentator was attacking "spiritual contamination," warning that America had started a "spiritual and economic Opium War" against China. "In the economic invasion," he said, "junk food like Kentucky Fried Chicken and cheap California wines will be forced on China like opium during the 1840 Opium War with the British; sexually explicit magazines, books, and films will be flooding into China to poison the Chinese mind. Some people call Fang

Lizhi China's Sakharov. Who is Sakharov? A man who has been trying to poison the minds of the Soviet citizens since 1968. That is why the Chinese government prevented Fang Lizhi from attending the American president's banquet on . . ."

Suddenly, the program was cut off and the picture became scrambled. Yun Mei turned off the TV. "Mark," she said, shaking her head. "Now you can see how divided we are. The anti-America and the pro-America factions are fighting and scrambling each other's signals, even at the national broadcasting station."

34

After another tour of Tiananmen Square, Hansen returned to his office to file a report about the surprise editorial in the *People's Daily* and Beijing's media war between the liberals and the hard-liners. Yun Mei had translated a few more articles and had gone to take care of a few personal chores. She had promised to be back to do more translations. They had planned to have dinner in a restaurant that, according to Yun Mei, could be material for another article.

The more he and Yun Mei were together, the more he found her services invaluable. During his previous visits in 1981 and 1983, he had only seen the surface of the drab city—the same department stores on Wang Fu Jing that displayed Parisian fashions, which the natives could only gawk at. The big news that all the foreign correspondents chased had been Arthur Miller's directing of his *Death of a Salesman* in Chinese, the Italians' remaking of Marco Polo's adventures, and Elton John's appearance in a Mao jacket, which had become a photographer's delight. Beijing had hardly become a real window on China; few foreigners had delved under the surface and researched the heart and soul of this mysterious city. Without a knowledgeable guide, a foreigner could only see the cosmetic showcase allowed by the government.

He felt extremely lucky that he had employed someone like Yun Mei, bold and willing, who had opened many secret doors and windows and introduced him to a complicated society full of odd customs and traditions and hidden emotions. With her, he had examined relics of Genghis Khan, the Mongol warrior who had become a Chinese emperor in 1215 and had almost conquered Europe. It was the khan who had opened the silk road and started trading with the outside world; it was Marco Polo who had traveled to China and marveled at the Chinese inventions of gunpowder, paper, printing machines, and paper currency. Going native, he had discovered the Chinese northern foods, jiaozi, laobin, and noodles, which he had taken back to Venice and renamed ravioli, pizza, and spaghetti.

While in China, this Venetian adventurer had not only landed a job in the palace, but had sewn many wild oats in Chinese soil. Even today, many Chinese with large noses were reputedly the descendants of that Venetian merchant. Hansen had even interviewed a few of them.

Yun Mei had told him that not all the large noses in China were related to Marco Polo; many were the offspring of thousands of Jewish immigrants who had settled in China, as they had in Russia and Eastern Europe. The only difference was that China had absorbed them all, and the melting pot had produced nothing except some large noses.

Recently, when he and Yun Mei had revisited the Forbidden City, she had given him the most vivid picture of Tse Hsi, the notorious empress dowager who had plundered the Treasury. She had stolen the money earmarked for China's modern navy to build her Summer Palace; she had her own niece murdered by having her thrown into a well; she had slept with many handsome young actors; she had carried out the annual act of mercy by releasing thousands of caged birds, which were promptly recaptured by her eunuchs so that Her Majesty could release them again the next year. With those colorful tales, Hansen found the revisit to Tse Hsi's Forbidden City doubly fascinating.

Yun Mei had helped him in many other areas. By explaining the intricate and hard-to-pronounce street names in Beijing, she had made them easier to remember and to find. Knowing the meaning of those names, he found that Beijing had really been designed in an orderly fashion. The large boulevards had been laid out like a chessboard. The major east-west boulevard was Chang An, the Avenue of Eternal Tranquillity. He had always had trouble with one tongue-twister, Chong Wen Men Wai Dajie, an important, much traveled road. Since Yun Mei had translated it, he found it simply meant "the Avenue outside Chong Wen Gate." Most of the important street names included directions. Only the hutungs, or lanes, were a total puzzle, but Yun Mei seemed to know them like the back of her own hands.

This evening, Hansen wanted to have a change of pace and get away from the student problem for a while. He had suggested that they go back in time for a few hours and totally relax.

Yun Mei was efficient and thorough. She called and said that to save time she would be outside the hotel in five minutes. He went down in five minutes, and there she was, waiting at the curb with her little umbrella hanging from an arm and her briefcase clutched in her hand. They walked to his car.

"Where are we going?" he asked.

"Did you say you want to go back in time for fifty years?" she asked.

"Oh, yes." He smiled, starting the car. He followed her directions, and soon the car entered the intricate little hutungs. Some lanes were cobblestoned, many were still unpaved, full of holes. The low brick houses with black tiles and vermilion doors were aged, whitewashed walls were peeling and cracked. Dirty-faced children in colorful clothes chased each other, laughing and screaming. Hansen honked merrily, like all the Beijing drivers; he patiently braked and accelerated, shouting greetings and warnings in Chinese. Some urchins ran after the car laughing and yelling, "Son of a gun!" "How you do!" "Motherfucking good!"

Weaving in and out of the hutungs, they finally reached a gaudy restaurant called Su Ho Yuan in a massive walled building with four houses on a huge courtyard. The front double door was open. Inside the yard, dozens of people in rattan chairs were watching an opera on a little stage. Two actors in colorful costumes were singing to the beat of a four-man orchestra—a gong, a drum, a Chinese clarinet, and a *fu chin*, the two-string Chinese violin.

"Birthday celebration," Yun Mei said as they entered the main building in the yard that faced the entrance. The hall was full of people dining at round tables. There were numerous small private rooms on the sides, each bearing a gilded name above the curtained door. The restaurant was brightly decorated with red and green lanterns, crowded, noisy, and warm. Uniformed waiters were darting about, carrying food, drinks, and hot towels. A smiling maître d' in a long gown greeted Hansen and Yun Mei with little bows and guided them to a private room named Moon Palace.

A waiter came in with tea, hot towels, and an impressive menu. Yun Mei opened it to a page full of strange names. "This page is designed for the Spring Festival," she said. "For good luck, they change the names of the dishes." She read out a few dishes and translated them; all sounded like poems. Chicken was no longer chicken but phoenix; snakes became dragons. She said that the restaurant was recently opened by an enterprising family. It catered to people who wanted to go back in time and enjoy a few hours of nostalgia. She ordered three dishes and a jar of white rice wine.

There was a lot of shouting in the next room. "Finger-guessing game," she said. "Do you know how to play?"

"Teach me," he said.

She filled two cups with the warm rice wine, then flung two fingers at him and shouted, "Five sons pass the imperial examination!"

"What do I do?" he asked.

"Put out any number of fingers on one hand and shout a Chinese phrase with a number in it. If the combined number of our fingers coincides with the number you've shouted, you win and I drink. The one who gets drunk first is the loser. Shall we try?"

Hansen knew a few Chinese phrases with numbers in them. He flung out two fingers and shouted, "Five generations under one roof."

Yun Mei put out two fingers and shouted, "Prosperity in four seasons!" She won.

After a few more games, Hansen had exhausted his Chinese phrases. He put out a fist and shouted, "My two aching feet," and won. They laughed and played the game until the waiter brought in the food.

She filled his bowl with a thick soup called Phoenix longevity soup made of chicken claws and turtle meat, turtle being the symbol of longevity.

Besides the soup, she had ordered two ordinary dishes, pork and chicken. He was thankful. He had attended elaborate Chinese banquets before and had dreaded bears' paws, sea slugs, and other weird dishes. Once he had eaten a delicacy called bull whip stewed in miracle grass. When he learned it was a bull's penis stewed in herbs, he had had to gulp down some strong tea to suppress his rising nausea.

In the next room, there was a disturbance; it sounded like an argument. "This was how a successful dinner party ended in the old days," Yun Mei said with a little laugh. "Everybody is fighting to pay the bill. It's up to the waiter to decide whose money to take. The one who pays gains a big face. Listen again."

Hansen listened. The people next door were leaving. Someone shouted at the top of his voice, "See the guests off! Mr. Wong has tipped twenty-three yuans! Thank Mr. Wong!" Immediately, several other voices echoed, "Thank Mr. Wong!"

"That's the waiters," she said. "An age-old custom."

When Hansen and Yun Mei were leaving, he also heard the waiters shout how much he had tipped. He shuddered.

"You have nothing to be ashamed of," she said, laughing. "You've tipped even more than Mr. Wong."

Back at the Beijing Hotel, Yun Mei translated two more articles, and Hansen finished a report on Beijing nostalgia. It was about ten o'clock when they finished. Night in Beijing was day in New York. He decided to call his head office. He talked to his editor, Jim Hawkins, who praised his latest pieces on the student movement, especially his report on the change of attitude of some of his Chinese friends, who had suddenly become cool and distant; some had begun to support the government line to save their own necks. Hawkins wondered if Chinese history was repeating itself.

He said that during Mao's declining years, Mao was bedridden, hardly able to articulate words; the Gang of Four, especially Jiang Qing, his wife, almost seized power, manipulating the party and the government in Mao's name, murdering and imprisoning thousands of their adversaries. Was Deng Xiaoping suffering the same fate in his last days? Hawkins wanted Hansen to arrange an interview with Deng, or at least with Yang Shangkun or Li Peng, the so-called Three Musketeers of Zhong Nan Hai.

"I'll try," Hansen said, "but don't hold your breath."

"Do your best, Mark," Hawkins said. "Find out directly from the top leaders what is really going on. We depend on you to beat the competition to the punch. And we all appreciate your details, full of atmosphere, a lot of local color. Do you still have that helpful Chinese gal?"

"She's my source of atmosphere and color. She's right here. Yun Mei, say hello to my boss, Jim Hawkins."

Yun Mei picked up the extension and greeted Mr. Hawkins.

"Miss Yun," Hawkins said warmly, "Mark has the highest praise for you and your help. We here at the head office all owe you a big thank-you. Keep up the good work! Tell Mark to give you a big hug for me."

Hansen heard the request. As soon as they had hung up, he gave Yun Mei a big, long hug. As he felt her soft yielding body and her tickling fragrant hair, an uncontrollable desire for her surged. Forgetting his own professional code, he kissed her on the mouth.

The kiss caught her by surprise. But she was more surprised to find herself responding to it with equal passion. When Hansen started moving his hands downward to massage her hips and thighs, she felt her heart melting. Oblivious of everything but him, she allowed him to carry her to the bed.

It was intense and noisy, the bed shaking. When it was over, she lay beside him, thinking. In the dim light, Hansen looked exhausted and relaxed; despite his long nose, he was lean and handsome. His head, framed by the soft cream-colored pillow, looked like a Roman sculpture. Feeling the warmth of his body, Yun Mei remembered how tightly she had clutched him and how she had wished she could swallow him whole and keep him in her forever. He was so different from the other two lovers she had had in the past. They were men of flowery words, in action only a quick slam-bang. Perhaps that was why she had not fallen in love with either of them.

But with Hansen she worried. She recalled that her friend Lily Liu had told her, "Don't ever fall in love. It's dangerous." Lily had fallen in love with a foreign correspondent. One night, after lovemaking, she had asked, "What if I'm pregnant, John?"

John had kissed her and said, "If not, we'll do it again and again until you are." But he had never mentioned the words Lily had wanted to hear the most, "Let's get married." As a foreign correspondent, John was transferred often. After he was gone, Lily had never heard from him again.

Yun Mei looked at the soundly sleeping Hansen and felt an ache in her melting heart. She climbed out of the bed, got dressed, and left quietly. Pedaling home on her bicycle, she saw herself as a poor girl looking sadly at a diamond in a locked case . . . something she could never own.

"Don't fall in love," she told herself, pretending that nothing had happened. She blinked a few warm tears out of her eyes and pedaled energetically, trying to forget.

35

Tiananmen Square was lively again, but the mood was solemn; the smile, the gaiety, found during the previous demonstrations had all disappeared. Two thousand students started a sit-in in front of Zhong Nan Hai. Some of them shouted slogans and demanded that Li Peng come out to talk to them. When Mark Hansen and Yun Mei arrived, the students were chanting, "Li Peng, Li Peng, come out!"

The crowd was growing rapidly; there were individual orators giving antigovernment speeches. Hansen listened to the nearest one, who was demanding the kind of democratic reforms that were advocated by Fang Lizhi. Meanwhile, a government loudspeaker overhead began to drown out his speech; it urged the students to go home. It said that rebellion against authority was fine in the past, but was no longer permitted.

Hansen and Yun Mei moved to the base of the Monument to Communist Martyrs, where another man was shouting in a loud but cracked voice, demanding the resignation of the Politburo. Nearby, a group of students was singing the "Internationale." A third man, standing on a stool, was talking about Hu Yaobang. His listeners cheered and called for Deng Xiaoping to reassess Hu's place in history and apologize to Hu's spirit for having mistreated him. Some chanted, "Little Bottle, Little Bottle, wake up! How muddleheaded you are!"

A short distance away, an older man—perhaps a professor—was lecturing the crowd. "Someone says that the only good communist is a dead communist. Not so! There are countless good ones. Zhou Enlai and Hu Yaobang were capable and humane. Because they did not believe in dictatorship, they did not become dictators. But they were hampered by dictators. That's why their noble ideals could not be realized. Today we see what is ailing China. We are here not to oppose communism. We are here to plead reform!" He ended his speech by leading the crowd to shout some anticorruption slogans and sing the "Internationale."

Hansen recorded as many speeches as he could, noises, slogans, and all. He wanted to capture the atmosphere, the mood, and the various opinions of the rather divided crowd. Yun Mei was also busy taking notes. In the afternoon, the crowd grew ugly; their attack concentrated on the *People's Daily*, which had published the controversial editorial. They demanded that the government answer the slander. Using loudspeakers, the Beijing government answered them by banning public gatherings, including giving speeches, collecting donations, and handing out leaflets. Soon thousands of students and supporters burst past the police line and once again occupied the entire Tiananmen Square. Thousands of workers also joined the crowd, pushing through the police lines to distribute food and water to the students.

There was talk of a military crackdown. When Hansen saw a line of trucks full of soldiers beginning to circle the square, he looked at Yun Mei apprehensively. "What's going on?"

"Let's get out of here!" she said.

They hurried out of the square, but at Chang An Boulevard a line of police stopped them. One officer demanded Hansen's tape recorder. When Hansen refused, the officer grabbed it, and another officer pushed him away. "Go, go!" they yelled at him. Yun Mei was struggling with a policeman who tried to wrestle her notebook away. As Hansen reached her, one of the policemen hit Yun Mei with his stick. She staggered, and Hansen caught her. Controlling his anger, he helped Yun Mei out of the square.

A large bump was growing on Yun Mei's head. "Let me

take you to a hospital," he said as they walked toward his car. "Where's the nearest one?"

"No," she said quickly. "It's only a bump. Take me home. I'll put a compress on it."

"My grandmother said the best cure for a bump is a raw steak."

"Who can eat a steak?" Yun Mei said with a grimace. "All I need is an aspirin and sleep it off."

"The steak is not for eating," he said. "You put it on your head to reduce the swelling. You can eat it later."

"If you want to buy a steak in Beijing, you have to know the mayor or the police chief. I don't think they'll help you after they've confiscated your recorder and my notebook."

Hansen forgot about the steak and drove Yun Mei home. He walked her to the door of her apartment building. At the door, he held her shoulders, looked into her eyes, and confessed, "I love you, Yun Mei. This is something I've wanted to say for a long time."

She looked at him tenderly for a moment. Just as he was about to kiss her, she turned away and ran into the building. He stared after her, puzzled and hurt.

Back at the Beijing Hotel, Hansen called her. The phone kept ringing. Giving up, he called Edward Robinson, the cultural attaché. "Ed," he said, "what are the chances of a foreigner marrying a Chinese in this country?"

"If Cupid hits a bull's-eye," Robinson said. "Chances are good, but the road is distant and hazardous."

"What do you mean?"

"Have you heard the Chinese legend 'The Ox Boy and the Weaving Girl'?"

"No."

"Ask a Chinese friend. He'll tell you. Why do you ask?"

"Never mind."

"Mark, if you've been hit by Cupid's arrow—God forbid—take the next flight out of the country. It's almost an impossible dream that you two will ever walk to the altar. Remember that New York girl who taught English in Hunan? She fell in love with one of her students. For three years, they hacked through red tape trying to get married. They didn't tie the knot until finally Deng Xiaoping pitied them and approved it. That's how hard it is. I haven't heard of an easier case. Usually, it winds up with the guy giving up, and the girl going back to Mother with a shattered heart."

Hansen called Do Do and Jimmy. They were not in. Disheartened, he went downstairs and ordered a whiskey on the rocks. Every night foreign tourists and businessmen relaxed in the lobby, chatting and drinking. A man sitting nearby approached him.

"Say, you look pretty depressed. If you're worried about China, you've got plenty of company. No amount of whiskey has drowned my worries yet."

Hansen forced a smile. "China will take care of itself. My trouble is personal."

"I can't see how you can separate the two."

"By the way," Hansen said, "have you heard of the Chinese legend 'The Ox Boy and the Weaving Girl'?"

"That has something to do with their Moon Festival," the man said. "An ox boy falls in love with a weaving girl in the moon. They can't get married. Too far away. A trillion birds pity them. They build a bridge between earth and the moon so the ox boy can go visit his gal. Something like that. A silly love story. I like *Romeo and Juliet* much better."

36

Do Do opened a letter without a return address. It was addressed to both of them. Inside, she found a short message scribbled on a napkin: "Dear Jimmy and Do Do, Don't let Raymond return to Hong Kong. This is important! Explain later. Love, Pang Sin.

Do Do gave it to Jimmy, who was watching television. "Read this, Jimmy," she said. She never took Pang Sin seriously, always suspecting there was a shady motive in whatever he did.

Jimmy's reaction was the same. He read it and ignored it. The front-page news in the morning paper was STUDENTS POLICE CLASH. She read the news. It reported that in the confrontation, scores of troublemakers had beaten up some policemen. Four were seriously injured and hospitalized. There was no mention of the student injuries.

Do Do had witnessed the clash. What she remembered vividly was the police beating the students, who were unarmed. Not one policeman was bloodied. "Goddamn liar!" she cried angrily, smashing her teacup against the wall. Jimmy had never seen her so angry, her face white and her hands trembling. She was unable to speak for a few moments. He thought she was going to do something irrational, such as seeking out foreign correspondents and telling them horror stories about police brutality.

"Do Do," he said as he picked up the pieces of the teacup.

"I believe in the old saying 'Think three times before you act.' This is the only way to avoid regrets."

"What is there to regret?" she said. Without another word, she picked up her handbag and left.

At Tiananmen Square, she joined a group of protestors who were also furious about the distorted report. People were still boiling about the previous controversial editorial; the new report was like salt rubbed into an old wound. Hu's death had also been kept alive. Tens of thousands of students from different universities roamed the square, shouting slogans, waving banners and portraits of Hu. A long streamer called for Hu's rehabilitation.

She followed a group of students to the Great Hall of the People, where the student leaders had sunk on their knees on the steps of the ornate building and were pleading for Li Peng to come out and have a dialogue. An official finally came out and told them that the premier was unavailable. Do Do felt angrier than ever and wished someone would throw a firebomb through the gate. She took a lot of notes, scribbling rapidly about what she had seen and heard, and what she felt. She would have everything published one way or another.

She saw Jimmy jostling in the crowd, trying to approach her. She looked away. They had argued a lot lately, and she wanted to avoid another confrontation in public. While the three student leaders were still pleading with the official, a few others were getting more militant, loudly demanding that all the old hard-liners in Zhong Nan Hai resign. One shouted, "Tell the old fogies that the people are angry everywhere— Nanking, Changsha, Guangzhou, and Shanghai! Tell them to wake up! Or else they must be responsible for the consequences!" A second man shouted, "Li Peng, come out!" A third waved a fist and screamed, "Little Bottle, why are you so stubborn? Come out and talk to us! People have rioted in every city. Are you deaf and blind?"

She saw Jimmy touch the man's shoulder, trying to stop his screaming. "Wei, Older Brother," he said, "Students will not riot. We must keep this demonstration nonviolent."

The man turned to him and screamed, "How else can you get them out from their lion's den? They refuse to talk to us!"

When Jimmy tried to argue, he was shouted down. Then two men grabbed him and started pushing him away. Do Do could not stand watching the men rough Jimmy up, yet she herself was getting more militant. Clutching her notebook tightly, she left Tiananmen Square.

In the afternoon, three thousand students started a hunger strike in the square. Jimmy did not see Do Do all day; he prayed that she did not join them. In the evening, he cooked several dishes, all Do Do's favorites, hoping she would come home for dinner. He was ready to apologize and acknowledge the fact that he, too, was stubborn. She did not come home.

He called several of Do Do's friends. Nobody had seen her for days. He started to go to Tiananmen Square to see if she had joined the hunger strikers, but almost immediately he changed his mind. He did not want to be shouted down and roughed up again. He suspected that some of the protestors were not students, but he had no idea who they were. They looked like street toughs with tattoos.

After he had eaten his dinner alone, Joan Wu, one of Do Do's co-workers at Radio Beijing, called saying that dozens of her colleagues, including Do Do, had been enlisted as interpreters for Mikhail Gorbachev's state visit.

"Who enlisted them?" Jimmy asked.

"Well, the movement," Wu said. "She told me to tell you not to worry."

"Joan," he said, "please ask her not to talk to foreign correspondents. Between you and me, she is too heated up and too straightforward; she might say things that are untrue. And tell her that my father has invited us to Hong Kong for a vacation. Where is she now? What is she doing?"

"Well, some of us have been busy writing slogans in English and Russian. Don't worry, this is a peaceful demonstration. We just want to tell Gorbachev that we are all for his *glasnost* and *perestroika*."

37

On May 17, the square was a sea of colorful banners fluttering in the wind. Raymond Hong carried a large one that read in English, I HAVE A DREAM. Yin Yin and May each carried a flag of the People's Republic of China. By noon, more than a million people had taken to the streets, many joining the students waving flags and banners.

Do Do, wearing jeans and tennis shoes for action, sought out foreigners in the crowd, offered to translate Chinese slogans, and answered questions, urging them to take pictures and write reports. "Winds of Change are blowing in China," she shouted in English. "Thanks to Soviet leader Mikhail Gorbachev! The students have started a hunger strike to bring the message to Deng Xiaoping!"

As she talked, she kept pointing at the banners that said in Russian: LONG LIVE DEMOCRACY! LONG LIVE GLASNOST! LONG LIVE PERESTROIKA! When she shouted those slogans, hundreds of voices joined her.

Jimmy was in the crowd, trying to tell some of his students not to participate in the hunger strike. They were already undernourished, looking pale and gaunt. But they were so excited that no persuasion could sway them. They had vowed to starve in front of Zhong Nan Hai, and to die if necessary.

"It's the most effective weapon in nonviolent protest," one of them told him. "Back off, Professor Hong. It's our fight."

Knowing that there was nothing he could do, he rushed home to make some phone calls. He had quite a few friends working in various government departments. He wanted to monitor the party's leaders' reactions to this unprecedented democracy movement, perhaps the biggest in Chinese history.

Tens of thousand of anxious demonstrators in Tiananmen Square were disappointed when Gorbachev and his entourage were whisked away by government limousines to another destination. He never had a chance to see Tiananmen and the student demonstration, or many monuments that the party leaders proudly regarded as symbols of Communist conquest.

For three days, Jimmy watched Gorbachev's visit on his television set, listened to his ideas, and envied his warmth and charisma. To his pleasant surprise, all the media gave the visitor a straightforward report; even the student protest was hardly censored. The winds of change were indeed blowing through China. In a moment of exhilaration, he wrote a letter to Deng:

Dear Comrade Xiaoping:

Mikhail Gorbachev's reforms are stirring global excitement. This historical meeting between the leaders of our two nations will lay the foundation for world peace.

Here are a few humble thoughts:

1. Gorbachev dramatically altered his country's relations with the West, turning what Ronald Reagan called the "evil empire" into what George Bush hails as a "partner for peace." If everything goes well, Gorbachev will be remembered in history as the man who ended the Cold War.

2. His reforms, including the respect for human rights, have deeply impressed the intellectuals in our country. I am confident that all the Communist countries will step into line and wipe out the hateful term "Communist threat." He will replace "balance of power" with "balance of interest." He will abandon class struggle in search of cooperation and mutual re-

spect. His visit brings a fresh wind that is now blowing over our country. It is regrettable that he has missed Tiananmen Square, where a million people would have applauded him and welcomed him.

Comrade Xiaoping, you are in the position to do the things that Mao Zedong would have loved to achieve if he had lived. Our people are still anxiously awaiting the arrival of the true communist Utopia that is based on peace, harmony, and prosperity.

He signed the letter and mailed it, wondering if Deng would ever receive it.

38

It was a foggy morning. Jimmy went to Tiananmen Square, praying that the hard-liners had yielded to the students' two basic demands . . . freedom of speech and the stopping of corruption. He found the square filled with excited young people. Loudspeakers from both sides were blaring. Foreigners armed with cameras and tape recorders threaded through the crowds, talking and listening. The hunger strikers had grown to more than three thousand. Part of the square had become a field hospital, with doctors and nurses in white gowns attending the increasingly weakened ones. Those who had collapsed from dehydration were rushed to various hospitals by ambulances, their sirens screaming.

He found Raymond, Yin Yin, and May inside a tent that was occupied by a dozen hunger strikers. May looked sick, her face pale and eyes bloodshot, almost lifeless. She had refused even water. When a doctor attempted to send her to a hospital, she refused.

Jimmy tried to persuade Raymond to leave the tent, but he was shouted down by other strikers. "Raymond," he persisted, "come with me. You have no business here. You are not even a Chinese citizen."

"You traitor!" one man said.

"Get out of here!" another shouted.

There were several other hysterical parents also pleading

with their sons and daughters to end the strike, but they were all ignored. One young woman told her parents, "Go home! Our demands are not excessive. The authorities will give us an answer soon. Please go home!"

"We have no other recourse," the skinny young man said, his voice so weak that it was almost inaudible.

"That's right," another echoed. "We are doing this in front of the Monument to the People's Heroes and Mao Zedong's tomb. We've all pledged to fast until the government gives us freedom or death. There is no other way!"

One hunger striker struggled to his feet and chanted, "Freedom or death," and collapsed. The student marshals begged the friends and relatives to leave the strikers alone, then cordoned off the area with ropes, only permitting ambulances and delivery trucks to enter. Nearby student leaders huddled over strategy, and media representatives held press conferences.

Do Do was running between two groups, offering the student leaders information. She told them that the government was ready to accuse them of plotting an armed uprising.

"Keep singing the 'Internationale,' " she advised.

The students not only sang the "Internationale" but made banners proclaiming their support of the Communist party. One quoted Mao Zedong, "Whoever opposes the student movement will come to no good end!" Another recited an old quote from Deng Xiaoping: "A revolutionary party must listen to the people, and should never keep people silent."

In a corner of the square, some students had set up a print shop, turning out flyers and handing them to visitors and sympathizers. Some set up rudimentary radio stations to broadcast news of Tiananmen Square and deliver commentaries that alternated with music and songs. Jimmy watched for a while and donated some money to a collection box under a makeshift tent that had been built out of scaffolding and tarpaulins. He was worried about Raymond, wondering how long the hunger strike would last. Were they serious about "Give me freedom or death?" What would he tell Aimee?

He picked his way out of the square where weary students, pale and gaunt, lay sprawled on the cold pavement, some bundled in cheap blankets and padded overcoats, others covered with plastic sheets. Many curled close together to keep warm on the chilly morning.

The cold weather in early summer surprised everybody. Many soothsayers predicted bad news, for the weather was *fan shang*, or unnatural, a phenomenon that always indicated disaster. But the mood was still optimistic. Many students played cards or chess, others practiced English, plucked guitars, and sang both Chinese and English pop songs.

The broad avenues surrounding the square were full of sympathizers who applauded and shouted slogans and flashed V signs with their fingers. Many dropped money into collection boxes and tossed candied, home-made biscuits and rice cakes at the students. Food peddlers declined payment; taxi drivers ferried strikers and marchers free of charge.

More army trucks arrived, but the citizens quickly surrounded them, trying to talk them into retreating. They reasoned with the soldiers, praising their past record and their patriotism. Some army officers even put out their own signs supporting the students. Jimmy was so encouraged that he shook hands with a few army officers, telling them that the wind of change was blowing all over China. It would blow away all obstacles that had hindered China's progress.

Every day, Jimmy monitored information in Zhong Nan Hai through various channels available to him. At home he sat beside his phone, dialing or waiting for it to ring, his hair disheveled and meals unfinished. He had not seen Do Do for days. Party chief Zhao Ziyang had been quiet; from inside information Jimmy learned that leaders in Zhong Nan Hai had been feuding, arguing what to do with the protest.

He was heartened when he heard that Zhao still insisted on a soft approach in dealing with the students. But two days later, on May 19, the news was not good. The hard-liners were gaining the upper hand. It was reported that Deng Xiaoping was getting increasingly impatient. "We cannot retreat," he said. "A retreat of one inch will lead to a retreat of one foot!"

Yang Shangkun, the president, also believed that retreat would mean the collapse of the Communist party and socialism.

But Zhao Ziyang insisted on paying the striking students a

visit. Jimmy rushed to Tiananmen Square to witness the meeting. He found Zhao in one of the makeshift shelters—a bus provided by the Chinese Red Cross. Zhao was so moved by the hunger strikers' plight that with tears in his eyes, he apologized for having come too late.

Jimmy was heartened by such a gesture. Later, he watched a group of student leaders hold an urgent meeting. They resolved to end the hunger strike and call an end to the protest.

Unable to find Do Do or Raymond to tell them the good news, he returned home and called his father. He reported to Charles that in a day or two the protest would be over. He, Do Do, and Jimmy would make the Hong Kong trip in early June, as planned. He also spoke to the hysterical Aimee; he comforted her by telling her that he saw Raymond every day and that Raymond was not involved.

"Where is he?" she demanded. "Why can't I talk to him?"

"He's busy with his girlfriends," he said. It was a lie, but it prevented Aimee from calling every day.

In the evening, while eating a bowl of noodles, he turned on the TV and saw both Li Peng and Yang Shangkun appear on national television. Peng still believed that a handful of people were seeking to destroy the Communist party and the socialist system.

"We must adopt strong measures to end the turmoil swiftly, so we have called in the military!"

"That's not true!" Jimmy found himself shouting at the TV set. "The protest is over!"

He quickly turned off the TV; he couldn't bear to see Li's rigid face and hear his belligerent voice announcing a military crackdown. Feeling crushed, he clutched his head in both hands and moaned. Now the protest would flare up again.

Two armies were called in. Martial law went into effect on May 20, banning public speeches, marches, strikes, class boycotts, and the spreading of rumors. Foreign reporters were barred from conducting interviews. Zhao Ziyang offered to resign.

Jimmy, to his surprise, found that the people of Beijing were defying the martial law. Thousands of them took to the streets to block the military advance. Office workers, women with children, elderly men and grandmothers and factory workers stood in the paths of army vehicles and pleaded with the soldiers to retreat. They shouted the praise of the People's Liberation Army. "You are the people's army," they waved and chanted. "Patriotism is no crime!"

Jimmy rode around on his bicycle trying to find Do Do and Raymond. He saw that most of the major roads had been blocked with trucks and buses. People were carting cement blocks, garbage cans, barrels, and pipes, and piling them high at intersections to allow only bicycles to go through.

Jimmy recognized the well-dressed and well-fed units from the 28th Army. They were young and calm, some even friendly. "Don't shoot the people," one woman said, wagging a finger at them. "Go home, comrades! You were people yourselves once, don't shoot them!"

At Tiananmen Square, Jimmy found that thousands of protesters had returned, and the mood was ugly. They had gathered around one of the student leaders, who shouted into a loudspeaker, "We will not retreat! We will not give up our struggle until our demands are met!"

The crowds grew again. From their banners, Jimmy could tell that almost every organization was represented, including the Communist party members. The *People's Daily* published letters from military leaders, calling for martial law to be lifted. One general declared publicly that he would never harm the people. On May 23, more than a million people paraded to demand Li Peng's resignation. They accused Li of staging a military coup against Zhao Ziyang. Rumors were flying. Jimmy learned that Li had been shot and Zhao was on his way to a political comeback. The rumor brought cheer to the entire city. Thousands of students were again leaving the square, exhausted, filthy and starving. But the students from other provinces poured into Beijing by trains and buses; they immediately filled the square again, and the greatest student movement in China's history went on.

At night, Jimmy listened to the BBC and the Voice of America to get unbiased reports; he was constantly on the phone talking to friends and colleagues, trying to find out what was really going on. Most of his friends were optimistic; the hard-liners would resign, they said. It was only a matter of time. According to inside information, a member of the Old Guard had praised Zhao Ziyang and declared that the government could not function without him. Another powerful member of the Old Guard also lobbied to reject Zhao's resignation.

Jimmy listened to rumors about the bickering in Zhong Nan Hai with mounting anguish. Everybody was waiting for Deng Xiaoping to speak. The fence-sitters were anxious; they wanted to know Deng's decision so they could swing with the wind.

Do Do finally returned home, haggard and exhausted. But she was not optimistic. She said that new troops had arrived. They were units from the 27th Army. They were farm boys from faraway provinces, highly indoctrinated and having no relatives or friends in Beijing. They despised intellectuals.

Jimmy offered her a cup of coffee, happy that she was no longer fiery and excitable. "Do Do," he said, "despite the saber-rattling, Zhong Nan Hai is changing. I've heard that many hard-liners are changing their minds. Some of them even lobbied against Zhao Ziyang's resignation."

"That's not good news," she said. "They all hate his guts. My source heard one of them say, "If we let Zhao go, we'll make a hero of him, like Hu Yaobang. That will further shore up his popularity. He made a mess . . . let him clean up the mess.' "

"What about Deng Xiaoping?"

"Deng is the number-one hard-liner," Do Do said. "He always has been. We ought to find Raymond and send him back to Hong Kong as soon as possible."

"Where is he? I looked for him all over."

"He could be in one of those hundreds of tents in Tiananmen," she said. "Nobody is safe. There is a three-way war going on. I hear there's a third force trying to stir things up. They have organized the unemployed, the street thugs, and a lot of ex-Red Guards to beat up army officers in the name of democracy. All they want is a bloody clash between the government and the people. When the government is weakened, they will take over. There's a rumor that they will enthrone Jiang Qing as the new empress dowager of China."

Jimmy shook his head. It was incredible that Do Do should believe such nonsense. But he kept quiet.

39

At noon, Mark Hansen had had a quick lunch of bean milk and meat-filled buns at a food stall in the Farmers' Market. He had been calling Yun Mei, but there was still no answer. Do Do had told him that Yun Mei might have gone to Shanghai to visit her aunt. She used to take such a trip during Chinese holidays, or when she was unhappy. Mark was still puzzled by her sudden change of attitude.

For two weeks, he worked alone, missing her weird tales, laughter, and companionship. He had meant to discuss with her his future and ambition, and her possibility of visiting America. Several times the word *honeymoon* had almost popped out, but each time he had swallowed it, thinking it was premature to mention it. Perhaps he should have proposed marriage on that day instead of simply saying, "I love you." He had been told that Chinese women were more practical; they simply could not separate love and marriage. If a man offered one without the other, they would retreat without explanation to avoid getting hurt. If that was the case, the Ox Boy and Weaving Girl theory did make some sense. A trillion birds building a bridge from earth to the moon was indeed an impossible dream.

With his new camera and new tape recorder, he visited Tiananmen Square every day. The mood in Beijing changed so often that he was unsure if the government would yield to the

252

students' demands. Fresh troops had moved into the city, occupying many strategic areas. The international airport, several buildings that housed the *People's Daily* and Radio Beijing, had all been seized and many workers dismissed. There was a renewed wave of unrest in the entire city. Thousands of students still remained in the square, giving hysterical speeches and shouting slogans; thousands of ordinary citizens had also returned to show solidarity. He saw three men climb a ladder and throw paint on the portrait of Mao Zedong that hung permanently on the Gate of Heavenly Peace. To his surprise, some students grabbed them and handed them over to the police.

He slept fitfully, like everybody else. One moment he was exhilarated, the next he was full of uncertainty and fear. As a reporter, he was supposed to be objective, writing with an unbiased mind. Why was he so involved emotionally? Was it because of Yun Mei? He talked to some other foreign correspondents. They were all full of apprehension. "The unrest is bubbling like boiling rice gruel," Edward Johnson at the embassy told him. "It might boil over at any moment. If there's anything I can do, don't hesitate to call."

Johnson was a good friend; they had been raised in the same neighborhood in Berkeley and had gone to UC Berkeley during the same years. It was comforting to think that he had such a good *gwansi* in the embassy, that almost all grapevine information was only a phone call away. According to Johnson, there were two schools of thought about the turmoil. One was that it was a power struggle, pure and simple. The other was that a third force was trying to stir things up to undermine the government and divide the party. No matter what happened, the students would be the victims. The brutal Cultural Revolution was a good example. It had been created by Mao and the Gang of Four to consolidate their own power. The rightists had won, but millions of students, used as tools, had abandoned their education for more than ten years, a terrible national tragedy that had set China back decades.

Getting more deeply involved emotionally, he was heartened to see thousands of citizens blocking the streets to prevent the troops from entering Tiananmen Square. Pennants and banners of all colors and sizes once again fluttered in the breeze.

Some of the students were on the outskirts of the crowd lecturing the soldiers in the army trucks. A few even were making friends with the officers, who showed support by making victory signs. Hansen took pictures of citizens offering meat buns and water to the soldiers and praising their patriotism.

While snapping pictures on Chang An Boulevard, he saw a huge white statue being rushed to Tiananmen Square on a cart pulled by hundreds of students. Some of them were shouting, "Long live the Goddess of Democracy!" He looked at it closely. It was a gigantic Chinese version of the Statue of Liberty, made of Styrofoam and covered with plastic. He ran after it, snapping a series of pictures.

At Tiananmen Square, the students erected the statue to thunderous applause. Facing north toward the portrait of Mao Zedong on the Gate of Heavenly Peace, it stood proudly with its raised torch, surrounded by hundreds of white and blue tents and colorful banners.

The upper balustrade area was now jammed with people waving and shouting. Their demands were the same: "Implement democracy!" "End censorship of the press!" "Dismiss Li Peng!" and "End martial law!"

Suddenly, a man jumped down screaming, "The tanks are coming! The tanks are coming! Get out! Get out!"

In the distance, guns were heard. People started running. A few students mounted benches and stools to urge the protestors to stay. One student leader argued with another, trying to shut him up. Hansen could not hear exactly what they were saying, but it was clear that there were two factions among the protestors, each espousing a different strategy. He was quickly engulfed by people leaving the square. He moved along and joined those who were pouring toward Chang An Boulevard. Gunfire became sporadic; several helicopters hovered overhead; loudspeakers blared messages that drowned each other out.

The street was now packed with people from the neighborhood. There were clashes between angry workers and troops. Many buses had been overturned to block the army vehicles; some army trucks were burning. As Hansen moved along the boulevard, snapping pictures, he saw people tossing Molotov cocktails at army trucks, setting more vehicles on fire.

A short distance away, he saw a skinny young man trying to stop a column of tanks that was heading for Tiananmen Square. Bare-handed, he stood in front of them, blocking their way. The lead tank tried several times to move forward, but the man did not budge. Fearful for his life, Hansen and several others rushed to him and dragged him out of its path just as the tank was about to crush him.

His shirt soaked in sweat, Hansen tried to shoulder his way out of the crowd before the violence spread. While passing an army vehicle, he saw a young man arguing with an officer. From the insignia, Hansen could tell that the officer was a major general. The young man was shaking a finger at him and shouting profanity. Suddenly, the young man slapped the general and spat at him. The stunned officer glared, his nostrils flaring, trying to control his anger. Across the street, a gang of rowdies were beating a soldier with sticks. Several students rushed to rescue the soldier, but they were too late. The unruly crowd hung the dead soldier from the window of an army bus. One of the rioters took out a knife and slashed open his stomach. Hansen heard cameras clicking around him. He looked away quickly and staggered out of the crowd, holding his mouth. He rushed back to his hotel and threw up in the bathroom.

40

The fifteen hunger strikers in the small tent were quiet and gloomy; two of them started groaning. A doctor came in and urged them to sip a bit of water, but they declined.

Raymond avoided looking at them. Every day they looked worse, their cheeks sunken, their eyes red and hollow, and their bony hands trembling. He lay between Yin Yin and May. May, lying on a horse blanket, stared blankly. Yin Yin had been restless, twisting and turning. Now, so weakened by days of fasting, she, too, hardly moved.

Raymond was the only one still energetic, for he had carried candy bars in his pockets. Late at night, he forced a bar into Yin Yin's still hand, and a few minutes later he heard her unwrapping the candy under her blanket. He tried to put a candy bar into May's hand, but she pushed it away angrily.

After the area was cordoned off with nylon ropes, there were no more visitors except the few doctors and nurses monitoring the hunger strikers' general condition. The smell of alcohol and urine was getting stronger, and noises outside the tents louder. Loudspeakers kept blaring. Slogans became more negative. Besides demanding the resignation of Li Peng, some insulted Deng Xiaoping personally with teahouse humor.

Raymond felt increasingly uncomfortable as he lay between his two girlfriends. At first, he had accompanied them during the strike mainly for excitement. Now he realized that he had done so to support May. He wondered if Yin Yin had joined him just to keep him company.

"Raymond," Yin Yin whispered, "are you hungry?"

He was so famished that he started having stomach cramps. "Why do you ask?"

"I miss red-hot beef noodles," she said. "Meet me at the latrine. I know where to go."

Pretending to go to the bus where temporary toilet facilities had been set up, they left the tent quietly, one at a time.

The temporary noodle stand on Chang An Boulevard was doing a good business. After waiting almost half an hour, they were served two bowls of noodles heaped with red-cooked beef and red-hot peppers. They ate ravenously and gulped down many cups of strong tea.

"Without your candy bars, we'd have thrown up everything we're eating," Yin Yin said gratefully. "Still hungry?"

"How about you?"

"Not for food," she said, giving his hand a meaningful squeeze.

Raymond felt a thrill running through his body. Such a verbal hint was more exciting than kissing or hugging. It always aroused him, causing him embarrassing moments when he stood up. "What do you have in mind?" he asked.

"Call your brother," she suggested. "See if they are home."

Two hours later, they lay beside each other in Jimmy's bed, listening to the Voice of America on the radio. It was giving a blow-by-blow account of the democracy movement in Beijing. Yin Yin nestled against him, her nude body still wet with perspiration, her breathing still heavy, as if she had just finished a marathon race. Raymond always enjoyed Yin Yin's passion, wondering if she was blessed by God with extra capacity for enjoyment. Normally, if time allowed, they would repeat the act a few times, with variations she suggested. But today he hesitated. He worried about May. The Voice of America was reporting that tanks had appeared in Tiananmen Square and that the warnings from the loudspeakers sounded ominous. Any moment now, blood would flow.

"Yin Yin," he said, leaping out of bed. "We have to go back."

"Go back? Where?"

"Tiananmen Square. May is still there. We've got to get her out!"

They rushed back on their bicycles. The square was in turmoil, with people running and crying; gunshots and ambulance sirens were screaming, carts and bicycles were overturned and abandoned; flags and banners on the ground were trampled.

As machine guns rattled, half a dozen tanks plowed into the square. They first toppled the newly erected Goddess of Democracy, then plowed ahead to crumple the stands and stalls, rolling over abandoned vehicles and crushing tents with people still sleeping in them.

"May, May!" Raymond was frantic, running in search of the tent he had been sleeping in. Frightened people fell as they ran, trampling each other.

Raymond found the tent. There was nothing left but a few hunger strikers' bodies, their flesh and bones crushed into a bloody mass. May's head had been cracked, her brains splattered like bean curd. Raymond crawled to the body, howling.

Yin Yin dragged him away as a second tank plowed into the debris.

With bullets singing past them, they hid behind an overturned truck. Suddenly, Raymond groaned. "I've been hit," he said, sinking to the ground. Yin Yin examined him and found two bullets buried in his buttocks.

"We've got to get out of here," she said, trying to help him up. Pale, bleeding, and half-conscious, he could hardly stand up.

A pickup truck was passing by. Yin Yin begged the driver to take Raymond, but the driver did not stop. Then an ambulance screamed by; it also refused to stop. She propped him against her side and walked. After several yards, both stumbled and fell, crashing into a bicycle cart that was carrying a wounded man. Yin Yin begged the young driver to take Raymond, but again there was no room for another victim.

The driver urged her to escape and save her own life. "Get out of here!" he yelled. "Follow me!"

She ignored him and made another attempt to prop up Raymond. They struggled a few more yards, their clothes soaked with sweat and blood. Finally, a truck picked them up.

Jimmy was searching for Raymond in the crowd. A young man had just finished delivering a speech. Jimmy recognized him as Yan Ping, an instructor from the Chinese Academy of Social Sciences. As he was shaking Yan's hand, gunfire erupted nearby. People screamed and scattered, ducking for shelter.

The killing had begun a few miles west of Tiananmen, along Chang An Boulevard. Bad news traveled fast; Jimmy learned from a man whose motorbike had broken down that the 27th Army was shooting at demonstrators at Mu Xi Bridge.

Jimmy knew that the bridge was one of the main links between the outer city and Tiananmen. It had already been blocked by trucks and buses that the demonstrators had overturned to stop the army vehicles from entering the center of the city.

The shooting stopped momentarily, but the crowd did not thin out. More people came out of the buildings and joined the demonstrators. Jimmy found long lines of disabled trucks and buses that made the city's center almost impassable. While the troops tried to clear the obstacles, they ran around hitting people with truncheons. The infuriated crowd fought back, hurling rocks, bottles, and Molotov cocktails. Many people brought out rugs from nearby buildings, doused them with gasoline, ignited them, and tossed them into the buses. When the buses began to burn, gunfire started again. The troops rushed the crowds, firing their AK-47s.

Chased by the troops, Jimmy ran into a *fu tung* with the crowd from Chang An Boulevard. Shouting angrily, some people braved the bullets and kept throwing rocks and firebombs. Soon Chang An Boulevard was an inferno. Guns cracked and bullets smashed into buildings and crowds.

Jimmy ducked into a small hotel where he found two bodies lying in a pool of blood in the lobby. They had been shot by the state security guards from the street. Bullets had also struck some guests upstairs, and the manager was frantically calling for an ambulance. As the battle raged on the street, several plainclothes guards dashed in, took positions in hotel windows, and fired out into the street. It was so chaotic that Jimmy did not know who was fighting whom. Some security guards seemed to be firing at the troops and vice versa. Some civilians had stolen weapons from army trucks and were now shooting at those in uniforms.

Jimmy rushed out of the hotel. He was shocked to find the street slippery with blood. Many pedicab drivers and freight bicyclists were braving gunfire to save the wounded and the dying. Remembering Do Do, Jimmy tried to return to Tiananmen Square. Bullets were flying, blasts of automatic rifle fire were deafening, hurting his eardrums. Many more tanks had arrived and were trying to push the burning vehicles out of the way. Angry shouts, terrified screams, and the wail of ambulances were heard all around him. Breathlessly, he struggled against the outpouring crowd.

Before reaching the square, he found thousands of people gathered at the intersection of Dong Dan Pai Lo and Chang An Boulevard and rows of buses parked there to block the military vehicles.

An officer standing in a jeep shouted orders, but the soldiers did not seem to hear him. "You idiots!" he bellowed. "Charge! Throw those grenades! Clear the way!"

Nobody obeyed; some soldiers fired into the air. It was not until the tanks had cleared a path that the military vehicles started moving in and some foot soldiers charged into a hail of rocks and bottles from across the street, firing indiscriminately.

The street was now a bloody battlefield. Pedicabs and bicycle-freight drivers pedaled madly, carrying the wounded to nearby hospitals. Jimmy frantically searched for his wife, looking at every bloodied face and asking anybody nearby if he or she had seen a woman of medium height and wearing short hair. He even described her clothes, but nobody paid him any attention.

He decided to follow some of the wounded being carried to a hospital. Most pedicab drivers avoided the Western section of Chang An Boulevard where the brutal 27th Army had started the slaughter. Some troops attacked the crowds from two directions, one column marching on the north from the Temple of Heaven, another slugging its way from the south section toward Tiananmen.

While fleeing, Jimmy saw many people shot in front of the huge Kentucky Fried Chicken franchise, with bodies lying curled in pools of blood. Rescuers were busy putting those who were still alive onto their flatbed pickup trucks. Jimmy asked a truck driver if he had by any chance picked up his wife. The truck driver told him to forget the description. He said that if she had been gunned down, she might be in one of the hospitals. "Climb up and find out," he said.

Jimmy climbed up among the wounded. Some were lying on their backs, some sitting. Many were groaning in pain, and a few were unconscious, all soaked with blood. The stench of sweat, urine, and excrement was overwhelming. When the truck drove north past the museums of the Chinese Revolution and Chinese History, it ran into a metal barrier erected earlier by the angry crowd.

While backing up, the truck driver deftly avoided a collision with a tank that was bearing down from the north. The tank stopped, its tracks caught in the metal barrier. The crowd rushed to it, screaming and shouting insults. Some picked up metal bars and smashed them against its side. The mob quickly piled clothing and blankets on top of its hull, doused them with gasoline, and set it on fire.

"Run, run!" a young man shouted. "It'll explode!"

As people backed away, Jimmy heard the terrified cries of the soldiers who were being incinerated inside the tank.

The truck finally arrived at the Beijing Union Medical College Hospital, where the doctors were frantically trying to save those who were still breathing. The wounded and the dying were carried in on stretchers, bicycles, planks, and portable beds. The dead were dumped in the hallways. The place, jammed with people, was in total chaos; moaning and the shouting of orders filled the air. In the operating rooms, the seriously wounded were lying on the cold floor waiting; some were in comas.

Jimmy found Do Do in one of the rooms. With a gaping

hole in her stomach, she was so bloodied that she was almost unrecognizable. Jimmy sank to his knees beside her and held her cold hands, his face twisting in anguish.

"Do Do," he called. She did not respond at first. When she opened her eyes, she barely recognized him.

"Don't go. Please don't go!" he pleaded, tears welling out of his eyes. "Father is waiting for us in Hong Kong, remember?"

She managed a weak smile. "Sorry, Jimmy," she said, her voice barely audible. "I can't make it now."

"Do Do, listen, all these years we have not had a vacation. We're going to Hong Kong."

"We've gone through so much, Jimmy. Now I'm looking forward to eternal peace. . . ." Her voice faded.

"You're all right!" he said, massaging her hands frantically to keep her awake. "You'll get well. Open your eyes! Please keep them open!"

"Remember how happy we were . . . when we rode the train to Beijing? The future looked so bright. Who would have thought . . ." She stopped again, grimacing with pain.

He got up and rushed to the nearest doctor, who was operating on a temporary table made of a door. Jimmy pleaded with him to save his wife's life. "This is an emergency! She's dying."

The surgeon said gently but firmly, "Everybody is an emergency case. She'll have to wait her turn. Sorry."

He rushed back to Do Do, but she was gone. He cradled her in his arms, buried his face in her short hair, and sobbed.

People were still pouring out of Tiananmen Square. Blasts of gunfire were heard sporadically; helicopters thundered overhead; pillars of smoke rose everywhere. Jimmy dashed around calling Raymond's name. Struggling against the flow, he tried to go back into the square, but the crowd, desperately trying to escape, knocked him down.

When the gunfire intensified, he followed the crowd, which quickly dispersed into the numerous *fu tungs* adjacent to the main thoroughfares. The Gobi Desert wind was blowing, churning up debris. He was half pushed by the wind into a small *fu tung* where many people were taking shelter in doorways. Sinking onto a doorstep, exhausted, he tried to blink some dirt out of his eyes. Cans and waste papers, blown by the wind, danced on the dusty ground. A flying piece of paper landed on his leg and wrapped around it.

He had become immune to pain, his emotions dead. He sat in the doorway, staring, his mind blank. He had desperately tried to find Raymond; his voice was hoarse from calling Raymond's name. Now he did not care. At any moment, he himself might die. He had left his fate to God. He even welcomed death.

A gust of wind blew into the doorway. The piece of paper was still clinging to his leg, as if begging him to save it from being blown away.

He picked it up. There was some writing on it . . . a poem, written in a slanting hand with a ballpoint pen:

> Mama, are you looking for me?
> My skull was crushed by a tank.
> Mama, are you calling me?
> My blood has become a rivulet.
> Mama, did you see me?
> I'm lying on the largest square in the world.
> I'm gone, Mama.
> But my love is still with you.
> Please wipe your tears and go away.

41

Pang Sin's wife, Ginger, was planning her thirtieth birthday in her new apartment in Shenzhen, the prosperous economic zone across the border of the New Territories. The penthouse was partially furnished, with a nice view of the skyscrapers in the fast-growing city. She read the guest list to Pang Sin, who was watching the TV news on a sofa nearby. The excited anchorman was almost screaming, reporting that the army had occupied Tiananmen Square; elsewhere in Beijing the troops were still shooting the unarmed people.

"Do you have any names to add to my list?" Ginger asked.

"Don't you want to watch the news?" Pang Sin asked.

"Why should I?" she said with a snort. "I know what is going to happen. Let them fight. My father will pick up the pieces."

"Like the fisherman who caught a dead clam and a dead crane. . . ."

"Pang Sin," she interrupted, her voice impatient, "please answer my question. Do you have any guests you wish to invite?"

Pang Sin had planned not to attend his wife's birthday. He couldn't stand all her chattering women friends who were only interested in gossiping and playing mah-jongg, a game he loathed. He had run out of excuses and he was racking his brains to find a new one. To avoid argument, he tossed out a few names at random.

"By the way," he said, "I have made an important appointment with a foreign businessman in Hong Kong. I'll be back next Saturday at the latest."

"What! That's my birthday!"

"I said I'll be back!"

"Is your appointment more important?"

"All right, all right," he said placatingly. "I'll come back Friday. He's an American businessman, he'll understand."

Back in Hong Kong, lying on his enormous bed, Pang Sin could not fall asleep. He glanced at his watch; it was 1:00 A.M. Tossing in the bed, he was torn between taking a sleeping pill and sneaking into Aimee's room.

Aimee had hinted many times that after midnight she always felt lonely. That was why she played a lot of mah-jongg at the Golden Phoenix. She usually spent weekends at home, for the Golden Phoenix was too noisy and crowded. "Why don't you come to my room and have a drink some time after midnight?" she had said the week before. The invitation had been ringing in his ears all week.

The temptation was so strong that he got up and paced. But as soon as he had put on his pants, he hesitated. Something held him back . . . something deeply disturbing. The house was dark and quiet. Through the window he could see a few lonely lights gleaming in the bay.

He paced the floor trying to make up his mind. He opened the cap of a bottle of sleeping pills several times, but he flopped onto his bed without taking any. While fighting the temptation, he could not help fantasizing about Aimee's panting, her passionate grunting, the warmth of her shapely body, and the explosion of her climax. They were so vivid and real in his imagination that he turned on his stomach and groaned in agony.

The torture became so unbearable that he leapt out of bed, pulled out his suitcase from the closet, and packed. The only cure was to leave, cut the mental burden and be free.

It was almost two in the morning when he drove down the Peak. It was not until he had entered the tunnel on his way to Kowloon that he noticed he was being followed. It was a large black American car, a 1980 Buick. Two men were in the front seat, Panama straw hats pulled down, hiding their eyes. The traffic was light. As soon as he drove out of the tunnel, the Buick sped past him, its taillight blinking, signaling him to stop. He kept driving, ignoring the signal; then he accelerated, watching the car behind. It followed him again, gathering speed. When it was passing him, one of the men pointed a gun at him, ordering him to stop.

Never argue with a gun, he told himself. He stopped on the quiet street, his back tingling.

"What do you want, Older Brothers?" he asked, managing a smile.

"Bean Cake Two wants to see you," one of the men said. "We'll follow you."

At the barnlike building in Kowloon, the men escorted him to Bean Cake's office and turned on the lights. One of them went to wake Bean Cake. The other man stood at the door, his legs apart and his hands in his trouser pockets. Pang Sin sat in the rattan chair in which he had sat many times before. He tapped the arm of the chair with his fingers, trying to appear casual and calm. But fear was gnawing at him, and he could almost guess what Bean Cake was going to say.

Bean Cake came in yawning, a cigarette between his nicotine-stained fingers. The other man followed and stood in a corner, leaning against a wall. He lit a cigarette. Bean Cake did not greet him. He sank into his chair behind the desk, took a long draw on his cigarette, and sighed. "His mother," he said in Cantonese. "I thought we were friends. But you turn out to be a pig. Worse, a skunk who steals from his own mother."

Pang Sin knew the problem, and he wanted to get it over with. "All right, make an offer and we will trade."

"Trade? There's nothing more to trade. We made two deals. You informed the police. You did not know we have spies in the police, did you?"

"Listen, Bean Cake," Pang Sin said, "I'll refute everything

I told them. Both kidnapping and opium smuggling were my inventions to get even with you. I can tell them I was drunk. . . ."

Bean Cake snickered, a dangerous sign.

"What happened to your old Red Guard spirit? We used to make people bash their parents' heads on cement floors without blinking an eye, remember? Suddenly, you are worried about your half brother. You not only threw ten million dollars into the toilet, you set the dogs on me!"

"Let the police take you to court," said Pang Sin, trying to sound sincere and remorseful. "I swear I'll refute everything I told them. They can't pin anything on you. I'll tell them I had a row with you. I was vengeful, a skunk. . . ."

Bean Cake kept snickering. "What do you take me for? A five-year-old child? Did you forget that you've given the dogs a tape? You secretly taped our conversation. That was not nice. Look at this place, all empty. We have to move, to hide, all because of your noble thoughts about your half brother. Before we abandon this place, we have a little ceremony that we must carry out."

He nodded at the two men. One of them grabbed Pang Sin by the arm and the other pointed a gun at his head. "Let's go," the gunman said.

Every Wednesday night Ginger hosted a hen party in her apartment. The guests were most of her friends in Shenzhen, wives and daughters of party members and high government officials. Sometimes relatives from Beijing came to enjoy a few days of sightseeing, savoring the real bourgeois life-style, which they envied.

This evening, Ginger had the living-room furniture removed and turned the spacious place into an intimate little nightclub, complete with colored lights turning and disco music blaring. Those who were tired of dancing could go to the family room to sip wine and gossip and laugh about men in general. Among the guests were some Hong Kong ladies, single and divorced, and a few man-hating spinsters. As the evening dragged on, they all drifted to the family room to gossip, leaving the men in the living room drinking by themselves.

The star of the party was Mona Wong, a Hong Kong actress who had recently been jilted by her American boyfriend. She was so depressed that she kept talking of jumping off a balcony. Ginger gave her a sleeping pill and told her to sleep it off in the bedroom.

In the family room, everybody talked about Mona. "All men are the same," Vickie Mao announced with a hiccup; she was quite drunk.

"Not all men," Melody Wing said. "Only foreign men. If you cut them open, you'll find all shit, no heart."

"I dated one of them," Grace Liu said. "He turned out to be a cat burglar. That's a handsome boyfriend for you."

The gossip and comments went on and on.

"Is Mona all right?" Pat Chang asked after a while. "She has slept long enough."

Ginger became concerned. "You don't suppose she has taken too many of my sleeping pills?"

"Let's go find out," said Vickie, hurrying to the bedroom. The other girls followed.

Mona was lying on her stomach. Ginger sat on the edge of the bed and called to her softly. No response. She shook her and called louder. Still no response. Vickie grabbed Mona's wrist and felt her pulse. Everybody was holding her breath.

"Is it still beating?" Melody asked anxiously.

Ginger opened the drawer of the bedside stand. "Oh, my God! She took the whole bottle! There's a doctor in this building. I'll go get him."

Back in the family room, the girls sat gloomily. They paced the floor. One twisted her handkerchief. Another kept biting her fingernails. They were all impatiently waiting for the doctor's arrival.

The doctor, a roly-poly short man, arrived with a satchel. Without greeting anybody, he hurried to Ginger's bedroom. The girls followed, but the doctor shut the door in their faces.

"Is he a regular doctor?" Vickie asked.

"He's a regular doctor," Ginger said. "His apartment stinks of medicine smell."

"He never smiles," Vickie said. "I don't trust that kind."

"If he's in there more than twenty minutes," Pat Chang said, "I'm going in. Fat men are quickies."

"Oh, Pat," Ginger said. "How can you talk like that while Mona may be dying?"

"The doctor will pump her stomach," Melody said.

"Oh, how embarrassing," Grace said. "I would rather die."

As they talked, the doctor came out. The women stopped talking, holding their breath. The doctor opened the front door and turned.

"Dead drunk," he said. "I suggest strong coffee or ginger-root soup. Lots of it!" Without another word, he marched out, slamming the door.

Soon after the doctor left, the doorbell rang.

A man delivered a gift for Ginger. It was a parcel wrapped in lucky red paper.

Ginger was excited, wondering who it was from. "Open it," the girls urged, all anxious to see what was in it.

Ginger opened the parcel. It was a red lacquered box. When she opened the box, she dropped it and let out a cry of horror. Inside was a bloody human ear packed in cotton. A card said, "HAPPY BIRTHDAY! From your husband."

The girls screamed. Ginger fainted.

42

Charles Hong entered the dark building through the back door about midnight. The driver of his office limousine parked the car nearby and went to sleep. Charles had told him that he would be spending the night in the building. The driver had been flabbergasted, for the building housed the infamous Golden Phoenix. But he was one of those trusted employees whose mouth was forever sealed about his employer's activities. In Hong Kong, a night of debauchery outside a rich man's home was commonplace. Still, a secret visit to the Golden Phoenix by the solid, perfectly behaved Sir Charles Hong was disheartening to the driver. He blamed it on the uncertain future of Hong Kong. Everybody was living from day to day.

Shanghai Mary was waiting in her secret office. Charles's visit was so important to the Alliance that she had instructed her staff to hold all phone calls.

For the first time, Charles looked haggard, as he had not slept well for several nights. The news from China had been bad; his son's phone line had gone dead. Aimee had been hysterical, pacing and tearing her hair, demanding that he send a plane to Beijing immediately to bring Raymond home. His worry about Jimmy and Raymond finally made him come to Shanghai Mary for help.

But he had decided to keep the visit a secret. He did not even tell his wife about his plans. Aimee was too emotional to be of any use. Besides, Shanghai Mary still did not want Aimee to know about her underground activities.

Charles was anxious to know what was going on in Beijing. Shanghai Mary said that the only reliable communications she had from Beijing were from fax machines.

"Come," she said. "Our network of information is the best in Hong Kong."

She took him to a side room where phones kept ringing and machines were humming. Two operators, a man and a woman, were busy working beside two fax machines. Shanghai Mary invited Charles to sit down on a sofa in a corner, then picked up a stack of fax messages and brought them to him.

"We have more than twenty sources of information from China," she said. "They keep us up to date on what is going on, especially in Tiananmen Square. These are the latest reports. After you've read them, we'll talk." She nodded and left.

Charles read the following messages from different sources:

Fierce fighting continues in streets of Beijing, with the demonstrators using bamboo spears, iron bars, and Molotov cocktails; the army using assault rifles, machine guns, and tanks. Corpses litter Temple of Heaven, Chang An Boulevard, and Mu Xi Bridge. Tanks crunched over abandoned vehicles. Blood, flesh, and brains spilled on Jiang Guo Men overpass . . .

Three sides of Tiananmen Square are sealed by army tanks and APC columns. Inside the square, demonstrators are still resisting. One student threw her hands in the air and shouted, "Foreign friends, please tell the world . . ." Before she finished, a volley of gunfire blasted, almost tearing her head off.

At Qianmen, an army officer shot several demonstrators to death. An outraged mob swarmed over him, kicked him to death, and hung him by the neck from the overpass. Cruelty worsened after each accident; hatred between the people and the army intensified as the battle raged.

Local doctors and medics from Hong Kong are trying to save lives under desperate conditions in the sealed square—no water, no medical supplies, no sterilization. Soldiers from the 27th Army have bayoneted several doctors to death for assisting the demonstrators.

In the square, government loudspeakers made a chilling announcement, branding the rioters as counter-revolutionaries attempting to subvert the People's Republic of China and overthrow the socialist system. It is a sweeping statement that automatically condemns all demonstrators to death. Defying orders, many soldiers fired into the sky.

The newest wave of troops seem doped; some are smiling and waving their weapons about, as if they're spaced out. A rumor has spread that the men of the 27th Army have been given amphetamines. They have been told that they need immunization against disease in Tiananmen Square.

Two factions of the students are feuding. One appeals for calm and nonviolence, the other insists on facing death. A mob has prepared more Molotov cocktails. Many have stolen weapons from army tanks. To avoid a bloodbath, the nonviolent students kept singing the "Internationale" over their loudspeakers. When bursts of gunfire started and the tanks rolled into the square, information became hard to get.

The freedom movement is finally crushed in Beijing. Now there are reports that the army is using flame-throwers and blowtorches to incinerate thousands of bodies in the square. Other reports assert that many casualties were taken to a nearby cemetery and cremated. A third report speculated that hundreds of corpses were incinerated in the military-security zone in West Hills. Now it is broad daylight. The mayor of Beijing has announced that more than a thousand soldiers have been killed and wounded. He made no mention of civilian casualties, which, according to Radio Beijing, are in the thousands. Actual numbers will never be known. . . .

Charles stopped reading. His hands shaking, his heart aching with anguish, he returned to Shanghai Mary's office.

43

Mark Hansen wished he could find out what was really going on in Zhong Nan Hai, the stately compound where China's leaders worked. The Forbidden City, the pleasure palaces of all Chinese emperors of Ming and Ching dynasties, had been opened to the public, but the Communist headquarters next door were more forbidden than ever, a mysterious black hole no outsiders had ever visited.

He knew all the problems that had grown out of Deng's economic reforms—rampant corruption, wrong selection of joint-venture partners, overbuilding of luxury hotels and office buildings—yet the shortage of housing for the common people was acute.

He also knew that the problems had become excuses for the hard-liners to wrestle power from the reformers, claiming that China could only be saved by returning to Stalinist policy.

He had made many attempts to interview Li Peng, the premier, Yang Shangkun, the president, and the elusive "Little Bottle," Deng Xiaoping. But all his efforts had been rebuffed.

Everybody was speaking cautiously. Foreigners met Chinese friends who suddenly became deaf and dumb. Nobody wanted to be interviewed. A few liberal Chinese friends talked loudly about supporting the army, as though invisible ears were listening everywhere. He had found Yun Mei, hospitalized for concussion, but he was afraid to visit her again at Fuxing Hospital for fear he might jeopardize her security. Every day he wondered how she was. There was no phone in her ward. When the phone rang, he was reluctant to answer, knowing that it was not Yun Mei calling. His Tokyo office had been pressuring him to leave Beijing as soon as possible, and the hot, humid days of June made his stay more unbearable, but he could not bring himself to leave. He also knew that the longer he waited, the harder it would be to leave. The airport had been jammed with people trying to get out of China.

He avoided venturing out, for Chang An Boulevard leading to the Beijing Hotel was still dangerous. How much he missed strolling the wide, tree-lined boulevards at night when the air was cool and traffic light.

He turned on the TV. The same anchorwoman on the screen was repeating that the government had displayed remarkable tolerance and that no students had been killed. She looked miserable but droned on, saying that only rowdy motorbike riders had been taken into custody, for they roared around town, creating a lot of noise. Hansen quickly turned off the TV, amazed that the government could lie so blatantly.

He worried about Zhau Ziyang, the party chief. It was rumored that he had been arrested. He shuddered when he remembered the fate of Liu Shaoqi, the liberal president who had died in jail during the Cultural Revolution. The fate of many Communist leaders depressed him. Those who supported reform had died in disgrace. How happy Yun Mei had been a few weeks ago when they visited the peasants in Hopei. They had laughed and talked, strolled along the Golden River, the little stream that flowed along the city's perimeter. It was a beautiful moonlit night. Yun Mei, with tears in her eyes, had said that after Liu Shaoqi had been murdered by Mao, his family had scattered his ashes into the Golden River. She had stared at the shallow water and murmured, "Never again, never again!"

Deeply touched, Hansen had said, "Amen!" and prayed that China would never again suffer such madness and repression. Now it seemed that the cruelest history was repeating itself. Poor Yun Mei, he thought. She was probably better off in a coma. Lying on his bed, thinking of her, he felt a tear on his cheek.

A colleague from *Time* called to say that he was leaving for the airport in an hour and asked if Mark would like a ride. He said no, and thanked him. They chatted for a few minutes. The reporter believed that China was now in the hands of five old men who did not know what they were doing; they were pushing the country to the brink of political and financial disaster.

Outside the hotel, most of the roads were still blocked, all the stores closed and lights turned off. The BBC and Voice of America became silent. He missed his morning paper, his daily mail, and his American periodicals. Even the local *South China Morning Post* stopped publishing. The heavy gunfire he had heard the night before was still ringing in his ears. So were the roars of the crowds, the screaming of women, and the terrified howls of children. He wondered . . . if Richard Nixon had not opened China's door, would China be better off?

He tried very hard to cheer himself up with pleasant thoughts. He recalled a bright Sunday morning when he and Yun Mei had gone to church, where many Americans and Europeans went for their weekly service. She was wearing a white summer bonnet and a flowing dress of white crepe de chine, a perfect picture right out of a fashion magazine. He had snapped many pictures of her, and like a fool he had kept the unfinished roll in the camera. They were all lost, seized by the police on the fateful day in Tiananmen Square. How he wished he had those pictures . . . some to frame and some to carry in his wallet.

Many Chinese friends had told him that if the troops started shooting at the students, the whole nation would boil over and the government would collapse. What now? Five old men were still clinging to power, still blaming everything on a handful of troublemakers.

Outside, sporadic shots were still heard. Hansen wondered who was fighting whom. Why did it take two armies to fight such a huge battle against the unarmed students? Why would the People's Army, which always claimed such warm friendship with the people, mow down its own people with machine guns and tanks? What was the true story behind the massacre?

Rumors were flying in the hotel lobby. People clustered in groups, waiting for buses and limousines to take them to the airport. Everybody wanted to get out. An acquaintance told him that another massacre was going on at Beijing University, with soldiers killing students at random. Those same troops had used fragmentation bombs in Tiananmen Square the day before. The noises coming from the street sounded as if the tanks were still trying to blast their way through the barricades of overturned buses and trucks.

He had lost contact with his head office in New York for two days. Before the massacre, he had been offered two choices: leaving Beijing immediately, or sitting in the hotel waiting for the whole thing to blow over. He had chosen the latter without hesitation. He loved China too much to leave. Perhaps he loved Yun Mei too much to abandon her. He wanted to believe, as some Chinese friends had told him, that some bad elements had infiltrated the student movement . . . that the government had to use force to defend itself against hired thugs who had fired at the troops and set fire to the army vehicles. He had listened to so many stories that he did not know what to believe.

But agonizing doubt gnawed at him. Could it be that those Chinese friends had defended the government to save their own skins? There were more than two thousand foreign correspondents in China, and he prayed that one of them would eventually lift the cover and reveal what had really happened.

He turned on his radio again. There was a report from a remote and unidentified station that the army had seized the Beijing Hotel and mowed down many Chinese who had taken shelter in its lobby. He knew it to be a blatant lie. He took comfort in the thought that many negative reports were probably false. The phone rang. It had not rung since morning, when Ed Johnson had called to tell him that there was a chartered plane leaving for Los Angeles that night. He urged Mark to leave. Hansen had told Johnson that he would call back. It could be Johnson again. He picked up the phone quickly.

"Yun Mei is on the government blacklist," a woman said. Her slightly accented voice was low and tremulous. "Get her out of Beijing as quickly as possible!" There was a click; she had hung up.

He called the operator, trying to trace it. He wanted to know if the anonymous call had been real or crank. Then he remembered that Yun Mei had many sources of inside information, provided by friends working in the inner circle of the government. He sat down and tried to calm his nerves. He must remain cool, he told himself, for he was going to make one of the most important decisions of his life.

It was 5:00 P.M. sharp when Johnson rang his room and told him that he was in the lobby. Hansen picked up his two suitcases and rushed to meet him. The lobby was crowded with Hong Kong tourists and businessmen, all waiting for transportation to the airport.

Johnson gestured to him when their eyes met. Without a word, both men walked out. The black Cadillac was waiting a few yards away, its engine running. The Chinese driver, a middle-aged northerner, tall and dark, put Hansen's luggage in the trunk. From the backseat, Hansen could see the little flag that identified the limousine as an official car of the American embassy.

Johnson, sitting beside him, handed a Chinese passport to him. "I've got her a temporary visitor's visa," he said. "This is a little irregular, but what the heck. It's an emergency. Tell the driver where to go. He knows all the little hutungs in Beijing."

As soon as Hansen said Fuxing Hospital, the driver gunned the engine and the car accelerated. He avoided all the roadblocks, squeezed through piles of debris and overturned vehicles, and entered one of the hutungs. From one hutung to another, the car threaded its way, and finally emerged in a wide boulevard. Within twenty minutes, he stopped in front of the hospital.

Hansen rushed in, followed by Johnson. The hospital was full of people, relatives and friends of the wounded and dying. Some of them were still lying in the corridor. Hansen went to the desk. In his best Chinese, he asked for Yun Mei's release. The nurse shook her head, saying that no patient could be released without her doctor's consent. Yun Mei's doctor was in surgery; he could not be disturbed. She was firm and businesslike.

While Johnson, who spoke perfect Chinese, was arguing with the nurse, Hansen went to Yun Mei's ward. The room was so crowded with additional beds that it took Hansen a few minutes to find Yun Mei, whose head was still bandaged and her eyes closed. Her face was pale as a sheet.

"Yun Mei," he said softly, touching her shoulder, "I'm taking you out."

She opened her eyes. The moment she recognized him, her eyes brightened. She tried to greet him, but her voice was almost inaudible.

"Don't talk," he said. He picked her up, blanket and all. As he carried her out of the ward, many eyes followed them curiously. A nurse rushed to them from across the room, calling, "Stop, stop! Who are you? What are you doing?"

He ignored her. He carried Yun Mei past the desk. The nurse ran after him, trying to stop him. Johnson joined them. He stuffed his calling card into the nurse's hand. He told her in Chinese that he was from the American embassy and that he was responsible for Yun Mei's release.

"Send me the bill," he said as he followed Hansen to the waiting limousine.

"The airport," Johnson said as soon as they got into the car. In the backseat, Hansen cradled Yun Mei in his arms. The car plunged into the traffic, its horn blaring. Avoiding the main thoroughfares, it was soon back in the intricate little hutungs of Beijing.

44

Raymond was lying on his stomach. He had been sleeping in this position for almost a week. Two bullets had been taken out of his buttocks. To kill time, he played gin rummy on the floor with Yin Yin in Jimmy's apartment. Each time he won a hand, he slapped the card on the floor and yelled, "Gin!," then grimaced with pain.

"Don't get so excited when you 'gin!,' " Yin Yin advised. "Take care of your behind."

Jimmy was sitting at the kitchen table, listening to the BBC on the radio. When the reporter's voice was scrambled, he switched to the Voice of America. No station was uninterrupted except the local one, broadcasting government propaganda. He switched the radio off, buried his face in his hands, and remained quiet. His shoulders were shaking slightly. Yin Yin glanced at him, knowing that he was trying hard to control his sobs. Since the massacre, he had been suffering waves of uncontrollable melancholy, and he had to hold his breath, waiting for it to subside.

The phone on the kitchen table rang. Yin Yin leaped up to answer. "I'll get it," said Jimmy, picking it up.

It was the mysterious voice with a heavy Shandong accent. The message was precise and firm, almost like an order: "We will take three. Be ready in twenty minutes. Wait for five knocks on your door, two slow and three fast. Don't open the door without this signal." Jimmy sighed with relief. "Yin Yin," he said, "we're leaving. Pack only a few things, no more than two bags each person."

While packing, he turned the television on. It was the same tiresome news program. The anchorwoman from the Central Broadcasting station was repeating herself. "Beijing is calm. Everything has become normal again. There has been no massacre. Only some patriotic soldiers have been wounded by hooligans and counterrevolutionaries."

"She changes her story again," Yin Yin said. "Didn't she say this morning that some soldiers were brutally beaten to death by hooligans? The station even showed a picture of a nude soldier hanging out of a bus window, his stomach cut open, his penis erect. . . ."

Jimmy hushed her. He wanted to listen to the different story.

"But the property damage is enormous," the anchorwoman droned on tonelessly. "Now thousands of the patriotic brave People's Army soldiers are diligently washing and scrubbing Tiananmen Square once again. The government is rolling out the red carpet for those friendly overseas Chinese and foreign friends to return to China."

"Goddamn!" Raymond cursed. "Hundreds of corpses were burned after the massacre by those patriotic People's Army soldiers. Who wants to come back? Gin!" He slammed down a card and grimaced. "Oh, my aching behind!"

Jimmy turned the volume louder. The anchorwoman asked the public to keep calm and to avoid gatherings, private or public. She said that the government encouraged people to report the whereabouts of those criminals and hooligans on the wanted list, even if they had escaped the country.

Within twenty minutes, Jimmy had packed a few essentials in a suitcase and a tote bag. His most treasured possession was Do Do's gift of the little Russian bear, which he kept in his pocket. He had no idea who this mysterious rescuer was. There was a fifty-fifty chance that the rescue was a trap. He decided to take the chance and follow the instructions, leaving their fate to God. Recalling those heated arguments he had had with Do Do while defending Deng Xiaoping, he still felt guilty and remorseful. Her death and her last words pained him doubly because she had been right.

The car arrived on time. The driver was the mysterious caller, middle-aged and swarthy. He wore a baggy Mao uniform and a duck-tongue cap that was pulled down to hide almost half of his face. Discouraging conversation, he put the three passengers' meager belongings in the trunk. He wanted two people to ride in the front beside him, pretending to doze. They put Raymond on the backseat, lying on his stomach. The car, a luxury sedan made in Shanghai, was filthy, covered with dust. But the windshield was clean, obviously washed before it came.

It was getting dark. The car smelled of exhaust fumes inside, and it was noisier than the foreign-made luxury sedans. The traffic was light; there were soldiers standing at intersections directing traffic. The driver avoided them by turning into a hutung. Jimmy was familiar with the area; he knew that the car was going east, on its way to Tianjin.

He did not have to pretend to doze. He was so tired that when he woke up, the car was stopping near the ocean. It was completely dark, with heavy clouds flying low in the sky, an ominous threat of storm. A small light gleamed. A man holding a flashlight was coming up the rocky shore. Below, the roaring waves were pounding on the rocks; Jimmy could feel drops of cold seawater hitting his face.

"I have three," the driver said to the man with the flashlight. Without another word, he took the bags out from the trunk and drove away hurriedly, as though he had just robbed a bank.

The boatman led the way down the bank, shining his flashlight on the rocky path. Waiting on the beach was a small sampan, held steady by a woman and a boy in his early teens. Jimmy and Yin Yin helped Raymond onto the sampan, which took them to a waiting fishing junk about two hundred yards off shore. The boatman tossed a rope to another man on the fishing junk, who held the rope taut while everybody climbed onto the junk, except the woman and the boy. The junk sailed, and the sampan disappeared into the dark night.

There were four other rescued dissidents on the junk. The

fisherman, a tall, weather-beaten man, told his passengers not to talk until the junk had sailed four or five miles from shore. The passengers all huddled in the middle cabin, some smoking and others sipping hot tea. They all looked pale and gaunt, their clothes wrinkled, their hair unkempt and faces unshaven for days. They welcomed the new arrivals and introduced themselves without mentioning their names. A student leader, a scientist, a professor, and a writer. They were all on the wanted list.

Jimmy had no idea who had rescued them; nobody was talking. The fisherman, his wife, and two sons supplied no information, either. Speaking a strange dialect, they sculled and cooked and fed the passengers with smiles.

The cabin was so cramped that the six men and one woman all slept sitting on the two built-in benches. Raymond was made comfortable on an air mattress on the floor. He slept on his side, saying "Ouch" each time he turned. He was cheerful, telling Yin Yin that this escape was like Indiana Jones escaping killers in his favorite movie. Somehow he cheered up the rest of the dissidents, and they all started talking after the junk had sailed all night. At dawn, they saw the first gunboat, a white speedboat armed with a small cannon.

Suddenly, the air became tense and quiet, except for the sound of the waves beating on the hull and the cracking of the cabin beams. Jimmy held his breath, his heart beating faster, gnawed by anxiety. Several dissidents were frightened, their faces pale and eyes closed, expecting the worst. One man said tonelessly that this could be the end of the journey.

As the gunboat approached, an officer and the fisherman exchanged a few code words. To everybody's surprise, the officer waved off the junk, and the gunboat sped away, churning up big waves that rocked the junk.

Raymond cheered and tried to rise to his feet. With a moan, he fell back on the air mattress, provoking some laughter. The professor said that they had finally arrived in safe waters.

The fisherman's wife, a sturdy woman in coarse blue cotton blouse and loose trousers, brought in a large bucket of steaming rice congee and dishes of preserved vegetables. She was followed by her daughter, a pretty girl of sixteen, who carried a basket of rice bowls, chopsticks, teacups, and a large pot of tea. The mother laid the food down on the floor, squatted, and ladled the congee into the coarse bowls, while the girl served them with a closed-mouth smile. In her strange dialect, the mother urged everybody to eat. The passengers did not need any urging; in a few moments the conversation stopped. There was only the sound of sucking, swallowing, and the clicking of chopsticks.

After breakfast, the passengers smiled and became talkative, enjoying, for the first time, freedom of speech. The writer laughed at what he had seen on television—high government officials visiting wounded soldiers, who wore snow-white bandages and crisp uniforms without any visible wounds. They all expressed gratitude for the opportunity to serve their country. The writer said he had been a drama critic; on his scale of one to ten with ten being best, he gave their performances a two minus.

They all laughed. The professor wondered where Deng Xiaoping was. The scientist said he had heard rumors that he was dead. Yang Shangkun, the old general and president, was now in charge. The student leader grimanced when he heard Yang's name. He said that Yang was the most faithful devotee of Mao's adage "Power comes out of the barrel of a gun." He was the one who had ordered the massacre.

The scientist said he had heard that Fang Lizhi, the leading dissident, and his wife had taken shelter in the American embassy. "That's why the soldiers fired on the embassy building. The government wants the couple to be carried out in pine boxes."

The student leader was sure that some troops had been ordered to burn their own vehicles. By destroying hundreds of its own old cars and tanks, and by murdering a few of its own soldiers, the government could show the world how cruel and destructive the rioters were.

"It's all the Little Bottle's idea," the student claimed.

It bothered Jimmy. Deep in his heart, he could never accept such accusations against Deng Xiaoping. Yet the doubt began to gnaw at him. Whenever he visualized Deng, he could see only a kind old man with a benevolent smile. For ten years, he had believed Deng was China's only savior, a patriot who had suffered tremendous ups and downs, who had been jailed and humiliated; his son had been pushed off a building.

Admiring Deng, Jimmy had read about his life. Denied medical treatment for his crippled son, Deng and his wife had massaged him and washed him daily, hoping to restore his severed nerves. During their detention, they had gathered firewood, carried water and night soil, raised chickens and vegetables like the rest of the poor farmers. For relaxation, Deng had played solitaire, taken long walks with his head bent down, his steps slow, a dejected man in deep thought. For a meager income, he had worked, under guard, in a small factory repair shop nearby, using a skill he had learned in Germany. He had known famine, wars, murder, and all kinds of tragedies caused by nature and human cruelty. How could such a man turn around and order thousands of unarmed people massacred? This puzzle caused Jimmy almost as much agony as Do Do's death. It made him uncommunicative; he often sat alone, staring into space in despair.

A seaplane was sighted. It quickly approached the fishing junk. The boatman signaled by waving his arms wildly. The sea was calm, with a few oceangoing ships dotting the distant horizon. Dozens of sea gulls dipping and circling the junk indicated that land was not too far away. When the plane touched down, the boatman maneuvered the junk close to it and helped the passengers climb aboard.

The plane took off smoothly, but the mood was tense inside. When they reached a high altitude, the turbulent air made the passengers more nervous. Nobody knew where they were going. Jimmy simply left his fate in the hands of the pilot, a total stranger who had not even shown his face. Luckily, it was a short ride. Before the plane touched down, he could see from the small window cargo ships, ocean liners, and smaller boats docked along an island full of tall buildings. Across the bay, the land was also crowded with skyscrapers. The harbor was buzzing with activity.

The professor cried out excitedly, "Hong Kong!"

The other passengers all heaved a sigh almost in unison.

Most of them had not visited Hong Kong before, but all of them had friends or relatives in the colony. Everybody smiled and talked again except Jimmy. He and Do Do had planned a second honeymoon in Hong Kong. Now the lure was gone; without Do Do, any place was a lonely place.

Raymond complained that he still could not sit down. He wished there were a miracle cure.

"I've got a miracle cure for you, Raymond," Yin Yin said.

"What is it?" Raymond asked anxiously.

"Just don't sit down," she said, laughing.

The passengers were transported to a building in a windowless van and escorted to a basement through the back door. A big fat lady met them and told them not to worry. But they would have to be in hiding for a few days. She had arranged for them to stay in a rented house. The van would take them there after dark. She said she was still not free to tell them everything and asked them to be patient. She also requested that they stay inside. They were not to write letters or make phone calls.

The rented two-story house was spacious and well furnished, with several bedrooms. Looking out from an upstairs window, the professor said that the skyline looked like that of Kowloon. Later they all sat in the dining room sipping tea and speculating about what was going to happen to China and to themselves. They analyzed the political situation and predicted Hong Kong's future. When they discussed the fateful 1997, silence fell. They were all hit by a gloomy mood and felt that they had not really escaped.

Jimmy was quiet. He sat alone in the large living room and brooded, feeling the little wooden bear that he always kept in his pocket. The rest remained at the dining-room table and aired their anger and frustrations. The phone on the coffee table became a focal point; everyone wanted to lay his hand on it but restrained himself. The biggest change in the house was that everybody had revealed his name.

Raymond had changed. He was serious and mature now, and he participated in discussions. The potbellied Professor Liu was the most talkative. He believed that the Tiananmen tragedy would inspire oppressed people all over the world.

"Mark my words," he said. "In a few years, Marxist total-itarianism will be fighting for survival. The Berlin Wall will fall, the people in Eastern European countries will rise again. The world will find that communism, with all its high-sounding jargon, is actually a system designed to benefit a few dictators." He talked and gesticulated as though he were lecturing in a classroom.

Woo Kan, the student leader, claimed that he and a few others had gone to see Li Peng. Raymond suddenly remembered that he had seen him on TV. Woo Kan, bushy-haired, had been arrogant and impolite; he had shaken his finger at Li Peng and lectured him like a schoolteacher scolding a wayward student. Woo seemed subdued now. He realized that high government officials could not stand losing face in front of millions of television viewers. Raymond told him that his finger-shaking had probably caused the death of more students.

Yee Wen, the engineer, asked Raymond why his brother was so gloomy, touching and staring at a little wooden bear as if his favorite pet had died.

"Can you blame him?" Raymond said. "He supported and defended the government all his life, and they killed his wife."

"Not all of them are heartless," Tall Mountain, the chain-smoking writer, said. Raymond also recognized him. He had seen May reading books by Tall Mountain.

"They've struggled for forty years," Tall Mountain said. "They've turned a small guerrilla band into the world's biggest army. They put China on the map as a major world power. Do you expect them to give up their power so easily?"

"I'm surprised at Deng Xiaoping," Professor Liu said. "He was ousted as general secretary of the party himself. He was denounced as a capitalist roader. I just can't understand how such a man can treat today's reformers the same way the Red Guards treated him . . . so brutally."

In the living room, Jimmy heard Deng Xiaoping's name and he started to tremble.

When Raymond said that he wanted to be a writer, too, Tall Mountain stared at him, shaking his head.

"Don't you enjoy being a writer?" Raymond asked. "You're pretty famous in China."

Tall Mountain told him that he would rather be a barber. What he had written was worthless as hair under a barber's chair. During the Cultural Revolution, he had written tons of stories, based on Jiang Qing's literary formula. "All my heroes looked alike," he said, "young, handsome, and scowling. They all had large noses like a foreigner's. They all talked dramatically with one fist raised high, looking upright and fearless. If they suffered a belly ache on a ship in the middle of a stormy sea, they rolled up their sleeves, picked up a kitchen knife, and performed an emergency appendectomy on themselves."

After a sip of tea, he went on, "Once I wrote a story in a moment of rebellion. I drew such a hero, but he was a little cross-eyed. When it was published, Jian Qing called me to her office in Zhong Nan Hai. She said angrily, 'I only allow villains to be bowlegged or cross-eyed!' She gave me a tongue-lashing and ordered me to correct my mistakes by cleaning latrines for six months. Many of my writer friends have jumped into the Pearl River and swum all the way to Hong Kong to avoid writing such heroes. Quite a few have drowned. But I was a coward. I continued to write about cross-eyed and bowlegged villains and scowling heroes with foreign noses. Obviously, Madame Mao loves big noses."

Raymond found the writer bitter but entertaining. Tall Mountain's patter relieved a great deal of tension in the hiding place.

45

Nobody wanted to miss the fabulous breakfast—five-spiced pork liver, braised duck feet, and a variety of other little dishes. There was also a choice of hot beef noodles or Cantonese rice gruel.

This morning, to everybody's surprise, a stranger joined them at the breakfast table, a short man in his mid-thirties, slightly balding, with deep-set, expressive eyes and thin eyebrows. He introduced himself as Su Kang, the communications chief of Zhang Nan Hai, who worked closely with the important players within the standing committee of the Politburo. They shook his hand gingerly, wondering how and why he had escaped from China.

After a long silence, Su Kang broke the ice. He said with a chuckle, "I can tell that you all wonder why I'm here and what has really happened in Zhong Nan Hai, but you're afraid to ask."

Jimmy was anxious to know who was responsible for the bloody crackdown . . . who had killed Do Do. He wanted to know everything that was not reported. So did the other dissidents, who all clamored to know the truth.

Su Kang said he had kept a diary, which he had smuggled out in a plastic bag tied to his stomach. With a bulging stomach, he had disguised himself as a pregnant woman and taken a train to Canton. He had stayed in Canton for two weeks in hiding. Finally, through the help of various people, including some government workers like himself, he had been able to reach Hong Kong. He refused to divulge the details of his escape, but he said laughingly that if he had not been a strong swimmer, he could have become dinner for sharks.

His story involved the most powerful men in Zhong Nan Hai, including Deng Xiaoping, the paramount leader; Hu Yaobang, the former party chief; Yang Shangkun, the president and deputy chairman of the Central Military Commission, of which Deng was the chairman; Wang Zhen, an old kung ho general who was very close to Deng; Li Peng, the premier; Zhao Ziyang, the party chief and a chicken bone in all the Old Guard throats.

Hu Yaobang, the former party chief, known as China's Gorbachev and a champion of reform, had been too soft on the student movement. The hard-liners dismissed him from his post on January 16, 1989. While most of the hard-liners were rejoicing over Hu's dismissal, Deng was sad. After all, Hu had been his right-hand man for many years. It was Deng who had installed Hu as secretary general of the party; it was Hu who had implemented most of Deng's economic reforms. It was Hu who had given him all the credit for China's new booming economy. Treated as a conquering hero, Deng had enjoyed the adoration of millions of people worldwide; he enjoyed seeing himself on television receiving world leaders, giving interviews and reviewing troops in an open limousine.

Hu had been openly pro-American; he had borrowed freely from America's example to form his own policies. He had even wanted to replace chopsticks with knife and fork. When he discovered rampant corruption within the Communist party, he insisted on exposing it and punishing the culprits publicly. Everyone in the party hierarchy had rotten apples in his family. Hu's demands had caused such a shock wave in Zhong Nan Hai that the Old Guard became alarmed. To placate them, Deng sacked Hu.

The students began to wonder if Deng was a wolf in sheep's clothing. Deng would not admit mistakes. He still believed that dismissing Hu was the correct course, good for the party, good for the country. After all, he had another right-hand man, Premier Zhao Ziyang, who was equally capable and equally re-form-minded.

On February 27, 1989, President Bush invited the Chinese government leaders to a banquet in the American embassy. He also invited Fang Lizhi, Deng's staunch enemy. Fang was the most prominent pro-democracy and anticorruption critic. At the bridge table, a hard-liner said to Deng, "How can you treasure Bush's friendship? He stabbed you in the back!" Deng said nothing, but secretly he ordered the Security Bureau to prevent Fang from attending Bush's dinner. On the day of the banquet, a carload of plainclothes agents did the job, creating a furor all over the world and driving a huge wedge between China and America. The students cried foul.

Ever since that unhappy event, Deng no longer treated America as China's friend. He started cultivating closer ties with the Soviet Union and Japan.

On April 15, Hu Yaobang died of a heart attack. Deng Xiao-ping, Yang Shangkun, and Wang Zhen, the three musketeers of the Central Committee, knew that Hu's death meant trouble. They held several meetings to discuss how to announce it. For a while they kept it a secret.

When the news was finally released, the party leaders held their breath, expecting great turmoil. To their pleasant surprise, what they heard were only some mournful messages expressing deep melancholy. Many reformers were a little disappointed; they had hoped that Hu's death would start a great political earthquake that would swiftly bring major changes in the government.

A shocking rumor crept out. When Hu was desperately ill, proper medical treatment had been denied him. Was this a premeditated murder? Many reformers wanted to know. But there was no proof.

One pleasant Sunday in May, a big character poster appeared in Bei Ta. Immediately, the Public Security police and the agents of the Ministry of Security were alerted. The poster announced a huge memorial service for Hu Yaobang. That morning, hundreds of flower wreaths appeared in Tiananmen Square. Meanwhile, Deng was enjoying a game of bridge in his residence inside Zhong Nan Hai. The mayor of Beijing called, suggesting increased security. Deng's hands started trembling. Unable to hold his cards, he ended the game. He had been expecting bad news. The students' poster was a premonition of a big storm in the making.

He called a meeting of his most trusted men: Yang Shangkun and Wang Zhen, the old general who always loved a good fight. Li Peng, the premier, was not invited. The meeting lasted two hours. The decision: "Don't give an inch!"

The crowd in Tiananmen Square was growing. Security guards were everywhere, taking pictures and recording conversations. Uniformed Public Security police stood guard by the railing near the Memorial, speaking into their walkie-talkies. Other armed police formed a line in front of the Great Hall of the People. Some students sat nearby, demanding to see Li Peng.

Deng was tense but feeling secure. Sitting in his living room, he glued his eyes to the TV screen. His aides had assured him that all the security agencies had been mobilized—the National Security, the Beijing Public Security, and the Secret Service.

During Hu's funeral, Deng heard many reports that angered him. The worst was a demand by the demonstrators that he and Li Peng both resign. He heard another rumor: "When people start criticizing Deng Xiaoping, the game is over. Better take your money and run." A professor said publicly in Tiananmen Square, "Remember Wei Jingsheng? He said that Deng was a dictator. Three days later, he was in jail serving a term of fifteen years."

The most painful remark he heard was, "Those who should die refuse to die; the one who should not die is dead."

He studied all reports, especially those from foreign newspapers and magazines. A face-loving man, he dreaded bad reports by foreign correspondents the most.

Newsweek: "Along the ten-mile march to Tian An Men Square, 150,000 students from 40 colleges joined the column. Workers poured from their jobs to line the route, climbing trees and crowding rooftops, throwing food and cigarettes to the march-

ers. Construction workers in yellow hard hats stood on scaf-
foldings banging chopsticks against their lunch pails and
waving their fists in solidarity. . . ."

The Wall Street Journal: "Forty years after Mao's 1949 revolution,
the Chinese people look to the riches and freedom of an open
market and democratic institutions which they see in the West.

"In their own government they see a group of old aristocrats
invoking a corrupt and stagnant system to tyrannize over a
nation. Says one American businessman in Beijing, 'These people know the emperor has no clothes.' "

Deng threw the reports on his desk angrily. Bush had
stabbed him in the back, now the American publications were
bad-mouthing him. He ordered that foreign correspondents be
restrained.

Wang Zhen paid him a visit, telling him that the students
were insulting him, calling him "Little Bottle." Some even
smashed bottles to vent their anger. He suggested that to crack
down with force was the only solution. Deng could not take
insults. He agreed. When Wang Zhen reported Deng's decision
to the Politburo, Zhao Ziyang was worried. He insisted that
there must be no bloodshed.

Deng waited. He wanted to hear more voices. He talked to
many generals, who never liked reform. They believed that
reform affected the army's morale; it reduced the soldiers to
the lowest rung of the social ladder, making them no better
than paupers. Mao had always emphasized military power and
had treated soldiers as heroes. That was why he had retained
power the longest.

Wang Zhen, the old warrior, said, "In China, one needs to
use a cattle butcher's knife to kill a chicken, because Chinese
chicken has thick skin and tough meat."

Deng agreed, but he still wanted to wait. His prostate problem was getting worse. He was depressed, often sitting in his
living room alone, staring blankly, his hands trembling.

He looked very sick, with dark circles around his eyes, his
puffed cheeks discolored and leathery, liver spots showing

prominently. The scheduled historical meeting with Mikhail Gorbachev on May 15 was only two days away.

His chief physician began to panic. He invited two of his colleagues to Zhong Nan Hai for an urgent conference. Could Deng stand the rigors of such a meeting? If so, what steps should be taken to make him look healthy and energetic?

On May 15, before breakfast, the doctors gave him several shots and made him take a dose of powerful tonic consisting of bear liver and snake gallbladder concentrate mixed with queen-bee honey. News had been leaked to the world that Deng was in robust health and had worked and played bridge all day as usual before Gorbachev's arrival. The news media had also reported that his swimming had strengthened his body, and his bridge had improved his mind. He was eager and ready to help seal the long-lost friendship with the Soviet Union.

But his doctors and handlers were worried. During the brief meeting between the two world leaders in the People's Great Hall, they stood in the wings with two nurses, watching Deng intensely and nervously, ready to leap into action at any moment. A stretcher and a wheelchair had also been ordered, with attendants standing nearby. Under the glaring camera lights, Deng, his facial spots hidden by makeup, indeed looked healthy and robust. His voice firm and strong, his words proper and coherent, he declared that he had retired from all his important government activities. Hiding his trembling hands, he did so well that nobody suspected he was very ill. His doctors all heaved a sigh of relief.

Meanwhile, the decision was made in Zhong Nan Hai to use military force against the students as soon as Gorbachev left China.

Zhao Ziyang was shocked; he tendered his resignation but was turned down. When he met Gorbachev, he dropped a bombshell by telling Gorbachev that while Deng had given up all his positions, he still was the man who approved all the major decisions. Deng, watching the meeting on television, heard it and was infuriated. How could Zhao have so blatantly revealed a party secret to a foreign leader? He felt that Zhao had betrayed him and made a liar out of him.

Zhao's enemies immediately started whispering into Deng's ear, "Zhao is engaged in a conspiracy with the students to seize power." It made Deng more determined to crack down.

When Yang Shangkun and Wang Zhen visited him again, they brought him a piece of paper. It was an order to declare martial law. Yang gave him a pen. Deng signed it with a badly shaking hand.

In the next few days, he read as many reports as possible, especially those from America. He knew that the inner reports from his own government sources were often whitewashed or censored.

Newsweek: "Martial law was declared in Beijing on May 20th. The story spread that Zhao Ziyang argued for conciliation, but 84-year-old Deng Xiaoping was adamantly opposed. 'I have three million troops behind me,' Deng was quoted as saying.

" 'I have all the people of China,' answered Zhao.

"Deng dismissed him. 'You have nothing.' "

The New York Times: "As a small military convoy rolled through eastern Beijing early on the morning of May 21st, an old woman street cleaner rushed up and lay down in front of the trucks.

"Several hundred students immediately dashed toward the convoy, asking the soldiers why they wanted to repress a democratic movement.

"'We are the people's soldiers,' an officer told the crowd. Then the troops, so moved that several were crying quietly, drove back the way they had come.' "

Deng had three residences, one in Zhong Nan Hai, one on Jade Spring Hill, in a Beijing suburb, and when he needed a rest, he went to Bei Dai Ho, a summer resort.

Since martial law had been declared, he lived on Jade Spring Hill, accompanied by his close aides, a doctor and a nurse who monitored his health daily. He missed his bridge game, but his home was full of visitors from Beijing, mostly founding fathers of the Communist party, old men still in power.

He never admitted mistakes publicly, but he confided to

one of his closest aides that if martial law had been declared a month earlier, all this could not have happened.

Zhao Ziyang, like Hu Yaobang, was speaking out against the use of force. His repeated plea for a dialogue with the students made Deng uneasy. Deng, more depressed, read more foreign reports.

Time: "Five miles west of Tian An Men, thousands flooded around a convoy of 50 trucks. Urged a young woman, 'The students are for the people. Please don't hurt the students.' Some vehicles departed, the soldiers flashing victory signs."

The Chicago Tribune: "In Tian An Men Square, the 27-foot-tall Chinese version of the Statue of Liberty has appeared. Nearly a quarter of a million people have defied a government warning in order to file past this proud lady with the raised torch.

"The crowds came on foot, by chartered buses, on the flatbeds of tricycles and in an endless stream of bicycles.

"A group of young factory workers studied the statue across a sea of bobbing heads. 'What does it mean?' All scratched their heads.

"One finally answered, 'I guess it means the people are no longer afraid of the government.' "

Deng stared blankly in his favorite chair, recalling the scene in Beijing when he had looked out a window in Zhong Nan Hai. In front of a noisy crowd, three skinny young students knelt on the steps, holding a piece of paper. Their demands were rather moderate. His heart softened. He almost yielded. But Wang Zhen's voice was still ringing in his ears: "Don't give an inch! Listen to the slogans! They're yelling that we are dictators, that you are an emperor! We've reached the point of no return!"

The scene was still vivid in his mind's eye. The students seemed decent; the rioters in the crowd did not look like students at all. Had he made a mistake?

He thought of George Bush and Fang Lizhi, the man he hated most. He wondered why Bush had betrayed him by inviting his enemy to a dinner of which he was the guest of honor. Had George Bush been influenced by Ambassador Lord and his novelist wife, Betty Bao Lord? Those two had been busy feeding the Chinese with ideas of freedom and democracy, and all kinds of American ways, including ballroom dancing. According to intelligence reports, the whole thing was an American plot to rid China of communism. He had been told that Betty Lord had often held "grass roots" democracy meetings in the U.S. embassy, and that the Voice of America was also feeding the Chinese public with "liberalization poison."

All those reports had been terribly disturbing. For his own health, he decided to ignore international opinion. He said to the elders, "If we're afraid of foreigners' opinions, we won't be able to do anything. Do you know why they put my picture on the cover of their magazines? Because we have three million soldiers and atomic bombs. Why should we fear foreigners?"

His voice was not very convincing, but the elders applauded him.

He decided to put the blame for the students' unrest squarely on Zhao Ziyang, who, like Hu Yaobang, was a major polluter with "bourgeois liberalization." The elders agreed. They would not retreat one step; they would not make the same mistake that Poland had. Poland had handled a similar situation badly, resulting in terrible chaos.

The students were getting more boisterous in Tiananmen Square, throwing little bottles and smashing them. It hurt Deng; he could not stand personal insults.

He received a petition from seven generals who pleaded with him to retract the order for martial law. Zhao Ziyang supported the generals, but Wang Zhen rebuked him, saying that the Chinese Communist party was so weak that it was frightened by a few students.

"Give me two companies of soldiers," he said publicly. "I'll take care of the rebels right now."

Zhao was not afraid of Wang Zhen's public utterances, but what Wang Zhen had whispered into Deng's ear was another matter. It was reported that someone had already whispered in Deng's ear, "The only way to save the party is to kick out the weak, impose rigid controls on the economy, strengthen the household registration system and the reporting system, encouraging individuals to report on each other. Only through thought control can the party survive," this man advised. "The people must be intimidated and made submissive enough that when you draw a circle on the ground it is a prison."

Deng glared at the visitor, who left, afraid that Deng might have a stroke. A few of Deng's aides also started whispering. Did the visitor have an ulterior motive? Was he trying to help Deng? Or was he trying to destroy him? Deng forbade them to talk about it. One of the aides believed that this man was Deng's deadliest enemy, a hungry tiger in sheepskin.

Deng also thought a lot of his crippled son, Deng Pufang. His son had been a target of criticism, for he headed the largest corporation in China, with branch offices in every province. Deng Pufang also whispered things into his father's ears. It was believed that he supported the reform . . . said good things about Hu Yaobang, Zhao Ziyang, and the student movement. But nobody talked about it.

Deng heard that Zhao Ziyang had repeatedly called Qiao Shi, the Public Security Bureau head, warning him not to hurt the students. Many leaders began to worry; what if the soldiers started shooting?

In a way, Deng wished that the soldiers would not shoot. All the eyes of the world were watching them. Besides, over a thousand reporters and editors had also taken to the streets, waving banners and shouting slogans to support the students. One of the banners said, "Don't force us to tell lies!"

Some party elders clamored to have the rebellious editors removed. New editors changed the government publications' tone immediately. One intellectual remarked, "The key to reading the newspapers is to apply a reverse dialectic. Whatever they say, believe only the opposite." It was reported that if a book was criticized by the government press as a bundle of lies, the book immediately became a best-seller. Something was drastically wrong.

Zhao Ziyang was on the attack again. He presented a set of demands to the Politburo: 1. retract the April 26 editorial that called the students troublemakers, and 2. investigate corruption and racketeering among families of high officials and party leaders; make their assets and income public, introduce greater democracy and give the press greater freedom of speech.

Such demands were like grinding hot pepper into old wounds; they caused loud groans among the Old Guard, who were determined to bury him. Zhao called Deng, asking for an appointment. Deng's office said curtly, "Comrade Deng is too busy."

Zhao needed the students' support; the students needed Zhao's patronage. But the students spent all their energy supporting Hu Yaobang, a dead man.

The students were noisy but peaceful; the hunger strikers became hollow-cheeked and pale. Some were in semi-comas. Zhao visited them twice, his eyes welling with tears. "My students," he said chokingly, "I've come too late." But the students were not moved or excited . . . except a young man who asked for Zhao's autograph. The hard-liners were heartened, and started digging his grave.

There had been rumors that a coup by some Young Turks in the army was being discussed. The elders immediately went to see Deng. They told him that it must be stopped at all cost. They all knew what had happened to the Gang of Four, the victims of a coup.

Deng was not too worried. He and Yang Shangkun held the key to the army. The Gang of Four had not had even one soldier friend when they were arrested. The elders insisted that as long as the students still occupied Tiananmen Square, nobody was safe. One of the old generals told Deng that the stalemate was hurting the party and the country. He wanted to see "bitter flesh" tactics solve the problems. Deng knew what he meant—killing his own soldiers and putting the blame on the rioters. Using that excuse, the army could start shooting. Deng's face whitened; his lips trembled. His angry glare silenced the general, who withdrew quickly.

In Building 202 in Zhong Nan Hai, the martial-law headquarters was buzzing with activity. Wang Zhen and Yang Shangkun were in charge, ignoring the seven generals' plea for leniency. They consulted Deng daily, reporting to him that the 28th Army was too friendly to the students. Deng already knew. The commander had declared that he would not shoot the students. He had also declared himself ill and checked into hospital number 301. But the 27th Army was trigger-happy. All it needed was a fuse to ignite the fire.

One afternoon, a soldier was beaten by a few civilians. Two columns of soldiers advanced to Xi Yuan Gate and clashed with the civilians, wounding forty-five people.

Zhao Ziyang, now powerless and pathetic, kept telling people that he could not repress the students even if he was being deposed. He was not afraid to die. But the hard-liners ignored him, treating his brave talk as a child's whine. The Voice of America and the BBC were jammed, but people still tuned in, listening and guessing. The Central Committee of the party met several times and issued two resolutions: The student movement was "insurrection," and Zhao was anti-party. Parachute troops were ordered to drop on Tiananmen Square. The commander of the 28th Army, living in Hospital number 301, was arrested. The air became more tense. More than a million people marched, holding banners and flags. Some harbored high hopes, believing that the government was about to cave in.

Wang Zhen, the old warrior, inspected the 27th Army. He said that to quell a rebellion quickly, only tanks would do the job. He declared he would lead the first tank to Tiananmen Square. When Deng heard about this, he immediately countered Wang with a directive called "internally frantic, externally relaxed." It said that the operation should be like a duck: On the surface, it glides on water smoothly, but beneath the water it paddles frantically.

Zhao Ziyang was under house arrest. The elders discussed his successor. Deng favored the Shanghai mayor, Jiang Zemin. Deng wanted a crackdown not only on the student movement, but on the party as well. Many military and party leaders were blacklisted.

The 27th Army was advancing toward Tiananmen Square from five directions: East Chang An Boulevard, West Chang An Boulevard, Capitol Airport Road, the Summer Palace, and the Jian Guo Men. All they needed was the fuse, an excuse to start shooting. Wang Zhen had volunteered to lead the attack.

About midnight on June 2, an army vehicle ran over some

civilians. The angered crowd beat some soldiers. Following the incident, a few soldiers were beaten to death and a lot of army vehicles were destroyed . . . enough excuse for the martial law headquarters to act. At 10:30 A.M. on June 3, Wang Zhen fired the first shot on Wanshou Road. The troops attacked, the war was on. On June 4, a drizzling gloomy morning, the bloodbath of Tiananmen Square began.

On Jade Spring Hill, the doctor gave Deng Xiaoping a shot of tranquilizer. Restlessly, Deng slept through the massacre.

On July 6, he fought off the effect of drugs and struggled to his desk to read the news. He brushed away the government inner reports and picked up the foreign reports:

Baltimore Sun: "They stood bravely together, about 20 students and workers, facing a dozen tanks. Some were crying, some shouting angrily.

"A column of soldiers carrying automatic weapons appeared suddenly from behind the tanks. The soldiers lined up and took aim at the protesters.

" 'They were just standing there,' said a witness who was watching as the demonstrators were gunned down.

" 'The leaders of our country are insane,' said a middle-aged man. 'They are insane.' "

AP, Reuters: "A girl of four was killed as she held her mother's hand.

"A man in his 50's took a copper bullet in his back as he cycled to work, as did many other victims.

" 'A girl in the crowd heard that her younger brother had been killed, and ran toward the soldiers,' a teacher from Beijing Language Institute said.

" 'We tried to stop her, but the troops opened fire. They shot her seven times, even as she was crawling.' "

Newsweek: "A woman had her arms around a soldier's legs. She was begging for her life. But the soldier just bayoneted her in the head. The soldiers threw people off the tips of their bayonets like bales of hay."

The New York Times: "Desperate as they saw their friends fall and crimson stains spread on their chests, students and workers sought out foreign journalists and tugged them toward corpses.

" 'We appeal to your country,' a university student begged as bullets screamed overhead. 'Our government is mad. There must be something that America can do.' "

Newsweek: " 'I don't cry often. I went through the Cultural Revolution and I've seen a lot. But I cried when I saw a tank run over a man and heard a kind of noise, like a PONG. His head was crushed.

" 'From where I stood, the sound of crying was louder than the gunfire. One line of students would get shot down, and then another line would stand, and the same thing would happen.

" 'What I saw was bodies, bodies, bodies.' "

Deng stopped reading, his face ghastly pale, his hands shaking badly. When the doctor and the nurse rushed in to give him another tranquilizer, he waved them off. His aides watched him closely from the next room. For the first time, they saw tears wash down his leathery, round face. Nobody knew if the tears were for the students, or China, or himself. They knew that the three were all terrible tragedies.

46

It was Monday morning. Charles Hong got up early and went to his study to make several important phone calls. He first called his personal secretary, Mrs. Ling, telling her that he would not go to his office today. He also instructed her not to transfer any calls to his home.

He picked up the morning paper. He glanced at the headlines; all the news had already been reported on TV. He leafed through the financial pages. An article attracted his attention. It said, "If brains were gold, Hong Kong has become a gold mine for foreigners and a gold rush is going on. Each time a Qantas Airways jet swoops down, gold diggers pour out to recruit Hong Kong technicians and management talent. Toronto's mating call has extended to doctors and radiation experts. The Portuguese government is also dangling carrots in front of would-be immigrants in both Hong Kong and Macao.

" 'Do you have $64,000?' they advertise. 'Buy a house in Portugal and you'll have a visa good for six years.' The ad also says that after 1992, when the twelve European nations become one big European community without borders, anyone with a Portuguese passport can settle anywhere in Europe permanently.' "

The news depressed Charles. Everybody was thinking of pulling out. A maid knocked on his door and announced breakfast.

Aimee was waiting for him at the breakfast table. It was rare

302

that she shared the chef's specialty in the morning, his favorite salted egg porridge. She looked haggard; she had been restless and quarrelsome. He kept calm and avoided subjects that might lead to confrontation.

"Charles," she said, "tell me how long we've known Shanghai Mary."

"Funny you should ask," he said. "I feel I've known her all my life. And I like her. I say that not because she's your best friend."

"She hasn't been acting like my best friend," Aimee said. "I'm very disappointed in her!"

Charles raised an eyebrow. "Why?"

"First," she went on, "she never told me she was involved in the freedom movement. Did you know that the Golden Phoenix is actually the headquarters for the Alliance for Democracy?"

"Well, I heard about it."

"You heard about it! Why didn't you tell me?"

"Why are you so disappointed?" he asked.

She did not answer until after Ah Hing had served them the salted egg porridge. "I heard that she got Raymond back. For two days, I've been asking her where Raymond is, and she never gave me a direct answer. Am I not Raymond's mother? Am I not entitled to know where my own son is? I want to see him, I want to know how he is! He almost got killed, you know. Why all this secrecy?" She was almost in tears.

"Aimee," he said sympathetically, "Shanghai Mary told nobody about Raymond's whereabouts, including me. I have two sons among the rescued dissidents. Their security is our first concern. Thank God they are safe! Shanghai Mary has done her best. For that we ought to be grateful!"

"But where are Raymond and Jimmy? Isn't it time that we know?"

"We'll know in time, Aimee," he said, glancing at his watch. "We have to make sure they're safe. Don't worry, Shanghai Mary knows what she's doing."

"I didn't sleep all night," she said. "This is Hong Kong, not China. We have law, we have police. If necessary, we can hire private guards to protect them. . . ."

"Aimee," he interrupted, his patience wearing a little thin, "Hong Kong is full of killers and kidnappers for hire. Before we are assured that the coast is clear, we'll have to wait. Then we can have a family reunion and celebrate."

"I heard you say that before. When will it be?"

"We'll know soon enough."

"It's all been a mistake! If we hadn't sent Raymond to China, we wouldn't have had all this agony!" She threw down her spoon and looked around. "I want my coffee. Where are the servants? Are they so lazy that they've all gone back to bed?"

As she picked up the little bell and started ringing it irritably, the doorbell chimed. Ah Hing hurried in with a pot of coffee as a maid went to open the door. When the maid greeted Raymond excitedly, Aimee leapt up. But she stopped, patted her hair, and straightened her dress hurriedly.

Jimmy, Raymond, and Yin Yin came in, followed by Shanghai Mary and a driver who carried their bags. Charles met them in the foyer, hugging his sons. Raymond introduced Yin Yin. Charles had heard a great deal about Raymond's two girl-friends. He greeted her with a warm embrace.

"Raymond, darling!" Aimee rushed to him, her arms outstretched. Raymond was embarrassed by his mother's smothering hugging and kissing.

Aimee examined his eyes, ears, and clothes. "Filthy!" she exclaimed. "You need a bath immediately!"

"Aimee," Charles said, "this is the happiest day of our lives. Before you ask them to do anything, let's have some champagne."

They all gathered in the living room. Ah Hing brought in two bottles of champagne and served it. Charles proposed a toast.

Everybody was cheerful. Raymond and Yin Yin sat close together on a sofa, holding hands. Charles asked Shanghai Mary to stay for a "dust-washing dinner"; she declined.

"What's a 'dust-washing' dinner?" Raymond asked.

"A dinner to welcome the loved ones," Charles said. "To wash off the dust of your trip. A Chinese tradition."

"Raymond," Aimee said with an exaggerated frown, "what's the matter with your Chinese education?"

"Before I leave," Shanghai Mary said, "I must express our thanks to Sir Charles Hong. Without his generous donation, it would not have been possible to get so many dissidents out of China. But there are thousands more still in hiding. We need all the help we can get. . . ."

"How come I don't know anything about all this?" Aimee asked.

Shanghai Mary smiled, shook everybody's hand, and left hurriedly, leaving the question for Charles to answer.

At four, the chef prepared a sumptuous "dust-washing" dinner. The round dining table was decorated with fresh flowers; the lazy Susan was loaded with Chinese appetizers, cold cuts, and fruit laid out in flower patterns. There were two extra pairs of chopsticks on the table.

"This evening, Do Do and May are with us," Charles said. "Raymond, you sit between Yin Yin and May. Jimmy, you sit between Do Do and me."

The five members of the family took their seats quietly. Jimmy looked at Do Do's empty seat and choked, his eyes red and moist.

Ah Hing popped open another bottle of champagne and poured it. Aimee was cheerful; she picked up her champagne glass and proposed a toast, "Happy reunion of flesh and bones!"

"Flesh and bones?" asked Raymond, frowning.

"Old Chinese saying," Aimee said. "Raymond, I'm ashamed of your Chinese education. You know nothing of our customs."

Raymond shrugged.

After the toast, Charles said, "Today, we have a decision to make, a decision that will affect our lives and our future. But we'll make the decision through the process of democracy. Let's vote whether we remain in Hong Kong or pull out and emigrate. We have five votes, including Yin Yin's. She is family. Agreed?"

Everybody nodded; Yin Yin beamed.

Charles went on, "Whether you vote to stay or to emigrate, a simple explanation is required, so we know why we are making this most important decision of our lives. We'll start with Jimmy and go clockwise. Jimmy, you first."

Jimmy thought for a moment. He cast a glance at the empty seat on his right, took a deep breath and said, "Do Do would have voted 'emigrate.' My vote is to emigrate."

Charles was next. He said without hesitation, "I go along with Jimmy. I trust his judgment. Your turn, Raymond."

Raymond stood up and squared his shoulders. Suddenly, he looked older. When he started talking, his voice was even and forceful. "May once told me . . . I quote: 'I have cherished the ideal of a democratic and free society in which all persons live together in harmony and with equal opportunity. It is an ideal which I hope to live for and achieve. But if need be, it is an ideal for which I am prepared to die.' She said she was quoting a man called Mandela. I didn't know who Mandela was, so I said, 'Phooey!' She said Nelson R. Mandela is a black freedom fighter imprisoned by the South African government for twenty-seven years. She said the Chinese people's ideals are identical. As long as they are not realized, there is work to be done. So I vote the way May would have voted: Stay!"

Charles stared at Raymond in surprise. Was this the same Raymond talking? He could not believe his ears. He suppressed a strong urge to throw his arms around his son and tell him how proud he was.

"Yin Yin, your turn," he said, trying to keep his voice calm.

"I go wherever Raymond goes," Yin Yin said.

"Tell us why," Charles said.

"I love him. Okay?"

"Good enough," Charles said with a smile. "Aimee, your turn. Yours will be the deciding vote. Think carefully. It may change all our lives."

"What is there to think about?" Aimee said. "I vote to stay. I'm with Raymond."

Looking tremendously relieved, Charles told Ah Hing to open another bottle of champagne. "Let's all drink to the winning votes!"

Outside, the sun was bright; in the distance, Shanghai Mary's girl crew was swarming over a shiny ocean liner, washing and scrubbing for leftovers.

As soon as the dinner was over, Aimee wanted to show Yin Yin the house. Charles took Jimmy to his study for a little private talk. It pained Charles to see his son so changed, so sad and gloomy.

"Jimmy," he said, "both of us lost our beloved wives. I've lived with the pain. So should you, and get on with your life. Let me show you something that may cheer you up a little."

He took out a letter from his desk drawer and gave it to Jimmy. It was written with a black felt-tip pen, the handwriting was strong and slanting, dated July 10, 1989.

Dear Charles:

I've been reporting sad and depressing news for a good many years. Now I can report some good news for a change. Yun Mei and I were married. Like a child, I'm still pinching myself to make sure it's indeed a dream that has come true. Yun Mei and I owe you, Jimmy, and Do Do undying gratitude for having brought us together. I have even adopted Yun Mei's positive attitude toward fate. Often misfortunes are blessings in disguise. We would not have had this happiest event of our lives today if Yun Mei had not been fired from her reporting job in Beijing. Even her concussion, caused by a policeman's club, may have played a hand in her rescue from further tragedy. I've started writing about it and you'll learn everything from my forthcoming article.

We have settled down temporarily in Berkeley, my hometown, and allow my family to spoil us. All my relatives want to show us their culinary skills, and we've reached a point where we're afraid to step on our bathroom scale.

We are not sure that our letters to Jimmy and Do Do will ever reach them. But we have not said anything in them that might jeopardize their security. Both of us pray that they will come out of this terrible turmoil safe and sound.

I'm waiting for a new assignment. I love the Orient, but Yun Mei has had enough of political upheavals, so we've requested Singapore, the most stable ship in a turbulent sea. Life could be dull there, but to me, as long as Yun Mei and I are together, life will be a long honeymoon anywhere.

Love from both of us,
Mark

When Jimmy finished the letter, his eyes were red. Charles watched him.

"Son," he said quickly, "in spite of your own loss, you have at least contributed a great deal of happiness to two dear friends. Now it's time to think of your own future. You have two choices. One, you can go back to teaching. The president of Hong Kong University is a good friend of mine. Two, you can join the family business. One or two, the choice is yours."

"I'll take two," Jimmy said after some hesitation.

"A wise choice," Charles said happily. "It pleases me, you know that." He picked up the phone and dialed a number. "I want you to work for Henry Ho, one of my most successful managers."

When Ho answered the phone, Charles asked him if he could use a young man from China, a political refugee, nice and healthy, with excellent references but unfamiliar with the hotel business. Ho said he could use an extra porter.

"That's fine," Charles said. "I'll send him over tomorrow morning."

After he hung up, he leaned back in his chair comfortably and said, "Jimmy, I want you to learn the hotel business from scratch. A porter is an excellent start. In two months I'll see to it that you become a desk clerk. I want you to climb the ladder step by step. In two years, you'll be qualified as a manager. By the time I'm ready to retire, you'll have learned enough to take my place."

"What about Raymond?" Jimmy asked.

"I don't know about Raymond. He's not a bit interested in business."

He looked out the window. In the bay, Shanghai Mary's girls were still swarming over the ocean liner, which glowed in the setting sun. He lit a cigar and went on, "Raymond is fascinated by Indiana Jones. He might be tickled to death to work for Shanghai Mary."

"I know what you mean, Father," Jimmy said with a smile. It was his first smile in a long time.